A Long Look Ahead.

A

LONG LOOK AHEAD;

OR,

The First Stroke and the Last.

BY A. S. ROE,

AUTHOR OF "JAMES MONTJOY; OR, I'VE BEEN THINKING," "TO LOVE AND TO BE LOVED," ETC.

NEW YORK:
J. C. DERBY, 119 NASSAU STREET.
BOSTON: PHILLIPS, SAMPSON & CO.
CINCINNATI: H. W. DERBY.

1855.

STEREOTYPED BY
THOMAS B. SMITH,
216 William St., N. Y.

PRINTED BY
PUDNEY & RUSSELL,
79 John Street.

PREFACE.

Having an errand one day, a short distance from my place of residence, I jumped into my one-horse wagon, and had just passed from the yard into the highway, when a gentleman on foot, with a small carpet-bag in his hand, attracted my notice, and as he was proceeding in the direction I was going, I asked him, according to country civility,

"If he would like to ride for a short distance?"

"I should be very glad to, sir."

Immediately a quantity of old boots and shoes were thrust one side, to make room for the feet of the stranger; for, to tell the whole truth, I was on my way to our parish cobbler, with some half-dozen pairs of youngsters' understrappers that needed "seeing to."

"Can you tell me, sir," said the gentleman, as he took his seat, and laid his carpet-bag down before him, "whereabouts the author of James Mountjoy lives? as I am told his residence is somewhere in this vicinity."

"That is the place, sir, which you have just passed."

The gentleman turned round, and gazed for some time, being only able to catch occasional glimpses of the house through the thick foliage of the trees, amid which it stood. And then, after satisfying his curiosity, began to descant upon the merits of the work, having, probably, not the most distant idea that its author was beside him. Being somewhat of a bashful temperament, especially when not well dressed, as was certainly the case just then, having dropped my hoe in the garden, and taken the reins just as I was, it was not very clear what was duty, whether to sit incognito, and listen to a stranger's remarks about one's own production—or just to tell him, "unauthorly," as I then appeared, the simple truth. The latter seemed the most honest course, and was at once adopted. What passed need not be repeated here; but when I reached my place of destination, and we were about to part, he grasped my hand, with the cordiality of an old friend.

"You cannot tell, my dear sir, the pleasure which this short interview has given me; it has gratified a strong desire which I have had ever since reading your book."

Now, there is no fiction about this, but only one among many kindred tokens in my own experience as an author. It may savor a little of self-complacency to some who cannot enter into the feelings of those who send forth the nurslings of their mind and heart abroad upon the changeful sea of public taste. But let such keep in mind, that gold is not the only stimulus which nerves to the patient toil of many months—unseen—unknown—by the lone fireside—in the still watches of the night, and through the long day. To know that we have made a lodgement in the heart—to feel assured that throughout our extended country, and in foreign lands, we have touched the chord that vibrates in unison with our own sympathies—and would feel the friendly grasp of the hand, and see the eye kindling with emotion, as we met, far distant from our homes, those who have embalmed our names as household words—is a part of our reward, which the poorest of us would hardly part with for a much greater amount of dollars and cents than the most favored have received.

And now, as I am about to send forth another production of my pen, I feel that there is due from me to those who by their expressions of regard have stimulated to the effort, a word in salutation. I cannot take you by the hand, nor shall we very likely meet, for I mingle not with the busy crowd, and the spot of country where I live is one side of the great highways of travel, so that few are the chances that we shall ever see each other face to face. But, if your heart can find anything in the pages of this book that it admires—if the time spent in its perusal shall not be judged by you as wasted—and if, when you lay it down, any feeling of interest for the writer is excited, just think that you can number him among your friends, if you wish to.

A LONG LOOK AHEAD;

OR,

THE FIRST STROKE AND THE LAST.

CHAPTER I.

"WELL, Charlie, I think you have been silent long enough. You wanted me to come down with you, and see the old place; and here you have been sitting on this log, and looking, and looking, without saying a word, this half hour."

"Well, Guss, and if I should sit here until the sun went down, and the stars came out and set again, I should, all the time, have enough to occupy my thoughts. But it is not very civil to you, I must confess. I have been thinking, though, about a matter that concerns you as well as myself."

"I hope it has not been about old times. You look so very sober, that one would imagine you were raking up everything that had been amiss in your past life. I should let old things be old things, Charlie."

"And so I mean to, Guss, although as to that matter, I believe I never went very far astray. I loved a frolic with the young fellows once in awhile, and, perhaps, went to a few more balls than our good uncle and aunt approved; and, perhaps, if they had said less on the subject, it would have been quite as well, for there is a perverse will in me, that fights for its own way the more it is opposed."

"You come round right, at last, though."

"Well, I hope there is some stronger principle now, to aid me in counteracting what is evil. But I have been thinking, just now, more about the future than the past."

"There is not much use in that—at least there is no use

in being so sober about it. We can't do much with the future, anyhow."

"We must make our plans for all that, Guss—for the future is before us, and we have got to meet it. But if I must tell you at once, I have been thinking about setting up for ourselves, here on this old place."

"Dear brother Charles, I beg of you to pause before you get your mind too strongly set about such a plan. Only think of the place and its condition—just open your eyes, and look at it; see this old rookery of a house, looking more like a stone cemetery, than a place to live in; and that old barn, one door fairly off the hinges, another hanging by only one, the boards in many places gone altogether, and others slapping about by every blast that comes along. Old Grumby lived here, until even he could stand it no longer; and if he, with his great boys to help him, could n't get pork and Indian meal enough to stand them through the year, what could we get, do you think?"

"What you say is all true, Guss; the place looks full as bad as you describe it, and the Grumbys were fairly starved out of it. But the difficulty there is very evident—they will ever grow poorer, the longer they live, no matter where they may be located; they have neither industry, patience, frugality, nor ambition—in poverty and wretchedness, they will probably live and die. Let us not, dear brother, despise our inheritance, because such persons have done no better upon it."

"Well, Charlie, let out your thoughts. You know there is but one track for us both. I shall stick to you, let things go as they may."

"And I to you, Guss. We are alone upon the earth, as to assistance from any human being, and we don't want it. Feeling, as I now do, with the strength of manhood in my arm, I ask no aid. But let us just look at the matter. Here we have fifty acres of land, all our own; ten acres of it are good wood land,—forty acres of it we can cultivate. Some of it, indeed, has been worn out, but the greater part suffers more from want of tillage than from too much."

"That is very likely, at least it has rather a wild look, the most of it."

"Yes, that 's true: the bushes have got a little too much

the upper hand, in some places. But for all that I cannot but believe, with this spot of land free from all incumbrance, ourselves owing nobody a dollar—with our physical strength, and the advantages we have had for education, that we can establish ourselves here, and in time gather around us all the comforts of a home. And where could we find a prettier spot?"

Augustus, the younger brother, made no reply, but cast a look over the place, as though wishing to be assured of the correctness of his brother's closing remark.

Whoever has travelled through that part of Connecticut which borders upon Long Island Sound, must doubtless have been struck with the picturesque beauty of those numerous indentations, or openings, through which the waters of the sea find access into the lower lands, winding, sometimes by different channels, through the long stretch of meadows, and, at last, uniting so as to form a little inland bay, where sloops can find shelter from the storms, and unload and receive their cargoes, beside the old mill, or the unpretending storehouse. The gentle slope of the land on either side of these openings, the clumps of trees that spot them over, with the snug dwellings clustering beneath, and the blue waters extending as far as the eye can reach, form altogether a home view scarcely exceeded by any portion of our beautiful country.

It was within the bounds of one of these snuggeries that the little farm these brothers owned was situated. It lay pleasantly fronting one of the arms of the creek which curved gracefully before it, rising, as it stretched back from the marsh, by a very gentle slope.

As their eyes wandered from spot to spot, either upon their own land, or their neighbors', a new and strange interest began to arise in their minds. Hitherto they had regarded it, with the old stone building and dilapidated barn, as but a useless possession. It had never yielded them any profit, and they would, doubtless, have sold it, had they been of age, for a small part of its real value. From time to time, indeed, they had come to look at it just as they had now. It was all that had been left to them, from the wreck of what had once been a good estate. It was all which they could call their own—it was associated with their days of childhood. They had never, indeed, lived on this spot—it was a piece of land disconnected with their early homestead. But they had always known it as their property, and therefore felt, on that account, an especial interest in occasionally walking over the fields, and strolling through the woods, or even hanging around the old buildings.

But, never before, had it seemed to them as now. The very idea which had been started, of their going to work upon it—of their making a home of it—however discouraging, to one of them at least, had still a charm about it, and the whole aspect of the place, and its scenery, were changed.

It was some time before either of them spoke. But Augustus at length asked,

"Well, Charlie, when do you think of commencing operations?"

"Right off."

Augustus looked at him a moment, to see whether he was in earnest, and then burst into a hearty laugh. Charles, full of life himself, and as ready to be pleased with trifles as his brother, joined with him. He well knew how ridiculous the idea must present itself to one who had not formed any definite plan, and, entering into his brother's feelings, enjoyed, perhaps as much as he did, the preposterous suggestion. For awhile, they gave vent to the explosion of their mirth, until, at length, Augustus recovered himself enough to ask—he did it with great difficulty, however,—

"Which place shall we begin to keep house in?—the house or the barn?" and another fit of laughter made the tears start from their eyes.

"Who will keep house for us? We had better get old Grumby back, and go board with him." Between each question, new peals of laughter arose, until the whole matter seemed to be got up for a joke, and to end there. Charles, however, had not been thinking in vain; he had thoroughly surveyed his ground, and all his plans were laid, even to minutiæ. As soon, therefore, as he had given full play to his lighter feelings, he commenced unfolding them.

"I don't wonder at your laughing, Guss, viewing it as you do; it must appear ridiculous indeed. I have, I can assure you, no idea at present of occupying our mansion, or any of the outhouses. I have, I think you will allow, a much better plan than that. You know the widow Casey, or Aunt Casey, as we call her, lives close by. She has no one with her, but her little daughter Hetty. She is poor, and her house is small, but she is very neat, and a good cook, and what is better, a good Christian woman. She has always appeared to be very fond of us, and I have thought of proposing to her, that we should live with her in this way—that we should have a room there to sleep ; we have bedding of our own, you know. Then, that we should buy all the provision necessary for the family, while she did the cooking, and attended to our room, &c."

Augustus had lost all inclination to laugh, and his countenance shone with delight.

"That would be the thing, Charlie ; most capital. We should feel so at home there ; and if we were sick, there is no one living we could so trust ourselves with. But will it not be very expensive buying everything so for all the family?"

"All the family will only be four of us, and the expense will not be so much as you think for. Of course you know we must have a cow, and we must have a yoke of oxen. The cow I can get for twenty-five dollars, and the cattle and second hand-cart I can get for one hundred dollars ; and clothes we have got enough to last us through the season ; so that my two hundred dollars, which I have saved, will be enough to give us a start."

"And my fifty."

"Well, if we want it, we shall have enough to start upon, and to keep us for six months, in which time, you know, if we have any crops, they will be available."

"Well, Charlie, you are not apt to make wild calculations ; but if this can be done, and Aunt Casey will take us, it will be the happiest day I have seen in this world yet. Oh, how snug it might be ; you could have all your books there, and when we were not at work, we could be reading ; and you can have your guitar, and I my violin, and no one to trouble us, and we could feel at home. When shall we see Aunt Casey about it?"

"Right off."

Aunt Casey, as the young men called her, was the widow of a seafaring man, who, as is most generally the case, left nothing behind him at his death, or next to nothing ; all his property being the house she occupied, a small tenement, with about an acre of ground attached to it.

The house, though small, and what might be called a poor one, was still a home for her and her little daughter, and she clung to it, even under many disadvantages. It was situated at quite a distance from the village; and, dependent as she was upon her own exertions for a living, it was a great labor for her to travel to and fro, with a little knitting, or sewing, or some work of that kind, and likewise to bring so far all the little supplies she needed; and sometimes, the difficulties she encountered, in her efforts to make an honest living, made a deep impression, and filled her with desponding thoughts. The world looked very dark to her ahead, and the few bright spots she could look back upon were almost obscured by the heavy mists that surrounded them. She had toiled hard, and gained little. She had shed many tears, and could remember but few smiling hours, since the sunny days of childhood.

That morning she had been upon a long and very muddy walk, and returned to her cottage wearied in mind and body. She had accomplished only part of her errand, and was mourning at the prospect of another weary travel on the morrow, when she heard the sound of footsteps approaching; and hastily wiping away the tears, stroked down her clean white apron, put aside a stray chair, and looked round the room to see if everything was in order.

"Aunt Casey, good afternoon to you. Why, what 's the matter? you look sad. Is Hetty sick?"

"Why, boys, where have you come from? Augustus how *do* you do? and oh my! how you have grown! Why, Charlie, if you aint a full-grown man. Do come and sit down, and let me see you a little while. It seems so good to see anything, or anybody I ever loved, or that ever loved me."

"Well, aunty, we have no kind of objections to sitting down, and letting you take a good long look. But, first, you must tell me what makes you look so sad. I always thought that you could put a cheerful face on, let the world go as it might."

"Did you? Well, I know, in the main, I have tried to be cheerful, and to put the best face on to things. But, somehow, it all looks so desperate now, that I feel about to give up;" and the old lady had to put her apron to her eyes.

She could think much longer about her troubles, than she could talk about them.

"Put down, put down! Aunty, come, none of that; how do you know but I have a plan to propose to you, that will be just what you would like? How would it suit you to take Augustus and me as boarders?"

"You, dear children! why, how could the like of me make you comfortable? Our provision here, you know, is hard to come by, and I aint no stock on hand, and no means to get any. And then the house is so small, and the place so lonesome like, you would clean git tired out, and homesick."

"Not in your company, aunt Casey, and a smile on your face. But I want you to listen to my whole story, and then, when I have told it, you can say just what you think about it."

And Charles related to her the substance of the conversation he had held with his brother, stating fully what he wished, and how it was to be accomplished.

The widow's countenance cleared up rapidly, as he proceeded, until a bright smile broke out upon it, and a tear of gladness fell from her eye.

"And can all this be true? and shall I ever see you two boys living under my roof, and all so snug and comfortable?"

"And you are perfectly willing that we should undertake it, aunty?"

"Oh, yes, I am willing enough; all I'm afraid of is, something will turn up to stop it; it's too good to be true. And when do you mean to begin, boys?"

"Right off. We shall be here, bag and baggage, to-morrow morning. And now, aunty, as we have quite a distance to walk, and plenty of business on hand, we will just take a glass of your good spring water, and be off."

The old lady jumped up, and opening a small, clean cupboard, took out a very large flowered tumbler, and running to the back part of the house, returned with the cool, delicious beverage, clear as crystal, and the drops already falling from the outside of the glass.

The next morning was a lovely April day, and the widow was up with the first streak of light. For there was a great work to be done that morning; the house was to be cleaned throughout; not that it really needed any such operation performed upon its spotless floors and wainscotting, but she thought it did; and as soon as the little breakfast-table was cleared off, the scrubbing commenced, and by the middle of the forenoon, she had gone through with the whole process, not excepting the little front porch; and then she and Hetty went to sweeping the grass around it, and to picking up any stray thing that might be in sight.

The house was rather a small concern, and finished in plain seaman style; and yet it had a pleasant air about it, both within and without. The principal room had windows on three of its sides, with two doors opening without—one on the east upon the porch, which ran the whole length of its front, and another on the south, and which was, in general, the most used. The porch alluded to was an indispensable attachment to all houses built by seamen; being in fact their chief place of abode, when on shore. Sheltered from the sun by its roof, the Old Salt can sit there at his ease, and mend his fishing-tackle, or smoke his pipe in full view of all that is passing on the water.

A shed, likewise, ran along the south side of the house, protecting their room from the direct rays of the sun, and adding much to the appearance of comfort, which, in spite of its plain finish, the little domicil presented. A large fire-place occupied the centre of the room, with doors opening into small bed-rooms, one on each side of the chimney; that on the south was occupied by the widow and her daughter, and the other was now to be given up to the young men. As soon as everything was in order, Aunt Casey sat down and began to look out for signs of her guests; but it was not until the middle of the afternoon, that the lumbering of a cart was heard through the edge of the woods, which ran between the house and the highway, and almost secluded the former from view.

"They are coming, mother," said Hetty; "but, oh me! what a load they 've got; just see, mother."

"Where the massy's will we put it all? but it 's the bed that heaps up so."

"Shall I drive to the south door, aunty?" said Charles, calling at some little distance.

"Yes, it will be the handiest place; but what upon earth have you got there? and are those your oxen, Charlie?"

"Oxen, cart, and all that 's in it, aunty; and it is all our own, and paid for too."

It was the bed, as Aunt Casey had said, which "made such a heap." But as soon as that was off, and carried into its place, such a variety was presented to view, as the good woman had never dreamt of having under her roof at one time; and as the different articles were brought in, and put away into some of the hiding places, of which the house had a good supply, exclamations of wonder were constantly breaking forth.

"Why, what upon earth! if he ain't gone and got two barrels of wheat flour? Why, you darling, we shan't want so much for cake and pies, for two years."

"Yes, but you see, aunty, I don't design it alone for pies and cake. There is no great difference in prices, and I think wheat bread is a little easier made, and a little better, don't you think so, when it is made, than rye. In those two bags you will find some rye, and some Indian, in case you might want to give us a treat of slapjacks."

"Well, well, darling, I 've nothing to say, I 'm sure, but try to do the best with the good things you 've got; but what is in these kegs?"

"That smallest keg, aunty, is white sugar, that is for our tea, and that half barrel is brown, and there is a half barrel of molasses—I remembered that you knew how to make excellent hop beer in summer time; and that small keg is lamp oil, and here is a keg of some very fine salt pork, and the other is fish; and there are four hams, and two pieces of dried beef; and now, aunty, don't you think we can stand it for six months? We shan't starve within that time, shall we?"

And Aunt Casey sat herself down, in her little rocking chair, and, instead of crying, went off into a little short laugh, shaking her sides, and chuckling to herself in the fullness of her delight and wonder, at finding so many good things, so unexpectedly placed under her control.

"And here, aunty, is a little package of spices of different kinds; all these I give now into your charge. This little roll contains two or three table cloths,—just let us see, aunty, how they will fit the round table; and the old lady, a little recovered from her fit of laughing, jumped up, and shaking her sides as she went, took down the table from its stand by the wall, and spread out its broad round face in the middle of the room. In a moment the cloth was laid over it, and she had like to have sat down again, and gone to laughing, but Charles interrupted her, by taking from its envelope a good-sized lamp, made of thick glass, placing it on the middle of the table.

"There, aunty, how will that do?" But there was no reply, other than a short dry shaking kind of giggle, that set Charles into a good round laugh, and Augustus and Hetty joining in, the little room, for awhile, was musical with their happy voices.

At about the setting of the sun, the young men came in from the barn, whither they had been to provide a place for their oxen, and the sight which met them, on entering the cottage, was enough of itself to have given them an appetite without their exercise and long fast. For there stood the round table, with its snow-white cover, the plates, and knives, and forks, shining their best, the tea-tray holding a small pile of cups and saucers, and a little pot-bellied silver teapot, shining brightly, with milk pitcher and slop bowl to match.

Charles stood a moment, admiring the arrangement, and then cast a significant glance at Aunt Casey.

"Where have they come from, aunty?"

"You remember them, don't you?"

"I remember something very much like them, my mother's present to you, when you was married?"

"And this is the first and only time they have ever been used; sometimes, when I have been put to straits, I have thought of selling them. But now, I am so glad I have n't; they will make the tea relish, won't they, dear?"

No one knew better than Aunt Casey how to prepare a good meal, if the materials were only on hand; and now she had done her best. The flour proved itself to be of the first quality, and as she took off from the griddle a fine puffy short-cake, and broke it in pieces, and piled it up on the bread plate, she could not help saying to Hetty:

"Wheat flour does make prettier short-cake than rye; and now, dear, put on that slice of broiled ham, and lay the eggs around the platter, and put that right before Mr. Charles' place, and I will fill up this teapot. Oh dear! how reviving it smells; it 's good tea I'll warrant you."

And all at once the table was filled with its dainties, and the chairs placed around it, and Charles and his brother neatly dressed, as though about to go into company, entered and took their seats. A moment Aunt Casey sat with her hands folded upon her lap. She knew not exactly the feelings of Charles, nor whether, with all his good qualities, he had any sense of his duty to God. She had hoped so, but she knew not.

But as he took his seat, he humbly bowed his head, and asked a blessing on their meal. It was enough; her heart was filled: she could ask for nothing more.

"Well, aunty," said Charles, as finishing his meal, he drew away from the table, "if all the articles prove as good as these we have had samples of to-night, we shall be fortunate; this is the best meal I have eaten for many a day."

"Or I either," said Augustus, who, not much given to conversation, except on extra occasions, put in a word.

"Well, there is one thing about it all, aunty, we can use them with the satisfaction of knowing that they are paid for; and if I live, I never mean to eat anything but what *is* paid for."

"You are right there, child; I've known many families come to ruin by keeping a book at this store, and a book at that. Things was plenty enough for a time, but the books eat 'em up."

"Well, we will see to it, aunty, that we shan't be eat up that way, anyhow. But are we not to have our lamp this evening?"

"Oh, la! yes; but I thought maybe you was going out—I see you all dressed up so."

"I dress myself, aunty, for my own pleasure, and all the rest of you; don't you like to see me in a snug rig?"

"And that I do. Dress makes a great difference in most anybody, but I was thinking how it makes you look like your uncle the minister. I never saw him but once, but I thought I never saw so fine a looking man."

Charles little thought of his question leading to such a termination, nor had Aunt Casey the most distant idea that her reply might have been construed into flattery. She merely spoke as she thought.

And if the uncle of Charles Lovell was a finer looking man than his nephew, no wonder that one sight of him had impressed Aunt Casey so sensibly.

Charles was but twenty-one, and yet to all appearance the full proportions of the man had been obtained. His broad, round chest, and well-fitted limbs, seemed calculated for toil and endurance, and the sprightliness of his step, and the elasticity of his motions, seemed to make active exercise a pleasure.

The countenance of Charles Lovell would not have found favor in the eyes of many of the softer sex. It was not distinguished for heavy eyebrows, thick whiskers, a square chin, or rolling lips. It was not a pretty face, with very clear red and white upon the cheeks, and fine arches over the eyes, and ruby lips, and flowing hair, curling behind the ears.

It was a countenance that beamed upon you with truth and earnestness. His clear, hazel eye, seemed a perfect window to the inner man; it could bear to be looked into, for there was nothing within to be concealed; and the feelings which sparkled from it were those which find a response in true and loving hearts. His hair was dark; his forehead open; his nose slightly arched; his mouth well set;—but you thought not of them: every feature seemed to be just right, as a part of the manly fellow, and you as much expected to hear from him sentiments that were noble and pure, and to find in him truth and virtue, as you would to inhale from the rose its rich perfume.

But we have left Aunt Casey lighting her lamp. It took, indeed, a little longer to perform the operation at first, as all lamps do; but when once fairly a going, and placed in the middle of the round table, which itself shone in all the glitter of the wax polish which Aunt Casey had that day put upon it, the whole set out was very satisfactory.

"And now, aunty, you must know that my motto is 'right off;' and, as I told you yesterday, it would give me great pleasure to assist Hetty with her arithmetic and geography, or anything that she wishes to learn. There will be room enough for us all round the table; you can have your sewing, and Hetty her books, and Guss, too, if he wishes,—but he seems to be busy with his fiddle-strings to-night."

"I am going to have a tune on the stoop directly; the moon is just rising, and I have eaten such a hearty supper, that I feel more like playing than reading."

That evening was but a specimen of a great many happy ones, spent in that little room; and when Charles, at the close of it, took down the old Bible, and after reading a chapter, knelt with them before the throne of grace, Aunt Casey felt too happy to go to sleep; but long after they had all retired, she sat watching the moonlight on the water, and thinking how strangely, how very strangely, things had turned up. "Heaven," she said, "seemed to have come right down upon her all of a sudden."

CHAPTER II.

In order to enjoy the pure delights of the country, the heart must be free from corroding care, as well as from the deadening influence of vice. To look abroad at the early dawn, and drink in the opening beauties of the waking day, to quaff, with delight, the freshness of nature, as the dews are dripping from tree and flower, the heart must be fresh from communion with its God, and feel that nature's opening beauties are but a reflection of His image.

As Charles Lovell came upon the front stoop of the cottage, fully rigged for the labors of the day, the scene that spread before him was indeed a treat to an admirer of nature. Streaks of light were stealing up from the eastern horizon, and the fleecy clouds that lingered upon the sky grew brighter every instant. A slight mist hung upon the marshes, and almost imperceptibly was moving upward. Like a long mirror lay the still water, not a breath to ripple its surface, and hardly enough to move the fog, which in spots spread from the marsh across its surface.

A sloop lay at anchor, with her sails partly hoisted, and waiting for the turn of the tide. The cocks were crowing merrily, and for miles across the water, from some barn yard, would distinctly come their clarion notes: while all around, from every bush and tree, the little birds sang joyfully, most joyfully, on this beauteous spring morning. Again and again, Charles turned his eye from point to point, over the fair panorama, watching each new phase of the advancing day with quickened interest, and his heart rejoiced in all the tokens of his Father's power and love, that met his eye; and he felt how happy was his lot, how privileged to labor, where all about him told him only of his God.

At this same moment, while this youth is thus drinking in pure and refreshing thoughts, inspired by the beauties of the coming day, at no great distance, and almost in sight from the point of view where he stands, another youth, but a few months his elder, has taken a glimpse of the same scenery—the same bright fleecy clouds, the same creeping mist, the same glassy river, but with far different feelings. He has not just risen from refreshing slumber, but from the card table, where, with boon companions from the city, he has spent the night. They have come about him as vultures for their prey, for he has just received his inheritance, a princely fortune. They are at a fashionable hotel, erected in a conspicuous place, where those who think they love the country, congregate in crowds during its hottest months. He has purchased a building site, and is preparing to erect a showy house, his country mansion.

He has chosen this region, because his eye has fallen upon a beautiful young creature, whose guardians reside in the vicinity, and he is doing all that wealth will enable him to do, to dazzle her with its glitter, and get within his grasp her pure and trusting heart. He looks with a sour aspect at the breaking day, and drawing the curtain to shut out its light, goes cursing to his bed, to dream away till noon, those hours which should have been devoted to some manly purpose. The lines of these two youths will soon draw nigh together; but their views, their feelings, their intents for life, are widely separate, as earth and heaven.

"And now, Guss, we must begin the tussle," said Charles to his brother, as they stepped from the house together. They were dressed alike, each with a short check shirt, and overalls of the same, good stout gloves on their hands, and boots properly prepared to resist the water, with which the surface of the earth was then plentifully supplied.

"And I think," said Charles, "that our first work must be to put our barn into some decent condition, if that is possible. Shall we go there first?"

"I think, first, we had better go and fix up our fence, on that farthest lot; it must be our pasture this summer, and it will not be much benefited by having a drove of cattle trampling over it, wet as it now is."

"No, that will never do," said Charles, springing to the

top of the stone fence, " that will never do; I wonder who can be so uncivil around here, as to turn such a drove of cattle out at this season of the year, before one can have a chance to fix the fences: there must be a dozen head of them."

" I will soon have them out, while you go and be making some figures around the old barn. It will need some studying out, I guess; it looks like a puzzler to me." So Charles continued his way to the barn, and Augustus, starting off on a run, soon came up with the intruders. There were, indeed, a dozen of them, and so accustomed did the cattle seem to be to the premises, that it was some time before they could be made to comprehend the fact that they were intruders. A few well-directed stones, however, sent them off at last, the way they had come, and a good frolic they made of it, kicking up their heels, and flirting their tails in the air, as though the whole matter was a joke. On coming to the opening by which the cattle had gone out, a person came out into the lot, close to Augustus, and demanded in a peremptory tone,

" What do you mean by meddling with those cattle? who *are* you?"

" I think, sir, I had better ask you that question, for if you are the owner of those cattle, I must request of you to take care of them."

" None of your impudence, sir, none of your impudence." And the man bristled up to Augustus, apparently about to deal him a blow.

Although the stranger was a large man, and Augustus but a good-sized youth of eighteen, he manifested no fear, but stood and surveyed him with perfect composure.

" Perhaps, sir, before you proceed any further, it may be well for you to know, that I am on my own ground, and that both you and your cattle too are intruders."

" That's right, my young man, that's right, stand up for your own, like a man. Aint I glad that the owner of this property has come at last to see to it."

Augustus turned his head towards the new speaker, and perceived a portly gentleman, advancing from the fence, near which they were standing. He appeared to have passed the meridian of life, and yet was doubtless not a very old man, for his step was quite elastic, although he walked at a moderate and even pace. His dress distinguished him as one who did not properly belong to the working class, for he wore rather a broad-skirted coat, with small clothes, and silk stockings, and a slight sprinkling of powder on his hair. His countenance beamed with kindness, although there was evidently a flush upon it, as if under some little excitement. He had a gold-headed cane in his hand, and by his side walked a large black dog.

"I say, I am right glad, my young gentleman, to hear you assert your rights as an owner; that fellow has practiced imposition long enough, and it has been a torment to my spirit."

If ever the demon of rage was depicted upon a human face, it was at that moment painted on his, who had so rudely addressed Augustus. His eyes glared wildly, his nostrils expanded, his mouth was distorted, and his cheek assumed a purple hue. At once he started fiercely towards the old gentleman.

Augustus sprang in the same direction, for he was not of a temper to see one injured, that had interfered in his favor.

"Don't be alarmed, my young friend, I am pretty well protected." And Augustus saw, indeed, that he was so, for the dog was near his master, and had his eye firmly and fiercely fixed on the enraged man, and evidently needed but a word of encouragement to have made short work of the matter.

"It's well you stopped when you did; Rover would like no better sport than a short tussle. I rather think he bears no good will to you."

The man had indeed come to a sudden stand-still, and even thought it prudent to retreat a few steps, and contented himself with threatening all manner of evil, in the shape of prosecutions against both the parties, besides letting off oaths enough to have satisfied any sea captain, in a gale of wind.

Augustus, thinking that he had better work to do than stand and listen to his profanity, at once proceeded towards the opening of the fence, with the design of fixing it, so as to prevent any further annoyance from the cattle. His opponent, however, advanced with him to the fence, talking in a very angry tone.

"I warn you, at your peril, not to put up a single rail or

pole there. This is highway, it 's been so ever since I 've been here, and it shall be kept so. Put it up, and I 'll take it down; and prosecute, if you will, and we 'll see who has got most money to spend in the law."

"I am not going to law with you," replied Augustus, "nor am I going to impound your cattle, if they get in here; but I shall fix the fence, and if you or any one else attempts to prevent me, and gets injured in the attempt, you or he may prosecute as soon as you please."

With that he commenced placing a pole, which he had dragged from a heap that lay near by, and was in the act of laying it on the fence, when the other seized it, and endeavored to displace it. Augustus was now excited to the very extent of endurance, and springing at the offender, wrested the pole from his grasp, and, in some way, he scarcely knew how, sent him reeling on to his own premises, where he finally came up on his back.

"And you served the puppy right at last; he is thoroughly frightened now, see how he goes, and you have not laid your hand on him either; he has played the bully here long enough. Old Grumby was afraid of him, and more than half his pasturing was upon your land. He is too mean to live in the country; he would like to establish a right of way across your lot, in order to save him a few rods of fence. But I 've kept a look out upon him. I knew that you boys were away and might possibly never live here, but it would be a great damage to the property; so every year, unknown to him, I have had the fence put up, and have evidence of his pulling it down, so you need n't fear his threats about the law."

"I thank you much, sir, both for my brother, and myself; but, surely, the man could not be so unjust and ungenerous as to wish thus to injure us."

"Ay, you are a young man, or you would not talk so. What does such a man care for but his own interest? But I must say, you won't find many such in the country. Though they are more troublesome here than elsewhere, the country is meant for peace and good will. We are all here in a measure dependent on one another, and one good turn deserves another. But I will tell you, for your comfort, that fellow is about leaving us; he has made himself so many enemies, that he finds it very uncomfortable being among us, and so he is going back to the city where he came from."

Charles had not noticed the doings of his brother, from the fact that he had been very much occupied. Things looked so much worse than he expected, that he began to be utterly hopeless as to his ability to fix the barn in any way that would make it serviceable. At first he thought to begin and straighten the yard, for the fence around it stood every way but the right; one post leaned too far in, and another too far out; in one length there were only two rails, and in another two boards. The gate was wanting, its place being filled by two long poles. The yard itself appeared to have been made the receptacle for all the broken posts, and rails, and pieces of board, that do so wonderfully accumulate on a farm, but have no business in a barn yard.

"It is a much more desperate case than I thought for. I fear the whole concern is past redemption; and without a barn, I may as well stop where I am. I have no means to build a new one, that is sure. I fear I have been too sanguine."

"Well done, talking to yourself, ha! ha! ha! How are you, Lovell?"

"Why, Slocum, is this you! Where have you come from?"

"It 's me, myself; how are you? looking at the old place, ha?"

"Yes, I 'm looking at it, but the more I look, the worse it seems."

"Pull it down, then, and let me build you a new one, ha! ha! ha!"

"We could pull it down easy enough, I think, if that was all. But as to building a new one, it can't be done. I have no money."

"How is the frame? aint that pretty stiff?" And Slocum, as he was called, walked up towards it, looking along its front, and was about to proceed to the other side of it, when Augustus, and the old gentleman who had befriended him, came up.

"Your brother tells me," at the same time giving his hand to Charles, "that you are about to do something with this old place, and I am very glad, for it can do nobody any good in its present shape. Are you going to build a new one?"

"I am not able to do it, sir."

"That is spoken like a man; and so you are thinking how to make the best of this. Where 's that fellow I thought I saw here? Ay, old ha! ha! ha! there you are: come along, and say what is best to be done here. That frame looks straight."

"That is what I was just going to say, colonel. I should n't wonder if it was in a pretty sound state."

"You should n't wonder! go right inside then, and look."

With a good hearty laugh, Slocum entered the building followed by Charles.

"That Slocum is a real smart fellow, and he has a warm and honest heart. He is a noble, generous soul. He has a foolish way of laughing, but he is a good workman, and understands work in the country. You know there is a great deal in that, or you will know it if you live long enough. Get some of these fellows from the city to do a job for you, and there will be as many ends to it as there are legs to a centipede. They would want you to put a mould board, all planed and fluted, to a cow stable floor, and they would fix one part so as to unfix another, and before you know it, you 've got to make all new to match, or have your place look like mother Bunch's petticoat, new before and ragged behind."

Augustus smiled at the old gentleman's simile, but he manifested such a hearty interest in their affairs, that his heart began already to yield him the respect due to a friend.

"Well, ha! ha! what 's the report?"

"I guess she 'll go."

"The frame," said Charles, addressing his brother, "seems to be quite sound and straight."

"There is no difficulty then whatever. Slocum, you tell these young gentlemen what is to be done, and in the cheapest way, you hear?"

"I have, colonel."

"Mr. Slocum tells me, sir," and Charles slightly bowed to the old gentleman, "that he has engaged to work for you for the next ten days. Could you conveniently allow him to spend a couple of days for us, before he commences your job?"

The old gentleman put his hand on Charles' shoulder,

"I was just going to propose to you that very thing; you need this work done soon, for you must soon be at other work, and I only wish I was young enough to come and give you a lift. But you shall have help; our motto in the country is, 'hang together—a long pull, a strong pull, and a pull together.'"

"Ha! ha! ha! that 's a good notion. Colonel, you send some of your boys along after to-morrow, and we will all see what we can do."

"I will see they 're here. Anything that I can do to give a boust to them that are just beginning the tug of life, I am glad to do—if its only stopping villains from taking advantages," giving a sly look at Augustus; and then bowing very politely, and being bowed to as politely in return by the young gentlemen, he called his dog and was about to proceed on his way, when appearing to recollect something, he turned to Charles,

"You are strangers here, are you not?"

"Somewhat so, sir; we were born in a distant part of this town, but have been brought up elsewhere."

"You see that chimney rising just above the hill there?" pointing with his cane.

"I do, sir."

"That is my house, and when you can make it convenient to call, I shall be happy to see you. But where under the heaven, do you live here? not surely in that stone building?"

"Oh no, sir, we live with Mrs. Casey, just round in the woods here."

"Well, well, well, that will do. Mrs. Casey is a good woman. I wish there were no worse folks in the world than she."

As the old gentleman went on his way, Charles could not but admire the dignity of his carriage, as he had the apparent kindness of his heart.

"That is the finest looking old gentleman I ever saw. How neatly he is dressed, and how well he manages that gold-headed cane."

"He is as good as he looks—he would walk a mile any time to help a neighbor, young or old."

"Has he boys of his own?"

"He has but one child, a daughter, and a fine one she is, as pretty as a pink, and as kind a heart as the old man has. No, he has no boys of his own; but if he only speaks the word, more than a dozen fellows that he has helped, in one way or another, will jump to do what he says."

"He must be a very happy man."

"I rather guess he is. But come, Charlie, now to business. The best thing for you and Guss to do right off, is just to go at the old thing, and strip her clean, take off every board on the building as careful as you can, and then we will see what can be done; it will take you to-day and to-morrow, tight work, and next day I'll be on, ha! ha! ha!"

The pulling off of old boards and piling them away, the picking up of rubbish, and clearing off a mass of unsightly materials, makes rather a dry and dusty subject for the pen, but to these young men it was a work full of inspiration.

The timbers appeared in such a sound condition, and the frame so little out of plumb in any part, that the prospect brightened before them continually, of having it put into a condition to suit their purpose.

"And what is this?" said Augustus, as he had just taken off some boards that exposed a part of the building which they could not get at before, "there seems to be some kind of lumber." Charles at once came by his side.

"It must be the shingles old Grumby was to purchase with our half of the corn last year. I supposed he had sold the corn for his own use."

"It is n't best to judge too soon, is it Charlie?"

"No, nor to judge the poor too hardly; the old man bought the shingles, but probably had not means enough to have them put on—there are quite a number of bundles."

"Enough to shingle it anew."

"I judge not; but there will be enough to make it perfectly tight."

So soon as they had exposed the frame fully to view, the brothers made a thorough examination, and to their amazement found nothing wanting but one new sill.

This, a few hours enabled them to procure from their own woods; a fine oak tree was felled, the branches lopped off, and the trunk cut off the required length, and by their oxen soon drawn to the place where it could be prepared for its destination.

Slocum came at the appointed time, and soon showed his skill in making old things new. Boards were turned inside out, and end for end, any way to make a snug fit; doors were hung straight, and well secured with large wooden bolts; the windows swung upon hinges, and fastened with hooks, enough of both articles having been found among the old rubbish. The roof could defy the rains, and the fence around the yard was straight, and made of uniform materials.

It took a complete week of working days before the whole was finished; and on the two last days six strong-handed young men labored cheerfully, refusing at the close to take one cent as remuneration.

"You are entirely welcome to all we 've done; we have all had the same turn done for us, and maybe shall want it again some time, and may have to call upon you to put your shoulder to the wheel."

"And I promise you," said Charles, speaking with much earnestness, "both shoulders, and both hands, and a right good will into the bargain."

And with light and happy hearts, much happier than money could have made them, off they started. They had done a deed of kindness, they had helped a brother youth in his first tussle with life, and they had received the cordial grasp of his hand, and the warm thanks of his heart. Their own hearts were lighter and happier too, and they have bound him to themselves by an enduring cord. These deeds of mutual charity, blest country life, are all thine own.

"And now," said Charles to his brother, as they were standing together, and looking up at the building, "I have another notion which I mean to carry out at our first leisure. The barn is now whole and straight, and fit for use, but the boards, you see, are of different colors, and it don't look as well as it really deserves to. I was reading last evening of a wash, easily and cheaply made, that will resist the weather, and can be prepared of any color. As soon as we can, after getting our oats in, and our corn and potatoes planted, we will fix some, and paint it."

One evening, just as he was about to stop his labors for the day, being alone at one end of the lot, his brother having gone to attend to their few chores, Charles was startled by hearing his name called rather loudly, and looking whence the sound came, he saw a cane waving in the air, as though beckoning him towards it. Although the person who wielded it was hidden from his view by a stone fence, he was well assured who the individual must be, as the wall formed the dividing line between his farm and that of Colonel Johnson, the old gentleman already introduced to the reader. At once he hastened to the spot.

"You will excuse me, Mr. Lovell, for calling you so unceremoniously, but I had no other way to get at you; the gate is away round the other side, my man is busy with his chores, and as to climbing this wall, at my time of day, it is out of the question."

"No apology is at all required, sir; I am but too happy to come at your bidding, and shall be glad to know how I can serve you."

"Well, I will tell you. I expect a couple of young friends to spend the evening at my house, and as they are the kind of folks I think you will fancy, I have brought a request from my daughter, that you favor us with your company."

Charles was taken by surprise, but he felt that it would be uncivil to say No.

"You do me great honor, sir, in thus distinguishing a stranger. I certainly cannot deny myself the pleasure of accepting your invitation."

"That is like a man again. But let me tell you one thing, you are not so much a stranger as you think for. I've watched you pretty closely; I have had my eye on you; but mind, and be with us this evening, and come in good season too."

As old Colonel Johnson will be often brought into notice in the course of our story, it may not be out of place to give the reader an idea of the domicil he inhabited, and his style of living. The man himself will be better understood as he appears in the scenes where he may bear a part.

It is an undeniable fact, that our ancestors had a better taste in the matter of constructing a home for life, than we of the present generation. Their edifice combined the beautiful and the enduring, and even conveyed the idea that for more than one generation did the builder erect the mansion that was to cluster the gems of his heart. It was no tawdry affair, got up for the purpose of attracting the gaze of the traveller, but a substantial resting place that could stand unshaken, amid the howling storm, and in spite of the wear and tear of time, even to a very old age, retain its respectability and usefulness.

The home of the Colonel had been erected by his father, in the days of his youth, and for aught that man could see, was as likely to continue, unshorn of its strength, for an hundred years to come. It was a substantial brick edifice, with heavy cornices under its eaves, and heavy mouldings over its windows, and heavy pillars supporting the massive roof that sheltered its wide porch before the front door ; and the door itself, divided into upper and lower, with its deep mouldings and heavy iron knocker, looked strong enough to be a barrier against the rage of the elements, or any other unwelcome intruder. It seemed to say, when barred, to all without, "Those sheltered here may sleep in safety." It was placed a little back from the road, allowing a neat court yard in front, and was shaded by trees, that had doubtless been growing ever since the foundations of the house were laid. It was two stories in height, and not very deep, but that deficiency was supplied by an ample addition to the rear, in which seemed to be combined all the little snuggeries that are so essential to the term comfort, as applied to a dwelling. Beside the court-yard, which projected a little on each side of its wide front, ran a carriage-way, leading back to ample barns, sufficiently in the rear of the house to allow of a good-sized garden, into which, from one door of the dwelling, its inmates might at once enter, and be among the flowers and fruits, with which it abounded.

Just as the twilight was becoming sufficiently dim to require the aid of lamps, Charles lifted the heavy knocker on the colonel's door, and was received by the old gentleman himself, and welcomed by a hearty shake of the hand.

"Just in time, my dear young fellow, just in time, walk in." Charles had barely time by the aid of the lamp to admire the ample proportions of the hall, and the broad low stairs springing from it, with their heavy balustrade and fluted rails, ere he was taken by the arm, and ushered into the parlor.

"Lucy, my dear, I have the pleasure of introducing to you Mr. Charles Lovell—my daughter, Mr. Lovell."

The young lady was seated beside a small table, highly polished, and just in the act of pouring out the tea. She rose and received him with such a cordial tone, and such a winning smile, that he could not help feeling that some herald must have preceded him, and won an interest for him with the fair lady.

"The Rev. Mr. Jamieson, our minister—Mr. Lovell, Mr. Jamieson. But perhaps you have met before, as I find our friend here, though of the blue order, favors us with his company on the sabbath." Charles smiled.

"I have not before had the pleasure of an introduction, although I cannot feel that Mr. Jamieson is quite a stranger to me."

"Nor you to me, sir," replied the reverend gentleman, "for I have noticed your attendance upon our services, and should have called upon you before if our good friend here had not promised me that we should meet here. Allow me, Mr. Lovell, to introduce to you my friend Lieutenant Montague, of the navy. You see" (speaking to the officer) "I have to give your title, as you do not carry your orders with you."

"Not when off duty, sir; but perhaps I ought to carry some of my insignia about me, that I may not be mistaken for a landsman, and shame my friends by my ignorance. Sailors, you know, are not expected to be very learned."

"That is all very well spoken, but I shall not treat you as you deserve just now, by proclaiming your excellences."

This produced a hearty laugh on the part of the colonel, and a pleasant smile from Miss Lucy, and at once drove from the mind of Charles all that stiffness attendant upon a first introduction.

As the colonel was a great stickler for old customs when they could as well be maintained as not, the handing round of tea was one that he had always kept up. He had an idea that it was a more sociable way of doing things, and perhaps he thought it a little more genteel.

Whatever its effect in general, certainly there was on that occasion no lack of social converse.

For some time the young clergyman and Charles had

quite a *tête-à-tête* upon some subject, in which both seemed much interested, with a word occasionally thrown in by the old gentleman, as their remarks might reach his ear. While the lieutenant and Miss Lucy were throwing playful shots at each other, on a subject of apparently minor importance, but upon which they differed. The old gentleman at length caught the run of their argument and broke in upon them.

"You may just stop trying your battery, Lucy, upon Lieutenant Montague; he is a heretic bred and born. I have no doubt now, much as he loves his friend here, our clergyman, he thinks it a sin for him to wear a gown, and had rather see him go into the pulpit with a pea-jacket on."

"Oh, my dear sir, not so bad as that. I appeal to Miss Lucy."

"Oh no, father, he has no objections to the gown; I think he rather prefers it."

"Then its the prayers; he don't like the prayers, I know he don't, for when I handed him the book last sabbath, he never said amen once. I suppose he thought it would be like hallooing 'ship ahoy,' or saying 'ay, ay, sir.'"

A hearty laugh followed this remark, both upon the part of the old gentleman and all the company. It had the effect, however, of drawing the conversation to a single topic.

"I think," said Mr. Jamieson, "I can answer for Lieutenant Montague on this subject. He has not much objection to our forms—he only fears their tendency, and we should all regret it, could we believe that they hindered the worship of the heart."

"Asking pardon of you, reverend sir, that savors a little—a little too much of the blue Presbyterian cant."

A smile was upon every countenance, for all understood the speaker well.

"Now, take the whole mass of you together; Presbyterians, Methodists, Congregationalists, and what not, and you are always dinging about the heart. No matter how you say your prayers, on your feet, or on your knees, or lying down half asleep, or on your head, so as you pray from the heart it is all well and good."

"Or clinging to a rope at the mast head, with the waves raging beneath, and the winds howling around you."

"But that's another case; prayer is very like to come out

of a man, pretty natural and pretty sincere, at such a time, at least it would out of me, but that aint the thing. I say there is very great fitness in having the worship of our God conducted in a solemn and careful manner, where everything is prepared reverently before hand. I don't like this one jumping up, and that one jumping up, and rattling off a prayer, sometimes with one idea, and sometimes with none at all, while the rest will, some of them, be leaning down, some standing bolt upright, and some staring round to see what the rest are about."

"Oh, father! father! it is so long since you have been in any other church besides your own, that you have forgotten, and your remembrance must be of some irregular proceeding a long time ago."

"Well, Col. Johnson," replied the lieutenant, "I am free to acknowledge that there are some parts of our service that I could wish were different. Many of our public prayers are too long, and not sufficiently reverent, and many appear more like addresses to the people than supplication to Heaven, and there may not be apparent reverence enough among the people, but still there may be as much purity of heart as where there is more external propriety."

"There you have it again—your heart piety. If a man has got any piety at all, won't he show it out?"

"Allow me, Col. Johnson," said Mr. Jamieson, "to suggest that, perhaps, no one can be a correct judge of a denomination with which he is not connected. I believe both you and myself have lamented over this fact, in reference to misconceptions, which have taken possession of even many otherwise intelligent people, and which have created, at least, an external coldness, if they have not turned aside the charity of their heart from us."

"Heart again; well, well, my dear sir, I don't know but you are right. I do believe there is a deal of uncharitableness going the round among us all. I hope we shall all turn out better in the end, than we give one another credit for here; if we don't, it will be a bad business for the most of us."

"And I think, father, we have canvassed this matter long enough, and with your leave I would ask Mr. Montague a question, in reference to the gentlemen who are, it is said, about locating in this vicinity. I have been just inquiring of Mr. Lovell, but it seems they are strangers to him. Do you know them?"

"I have been introduced to one of them in the city—the one who has purchased Roder's Point. He is said to be very wealthy—he has just came into possession of his estate. I think a friend of his is also looking out for a building spot."

"It will be quite an advantage to our place, or rather to its vicinity, to have gentlemen of wealth coming into the region."

"That depends, my dear, upon the kind of men they are; one good, honest, industrious working man, is better for the country than half a dozen men, with a million a piece, who could do nothing but set an example of extravagance to our young farmers, and teach them to gamble and violate the sabbath."

"And I fear very much, from what I have seen, that one of them, at least, is not in a very fair way to make a very useful citizen."

"Then we don't want him. A man who possesses wealth, possesses power; but it is power to do evil as well as good. If they are coming here to put up their fine houses, as mere places for summer resort, where they can idle away their time in fishing and hunting, and carousing at our taverns, and spending their sabbaths in dissipation with their companions from the city, who come out on that day as a day of leisure; in fine, when men of wealth come into the country, in order that they may act without restraint, I say we want them not; their fine houses may please the fancy of those who look at them as they sail along our shores, or travel through our roads, but one had better have good log huts, put up by hard-working honest young men—they would look a hundred times handsomer to me."

"Well done, father, why you are getting beyond yourself; you have no idea how eloquent you are."

"I think, Miss Johnson, he could not be eloquent in a better cause. The country seems to me, when I retire into it, after mingling with the crowds in our own cities, or those of foreign lands, to be the natural abode of purity, peace, and contentment, and those must necessarily have for their companions industry, sobriety, and religion. The country needs no ornament that man can add. The beauties are the result of a divine skill, they are complete in themselves; but to be enjoyed the mind must be in harmony with them."

"And," said Mr. Jamieson, his bright eye kindling with the theme, "how much they lose who forget the fine sentiment you have just expressed. That in obeying the precepts of our Saviour the mind is brought into that peaceful state, which fits it to enjoy the beauties of nature. Obedience acts upon the mind like an inspiration; the very airs of heaven play around the senses of one whose heart is fresh from communion with its God."

Charles was deeply moved, for the sentiments just expressed were fully his own, and his heart served to be drawn very near to both the speakers. And Lucy, too, from some cause, must have sympathized most deeply, for when the reverend gentleman paused, Charles, who sat near to her, observed a tear to start, and lose itself somewhere on her beautiful face.

As the evening was drawing to a close, the little party made a movement for separating.

"One moment if you please, gentlemen. Lucy, my dear, the prayer book, if you please," and as his daughter came with it, he merely pointed her to Mr. Jamieson. The reverend gentleman arose, and gracefully took it from her, and turning at once to the psaltery read an evening psalm, and then all prostrating themselves in worship, he laid the closed book as he did so on the chair before him, and offered up in simple, unaffected language, a prayer suited to the occasion. Whether the old gentleman recognized it or not as an extemporaneous effusion, he failed not to respond the amen in a good full voice. It had been a pleasant interview, and it closed as all social scenes should close.

"And now, my young friend, since you have found the way here," at the same time taking the hand of Lovell in both of his, "let us see you often, and I ask it not in compliment, but with all sincerity."

Charles replied as well as his excited feelings would permit, for the whole scene had been so agreeable, so much to his mind, and so unexpected, and the prospect of being a welcome guest among such friends was so pleasant to contemplate, that he felt it indeed to be an era in his life.

As the three gentlemen walked along on the road, which led by the residence of young Lovell, their conversation was interrupted by the trampling of horses' feet, and presently one came out from the woods, at some distance ahead, and crossing the road, stopped at the opening of a narrow lane. One of the riders sprung from the horse, evidently a female, and started off in much haste down the lane. The man paused a moment, and then came rapidly forwards on the road, by the side of which the gentlemen were walking. As he approached, they could see him draw his cloak around him more closely, so as completely to screen his countenance.

"What is it," said Lieutenant Montague, "which so distinguishes each individual from another, that whether we perceive his features or not, if we have been in the habit of seeing him, we can recognize him, either by some peculiarity in his walk, or in his manner of sitting, or even of wearing his clothes. Now, that man I am very sure I know, merely by the way in which he wears his hat, and carries his head. I don't much like the fact of his hiding his face from us."

"Perhaps he merely shields himself from the night air."

"Thank you, Jamieson, for reminding me of an important principle,—to think no evil."

"I hope you do not suppose that I intended to administer a reproof."

"By no means; and if you did, I should consider it but the privilege of a friend. But do you leave us here, Mr. Lovell?"

"My home is just behind this clump of trees, so lonely that it is easily hidden."

"If what I hear of it be true, it is one that neither you nor your friends need be ashamed of."

"Neither am I, sir, but enjoy it, I have no doubt, much more than many do a palace. But may I not hope to see you there?" addressing Mr. Jamieson.

"You may, my dear sir, and that very shortly. I fear only I shall be tempted to come too often."

"And you too, sir. Is this to be our last interview?" turning to the officer.

"Not if you will allow me to visit you;" and taking the hand of Lovell, "I meet with too few congenial spirits as yourself and my friend here, not to wish to enjoy your company while I may. May I come when I please? Will you treat me without ceremony?"

"Without ceremony I promise you, beyond what we exercise towards each other. I hold that proper ceremony tends to strengthen friendship, and make its communings more agreeable."

"I cordially agree with you in that. I will come, you may depend upon it."

The three friends parted, for so they might now be called; Charles crossing through the grove, and they winding along the road that led towards the village.

CHAPTER III.

"WELL, Slocum, how are you?" said the old tavern keeper, who owned the hotel most generally frequented by those who came to Wellgrove, not as travellers, for it was at some distance from the public road, but for the purpose of spending their time in amusement. It was situated near to the water, and was therefore convenient for fishing and shooting, as most of the wild fowl in that vicinity frequented the creeks and marshes. It was, moreover, a pleasant retired spot, well shaded with some large willows, and commanded an extensive view of the Sound, and of the adjoining inlet, and what was of some consequence to pleasure-seekers, was very well kept. The tavern keeper was just coming from behind his bar, and about to take his seat in the big arm chair by the window, when he thus addressed the gentleman named above.

"Well, Slocum, how are you? what's the news from Milton this morning?"

"Ha! ha! ha! Uncle Jo, how are you? how do you get along in Wellgrove?"

"So so, pretty much after the old sort."

"Plenty of rich boarders this summer, ha! ha! ha!"

"Well, we 've got a few, but whether they 're rich or not, I can't answer for. One thing I should 'nt be afraid to swear to."

"Ha! ha! ha! what's that?"

"That if you and I live long enough, we shall see some of 'em with very little loose change in their pockets. I 'll swear to that."

"Going it strong, eh, Uncle Jo? ha! ha! ha!"

"Well, you can see as well as I can, Slocum. Have n't you seen Vanderbose yet?"

"Not I, and I've come again for to see him, I must—is he up yet?"

"Not yet."

"When will he be up?"

The old man drew a large silver watch from his pocket, and holding it up before the face of his visitor,

"There, by the time the big pointer and the little pointer both get up here to the top of the hill, and stand together, then you may expect to see him and the rest on 'em come out rubbing their eyes, and swearing about there being such a glare of light, and asking for some morning bitters to take the bad taste out of their mouths."

"They 'd better not have taken their evening bitters, may be, if they did n't like the taste of it in the morning. But you aint in earnest, Uncle Jo, that they won't be out till twelve o'clock?"

"All I know is, that they have n't yet. Why, la! Slocum, how could you get up in the morning and go about as spry as a lamp-lighter, as you do, if you was up, maybe, till break of day, guzzling down wine, and rattling the dice box, or shuffling cards and dominos; you would n't feel like work, would you?"

"You don't say? it can't be so?"

"It is none of my business to be telling tales out of school. They board here, and pay for their rooms, and for what they eat and drink; and when they go to their rooms at night, and aint too noisy, it aint for me to go and knock at their doors like a college tutor, and say 'go to bed.'"

"Well, Uncle Jo, what shall I do? here have I been three days running to see this Vanderbose. The New Yorkers, you see, have jobbed the main house; they know what they are about, and have a written contract, when so much of the work is done so much of the money must be planked down, and there is no get away from it. But here he comes to me, and wants me to go to work, and to bring three or four good hands with me—putting up a boat house, and a billiard house, and a dog house, and ever so many little rookeries round, and we 've been at work pretty lively for about six weeks, and some of the fellows want their money, and they must have some, they want it for their families."

"Oh, la! if that 's all, there can be no difficulty. He 's

got money enough, so they say. He pays me regular once a week. I tell 'em all when they come, 'Saturday night must see us all square,' and they toe the mark. He 'll pay you, no danger."

"That aint the thing of it, Uncle Jo; I suppose there is no danger in the long run, at least for some time yet, but such fellows as Ringold and Slaton want their money; they are good fellows to work, but they both had a long sickness last winter, and they 've got pretty much ashore, and you see he has n't yet paid us one copper."

"Have you asked him?"

"Why, yes, I told him when I hired them for him, that they were poor men, and would like to have their money once a week. Well, he did n't make no reply to that, and when I came to ask him for fifty dollars a week ago, he gave me a kind of grave answer, and said something I did n't very well hear, about paying when the work was done."

"Well, I don't know much about it."

"I don't see, Uncle Jo, what such folks want to come to the country for; why don't they stay in the city, where they can lay abed, or do what they please inside their old brick walls. What pleasure can they take here?"

"Well, it is n't for the country, Slocum, that they come. But the fact is, they don't know what to do with themselves. They aint got no business—nothing in the living world to do, but to seek their pleasure. Well, they git tired of their balls, and shows, and parties, and theatres, and what not, and it's kind of fashionable, and sounds large, to have a country seat, or mansion, as they call it; and then there is another thing, they think in the country they can do jist as they please—there aint no police to see after them, they can spend their Sabbath lounging along shore, or lying under the trees, or drinking and carousing in their houses."

"I don't think such folks do us much good."

"Good! no—but here he comes."

From a wide passage which led into the bar-room, was now seen approaching a young man, not much past twenty-one years of age, his countenance not bad looking, and yet not very prepossessing—in fact, but little expression to it. He seemed, however, hardly yet in the wide-awake world; his eyes were nearly closed; and a scowl was on his brow, as though the broad light of the bar-room was painful. His hair uncombed, stood in all directions, not at all adding to the composure of his appearance.

A scarlet dressing-gown, and red slippers, composed the principal part of his dress that was seen. As he entered, he turned immediately to the bar, without saying a word, and the old tavern keeper arose to wait upon him. He went behind his bar, placed a decanter, a tumbler, and a bottle of bitters on the counter, and then stood looking across the room towards Mr. Slocum, to whom he found a chance to give a sly wink. Not a word was uttered by either party. The gentleman helped himself to the dose he wished, and then turning round, was about to go the way he had come, when the landlord remarked:

"There is a man here waiting to see you."

"To see me?"

"Yes, there he is;" with that Mr. Slocum arose, and walked towards him.

"Good morning, sir."

The young man looked a moment as though not able to comprehend the identity of the person before him; but after rubbing his eyes a little, replied:

"Ah! it 's you is it? how do you get along?"

"We are getting along, sir, slowly."

"You may well say slowly. I thought you would all be done, and cleared out long ago."

"Then you must have thought we 'd have wanted our pay."

"Yes, no danger of that. You fellows are greedy enough for your pay."

"Well, I suppose we have a right to it, if we earn it"

"Earn it! Well, did you want me? be quick; I can't stop here all day."

"Well, sir, we have been waiting these two days to put up the boat house. You agreed to come on Monday, and here it is Wednesday, and you have n't come yet."

"Well, suppose I have n't, and suppose I choose to keep a parcel of fellows at work doing nothing, whose business is it so long as I pay them for it?"

"That 's all well enough, sir; still there are other persons waiting for us, who need our services, and it is a little pleasanter for us to be busy than idle."

"Well, I 'll be there some time to day;" and he was about to retire, when Slocum continued,

"I should like to say a little something to you about money."

"Well, what about it?"

"You know I told you about the last men I hired, that they were poor, and needed their money every week."

"Well, give it to them, that 's the way my builder does. I should be nicely set to work, settling with a parcel of laborers every time they wanted money."

"Your builder from New York is responsible alone to his men, and his men to him. Mine is a different case. I hired these men for your accommodation, and not mine. I get no benefit for it, and do not feel disposed to advance money for a rich man."

"I tell you what it is, Mister, you need n't think to hold your head up to me with your independent airs. I shall teach you country folks manners. You have undertaken your job, and you shall finish it; and when you have finished it, you shall have your money, and not a cent shall you have beforehand; so you hear the last I have got to say to you."

"You will find, though, that it is not the last that I shall have to say to *you*;" and Mr. Slocum was about turning away, when the young man came towards him in great rage.

"What was that you said, sir?"

"I said," replied Mr. Slocum, in a very calm voice, "that it would not be the last I should have to say to you."

"And what did you mean by that, you puppy?" shaking his fist at the same time.

"I advise you, sir, to keep your fist down, for if it should happen to touch me even slightly, it might not so be so well for you; and at once take back that insolent remark; take it back quick, sir."

The young bully now began to feel that he had been too hasty, so he began making retrograde movements towards the passage. But the landlord stepped up and laid his hand npon them both.

"Now you see there can't be none of this here. You, Mr. Vanderbose, just ask his pardon for calling an honest man a puppy—people in these parts can't stand that—or else

I shall just leave you to his mercy; and Slocum aint a man to be trifled with."

The young man indeed began to feel so, for he was already under the grasp of Slocum, and he saw the fire flashing from his eyes.

"I'll take it, I'll take it back; let go of me, let go of me."

"Very glad to do so; and now, sir, your decision as to the money; for after what you have said, I shall not apply to you again, but shall leave you to settle the matter with the sheriff."

This brought forth a long string of curses on the country, and upon himself for even dirtying his fingers with it, until after unloading his foul cargo, he demanded how much money was wanted, and when told, opened his purse and handed the fifty dollars.

"And now," said Mr. Slocum, "if you wish your work to be done by me, you must come and give your directions, for I have other persons who are waiting for my services."

"I suppose my money is as good as theirs."

"Perhaps it is; your manners are not, and I like not only good pay, but civil treatment."

"That's it, that's it," said the landlord, now acting as umpire; "you see, Mr. Vanderbose, you don't quite understand our folks; we country people feel all, that one is about as good as another. We will do anything to serve in a civil way, but we can't be druv—we can't be druv, *no how*. You are used to have people bow and cringe for your money, and fly at your bidding, and you get to think that if you have only enough in your purse, earth and heaven too must both be your humble servants. But we can't go it, sir, we can't be druv—and you'll find it so; so you might just as well speak civil, and jog along quiet."

And finally, the young gentleman began to be of the same opinion, for his deportment was much more deferential, and he engaged in about three hours to be at his place, and attend to their requirements; and then he shuffled off to his room, doubtless to pour out the abundance of his wrath in deep curses upon the country, with its hot and glaring sun, and its impudent and self-willed people.

Roder's Point, the site which young Vanderbose had selected, was indeed one, which if not suited for a truly rural taste, was well designed for the public gaze—being a long tongue of land running out into the sound, with a gradual rise from the shore, until at its highest point a considerable eminence was attained, affording an extended view of the water. It was a rolling plot of land, with no tree upon it, except a few dwarf cedars sprinkled along among the rocks that lined its base. On the very summit of vision, Mr. Vanderbose had chosen to place his mansion, a high staring square house, with porticos and large pillars in front and rear, for the rear was as visible from the highways of the land as the front was to the passers-by upon the water. A wide hall ran through its centre, with two rooms on each side of it, opening into the hall and communicating with each other by folding doors ; windows in abundance on every side, and from each the same extended view, until to an observer from within, it was evident that the grand idea of its owner was to see and be seen as far as possible. A straight flight of stairs conveyed you to the second story, into the same wide hall with the same four rooms opening into it. The kitchen and cellar, and all the et ceteras for domestic purposes, were in the basement. There were no little attachments, such as we often see connected with our snug little country houses, conveying to the mind of the beholder ideas of convenience and comfort, and home enjoyment. It stood all alone in its glory, a square well-proportioned building, but looking as much like a place to make a home in as the light-house that loomed up on the distant headland. Not a tree, nor even a shrub was there to cast a shadow that a butterfly might shelter under. These were all yet to be planted, if at all, and how many long years must pass before this vast white pile would have its comfortless aspect softened by the graceful foliage of towering trees. But it answered the design of its owner. It had a majestic appearance as it stood thus in bold relief upon the distant sky. It would catch the eye of passengers, and through the crowded deck of the steamers, his name would be passed as the happy owner. A home he thought of not establishing, he merely wanted a place to attract the admiration of the stranger, to call his mansion, to exhibit to obsequious acquaintances, and to revel in at his pleasure, without the annoyance of a prying neighbor. But in addition to all this, he had fallen in love. Now, dear reader, don't be alarmed, and don't begin to scold. We shall not indeed think hard of you if you do, for if our estimate of his character is correct, and if we have introduced him to you in a fair light, you might very properly turn upon us and say, "In love! fallen in love! such a man fallen in love!" But mercy on us! how you stare! are there not many kinds of love? Think not, gentle reader, that we have the most distant allusion to that fire which comes from heaven, and only kindles in a pure breast—which throws its genial warmth through every avenue of the heart, and before it flies away all that is selfish and debasing. Oh no! we mean no such thing. He has fallen in love in this same way many times, and with many different objects. He fell in love with a very fine span of horses, and because his purse was large enough he bought them. He fell in love, too, with a dashing curricle, and he bought that; and then a beautiful spaniel caught his eye, and because his owner did not wish to part with him, he paid him many fold the value of the brute; so strongly was his heart attached. And now in the same way he has fallen in love with a very pretty girl. Poor thing! you say, surely he does not think to buy her!

If he gets her at all it must be in some such way. He has no heart to offer in exchange for hers. No pure and generous heart, such as lovely woman fancies she obtains, when she gives her own unselfish love to man. All he can offer is a large rent-roll in the city; splendid rooms at the most fashionable hotel, to spend some winter months; jewels to adorn her person, already one of nature's most finished pieces; an elegant carriage and fine horses to carry her in style, the admiration of all eyes; and, lastly, and perhaps the thing most alluring of all, this mansion on its airy height, the proudest building in the region.

But again you say, Has she a heart? and will she be likely to barter it for such trash? She has a heart, warm and loving, and pure as earthly innocence can be; and with one who could command her respect, who could guide her opening mind, who could cherish her warm affections, she would be all that man could ask for. But she is young, scarce eighteen, an orphan, and although kind friends protect her, and provide for her, yet no father screens her with his jealous eye, no mother listens to the tale of all her little feelings, nor teaches her what woman wants to make her happy. Poor thing! you say, and you well may; an orphan, a female orphan, demands the sacred sympathy of all. But we are going too fast, and must return to our story; this digression, gentle reader, was only made for the purpose of explaining the reason why this mansion was erected; a splendid cage to catch some eager bird.

CHAPTER IV.

"I THINK, brother Charles," said Augustus one evening as they were returning from the labors of the field, "we ought to be thinking about providing ourselves with a horse; we need not get a high-priced one, but something in the shape of a horse, that we can at times use on the farm, or ride off with a little."

"I have been thinking of the same thing, Guss; we must have a horse before a great while; at the distance we are from the village, and from church, we must have some means of conveyance. But I do not exactly agree with you about the kind of beast. It will cost as much to keep a poor horse, as a good one."

"Yes, but I only spoke of a poor horse, because I thought we should not be able to pay the price for a first-rate beast."

"Well, Guss, I will tell you what I have been thinking of. That if, when we get our crops in, we could find a first-rate colt of about three years old, of the right breed and quality, we could probably get it for half the price which the same quality of horse would bring when trained, and we could train him ourselves."

"And train him just to our mind. And I think I know of a first-rate creature. Slocum spoke to me about it the other day, when he was looking at our oats. He said that Folger had a fine colt, which he would be willing to trade either for hay or oats, and he would take them in the shock right out of the field."

"Why did you not speak of it? you know to-morrow we shall begin to cradle our oats."

"I will go this very evening and see Folger, if you say so."

"And I will go and get the cow, and attend to your chores. If you can, get Folger to bring the colt, and let us see him;

and as we shall be at work at the oats to-morrow, perhaps we can make a bargain on the spot."

After Charles had finished his supper, he had occasion to visit a lot on the further part of his farm, where he had heard that a spot of fence needed attention. He repaired the trifling damage in a few minutes, and was about returning, when his attention was arrested by perceiving a horse standing apparently tied to the fence, in a by-lane that led from the main and travelled road; and close at hand were two persons, a man and woman, both quite young. The female was evidently pleading earnestly with the man, who seemed perfectly unmoved, and kept gradually retreating from her towards his horse, as though anxious to get away from her importunity. Charles had some strange suspicions at once arise in his mind. He felt very sure that this man was the same he had seen pass, often late in the evening, now for some months; and that young woman, he felt very sure, was one that he knew or had known years ago when he and she were boy and girl. But he could not distinguish features. His mind was strangely excited, and he determined to see the end. He was secured from observation by the hedge near the fence, but he could distinctly see them, and hear the sound of voices, although he could not distinguish words.

In the urgency of her plea, the female at length clasped him by the arm, and fell upon her knees, and then a cry of anguish arose on the still night air. Charles trembled through his whole frame in sympathy with that bitter cry; but the man she grasped seemed perfectly unmoved, only endeavoring to undo her hold. At length he drew forth what Charles supposed was a purse, and offered her its contents. But her cry only became more agonizing. She thrust the offering from her with violence, and clung the closer to the man. In an instant the wretch rudely tore himself from her embrace, and she fell prostrate to the earth. With as much indifference as though he had thrown off a reptile, he mounted his horse, and galloped down the lane, and into the highway, and was soon out of sight. It was not in Charles' nature to see a female in distress, and not fly to her help; and without a thought whether his presence might or might not be welcome, he sprang over the fence, and through the hedge, and hastened to the spot where he had seen her fall. A stone wall interposed between him and the object of his search; as he sprang over that, he stepped up with a slow pace. She still lay there, probably just in the position she had fallen. Charles stood and gazed at the piteous spectacle. Her face was partly exposed, her arm merely shielding her head from the green sward, her hair in long ringlets lay spread partly on her arm, and partly on the ground, mingling with the grass, that in that unfrequented pathway was of considerable growth. She was neatly dressed, even genteelly, and beautiful was her form and face, although he could perceive that the latter was deadly pale. He had no longer any doubts as to whom she was; Margaret Simmons, the daughter of the poor widow who lived at the old landing; who had once been his playmate, whom he had occasionally bowed to, as he had met her since taking up his abode at Aunt Casey's. His fears for her had been excited, he scarcely knew why. He fancied she was a little too fond of dress, a little too conscious of her powers of attraction, and a little too ready to accept the attentions of his own sex. He had, therefore, not taken any pains to renew their intimacy; and he had noticed that at his last meeting with her, the salutation he received from her was a very reserved one, as though she resented his unwillingness to acknowledge their former intimacy.

But all other thoughts were now merged in distress for her present condition. He came close to her side, and bending to the ground on one knee, called her gently by name, but no answer was returned. Again he spoke in a louder tone, but no sign of recognition came back. He felt her hand, it was cold; he laid his hand against her fair cheek, there seemed no life in either. Thoroughly aroused to do something for her relief, if possibly life were not yet extinct, he gently raised her from her prostrate position, and resting her head upon his arm, rubbed her forehead, and temples, and wrists, speaking occasionally her name, and doing whatever his judgment dictated to arouse her, and restore her consciousness. Presently he thought there was a slight sigh, and he redoubled his exertions; a heaving of the chest, and a convulsive movement of the arm, encouraged him—consciousness was returning; and that she might not be alarmed on recognizing him, he again spoke to her and called her by the name which he had once familiarly used:

"Margaret."

Her eye unclosed, and its gaze was fixed upon him.

"Margaret, don't be alarmed, an old friend is by you; do you remember me?"

"Yes," she answered, but in the feeblest manner.

"You have been ill, Margaret, and as soon as you are able, must be taken to your home."

She made no reply, but in a few moments attempted to raise herself. Charles assisted her to an erect position, but immediately caught her, or she would again have fallen.

"Margaret, you must yield yourself to my care, until your strength returns; trust to me as you would to a brother."

She burst into a flood of tears, as again her head rested on his arm; long and bitterly she wept. Nor did Charles attempt to restrain her, knowing as he did, that it was nature's own way for restoring the physical power which had been laid prostrate by the agony of a bruised heart.

"I shall remember your kind attention to me, Mr. Lovell, in this sad hour, but I feel my strength is again returning, and I should be sorry to detain you any longer."

"But I cannot leave you, Margaret, until I see you safely home; and if in any way I can serve you, let me know it; at least you must not ask me to leave you here at such a time, and under such circumstances."

"You are very kind, and have been very kind, or I fear I should not have survived the scene I have passed within this last hour. But upon you, surely, I have no claim."

"You have the same claim, Margaret, that the helpless and the injured have on every man that has a heart to feel and a hand to do."

"I will ask your aid then so far as the beginning of the causeway; the distance from there to my home is short."

Few words were spoken by either, as Charles aided her trembling frame through the lane, and across the highway, and down upon the marsh, through which the causeway passed to her solitary dwelling. She had gained strength, however, as they proceeded, and when in sight of her home released the arm of her companion.

"I shall not need your assistance any further, Mr. Lovell; you have been very kind to me, but I have one favor more to ask. I have been in a state of unconsciousness, I know not whether you witnessed the scene which led to it, but I ask of you as a final favor, that you retain within your own bosom what has transpired."

"If you request it, I will. But can I do nothing for you? You have no father, and your brother is but a boy; you are in some great trouble, Margaret, and I would aid you if I can."

"Oh, you are very kind; but I fear my wrongs cannot be redressed by man; perhaps you may hear from me. I cannot explain all to you now, but I would wish, if possible, that Charles Lovell might not judge hardly of me until he knows the truth."

As she seemed desirous of returning to her home without an attendant, Charles bowed to her and went on his way. He he could not, however, help looking across the marsh as he proceeded to his home, for he could by the light of the moon perceive her in the distance, as she walked slowly along towards the old ferry-house, standing alone amid the extended area of low land that lay beneath the higher grounds upon which he was walking.

Aunt Casey had not lighted her lamp yet, but was sitting on the stoop, cheerfully chatting with Hetty, and Charles, without saying a word, took his seat near to them.

"I guess you must be well tired with your day's work. Augustus tells me you have got in all your hay."

"Yes, aunty, it is all in, and to-morrow we begin at our oats; tired! well, I don't know but I am, but I had n't thought about it until you spoke."

"I tell'd Hetty, the other day, that I wondered if you ever did get real tired, for you never said nothing about it, and you always walk as spry when you come home at night, as when you went away in the morning."

"I ought to walk quicker, aunty, for I can think all the time how nice and clean everything will look here at home, and how pleasant it will be to wait, and dress, and sit down to a good supper, and smell that fine tea of yours, and then to rest out here, and enjoy a good long chit-chat."

"But I should think you would get tired for all that. In haying time people have to work dreadful hard."

"That is pretty much as they manage it. Augustus and

I, you know, have no one to drive us, but our own wills, and so we just take our own time; we work steadily on, and never mean to get more grass down at a time, than we can take care of easily. You see I work, aunty, because I prefer to, and expect to keep on working for many years, and therefore don't mean to wear myself out while I am young."

"You are right there, dear; oh, how many young folks have I known just destroyed themselves by doing two days' work in one. They will want maybe to have a holiday, or maybe a number of them will get together, and try who can do the most."

"I hope I shall never think of holidays, aunty, when there is work that needs to be done, any more than a merchant would when customers were in town. But, as I was saying, Guss and I have worked steadily, and we have kept ahead of our work, and have never felt driven, only about the time of getting in our oats, and that was on account of fixing our barn. But have you seen the barn, aunty, since we have put that wash on?"

"Yes; and do you believe me, I thought as much as could be, you 'd gone and put up a new one."

"It looks better to me than a new one, because it seems to be so much property redeemed from destruction. I have no doubt I enjoy it more than those from the city, who are putting up their elegant establishments."

"It will be well for you if you always keep the same mind. The more we get sometimes, the more we want, and sometimes we despise what we once tried to get. I 'm afraid the elegant houses they are building, and the elegant horses and carriages they 're a drivin' round here, and the servants, and company, and what not, will maybe do a deal of harm to our young folks, and put high notions in their heads, and make them uneasy. I tell'd old Colonel Johnson t'other day, that it did n't give me no pleasure to hear that such fine places are building, as they say there are."

"Well done, aunty, I 'm afraid you think I need a little preaching; I never heard you deliver so long a discourse before. But you have no objections, aunty, to us country folks making the very best of what we 've got, and having things neat and comfortable, and convenient and tasty too. Now, don't you think that this stoop, and the house too, look all the better for my having fixed this frame at the side, and put these vines here?"

"Oh, la! that it does."

"And don't you think our room looks all the pleasanter for these paper curtains I put up?"

"Oh, la! yes; but I did n't mean the like of that. What I mean is goin' to 'xtremes; it 's that goin' to 'xtremes that makes the ruination."

"Well, aunty, I don't know when I shall ever begin to build my house, but you will see a curiosity, I guess. I mean to have it plain, and roomy, and convenient, and home-looking, and as pretty as a box if I can; but there is no use in talking about that for a good while to come. I have got my barn, and got my hay in it, and there is room enough for my oats, and my corn-stalks, and all we shall have to put in it; and I mean to feel contented and quiet for the present."

It was a beautiful morning when Charles and Augustus commenced swinging their cradles among the oats; and they felt solicitous to get down as much as they could, the air seemed so dry and pure.

"Did you say, Guss, that Folger would be here by ten o'clock?"

"That 's what he said, but it has turned out such a hot day, perhaps he won't feel like it; it is the warmest day I have felt this season."

"It is rather warm, but that is not all; our labor is probably the hardest we have done yet, and it is much harder for you than for me, as I am more used to it. I think, Guss, you had better stop and take the rake, and be getting it ready to bind."

"I think you had better stop too, Charley; we have got down nearly one-half the piece, and from the looks of things we may expect a shower this afternoon."

Charles turned his eye to the west.

"Ay, ay, I see. I thought to be sure we could hardly have rain to-day. But this is August and not July."

At once, he seemed willing to yield to his brother's suggestion, and taking their cradles to the tree which shadowed a favorite spring, hung them up, while Augustus proceeded on his way to the barn for their rakes. Charles threw his hat upon the ground, and was about to take a drink, after his own fashion, when a troop of riders suddenly reigned up to the fence. There were two ladies, accompanied by a gentleman, all mounted on fine horses, and had been riding from the appearance of their steeds at a pretty fast rate.

"May I take the liberty of asking you, sir," said one of the ladies, "how I can obtain a drink of that spring water? I am so thirsty."

"I have no cup, Miss," replied Charles, "but if you will allow me to wait upon you, I think, I can supply your need."

"Thank you, sir, I accept your offer."

Charles immediately selected a large plantain leaf, and folding it so as to make quite a decent cup, dipped it into the cool bubbling spring and presented it to the lady, who having thrown her reins upon the horse's neck, stretched out her hands to receive it.

"But how shall I ever get it to my lips?"

"Please take hold of the corners above my hands."

"So!"

"Yes, Miss, now you have it." The little quivering cup was raised, and its contents quaffed at a single draught.

"Oh, most delicious! Julia, dear," addressing the other lady apparently of her own age, neither of them probably exceeding seventeen, "will you have a drink? But I forget," bowing pleasantly to Charles, "we are dependent upon your services."

"And they are perfectly at your command," returning her salutation with a graceful bow, and then addressing the other lady, "will you allow me to wait upon you, Miss."

She blushed deeply, and courteously declined the offer, having been evidently checked by a word from the gentleman, who was close beside her, and who seemed restless and displeased.

"Well may I," said she, whom Charley had waited on, "whenever I pass this way help myself to a drink—it is so deliciously cool. I think I can make a cup for myself next time. Is that the spring where that little mound rises in the shade there?"

"It is, Miss, and it is a great curiosity; would you like to see it? there are few such boiling springs to be found."

"Don't be impatient," said the lovely girl, looking towards her companions. "I won't hinder you but a minute."

And she was about to spring from her horse, when Charles, who had just thrown off the two rails, which formed the fence on the top of the stone wall, interposed,

"A moment, Miss; rein your horse by this wall, it will afford you a convenient place to alight."

"And to get on again, too; but you have thrown down your fence now to accommodate me."

"Oh, that is of no consequence; it is rather an uneven horseblock; may I assist you?" The frank girl accepted his hand at once, and springing to the ground, was in an instant beside the little fountain.

"Oh, how beautiful! how brilliantly clear! a boiling spring indeed, and the whole of the white sand at the bottom is in motion. But this is not all nature, you have helped it a little?" looking at Charles.

"I have put the curb in, and arranged the turf in the vicinity, and guided the little stream to please my fancy."

"One, two, three little pools, or springs besides! then the one from which you gave me drink was neither of these that attracted my attention as I rode by."

"I gave it to you from the fountain itself, the purest and the coolest."

And while she spoke to him, and he to her, her bright, soft, hazel eye was steadily fixed upon him, and yet there seemed not the slightest approach to forwardness, but as if she felt herself to be in the presence of one who bore upon his fine face, and in his courteous manners, the mark of the true gentleman, and therefore her own pure mind felt free to indulge without restraint in communing with him.

"Come, Addie, we are waiting."

"I am coming;" and accepting the hand of her rustic gallant, was on the wall, and in the saddle, in an instant.

She bowed her head, and smiled her thanks, which was so handsomely responded to by Charles, that her companion was evidently taken by surprise; and although the gentleman who kept close beside her, did not deign to turn his head that way, *she* did and very gracefully saluted him as they started off.

Charles sat down by the spring in a strange kind of flutter, thinking over all he had said and done, and all that had been said to him. How pleasantly she accosted him! how delighted with the cup and the water! how ready to examine the spring! how gracefully and frankly she accepted his attentions! how perfectly natural seemed every word and act! But these were not all. The loveliest countenance he had ever beheld had just been beaming upon him, with its bright smile, kindling apparently at what he had said, or at something in connection with him. And when the smile passed off, there was an earnest, serious gaze, a look that almost had a tinge of sadness—the slightest shadow on her sweet fair brow that he felt to have a power, he never knew that woman possessed before. It went directly to his heart, and kindled an intense desire to do anything that she might ask, to do it with alacrity and delight. And then, strange effect of the imagination! he fancied a peculiar expression in her last look, as though it spoke of an interest in him—mad and foolish youth! O, Charley, we should not have suspected you to be thus open to delusion. But there he sat by the spring, as lost to the business of the day, as if there were no oats to be gathered, no shower to be feared, and even no such thing as a colt in the world.

"You seem to be pretty busy thinking."

"O, is that you, Augustus! do you know who those folks are that you met?"

"No; nor I should n't want to know who the man is. I guess he is some upstart."

"Why?"

"I heard one of the ladies' reply to some ugly remark he had made, I suppose, about you; for I saw that they stopped here. 'You may if you please,' said she, 'call him a clodhopper, but I never in my life felt more sensibly that I was in the presence of a true gentleman.' But here comes Folger." Charles sprang to his feet; all his feelings of interest for the colt reviving at the mention of his owner's name.

There is something peculiarly attractive to a man in the ownership of a horse, and especially his first horse. There is no animal, not excepting the dog, who seems so nearly allied to man. His intelligent eye and ear, his lofty carriage, his free and graceful motion, his vast strength, his obedient temper, and his indispensible use, all endear him to us. We love to look at his fine proportions, to take in the inspiration of his energy and power. We love to feel our power over him, and think more highly of ourselves, as we bound through the air upon his back, and guide him, and curb him at our will.

Mr. Folger was on horseback, and the colt was beside him held by a halter. He was of a dark chestnut color, his mane and tail a shade lighter, and disposed to curl. His body was well put together, round and snug, his chest full and broad, his legs straight and well set, with a white streak around one fore-foot, his neck and head slender, with a bright, clear, kind eye, and a white star in his forehead.

The owner, who, although keeper of a tavern, was no horse-jockey, said nothing, while the young men were looking at all points of the horse, but handing the halter to Augustus, allowed them to satisfy themselves in every respect.

"He looks well enough," said Charles, coming up to Mr. Folger, as though he wished to hear his account of him.

"He is a colt; has never had a bit in his mouth. I have not broken him yet, because he is too young to be put to hard service. If I was to get him so as to be driven, my boys would have him off, and perhaps in one day ruin him. I have, therefore, let him remain, except merely halter breaking him, and you see you can do what you please with him; he will lead like an old horse."

"Will he not be too young for us to use?"

"He is too young for anybody to use much; he ought to be bitted and broken, and used a little every day, until he is under perfect control. It will take a year at least to get a horse trained as I should wish. I should think if you wished to train a horse for your future use, and to train one to your mind; if you wish a horse that has kind feelings, and likes to be petted and made much of; I don't know where you can find such another, for he has the very best blood in him; his mother would all but talk."

As Charles had every reason to believe what was told him, he invited Mr. Folger to alight, and walk into the oat field.

"I told Mr. Slocum that I was willing to trade either for hay or oats, but would prefer oats, and would like them unthreshed. My price for the colt is fifty dollars. How many acres have you in oats?"

" A little over six acres."

" They will yield about thirty bushels to the acre, some a little more, and some not quite so much. You have cut down the best of them. I have noticed the field while they have been growing. I will tell you at once what I will do ; you shall cut and bind, and shock up one half the piece ; you have pretty much one half cut now ; and I will come with my teams, and take it away, and you shall have the colt."

The brothers looked steadily at each other a moment.

" Just as you say, Guss."

" Just as you say, Charley ; I 'm agreed if you are."

" It is a bargain, sir."

" When shall I send my teams ?"

" This afternoon, as soon as you please; we shall go to binding immediately."

As there was no time to be lost in looking at their prize then, Augustus ran with him to the stable, and in a few moments they were binding away in earnest; but it looked rather discouraging; three acres all spread out on the ground to be raked and bound, and carried together, and in two hours a load to be ready.

" Hulloa, boys, what are you up to, ha ! ha ! ha !"

" Slocum ! I declare," said Augustus to his brother, " and who has he got with him ?"

" You want any help, boys ?"

" We should like some help, but we should n't dare to ask you."

" Why not ? ha ! ha ! ha !"

" We should get no chance to repay you; we are not joiners, you know."

" You aint, ha ! well, no matter for that; where 's your other rake ? here, Joe, you and Guss rake, and Charley and I will bind ; now work away, boys, for we shall be after you."

And " work away " it was; the rakes flew, and the little heaps rolled together in rapid succession, and the binders kept close behind them, and not allowing the space to increase that separated them from each other.

" You see I met Folger up street away, and says he, we 've traded for the colt. Glad of that, says I. And I am to take the oats, but I must hurry home, says he, and send the teams along, for there will be rain before night. So on I came;

I was going to the colonels to set Joe at a little job, so I looked over here and see what was going on; says I, Joe, those fellows want help; the colonel won't scold much, I guess, ha! ha! ha! Come, boys, we are gaining on you."

"We 'll risk it, bind away as fast you like, we 'll keep you going."

"Well, I don't know, Slocum, how I shall ever return this favor, for I have never been in quite such a pinch before; I have wasted a little time this morning."

"You can't have wasted much, Charley, if you and Guss have cut all these down to-day."

"We have."

"You have done well; but it will be a great thing for you to get them bound up, and ready for Folger's teams. And as to paying me—I 'll get my pay out of you yet, in some way, ha! ha! ha!"

An hour and a half steady work, with the speed which they held, made a very sensible gain upon the piece.

"And now," said Charles, "it is half-past twelve, we will run down to dinner, it will be all ready, and then Augustus and I can finish it."

"I sha n't leave you, boys, in such a drive, no how; and if you will let me give you a little advice, as an old manager, it is this—don't let us all stop and go to dinner. There will be driving times pretty soon, you will see, for Folger will send all his teams together; he can see as well as any one that rain is brewing, and it will be here by the middle of the afternoon, and Folger won't wish to have his oats wet. If you want to eat, let Guss run down and bring up a bite, I 'll set Joe to throwing the sheaves into heaps ready for shocking, and you and I will take the rakes, and get a good parcel raked up, then no matter what comes, we can be ready for it."

No time was lost in arguing, so Augustus went off with right good will to obtain the supplies. He could not come back, however, quite so fast as he went, for Aunt Casey had fairly loaded him down. She heard how it was, and determined, for the honor of the house, that there should be no stint, even the white table cloth and all.

"Well, well, ha! ha! ha! well done, Aunt Casey, if here aint dinner enough for a dozen; I tell you what, boys, if you live so every day I should like to come and board with you."

It did, indeed, look refreshing to a hungry man, for Augustus had, according to the old lady's instructions, spread out the cloth half-way, and there stood a plate with slices of cold boiled ham, and cold boiled pork, a dish of mashed potatoes, good thick slices of fine white bread, a roll of butter, and two dried apple pies. The spring was close at hand, and cups were plenty; there was no lack of appetite, and before all were satisfied, it was very evident that Aunt Casey was not a bad calculator as to the ability of four stout young men. There was, however, some to spare.

Things turned out pretty much as Slocum had said. By two o'clock three double teams were passing into the field, and the work of loading commenced. While one of the teams was loading, one of the three teamsters went lustily to work with the binders; all were in fine glee, and it would have been impossible to tell from the interest manifested by each, who were the individuals to be benefited, and probably there was no difference in their feelings. The circumstances had excited each one. A quantity of grain was to be secured, and a dark cloud was gradually rising in the west, and occasionally a low distant murmur could be heard, the faint echo of the far-off thunder.

Two loads have at last left the field, and nothing now remains to be done but to despatch the third and last. The raking and binding are finished, and all the hands in the field are busy besides the loaders, with gathering into shocks, and that is soon completed.

"Well, Charley, we 'll go now."

Charles came up almost out of breath.

"Mr. Slocum, what shall I do or say to you? we never should have done the thing without you."

"I knew you would n't, ha! ha! ha! I knew you would n't, and so I was determined to stick by you. We must go up to the colonel's now—but here is the old fellow himself."

"Ay, ay, I 've had my eye on you; I've had my eye on you—a pretty fellow you are! I 've seen you."

"Well, colonel, you see I found the boys here had got into a little scrape, and you know I must help folks when they get into a pinch, ha! ha! ha! But I'm going right up now."

"Well, well, Slocum, that 's all right; but I 've been very angry, and if it had n't been that I saw you here working like a good fellow for these young friends of mine, you would have taken it, mind me. But where is your oats a-going?"

"Oh, we have sold it, sir; we have traded some of them away for a colt."

"To break your necks! yes, yes; you need n't tell me; I know all about it already, and I guess you aint far wrong, after all. And now old ha! ha! just come along, for I must waddle home again. That cloud begins to look rather black."

Charles and Augustus were now left alone in the field, the last load being well on its way to a shelter.

"I think, Guss, that we shall have a hard storm, and it is coming fast; you had better go and secure the doors and windows of the barn, and I will carry the tools, and then we will both hasten home, for Aunt Casey is timid, you know, and there will be no more cradling to be done to-day."

Augustus made speed towards the barn, and Charles took a shorter cut across the field towards the house. But the storm was much nearer than he had anticipated, for the sudden darkening of the air caused him to look up, and he saw the huge mass of vapor that had been slowly gathering now rolling along broken into rugged heaps, and flying as though impelled by the force of a hurricane; he immediately hung his cradles within the thick branches of an apple-tree, stacked his rakes against its trunk, and then made his utmost speed for the cottage. As he reached the gate, as though impelled by instinct, he immediately threw down a pair of bars adjoining it, for he saw coming up the road, and on full gallop, the two ladies who had stopped at the spring in the morning.

"They must stop here," he said to himself, "for where else can they go for shelter?"

And he was right in his calculation, for the leader of the two at once reined up to him. She did not appear to recognize him, but speaking as if almost out of breath:

"Good sir, can you show us to a shelter?"

"Please ride through the bars, and follow this path, and just through the grove you will find the house. I will be there. Have you not a gentleman with you?"

"His horse loosened a shoe, and he was obliged to dismount; but he is coming." And as Charles looked, he saw him just ascending a small hill. Leaving him to follow or not as he pleased, Charles ran with speed to the house. Augustus was already there, and had assisted one of the ladies to dismount, and Charles immediately offered his services to the other.

"Please excuse me," said she with that sweet smile again, "I did not recognize you at first; I was in such a flurry, for the clouds looked so threatening, and I knew of no place for some distance that we could get to. You must have thought I had soon forgotten your politeness."

Charles did not reply, for the gentleman just then rode up in great haste. He was very pale, but whether from fear or displeasure, it would have been difficult to decide. He looked up at the clouds, and then at the circumstances around him, as much as to say, "It looks awfully black; but what kind of a place is this to shelter in?" And Charles felt just mischievous enough to enjoy his dilemma. One of the ladies, however, came to his aid.

"Are you not going to dismount? there is a terrible storm coming; how fearfully it roars!"

Without replying, he jumped from his horse, and stood beside him.

"Who is there here to take my horse? What kind of a rookery have you got into! is it a tavern? or what is it?"

"Oh, Julia dear, do speak to him," said her companion in a whisper, "do ask him not to speak so."

She who was called Julia looked indeed much distressed. She seemed to be equally sensible of the rudeness, but yet afraid to administer reproof; blushing very deeply she ventured to say:

"Had you not better tie your horse and come in?"

"I should advise you, sir," said Charles, who had just come from the shed, where he had gone with Augustus to secure the ladies' horses, "to remove your saddle under cover, and then tie your horse, and you have no time to spare."

"Take off the saddle! I don't know anything about taking off saddles."

"Oh! I can show you," and the lovely girl was about to put her knowledge into practice, but Charles immediately interposed, and the saddle was off in an instant. "You had better tie your horse quickly, sir." But at that moment a vivid flash of lightning, followed instantly by a deafening peal of thunder, caused the horseman to drop his bridle, and spring into the house; Augustus happily was near and caught the rein, as the affrighted animal was about to tear away. Immediately the tempest came sweeping on in its fury; there was a darkening of the air, a loud and sullen roar, a twisting about of the limbs of the large trees, a whirling of dust and small branches through the air, flash after flash, and peal after peal, and then the pouring rain dashing against the little tenement, as though it would be beaten to the earth, or removed from its foundations.

Aunt Casey was never very courageous in thunder storms, her plan had been generally to run to her bed and cover up; Charles had laughed her almost out of this habit, so that she had braved most of the summer showers, without having recourse to her old expedient.

But this storm was something more than common, and the first clap of thunder not only started the young gentleman, as before stated, into the house, but also started Aunt Casey towards her room; just as she was going, one of the young ladies, who was called Julia, caught her arm:

"Oh, is n't it dreadful!"

Aunt Casey whispered to her, "The bed I always think the safest place; if you are afraid, dear, come with me," and presently they were both out of sight.

The other young lady, and she with whom we have had most to do, appeared to be quite self-possessed, and seemed to enjoy the very uneasy situation of their gentleman attendant, and perhaps this will be as convenient an opportunity as we shall have to give a description of him, at least of his dress; and in his own estimation, this seemed to be the most important part of him. His coat was a green frock, very tastily made, and an excellent fit, but designed no doubt as a riding-coat, as it was shorter than was then fashionable for common wear. His trowsers were of yellow jean, or more properly a dingy buff color; they were made to set easily over boots, and were confined down closely by straps, and a row of buttons, about half way from the knee to the foot. These were of pearls, and gave a showy, and rather military appearance, in connection with the glittering spurs. The foot was small, and very neatly encased in morocco boots, and from the manner of his looking at them, and twisting them about, and thrusting them into notice, it was evident that he prided himself much on account of them. His vest was somewhat of the color of his pantaloons, only more delicate, both in hue and texture. It opened widely, and displayed linen of the finest texture, elaborately worked, and faultlessly white. A splendid diamond broach shone conspicuously upon the ends of the light silk cravat, which it seemed to confine in a smooth cross fold upon his bosom. Watch, chains, and seals, very costly, no doubt, were drawn across from his watch fob, and hung in full view from the lower button of his coat; a neat riding whip, and a light colored beaver, closes the inventory. It is said to be the mark of a true gentleman, that however well he may be dressed, he never appears to be conscious of it. This mark, if a true one, it must be confessed did not characterize the present individual, for in spite of thunder, lightning, wind, and rain, he would find time to look down at his feet, strike his heels with his whip, and cast his eye over the lappels of his coat, and down into his bosom, and so on, and doubtless had there been a looking-glass, he would have peeped into that.

As to the man himself, he was of medium height, his hair dark and bushy, rather neat whiskers, his face pale and thin, and the expression tame. The color of his eyes it would be difficult to define, as they were not very visible from a habit of keeping them nearly closed. You have the man externally. The interior will be developed in course of time. But while we have been attending to this description of him, the gentleman himself has not been either standing or sitting, for his likeness. He had probably not very strong nerves, for he appeared to be considerably excited. His first start, as we have seen, brought him from the stoop into the middle of the room, and grasping the arm of the lady to whom he seemed most attentive, exclaimed:

"Don't be alarmed, Julia, it is terrible, aint it?"

The young lady, however she may have preferred his attentions in quiet times, seemed now not to put much value upon them, but rather to feel safer with Aunt Casey, and clinging to her, retired as we have seen to snug quarters.

From the other lady, and the master of the house, Charles Lovell, he could get no sympathy, for after the first brush was over, they had settled down quietly in a kind of *tête-à-tête* over a volume of Johnson's Lives, which happened to be lying there, and seemed to pay no more attention to the terrible peals of thunder that were rattling over them, than if the whole thing had been nothing more than an April shower.

Augustus had ensconsced himself on the stoop, and appeared to be enjoying the vagaries of the storm in a very quiet way; so that the gentleman felt absolutely alone, and had to amuse himself as he best could. Charles had, with all due politeness, offered him a seat, which he declined, and preferred standing with his hat on, as though ready for any emergency, and he seemed to be divided between two causes of fear,—the coming down of the old house upon his head, and the crinkling fire without. One moment, as the wind howled across the chimney, he would turn his head up and look round to see what was coming, while he stood holding the door with one hand, partly open, and ready for a spring; and then, as a blinding flash of lightning would glare among the trees of the little grove around the house, he would dodge in again, and look round the room, casting his eyes over his person, and down towards his feet, as though there was nothing at all the matter, and no danger to be apprehended.

Charles had found time during the confusion of the shower to slip into his little room, and exchange his check frock for a white linen round-about, that he was in the habit of wearing in the house; and dropping his overalls, the work of a minute, he had come out so metamorphosed that the strange gentleman himself had to cast one or two curious glances at him, as though uncertain what to make of him. The young lady, too, was evidently taken by surprise; and although from the first her conduct had been marked by the most lady-like deportment towards him, yet the change in his dress was so becoming, his fine, manly countenance, bronzed by exposure to the sun, and his well-proportioned form, were exhibited to such advantage in his light and airy, yet snugly-fitting garments, that whatever other feelings she might have had, it was very evident that she derived great pleasure from having one whom she had boasted as a gentleman in his bearing, appear in the present company to so much advantage. But there were other feelings at work, too, in the young lady's mind. She was evidently at a loss how to make things harmonize. Was this the real home of this young man? was that old lady his mother? But she could trace no resemblance. The little case of books, too, had caught her eye. She had seen the same elsewhere, but never before under such a humble roof. And the guitar, which stood in one corner of the room, did he use it? or the young girl? and she thought it could not be the latter; nor could she be his sister. All this, however, is but fancy; we can only judge of her thoughts by the expressive glance of her eye from him with whom she is conversing, to these different objects, and then back again to him. That she was interested in his conversation, she took no pains to conceal. There is a charm in a cultivated mind, that is all powerful with the female heart; it throws a drapery of its own fancy's weaving about the whole person, and clothes even forbidding features with beauty. But a cultivated mind throwing out its witching thoughts from lips that seem made for love, and sparkling from eyes that seem but the windows of purity and truth, no female heart, that has in itself the holy fire, but must kindle by it. How much was felt, how deep the admiration, and how warm the sentiment inspired, it were almost impious to ask, and worse impiety to tell.

But was the youth a mere entertainer in this scene? and are there no peculiar feelings working within, while he enjoys this rare and unexpected opportunity? The smile upon her lip, the slight shadow on her brow, had in the morning touched him most strangely. But now she sits before him face to face; the light riding cap is thrown by, and the whole of these fine features are shining full upon him. We speak advisedly now, and can, without the violation of any principle of duty, say what we know.

That there was enchantment in her presence, he had felt during the short interview of the morning; and now he was conscious, yes, verily he was conscious, that a chain was winding about his heart—that a spell was upon him. He wished the thunder and the rain to keep on their clatter, and he dreaded every lightning up from without, for fear the clear sky should put an end to the charm. He was deaf to all the whisperings of reason. "An elegantly dressed young lady, her manners more elegant than her attire; doubtless the scion of some aristocratic stock, accustomed to all the refinements of life, perhaps wealthy herself—how insane for him, so far down among the ruder things of life, to dream for an instant that she can be aught to him, but a beautiful vision that will soon pass away forever." Thus reason whispered to him, but he heeded not, and with all the infatuation of a doomed man, yielded his heart; yes, strange as it may seem, yielded his heart to the fair object, and set her image up before him, to be for life the idol of his earthly love. It was a mad purpose we allow, and utterly at variance with his whole character, but we cannot help it, nor can we help him; and if he suffers for his folly, it will be no more than many have done before him, and will doubtless do even after reading the development of his fate.

But summer showers seldom last long, and although this had been something more than common, yet in an hour it had spent its fury; the clouds began to break away in the west, the rain ceased, the sun blazed forth, and set the bow upon the eastern cloud. All was as still and bright as though nothing had occurred.

At the first intimation that they wished to go on their way, Charles and his brother proceeded to get their horses in readiness.

The gentleman appeared not to be in a very amiable humor, and yet he made great efforts to be polite to the ladies. Whether he could have saddled his horse was very doubtful, but Charles whispered to his brother, that perhaps he had better throw it on for him. As the first horse came up, the gentleman called out:

"Come, Miss Julia, your horse is waiting." She tripped it lightly out, and looking at Charles, smiled pleasantly, and thanked him for all his courteous treatment. "I fear if you had not hastened our saddles off so quickly, our ride home would not have been so pleasant as it now bids fair to be."

"Come, are you ready?"

"Oh yes, I am ready, my good sir, but you know ladies must have time to say their say out—now for it," and the lively girl, accepting his hand, bounded to her place.

"Will you accept of my assistance?" said Charles, as the other also came from bidding Aunt Casey good-bye.

"I will with pleasure."

"Miss Adelaide," the gentleman called out, "I will assist you in a moment, you need n't—"

"Thank you, I am on, and never had a better mount in my life."

Charles walked by the side of the ladies until they passed through the bars, and then taking off his hat, made a low obeisance. Their salutation was not less marked nor respectful. As the gentleman passed through he held out towards Charles a piece of money.

"George, George, are you crazy!" and Miss Julia caught his arm, "for mercy sake, don't."

Charles stood and looked at him a moment fiercely; a rush of thoughts crowded upon him; they had been gathering force through all the time he had been under his roof; for with all his rudeness of manner was added in Charles' mind the strong belief that he was the miscreant whom but the evening before he had seen maltreat a lovely female, and leave her for aught he knew in wretchedness to die alone. He could have torn him to the earth, and trampled him beneath his feet, if he could have forgotten his own character, and the company upon whom the vile creature was an attendant. In a calm and steady tone he addressed him:

"Respect for myself, sir, and especially for those you wait upon, prevents me from treating your insolence as it deserves. Remember, sir, that money will not always pay for acts of kindness, nor will it always heal the wounds of a broken heart."

He was doubtless about to answer Charles in a rude manner, for his looks betrayed great rage; but as the last sentence was uttered in an undertone, and its meaning broke upon his mind, he seemed like one stupefied. His countenance became deadly pale, and turning his horse's head, prepared to go on his way.

Not so the young lady, who had received so much of Charles' notice. She rode up to him:

"I little thought, sir, when entering your hospitable roof, that your kindness would have been thus requited;" her lip trembled, and a tear fell upon her cheek.

Charles could not reply; he was too deeply agitated, and the lovely girl, with much emotion, continued;

"I trust you will not in your remembrance, of either my cousin or myself, charge to us the improprieties of another."

"I assure you, Miss, not a thought but you might read will ever pass my mind in reference to yourself," a slight pause, "or your cousin either."

She looked steadily at him as he spoke, and for a moment seemed to be spell-bound. Then, with that shadow on her brow, that token of thoughts that came from her heart, she bowed gracefully to him and departed.

Charles watched her beautiful form as she urged her horse to overtake her companions. He knew not that he should ever see it again; he could not hope that he would. He had learned but little respecting her place of residence, or kindred, but from what he had gathered he concluded that her home was in the great city, and her stay in the country but that of a visitor. Among its thousands there would be no doubt splendid suitors for her hand, and happy he who should be the favored one; "yes," he spoke aloud to himself, "he must be a happy man."

CHAPTER V.

The training of the colt was a matter not to be thought of during their harvest season, and nothing was done, therefore, further than to win his confidence, and get him to be familiar with him. A handful of oats dealt out whenever they went up to him in the field, and gentle treatment in handling him, very soon accomplished that. Naturally of a confiding temper, he appeared delighted when either of the brothers approached him; winnowing and pawing as he heard their steps drawing nigh to the stable, and fairly starting off at a gallop to come up to them in the field.

"How soon!" said Charles to his brother, as the confiding creature one day stood with his head leaning over the shoulder of Augustus, "has he become acquainted. He has certainly an excellent disposition, and if we can only manage to make him obedient to our will, without destroying his confidence, he will be trained to some purpose."

"We shall have to manage very carefully to do that, they are so fractious sometimes."

"Yes, no doubt they are; but I don't wonder at that. Many begin with harshly treating them, swearing at them, and knocking them round; at any rate, I mean to try a different method with Pomp; (I think we had better call him Pomp), there are so many Toms, and Billies, and Charlies round. He is a beauty; and if we only manage rightly with him, he will soon be worth double what we gave for him."

"Well, I am so fond of him already, that I should n't wish to part with him for double that now."

"Nor I either, Guss; but it won't do for us to stay here any longer. If you will go to work cutting up the corn, I will run up and see the colonel, as he has sent for me to come and see him about a harness."

The colt followed them both to the bars, and for some time stood with his neck stretched over them, until they were out of sight.

"Lovell, how are you? ha! ha! ha!" Charles was just entering the alley which led towards the barns of Colonel Johnson. He turned, and met the good-natured Slocum.

"Look out! ha! ha! ha! don't you squeeze my hand so. I hurt it with a chisel the other day. Is the colonel at home, do you know?"

"I think he must be; for he sent word to me yesterday, that I must be at his stable by nine o'clock this morning."

"Then he will be there, no doubt; yes, there he is, shaking his cane at us."

"One at a time—one at a time, you rogues, you, how can I attend to two people at once? and Mr. Lovell must be the one, for I sent for him expressly."

"Not this time, colonel; Charlie is a good fellow, and I know he will wait awhile. But I want you, colonel, just to get somewhere that you can sit down, for I have got quite a story to tell, and you will get out of patience if you stand."

"You are a very pretty sort of a fellow, Slocum; I am glad I don't owe you any money though, so it can't be on any dunning business. Sit down, ha! must I! But what is that young man to do, that I have sent for to come and see me this morning?"

"Oh, he 'll amuse himself some way, no doubt; and if he knew all about it, he would n't mind waiting a little."

The old gentleman walked a few paces, until he came to a hen-coop; that being flat on the top, offered a pretty fair seat, and taking his station upon it, motioned to Slocum to bring along a saw-horse which stood near by.

"You can sit straddle of that, or sidewise, just as you please."

"Ha! ha! ha! just the thing, its my natural seat."

"Well, only keep quiet on it, if you can, and let out your budget. I want to know what 's the matter; for you seem in such a stew about it, that I am all fidgetty myself; begin your story, and let it be short."

"You know Serle."

"What, the fellow that married that pretty girl there; the daughter of—of—"

"Polly Gaines, daughter of the widow Gaines."

"Yes, yes, yes."

"Well, Serle is a good fellow, he is as steady, honest, industrious a young chap as there is any where round, and a real good mechanic too, ready to do a job whenever he can get one, and willing to work early and late, so as to make a living. I know, you see, for I am about these young fellows, and see all their actions."

"Is he dead? or has he broke his limbs?"

"No, but you see he had a long sickness last winter, that has pulled him back bad."

"Sick! was he? and why did n't you tell me of it?"

"Well, it was n't a case, colonel, you know, where one can go very well, and offer anything like charity; they feel, you know, a little spunky like, as though they wanted to take care of themselves."

"I honor them for *that*."

"So do I, colonel, they are the right kind of folks after all; them that want to stand on their own feet, and take care of themselves, so long as they can. But you see when spring came, and Serle got out again, I found out because he came to me for work, he 'd got clean used up; he had spent the last dollar he had in the world. Well, I gave him a job, and he has worked like a good fellow; and he 'll do well enough, there 's no danger of that; but you know, colonel, it 's a great thing for a man here in the country to have a house over his head."

"That it is, whether in the country or city."

"But especially in the country; you know there aint many houses to spare, and when there is one to let, it brings a high rent for us country folks. Now, Serle has to pay forty dollars a year rent, for only half the Gage house; it don't seem much, I know, to you, colonel, but come to take forty dollars a year out of a man's wages, just only for rent of the house to live in, and it makes a hole, I tell you."

"Don't he have a garden spot with it?"

"Nothing but just the bare house."

"Well, come go on with your story; tell me at once, Slocum, what you are driving at."

"I will, colonel. Well, there 's a grand chance now for the poor fellow to get a house all his own; and would n't that be good? and a nice garden spot, and a place to keep a cow; why it would be half his living."

The colonel raised his cane, and shaking it very significantly, "I'll lay this stick on to you in short order, if you don't tell me quick what it is you want; where is the house? where's the land? and where's the money to get it?"

"Well, you see, colonel, the case is this—there is a good building down on the French place. You know that place has been sold lately to the New Yorkers?"

"I don't know anything about it; go on with your story I tell you."

"Well, it's just as I say, they have bought the French place, and they are going to build all new. Well, the old house is a good snug tight building, all right for a small family, as snug as a mitten, and they are going to pull it down. Thinks I, that is too good a house to pull down, its a sin and a shame to do it, it's a wicked waste. By jingo, if I don't ask the fellows what they'll take, and have it moved right off smack and smooth; so up I goes and pops the question. I did n't know how they'd take it, but thinks I to myself, they can but say no, and there's an end of it."

"Oh, body a me, if you aint enough to drive the patience out of a saint; you are worse than old Nab Moneypenny, who will begin telling you about a cut on her finger, and end with a hanging match."

"Well, colonel, the long and short of it is, says the fellow to me, what is it worth? will you give me twenty-five dollars for it, and move it off, and have it out of the way by day after to-morrow? How long may I have, says I, to give you an answer? to-morrow, twelve o'clock. Thank you, sir, says I, I'll be here by that time, and if I aint, you may begin to pull it down. It is dirt cheap, colonel. The house could n't be put up for three hundred dollars; it's as cheap as dirt."

The colonel very deliberately took out his handkerchief, and wiped his brow.

"Well, you see, colonel, I goes right down to Serle, and tells him of it. I never see a fellow look as he did; he jumped right up, Slocum. Says he, I've got forty dollars, it's all I've got, and fifteen I owe for rent; but here is twenty-five; only what shall I do for a place to put it on? I can't put it on the commons. And the poor fellow sat down on his chair, clean discouraged. I never see him look so bad. And I must say the thing looked awkward. A house, you know, colonel, when we get it moving has got to go somewhere."

"Without it would keep moving like your tongue? it would n't need any stopping place."

"Ha! ha! ha! well, colonel, says I to him, Serle hold on, there 's that four-acre lot that used to belong to the old Hawthorne family; it 's got an old shell of a barn on it, and it 's got an old foundation of a house, and brick and stone enough for a good cellar, and it 's as pretty a buildings pot as there is in town, right by the little river. The land is good, and there 's wood enough on the run, on the back part of it, to help along in a family for a good while. Says I, Serle, that whole four acres, and all that 's on it, can be bought for one hundred dollars, and I have no doubt young Hawthorne will give you time to pay it in. So off we went, Hawthorne was ready to sell it, and it was pretty much all agreed upon. Serle was to have two years to pay it in, and Hawthorne was to let us know in the morning. So this morning I called there pretty early, I tell you, for I know we had business on hand if we did the thing. Serle looked as if he had n't slept a wink all night, and his pretty wife, I see, kept wiping the tears; oh, said she, Mr. Slocum, if we could only get it, and have a home of our own, I shall never forget you the longest—"

Slocum was now obliged to use his handkerchief, and the old colonel, to keep him company, began to use his.

"Well, what do you think? at last Hawthorne came along, and I see at once he was going to be off. He made some kind of excuse, but the upshot of it was, that he would sell it for the one hundred dollars, but must have the money down; I see how it was; Serle turned as pale as a sheet, and his wife I see in the buttery wiping away the tears; thinks I, good folks I know how you feel; I have felt so too. Says I, Hawthorne just step out here, and so out we went. now, says I, Hawthorne, you see how they feel; must you have the money down? says he, I must; it belongs, you know, part to my sister, and that fellow Lucas some way got wind of this matter, and he don't want Serle to have it, and

and he came over last night, and offered the hundred dollars cash down; but I told him you had the first offer. 'How long will you give me to have an answer?' 'Two hours,' says he. 'Done,' says I: 'I'll be at your house in two hours.'"

The Colonel had been wiping the perspiration away for some time, having given up the idea of making a short story of it: he was trying to wait as patiently as possible.

"And now, Colonel, that's the end of it."

"I am glad of that: and now tell me what you mean by coming and pouring into my ears such a long rigmarole about this concern."

"Well, Colonel, I don't hardly know myself; but I came right off here, because it seems so natural to me, if there's any trouble anywhere, to run to you, you know."

"It is, eh? well, I'll tell you what to do: go right straight off to Hawthorne, and have a deed made out for the land, and as soon as it is done, the money shall be ready for him."

"Oh! Colonel, may you be blessed,—"

"Hold your tongue, sir, will you? you've talked enough for one day: you want to set a man crazy? And hear what I say now: let the deed be made in Serle's name. He'll feel all the more encouraged to have the title for his house and land in his own name. And the twenty-five dollars shall be ready at the same time to pay for his house. But don't you say a word about it—you hear—only to Serle himself; and let him keep the little money he has about him: he will want it to fix up with. And now be off, do you hear? and not sit there, blowing your nose, like a great baby."

Slocum arose, and taking the hand of the generous old man, gave it a hearty squeeze.

"God bless you!" and he tried to get out something further, but it would not come.

"Well, well, well! just go along and see to the thing."

"Just see that fellow!" said the old gentleman to Charles, who was now approaching; "just see that fellow, how he goes!—blowing his nose, and swinging his arms—aint he a sight! I tell you what it is: that fellow ought to have his bust taken, and there ought to be a monument of gold erected to him. He deserves it more than many who receive them. Just see him! he has started off on the full run. Oh, you good soul! I wish I was young enough: I'd see who would run the fastest. And now, my good fellow, I think you have been kept here waiting long enough. You see, I found out all about your colt before you told me of it. I don't forget how young folks feel. You think as much of that horse, now—I know you do—almost as if he was a relation. You may laugh; but it is just so. And now, do you come in here, and see what we can find."

The place where they had been conversing was an open space at the end of the lane, which led into the barn and carriage-house. Everything about it was neat and clean; and as they entered the building, no more dirt was to be seen than in many a private dwelling.

The Colonel led the way to a small room, partitioned off by itself. It was lighted by a window; and in it were several sets of harness, apparently new; although, upon further inspection, Charles saw that they had, no doubt, been long in use, but were in good condition, and nicely cleaned.

"There," said the Colonel, pointing to one hanging by itself, is a harness I had made more than twenty years ago, for the purpose of breaking a very fine colt. It has been used since, to break half-a-dozen more. I shall never break any more for my own use. If you will accept of it, you are very welcome to it."

"It is a great present, sir, and one that I had not the most distant idea of. When you spoke about helping me to a harness, I thought, possibly, you might have something to loan that might suit me, until I was able to purchase one."

"No, no: I have loaned it to several, but I'll give it to you. But I want to talk with you a little about breaking a colt. The chief things you will need are kindness and care, and some little resolution into the bargain. There is no use for harsh words or harsh actions with a horse. You must be careful in first putting on the bridle. Do it moderately, and see that it does not chafe him; and, after he is well bitted, put the harness on with a great deal of care. Do it gently, and let him stand and get used to it, and so by degrees manage him; and when he finds that he is not going to be hurt, he will go along quietly. But be sure of one thing: don't let him get away from you, or get the upper hand. Treat him with all kindness, but let him see that he has a master that he must obey. And now, I've not only given you a harness, but a lecture into the bargain."

"And I assure you, sir, I thank you truly for both. I only wish I knew in what way I can do any thing for you, sir—not to pay you for your kindness, but to convince you that I feel it."

The old gentleman took him by the arm,

"I 'll tell you what you can do, just continue to go on as you have, work manfully with your hands—improve your understanding, as I have good reason to know you have, and with all, cultivate a liberal heart. All I want is to see you and your brother, for whom (I cannot tell why) I feel a kind of fatherly interest, doing well. And now come, just take the harness out and hang it on the fence, and come into the house, for Lucy wants to say a word to you."

Charles wiped away a tear that had come, in spite of every effort to keep it back, and taking down the harness, was about to put it upon the fence, when a thought suddenly occurred to to him.

"I should be most happy to wait upon Miss Lucy, at any moment's warning. But I had no expectation of entering your house, when I came, and especially of receiving a summons to a lady's presence. I am in my working-dress, as you see, sir."

"Some would say, never mind that, go in just as you are, and so would I, if I thought your objection was founded more upon shame for yourself than respect for the lady. But I do not believe so, and as I am convinced that a great deal of our happiness depends upon proper respect to the female sex, and attention to decorum in their presence, I therefore uphold you in your objection. Only keep the request in mind, and come as soon as your business will allow."

Charles bowed his adieu, and taking the harness on his arm, was walking down the lane to the road, when a horse on the full gallop, with a rider upon him, turned suddenly in. It was Slocum—he was almost out of breath, but made out to tell his wishes.

"To-morrow morning, Charlie, by sunrise, I want you and Guss to be with your team at the French farm down on the point. We are all going to give Serle a lift to get his house drawn down by the bridge across the little river."

"To-morrow, by sunrise, we will be there." Slocum then dismounted, and went into the house, and Charles went on his way.

"Well, Guss, I am sorry that you have had to work so long alone. Why, what a piece you have cut down!"

"I 've worked steadily along, but what have you got there, a harness?"

"Yes, and it is ours. The old gentleman has made us a present of it."

"It is a beautiful present. How strong it is, too! Pomp can never break that, and it is not clumsy, either; and he cannot hurt it if he should lie down and roll in it. How very kind he is! you have done a better morning's work than I have."

"Well, I will lay down the harness and take hold with you. We must not get down more corn than we can bind and stand up this afternoon, for Slocum wants us to-morrow, with our team, to help to move a house for a friend of his."

"That's good, I want to do something for that fellow—he has a noble soul, and he has done so many little things for us."

Charles did not delay his visit to the Colonel's any longer than was necessary, and as soon as he arose from supper went on his way there, wondering a little what commands Miss Lucy could have for him. He found a little circle of ladies there, busily engaged around a table, sewing.

"You see," said Lucy, "I am not at all backward in calling upon you, when I need a gentleman's assistance."

"And my services, Miss Johnson."

"There now!" and she put her finger up playfully, "have I not forbidden that? recant at once."

"Miss Lucy, my services to their very utmost are at your command."

"Very gallantly said, and I believe honestly, too. But do not look so suspiciously at all this black silk, and the sewing apparatus; the service I shall ever demand, I promise you, shall never be inconsistent with my respect for the feelings of a gentleman. We want you, Mr. Lovell, to be our almoner on this occasion."

" Any thing that you request." Bowing to her, and the circle of ladies.

" Well, it is our wish then, that you be the bearer of a little token of regard for our minister. I suppose you are no great friend of gowns—I mean the clerical gowns."

" I am not an enemy to them, I assure you."

" And you would rather see one that was new and decent, than an old faded garment, and a little darned ? "

" By all means."

" So I have thought, or at least, so we have thought, for these ladies are united with me in this matter."

" In doing the work, Lucy," said a pretty black-eyed girl, who looked up from her work very archly at Lucy.

" In the whole matter, I say ; so you, Jane, keep to your work, and let me do the talking. You see," looking again at Charles, " a few of us ladies thought we would like to see our minister in a more becoming dress on the Sabbath, so we have purchased the silk—"

" Oh Lucy ! "

" And we have made up a new robe, and it is all but finished. But we felt delicate ourselves in presenting him with it. And as I know he looks upon you as a friend, and would rather receive it from you than from any one else, I ask the favor of you to present it for us."

Charles blushed a little, for he felt that he had been distinguished beyond his merits.

"I must obey you, Miss Lucy, as I have said I would. But I must think Mr. Jamieson would feel infinitely happier to receive it from your own hands."

" So we all say," spoke several of the ladies at once. Lucy blushed, until even her fair forehead was tinged with the crimson hue. Charles saw her confusion, and with promptness at once replied,

" But it will be highly gratifying to me to be the bearer of such a beautiful gift, if you desire it ? "

" Thank you," said Lucy, struck with the sensibility that had prompted him to come to her rescue, " then all we have to ask of you is to wait until we have completed our task, and it shall be committed to you."

CHAPTER VI.

The Rev. William Jamieson, whose name has been incidentally mentioned in this narrative, was a native of the State of New York, and a descendant of the De Lanceys, of Westchester county. His parents belonged to the Reformed Dutch Church, and he himself had been educated in the doctrines of that persuasion. He had, from his boyhood, looked to the clerical profession as one which he should wish to follow. This boyish feeling originated in a romantic turn of mind; but had, by a very different process, as he arrived to maturity, become the settled purpose of his heart.

What led him to unite with the Episcopal Church, it would not be worth our time to inquire into. Suffice it to say, he looked not at her as the true church, in distinction from any other persuasion that held the main doctrines of the Gospel; but he liked the decencies of her service—the order of her government, and, moreover, he liked some ideas which she held, and which he thought other evangelical churches had relinquished, in reference to the power of the ordinances which the Great Head of the church had established. He believed in the fullness of the Pentecostal Gifts as the inheritance of the church, and mourned in secret that she had lost the faith which could make the promise effectual. He believed that the ordinances of the church, entered into by a true spirit, were something more than a mere form of admission to outward union. Thus believing, he felt a greater sympathy with that persuasion, which, at least, acknowledges a belief in the power of the Spirit, accompanying the external rite. He had, therefore, enlisted under the Episcopal banner; but with the feeling uppermost in his heart, that in other signs must be sought the marks of the true children of the church, than in the outward banner under which they were marshalled; and whenever he saw these marks, his heart yielded its brotherly affection. He was a fine scholar, as well as a pure minded Christian, and his talents as a preacher would doubtless, had he thrust himself forward, have placed him in a very conspicuous station. But, modest and retiring, he had rather shunned notoriety, and contented himself with the charge of a small parish in the town of Melton.

A place of worship had been erected for him at some remove from the centre of the town. It was a neat, tasty, stone edifice, in a retired spot, amid fine large elms, whose long, sweeping branches almost touched its roof, and whose refreshing shade, in the heat of summer, provided a pleasant resting spot for those members of the congregation, who came from too great a distance to think of returning to their homes, during the intermission of worship.

As Mr. Jamieson had not yet entered into the married state, he could afford to live on a very small salary. It amounted, in all, to only three hundred dollars, but was sufficient for his wants. He had but little occasion to spend much for books, for a valuable and complete library had been presented to him by a friend; and he boarded with a pleasant family near to his church, who provided him with two good-sized rooms, and at a reasonable cost.

He had a sincere desire to fulfil the duties of his station. Over all to whom his watch properly extended, he exercised a truly pastoral care; and he would gladly have extended his labors to many a family in his vicinity, who sadly needed ministerial faithfulness; but motives of delicacy restrained his efforts to those, alone, who constantly attended the services of the Sabbath in his church. He doubted, indeed, the validity of that title, which any particular denomination might set up to a district of land, whether large or small, as peculiarly theirs; but his was not the temperament to strain for a right, or to contend against a wrong. His Master's work he loved, and was ready to do it as he could, without contention. His forte was rather by the bedside of the sick or the suffering, than in the public arena where disputants contend; rather in proclaiming a Saviour's love, in tones of gentleness, to the little flock that gathered round him on the Sabbath, than in thundering forth through the land the strong dogmas of some peculiar system of divinity. He was not up to the tone of the sectarians of the day; nor did he think it necessary to take up the cudgel against every error that arose. But he often said to those with whom he was most intimate,—"Let the heralds of the Gospel but preach the truth, the pure, simple truth, and I believe error will die away before it. Active love was characteristic of our blessed Redeemer. Let it be, also, of all his followers, and a fire will be kindled in our world that will do more to melt down the hardness and wickedness of the human heart, than all the elaborate arguments, either in support of particular systems, or against them."

In personal intercourse, he was equally engaging, as in his discourses from the pulpit. His manners were highly polished. Free from all affectation of politeness, they seemed to be the legitimate effect of a kindly disposition, directed by a nice sense of the proprieties of life. Far removed from hauteur of station, yet never, to his most intimate friend, so demeaning himself in private, as to lose aught of his sincere respect.

That Charles Lovell should have become attached to such a man, when admitted to intimacy with him, is not to be wondered at. Although his senior by some years, Mr. Jamieson had treated him as an equal; and Charles duly valued the friendship of one to whom he could unfold his views and feelings with freedom—whose advantages had been so much superior to his own, and in whose sincerity he could confide without a doubt.

Charles had been educated in the forms and doctrines of the Congregational Church, and had no idea of leaving that persuasion because of any change of views. He loved his own denomination, and had now been, for two years, a member of the church by confession of his faith.

But where he now lived was some miles from his church, too long a distance to walk with comfort, even in fine weather, and he had no means of riding. The Episcopal Church was within sight of his dwelling—a pleasant, shady path led to it. No weather need detain him from the house of God, and his Sabbath would be, what it ought, a day of rest. He resolved, therefore, to make the trial. Both minister and people were strangers to him; but his main object was to attend the sanctuary, that he might mingle with the people of God in public worship. He did not anticipate such discourses as he had been accustomed to hear, and he thought that he might find difficulty in engaging comfortably in their manner of worship. This last objection, however, almost immediately vanished. With a heart ready for devotion, he found the service, at least much of it, well calculated to bear the desires of his heart, and his wants as a sinner before the throne of Grace. And great was his surprise to hear the same truths he had been accustomed to, brought out in all their striking points, boldly and prominently to view, and the sinuosities of the heart followed through every avenue; and every thought and feeling brought into close contact with the word of God. Each Sabbath had increased his interest, and strengthened his resolution to make this his home for public worship.

Mr. Jamieson had returned from his evening walk, had lighted his lamp, and placing it on the round table in the centre of his room, took his seat in a very neat arm-chair by its side. It was just such a chair as one could feel at rest in, and let his thoughts work while his body was unconscious almost of its own existence—so nicely was it poised, and so perfectly were the limbs sustained in ease. Neatly arranged on shelves, that covered more than one side of the room, were his companions—the best of many ages; the mighty, the wise, the witty, and the good. Man, as he appeared through the ages that are past—his mighty works, and all his beautiful thoughts.

Beside him lay his Bible, and a paper that he was about to read. But he seemed just then not quite ready for it, for he has drawn from his pocket a note. How neatly has it been folded! And as he holds it to the light, what a beautiful hand-writing is displayed! Did the hand that traced the letters of the name, his own name, feel that it merited the best that it could do? But why so long in opening it? it has been opened many times before. Ah! he has pondered long enough on the envelop; and now it is unfolded, and his eye turns instinctively to the signature. There seems to lie the charm. The note itself is formal as need be; it might have been addressed from one angel to another, so free is it from aught a lover's heart could take hold upon. But the name there—in full—"yours, with sincere respect." Ah! there must be some charm in that, to cause that look so long, so full of meaning. A rap at the door, and the little note is carefully put away, and a well known voice brings a bright smile upon his face. He rises to admit a friend.

"Ah, Mr. Lovell! come in, you are welcome, indeed; come in."

"I expect, my dear sir, I shall be welcome to-night, as I have never before been. I have a token here that ought at least to give me a favorable introduction." And handing a parcel to the reverend gentleman, pointed him to a paper fastened upon it.

"To the Rev. Wm. Jamieson, from the young ladies of his parish." It was but the work of a moment to undo the precious bundle, and the elegant new silk robe hung upon the arm of the young pastor. He looked steadily at it. A tear moistened his eye, and his voice trembled as he spoke.

"May the hearts that devised, and the hands that executed this precious testimonial, receive a recompense from above."

"Say *the* heart that devised, for although more than one pair of hands have accomplished the work, I am rather inclined to the opinion that to one heart alone you are mainly indebted."

"Ah! think you so? and may I know to whom, in particular, I am indebted?"

"We can often, you know, give a guess, without being able to offer positive proof that our guess is a correct one."

"Then it is only a guess! well, come, sit down, my dear sir. I have been so taken up with my present that I have forgotten my manners."

"I wonder what it is!" said Charles, taking his seat, "that sheds such a charm around the room. It seems to me in such a place that I can bid good bye to the world with a good will."

"And turn monk, ha! Well, I cannot say that I should honor my room, for having accomplished such an end, and that puts me in mind, my dear sir, of an errand that I have to you, which I approve much more than I do your thoughts about a cloister."

"A message for me?"

"Yes, and while I feel that it would be a compliment to

any young man to receive it, yet in the present case I equally honor the judgment of those who have commissioned me with it."

And thus saying, he brought forth the little note which he had been looking at so tenderly, and placed it in the hands of Charles.

The young man blushed deeply, as he read it, and then laying it gently on the table,—

"Of course, sir, I hope you have discouraged such an idea. I could not think of such a thing a moment."

"I have not, I can assure you, for I most cordially approve of the measure. There has been but one consideration which caused me to hesitate a moment in delivering the message to you, and which would effectually have prevented me, if our intimacy had not hitherto been so close. But I believe I need not fear that you will misjudge my motives into a desire to bind you permanently to us. I love to have you with us, but I would do nothing to bribe you."

"It would take a great deal now, sir, to bribe me to leave you. I want to be useful among you, but with what face can I attempt to teach such persons. One of them, I know, is much in advance of me in intellectual attainments. She is herself much better fitted for the duty than I am; and other names she mentions, I know to be ladies highly educated."

"I know that well; they are all of them ladies of bright minds, and have had superior advantages, and it will require no common intelligence to keep ahead of them, and command their respect. But I must be plain with you. You are not aware of the advantage you have gained over most persons of your age, by the course of reading and study you have pursued. Few, even in more advanced life, have such an acquaintance, as you have, with the Scriptures; and the books you have read, as collateral to them, even few in the ministry have attended to. You have a better knowledge of Prideaux, and Calmet, and Josephus, and Lightfoot, than nine out of ten of those who have gone through a regular theological course, and your knowledge of profane history will gain you an immense advantage, especially in ancient history. And your attention to the study of the physical geography of the east, as well as its ancient civil divisions, are all calculated to give you a stand, as a teacher of the Bible, that few can take. You may smile, but I am myself pursuing attentively the very track you have been over."

"You almost surprise me with your catalogue. I have, indeed, derived much pleasure from that course of reading; but no doubt most persons fond of reading have made themselves familiar with the same books."

"I wish it was so, our young men and old men would be much more efficient. But I assure you that among all my acquaintance, of either clergy or laity, I know scarcely one who has so good a stock of Biblical knowledge as yourself."

Charles listened with all due respect to the reasoning of the reverend gentleman, and at times seemed disposed to yield; but the thought of having Miss Lucy Johnson sitting down before him as a scholar, presented an obstacle to his mind insurmountable. The high respect he entertained for her as an educated and talented lady—the deference he had always felt towards her, as one superior to himself, not only in intellectual acquirements, but on account of her superior station in society, had made an impression on his mind not easily effaced.

"It is very difficult for you, my dear sir," said Charles, "rightly to judge of my feelings. You, from your education and profession, stand in such a relation to society that you are on a level with even the highest class. They all acknowledge you as an equal and superior, and from your high place can deal out your teachings and admonitions with profit and freedom. With me, circumstances are entirely different. You are well aware that, in this place, society is of the mixed order. There are persons among us of wealth, who have been trained in a city, and have their own notions of what is respectable, and what is not. Then we have those, who have always lived here, who possess means above our common farmers and tradesmen. They have always kept, in a measure, aloof and by themselves. It would hardly do for me on the Sabbath, to set up for a teacher, and take a station of dignity before those who, on other days, might think it an act of condescension to acknowledge me as an acquaintance."

"Oh, my friend Lovell! you have gotten strangely out of your common course. Pardon me for interrupting you; but you are the very last person I should have suspected of indulging such feelings. You! who have deliberately made up your mind that to work, with your hands upon your own land, was just as respectable as to be a merchant, a lawyer, or of any other profession."

"And so I do, sir."

Mr. Jamieson smiled, and Charles began to perceive upon what rock he was running.

"My dear Lovell, you and I have been so intimate, that I may speak plainly. Now, for one moment, consider what position you are taking; how often you have combated it yourself; who has told you that these persons look down upon you? Does not the suspicion in your own mind bear a little witness against you? If you really believe your business to be respectable, why should you quail before the wrong feelings of others. Believe me, my dear friend, that this very thing is the incubus that weighs down the laboring man. It is not that others do not sufficiently esteem him, but he imagines they do not."

Charles laid his hand on the arm of his friend.

"Say no more about that, I am wrong. I am very wrong, and have been reasoning from premises that I have always denied."

"And you certainly have no reason to complain as to the treatment you have received. He who has been admitted almost to the intimacy of a near relative, by a young lady of such standing as Miss Lucy Johnson, surely has no cause to complain of want of respect."

"Please, my dear sir, to say nothing further about it. You never, I trust, shall hear a word on the subject from me again."

"And I sincerely hope I never may. For, do you know that I am looking to you for the accomplishment of great things in this very matter? Your conduct, from the first, has won my admiration. Ready with your hand for whatever it finds to do, and ready with your mind to enlarge its capacities by storing it with knowledge; and thus, by your manly labors in the field, and your intellectual power in the social circle, or the public assembly, commanding the admiration and esteem of all."

"I see," said Charles, "there is no use in contending

against my master; and therefore I put myself at your disposal, and leave responsibilities with you."

The evening was drawing to a close, and Charles rose to depart; but Mr. Jamieson concluded to accompany him part of the way.

As they stepped from the stoop into the road, a boy came up to them, and, addressing himself to Mr. Jamieson, said—

"Sir, won't you please come to our house? Mother wants to see you."

"Wants to see me? What is your mother's name, my boy?"

"Her name is Simmons: she says she wants to see the minister."

"Is your mother sick?"

"She ain't sick herself; but there is something the matter with my sister."

Mr. Jamieson looked at Charles: "Will you accompany me?"

"Certainly: it is rather a lonely walk."

Charles had heard nothing from Margaret Simmons, since the scene of suffering through which she had passed, and of which he was a witness. He said nothing to his companion, as they walked along the lonely causeway which led to the house, about the circumstances of that scene; for he had promised not to reveal them; but he felt very confident that the present call had relation, in some way, to that event. The house, from a distance, appeared to be situated in the midst of the large area of marsh land spread out on either hand; but, as they drew near, the river, or creek, upon which it stood, began to be visible. And the old dock, which once had been the harbor for sloops, was now a desolate ruin. The house itself bore visibly the same marks of decay with the landing. It had once been a respectable tavern, but it had long been useless as such, and was now only visited occasionally by the boatmen, as their craft might happen to anchor near the spot, or by those who might wish to procure a boat for the purpose of fishing in deep water.

"Many happy days have I spent here, when a little boy," said Charles. "It makes me sad to see such a change."

As they tapped at the door, a voice replied, "Come in." The boy, however, who had preceded them, opened the door, and admitted them to the room. It had once been the public room of the house. The old railing, which formed the little enclosure where the bottles of liquor once stood, was still there, but the bottles had vanished, and their places were filled with all that variety of baskets, bundles, boxes, &c., which somehow get together even in the poorest houses. The long bench still ran along one side of the room, and bore the marks of the loungers who had once dissipated here many hours of their wasted lives. The whole apartment bore the indelible tokens of the place where Intemperance had once held her orgies. A few articles of furniture were scattered about, showing that it was now bed-room, sitting-room, and kitchen.

As the gentlemen entered, the old lady raised her spectacles upon her cap, laid aside a garment she was mending, and, brushing off the loose threads about her person, bowed to Mr. Jamieson.

"Your sarvant, sir."

"I have come, Mrs. Simmons," said the reverend gentleman, as he took her hand, "at your request; and as my friend here was with me at the time, I took the liberty of inviting him to accompany me. I believe he is not a stranger to you: you once knew him when a boy."

"You remember Charlie Lovell, Mrs. Simmons?" said Charles, as he took her hand.

"Indeed! and that I do; but I should never have known you again. Oh, dear! what a change a few years does make in us!—but more in some than in others. Sit down, gentlemen. Billy! hand them seats. I am very glad you have come, and very sorry to have to send for you so, at night."

"We are very glad, madam, to do anything, whether by night or day, if it is in our power to be of service to you."

"You can go in the other room, child, and stay by your sister, and see if she wants anything, and tell her who has come. I thank you, sir, very much—both on you; but whether you can be of any service, it is not in me to know."

"Is your daughter very sick?"

"Well, indeed, sir, it is not in my power to say, nor what

kind of a sickness it is; but it seems to me to be an ailin' of the mind. Her heart seems to be all clean broken, and there don't seem to be no power to keep soul and body together."

" How long has she been in this state?"

" Well: it ain't long that she has been just as bad as she is now. But it has been a comin' on now for some time. The first I saw of it, she began to be very sober like: she didn't laugh and sing, as she used to do. She used to be just like a bird; but, all at once, I see she began to look down-hearted, and she did n't seem to care about her sewing nor knitting, but seemed to want to get off by herself; and so she would take long walks, and wouldn't sometimes get home till late of an evenin'; and then, again, I would often hear her give a long sigh. Sometimes I would speak to her. 'Margaret,' says I, 'what upon earth does ail you?' And then she would try to smile, and say, 'Oh! it ain't nothing, mother; only I feel a little sad just now.' But sadness, you know, sir, ain't natural for young people."

" Not in general, if they are well."

" But it 's about six weeks, now gone, that she came home one night from a walk; and such an altered creature I never saw. 'Margaret,' says I, 'what does ail you? You frighten me.' 'Oh, nothing! mother: only let me go to bed, and there let me die. I don't want to see the face of living creature more.' I see she had been a cryin', and I tried to get out of her what had happened; but it did no good. 'It ain't no matter, mother,' says she: 'it can't mend it to tell of it; and if you don't want to kill me outright, you won't say no more to me: only let me get away from human beings, and let me die.' But you know, sir, it ain't in a mother's heart to let a child die, if she can do anything for one. So I tried to comfort her; and I got her to bed, and gave her something warm; for she was all in a quake. And so it 's been, off and on, ever since. But these few days, she seems to take on worse: so I told her yesterday I shouldn't stand it no longer, and that send for somebody I would; but she held out till this evening; and then she told me I might send for the church minister; and so I didn't stop a minute, but sent right away, for fear she might get out of the notion of it, if I waited till to-morrow."

"Can we see her, madam?"

"Well: just wait a bit." The old lady left the room, but returned immediately, with the request that both gentlemen should come in.

As they entered the room, the mother and brother retired, probably at the request of Margaret. It had a very different aspect from the rest of the house, and told plainly of the taste of the occupant.

There was an air of neatness and order pervading the whole, and the very best seemed to have been made of its little furniture. The floor had no covering, except a strip of carpeting by the bed-side, but the floor was clean—half curtains of white hung at the windows, and the fire-place had a pot of flowers in it. They were, however, withered now, for the hand which gathered them had not plucked any flowers of late—and the little table which stood under the looking-glass had a clean white cloth upon it.

She was in bed, although raised so as to be almost in a sitting posture, with her head leaning back upon the pillow, as she had not power to support it. Charles had seen her in the hey-day of health; he knew how beautiful she once had been, what a sunny smile always shone upon her bright countenance. It was sadly changed now, although beautiful still with its pallid hue and cast of settled melancholy. And as he stepped up, and silently pressed her slender hand, he could not repress the signs of deep feeling. She looked calmly, sadly at him, a slight flushed tinged her cheek, "I will speak to you," she said, "before you leave; I have something to say to you." He retired to the window, and sat down, as Mr. Jamieson approached the bed.

"I know you, sir, although doubtless you have no remembrance of me. I have many times heard you preach."

He bowed assent.

"We have taken a great liberty," she continued, "but when death is near, you know, we cannot stand much upon ceremony."

He took her hand, it felt, indeed, as though it might soon be motionless.

"Do you feel yourself to be so ill?"

"I feel that I have not long to live, and so far as this life is concerned, I am well content that thus it should bé. But

I fear I have no suitable preparation for the life beyond; and I want you, sir, to tell me what to do, so that I may not go before my Judge, feeling as I now do."

"You think, my dear young friend, that you are very near to death?"

"I do feel it to be near."

"And you say, you fear to die?"

"I fear the great realities that come after."

"What great realities are you thinking of?"

"Oh, after death, you know, is the judgment—the body will return to dust, but my soul must go back to its Maker. And He will judge me, and I shrink from it. How can I go *there*, for I am a great sinner?"

"When you think of yourself as a great sinner, do you feel really distressed on that account? or do you merely feel afraid, that, because you are such a sinner, your Judge will condemn you?"

For some moments the poor girl lay with her eye steadily fixed upon him, who was endeavoring thus faithfully to do his duty, however painful to himself.

At length she replied,

"I never thought of that before."

"The Scriptures teach us that it is not enough that we be merely conscious of our sins, there must not only be a consciousness of guilt, but also a sincere sorrow of heart on account thereof. The same kind of sorrow that a child would feel who had done wrong to a kind, and faithful, and loving parent, and had become sensible of the wrong, and whose heart was melted with contrition."

With most intense interest was her gaze still directed to the speaker, and, as the last illustration broke upon her mind, she was evidently much excited.

"I can understand you now. Oh, I see there is a great difference." She paused, and wiped her forehead, for the big drops were gathering there.

"Oh, sir, under such circumstances, can you tell me what I am to do? Where am I to get that true sorrow from?"

"Christ Jesus is the mighty Saviour, to Him alone you must go. He died for you. His blood alone can atone for your sins, and His Holy Spirit alone can work in you the great work of repentance and faith. To him you must go—

pray to Him that he would save you—that He would give you a right temper of heart, and a right understanding of his great salvation. Have you ever prayed?" This last question he put in a tone so low as to be scarcely audible. She heard him, however, and a tear gathered as she replied—

"How could I pray? Sometimes in my agony, I have called aloud for mercy, but it was only because my misery forced me to cry out, as a wretch under torture, or a drowning man, with the waves breaking over him. But, sir, dear sir, will you pray for me? will you pray with me now?"

Without reply, he knelt down by her side. To heaven, with all the fervor of his feeling heart, he poured out his desires for the erring, suffering one. The prayer was plain and simple, and the desires expressed within the comprehension of the feeblest mind. Her eyes were closed, her hands clasped before her, and her soul seemed to enter into the spirit of the petition sent up for her. He arose, and stood again at her side. She looked up calmly at him. "I have never prayed such a prayer as that. Oh, that I had! Oh, that I could!"

"Try to do it. He hears the ravens when they cry, and gives them food. He hears the seamen, when, amid the tempest, they call upon Him for deliverance, and stills the storm. And, surely, to one who asks for his own Spirit, and to be brought into complete obedience to Himself, He will not turn away."

"Oh, bless you for these words, what you say I will try to do. For I feel that what you say to me is truth. Would it be asking too much of you, to request that you would call again?"

"I should feel very sorry not to see you again, and many times. May I come as often as I please?"

"Oh, do, do. I feel as if you had helped me to see a little way—a very little way, and I can't bear to think of losing it. Come as soon as you can."

As Mr. Jamieson left her bed-side, Charles, as she had requested, came up to her.

"You are surprised to see me so changed. You would not wonder if you knew all. You know a part, you have been a witness to some things; but you do not know all, and I want you to know all, for I don't know why it is, but I cannot bear that you should think worse of me than I deserve." And placing a letter in his hands—

"This I wrote since our last interview: your kindness to me in that dreadful hour has made me most anxious to reveal the whole. I want one heart to cherish just feelings towards me; especially I want, even in death, and after it, you to think well of me—as you can."

The tears flowed freely, as she brought out these last sentences, in broken tones.

He pressed her hand gently, and leaning over her, said in a soothing voice,

"Margaret, I offered to take a brother's place, and have your wrongs redressed."

"I know you did—Oh, how kind it was at such an hour—Oh, may you be blessed with love as pure, as lasting, as your noble heart deserves. But promise me one thing—you will do nothing in revenge when you may meet with him. Let him go, God is the avenger of the fatherless. All I have written is merely to let you know the truth—good bye." And covering her face, she gave him her hand, and received his parting embrace.

CHAPTER VII.

It was not often that the morning meal was eaten by the candle-light in Aunt Casey's cottage. It being one of the rules that Charles had established for himself, that daylight afforded sufficient time for all the work that was to be done. There were, however, occasional exceptions to the rule, and this morning was one of them. Charles had promised Slocum to be on the spot by sunrise, and he meant to be there; and Aunt Casey had the smoking breakfast on the table by the time which had been agreed upon the night before. And just as faint streaks of coming day were visible in the east, Charles and his brother started from their barn-yard with their yoke of cattle, on a good lively walk.

It was a clear October morning, the stars were yet visible, and they shone with that sparkling light which always indicates an atmosphere of peculiar purity. As the day advanced, the white frost could be distinctly seen, and although but a slight one, it made the exercise of walking rather agreeable than otherwise. The young men felt as if about to enjoy a holyday. Their minds were free and elastic, ready to enjoy the inspiration of pure air, and the rich beauties of a lovely autumnal morning.

No care, like a worm at the root, spoiled the full play of their best feelings. No gloom to shroud their spirit, such as throws its heavy mists around the morning hours of the idle and the dissipated. Strong in the consciousness of faithfully discharging the duties of the day, they hail, with manly joy, each rising sun.

But now, especially, is there a flow of joyous feeling. It beams from their bright faces; it shows itself in their quick and steady step. They are bound on an errand of love; and they are to meet comrades, who are also now hastening to the same point;—whole hearted, honest, and manly spirits, who have, like them, been born and reared amid the free and wholesome atmosphere of the country; who knew the blessings of a country home, and the sweets which embalm it in their hearts, however plain and rough its exterior. And they are gathering, now, on all the different roads, and walking gladly forward at this fresh hour, to give a long pull, a strong pull, and a pull all together, to help a fellow-townsman, just grappling with the cares of life, to rear himself a home—a place where he can gather his heart's treasures around him, and shut out the world—where he can feel himself alone to be the master, and all others guests. And it is worth all the stir and bustle of this morning, and the patient, steady labors of the day; for it will cause some hearts, even in the prospect of its blessings, to leap for joy.

They are two miles on their way, and broad day is about them. The blue jays are screaming through the wood, and flocks of robins are spreading among the cedars by the roadside; and the crows are cawing, as they sail steadily aloft on their way to some far-off corn-field. And now an opening in the hills, which skirt the east, presents to their view a broad sweep of the Sound, with its distant headlands. It is smooth as a mirror; and the bright streaks that gild the far-off clouds, old ocean's mists, are all reflected back. 'Tis bright above, and bright below; and now their golden tinge has lighted the hill-side; and the forests, in their varied hues, throw off a mellow tint.

Charles would have paused to look, and to admire; for his eye was quick to catch each passing beauty; but they must on, for a mile is yet to be traveled over, and the sun is near at hand.

"There they are, Charlie! there they are!" and Augustus pointed to the west, where a cross road came from an opening wood to meet the one on which they were walking.

"That's a fine sight, Gus! there must be forty yoke. Ah! they see us!"

A cheerful huzza greeted them, which they as cheerfully returned; and, quickening their speed, soon joined the company, receiving a hearty welcome from many a sturdy hand.

Slocum had been there the day before; and, long ere sunrise this morning, he was on the spot, with a gang of hands, getting the building in readiness for a start. With the immense power on hand, he designed to draw it along on timbers, prepared as the runners of a sled, depending only occasionally upon the use of slight rollers. At such a time, when probably seventy men, and fifty yoke of oxen, were to be brought into harmonious and instant action, everything depended upon the wise management of a few leaders. Slocum took upon himself the chief control; and under him was a leader, to watch the progress of the building, to fill up small hollows, and provide against obstructions of any kind; and a leader of the team; for it was of the utmost consequence that the whole should be made to exert their strength at the same moment, and at the orders of one man.

"Choose your own leader, boys," Slocum called out to the teamsters; "only let us have a ready, wide awake fellow, for we mean to make it walk lively."

With almost unanimous acclamation, the name of Charles Lovell was called out. Charles made all the objections he could, but they were of no avail; and Slocum could not wait for any scruples of conscience, or delicacy, so he called out—

"Take the best horse you can find, Lovell, and mount him quick."

This was not usually necessary; but choice had to be made of a route by which to carry their burden; and some one must be able to go from place to place with alacrity. As Charles had no objections to this part of the arrangement, in a few moments he was mounted, and ready for action.

The first pull was the important one. The building having been loosed from its foundation, and the heavy sleepers placed under it, the chains were fastened to them, and the long line of cattle, each yoke with a driver at its head, was arranged in the direction they wished to move. Lovell was stationed at the head of the line, and the eye of every teamster was fixed steadily upon him. At a signal from Slocum, he raised his hand, and every lash was, in an instant, swung across the yoke it guided. There was a slight creak, as the beasts bent their necks to the burden, and the house moved slowly from its long resting place, amid the hearty shouts of numerous spectators.

On and on, slowly, steadily, yet surely, traveled the huge hulk, behind the long line of bended necks; each teamster using such means as he knew his cattle required, to keep them doing their part of the work: some by a gentle word; others by a slight touch of the lash; and others, again, by a severer admonition. All, however, keeping on an even strain, and with their eye on their leader, that at once the signal might be obeyed, either to halt, or to quicken speed. Slocum had so managed matters, that, for some time at least, there should be no stop. But they will be compelled to have many halts until the long pull is ended; and we must go to the end of the route, and take a view of matters there.

It was about two o'clock in the afternoon of this same day, when Col. Johnson and his fair daughter Lucy came out of their fine, old-fashioned domicile, and walked down through the neat court-yard to the front gate.

There was just then standing there, one of the most respectable-looking establishments, in the shape of horse and carriage, that could have been found for miles around. Not by any means the most showy, dear reader, we have used the word respectable advisedly, and with due consideration of its meaning.

The horse was a large, strong-jointed, nervous-looking creature, who stood so firmly upon his four legs, and tossed his head about with such an air of independence, that one could not help forming the opinion that the matter of being harnessed to the vehicle, and carrying its two passengers, was altogether a holyday concern—he had rather do it than not; and if they would only let him know where they wished to go, the reins might be dispensed with; a whip would only be an insult; and, in fact, that old master would as soon have thought of taking a sword-cane with him.

And what a fit was that harness! how easily it seemed to lie upon his plump, black carcass. The polish on both so complete, that they might have been supposed to be rubbed off at the same time. And what a soft, dreamy kind of a place was that seat! what large, full, downy-looking cushions; and no chance of being squeezed—plenty of elbow-room, and leg-room, too! And if there had been any probability that the horse should behave naughtily, of which there was not the least fear, why, it would have been nothing to step out; it was nothing to get in.

What a pleasant contrast in colors, too! the dark olive without, and the light drab within. And how gracefully it hung on the curved braces! And what a nice proportion in the distances of its wheels! No danger, whether in getting in or out, going fast or slow, of being brought into contact with the mud and dust: they were left, just where they ought to be, without.

"Josey is almost tired of waiting for us. Whoa, Josey!"

Josey did seem to be a little impatient; for, as soon as he saw his master, he began to paw the earth, and throw his head up and down faster; and finally, as they were getting in, he fairly turned his neck, and looked behind him—as much as to say, "As soon as you are ready, I am."

"Whoa, Josey! now come."

Ah! that was gracefully done. Just the slightest toss of the head, and the carriage moved, as if it went by some power the horse had nothing to do with. He merely trotted on unconcernedly and playfully before it. The whole thing was a matter of sport.

The top had been thrown back, for the weather was so pleasant, and air so perfectly in accordance with one's feelings, that Lucy had said "she wanted to feel it," and the Colonel replied, that he "hated tops, at any rate, without it was raining hard." And, besides, there was another reason why tops should be down: it was one of those lovely autumn days which are often witnessed in the beautiful month of October, when, wherever the eye turns, there is something to attract and please. Now the far off mountain, with its purple hue, in rich contrast with the yellow sky—now the hill-side near at hand, spreading out its varied picture, where every hue blends in sweet harmony, and touches the finer feelings of the heart by its mild and peaceful radiance. And now the lone maple by the road-side in its brilliant red, or the golden hickory, or the rich brown oak, or a cluster of dark evergreens shooting up amid the spangled grove; and all around, wherever we may look, there rests such a mellow tint, like the halo from a better world, that the soul is hushed to peace, and the very earth seems a symbol of love.

"I thought that first we would ride down, and see the spot

where they are going to put that house—as far as I remember, it is very pretty place."

"But do you say, father, that the house is to be drawn two miles, and all to-day?"

"So Slocum said; he was at our house yesterday, and asked me for my oxen to help along."

"It is to be drawn by oxen, then? that will be a curiosity. I was glad you proposed a ride, father, for it is such a lovely day. But I almost wondered at your desire to have me see the removal of a house. I once saw a building removed, and it seemed a very slow, dull kind of business."

"That was upon rollers, child, and drawn by a windlass. This, you will find, is quite another affair. The fact is, it is just one of those scenes which I fancy. In the first place, a poor young man is about getting himself a house, and I feel a desire to see what kind of a place he is going to have. I had rather look at it, no matter how lowly, than I would at any of those fine, showy houses they are putting up around us. There is another thing about it I like to witness—whoa, Josey!" Josey was unusually disposed to go ahead; the fine weather seemed to have affected him, but his master's voice checked him; he did not like it though, for he tossed his head and shook his bits, as much as to say, "I could if I would." The old gentleman resumed, "I say, there is another thing I like to witness, and that is the kind feeling which it exhibits, to see so many united in giving a helping-hand. It is a side of human nature I like to see—we can see its dark and selfish aspects without riding for. But here is the spot where it is to be placed."

"Oh, I remember this spot well, and have often wondered why some one did not put up a good house here."

"Well, well, well, Slocum told me that he thought the man had got a good situation—I call it beautiful. Now just imagine, Lucy, when every thing gets fixed up a little snug, these bushes cut down, and the fences righted, and the trees trimmed, and the garden in order—what a pretty spot, too, for a garden!"

"And that grove, father! Oh, what a lovely spot it will be, and how many fruit trees; and such a pretty slope down to the water; really, if he did not give too much for it, and can afford to keep it, what a nice place it will be—what a pleasant homestead. Do you know what he gave for it, father?"

"What he gave for it? Well, I think Slocum said it cost him a hundred dollars. It is worth it though, well worth it."

"How good it will be for them to have a house. I am so glad you have let your oxen go, father, to help along."

"Well, that is no more than we ought to do. It is a great thing to give a little help at the right time. Have you never seen a boy try to climb a tree? the branches are, may be, some distance from the ground—up he starts with a good resolution, and tugs, and tugs, and scratches away till he gets almost to the branches; and then he begins to get out of breath; he holds on and rests a while, and at it he goes again; he is almost up, he can see the limbs just about a foot above him, if he could only get a grip of them once, he is safe; but his arms begin to tire, he tries again; but he can make no progress, and he feels that he must give it up. Now, if some one just at that pinch could just give him a little boost—a little boy might do it, may be--just so he can get hold of the limbs, and then up he goes, and nothing can hinder him from going as high as he wants to; for want of that little aid he must have gone to the root of the tree and staid there."

"I believe, father, your idea is the right one. And now, I think, all these farmers, who you say have given a day to help Mr. Serle, may be said to have given him the push at the right time; for when he once gets his house, and gets into it, and gets his land in order, he may fairly be said to have got hold of the branches, and can take care of himself. But, I suppose, he has had to buy the house, too?"

"Oh, yes, no doubt."

"I wonder who has helped him? Oh, what a pleasure it must be to know that one has been enabled to give a young family a start for life."

"Whoa, Josey!"

Josey was standing still enough, only occasionally giving a slight toss to his head. But the old gentleman seemed fidgety, and desirous of diverting attention to some other subject; for his lovely daughter, as she uttered the last sentence, turned her face full upon him. Very luckily for him, however, just then, the rattling of a carriage was heard behind them, and in a moment more a dashing barouche drove up, and stopped beside them. One of them, he who holds the reins, and was the owner of the establishment, bowed very low to the Colonel and his daughter, and with a very self-complacent smile attempted to introduce his companion.

"Mr. Roorback, Colonel Johnson, a friend of mine from the city, who is looking for a situation here for a country-seat."

Mr. Roorback, who seemed rather a plain sort of man, although pretty well dressed, made a dodge with his head, very strangely in contrast with the stately, graceful bow of the Colonel.

"Miss Johnson, Mr. Roorback." Almost a double jerk this time; it was acknowledged by a slight inclination on the part of the lady.

"I think it a great pity, Colonel, that Hawthorne should have sold this pretty building spot to that fellow, who is going to put up an old shanty on it."

"Ah, well, I have not seen the house; but I understood from Mr. Slocum, who is a pretty good judge of such matters, that it was a very decent house, a tight snug house for a young man who is poor to begin the world in."

"Oh, well, it may be well enough for a poor man, as you say, but it ain't such a building as we want to see around here. This is a beautiful building spot. I offered Hawthorne the price he sold it for, and cash down, but he'd given the fellow the refusal. I don't see where he got the money from. I don't believe he's worth fifty dollars in the world. He has borrowed it, likely, and he'll never be able to pay for it, and then some other devil will get it."

"Well, Mr. Lucas, I suppose poor devils, as you call them, want houses as much as rich ones, and they cannot get them so easily. The town's people generally seem to feel glad of the matter, for they have turned out, I am told, to help him get it here."

"Yes, the farmers have turned out with their oxen, but you know that's their way. They don't stand to ask whether it is going to help the place. They don't seem to care about that, and sometimes, I think they had rather see a plain, little bit of a building put up, and get a poor family in it, than have a man settle among them with two or three hundred thousand in his pocket." And, as he said this, he patted his companion on the knee, and gave the Colonel a very significant wink. The Colonel, however, was not at all affected by it, for he immediately replied—

"I think the farmers, if such is the case, show their good sense—one industrious working-man is a much more useful member of society, where the most are workers, than a dozen men with millions in their pockets, if they are not of the right sort."

The gentleman blushed a little, but he answered rather mildly—

"Well, that to be sure, we want people, as you say, colonel, of the right sort; but you don't think any less of a man because he has plenty of the stuff."

"By no means, sir, by no means, if he has come by it honestly and *honorably*." The Colonel laid marked stress on the last word.

"But such men, I have generally found, Mr. Lucas, have a great respect for those who are down in life, struggling honestly and bravely to get up. How many persons now can you count up from among your acquaintances, who may be rich now, but started originally from no larger nor better house than is about to be put upon that old foundation?"

"Yes, yes, that 's true. Well, I must be going, I am somewhat in a hurry. Good afternoon, Colonel." The gentleman bowed his best, his companion gave his head a jerk, the whip cracked over the horses, and on they flew.

"You spoke a little too plainly, I am afraid, father. But Oh, look yonder, what a pretty sight! how steadily they advance."

"I will turn Josey into the other road, I see they are upon this, and we can have a better view of them. Whoa, Josey."

The Colonel drove a few rods one side into another track, running parallel with the one he had been upon, and a full view of the cavalcade was afforded, as it came slowly, steadily along the winding road.

"That is a sight, father, worth riding many miles to see. How steadily those faithful beasts urge their way! every neck bending to the work, and how steadily the building draws on to its destined spot. There is a moral beauty in it too that goes to the heart. All that is a labor of love."

"That is it, dear, that is the beauty of it. And just look what a manly set of fellows, what good, honest jovial faces, and see that fellow on horseback, how finely he sits on his horse. With his frock on too—but stop! it ain't, is it? yes, it is our boy, the rogue! it's Charles Lovell; the leader of the band, is'nt he? ha! the rogue, he'll be a leader wherever he is. And there's that Slocum, with a red handkerchief round his neck. That fellow is in his glory now, he is happier than if he was getting a hundred dollars for the job."

The train had now reached them, when at a signal from Lovell it suddenly stopped. A young man was seen running up to Slocum, and the finger of the latter was immediately pointed at the carriage. With a sprightly step, the former at once approached, he was a good looking youth of about twenty-three, his hair light and curling, and his complexion of a clear red and white, such as is often seen in Scotch lads, his dark gray eyes sparkled as he came up, and taking off his hat bowed to the Colonel and his daughter.

"This is Colonel Johnson?" His voice trembled very much.

"It is, sir."

"My name is Serle," and he put out his hand, which the Colonel at once cordially grasped. Tears started from the eyes of the young man. He tried to speak, but he could only get out with great effort—

"God bless you, sir!"

"May the Lord bless you, my dear young fellow, and give you and your good wife as much happiness as will be best for you, and tell your wife that when you get all fixed, I am coming to drink tea with her, and get a kiss of the baby. Good-bye to you, now; and now see to your oxen."

Slocum had advanced so near to the carriage that he could see the deep feeling manifested by Serle, and hear the good-natured tones of the old Colonel's voice. He could keep in no longer, so he called out—

"Three cheers for Col. Johnson. God bless him!"

There never went up a more lusty huzza than arose from those hundred voices—it seemed to come from their very hearts. The Colonel was deeply agitated, but he could only say, "Whoa, Josey, whoa Josey."

"What does it mean, dear father! what does it mean?"

"Oh, tut, tut, tut, nothing but that Slocum. He's always a doing something, some mischief or other."

"Miss Lucy!"

Lucy turned, and Charles Lovell, with his hat off, and his fine face lighted up with a glow of excitement, bowed to her, and Lucy smiled, with that unaffected joy upon her face which might have greeted a brother.

"Ah, how *do* you do? Can you tell me what the people mean by all this?"

"Only letting out the fullness of their hearts towards one who has ever proved himself the helper of the helpless—and this is a new instance of it."

"Dear, dear father," and Lucy caught him round the neck, and without fear or thought of who saw her, gave him a hearty kiss.

"Tut, tut, tut, tut, you are all crazy together. Mr. Lovell, just help me up with this top. Whoa, Josey, we must get on our way."

"Not yet, sir, not yet, if you please. Miss Lucy, the young ladies in this vicinity have assembled a little back in the grove, and are preparing refreshments for those who have been at work to-day. The neighbors have sent in from all quarters, and I know it will be gratifying to you to be with them, and very gratifying to them to have you."

"Ah, I should dearly like it, but I should be so ashamed, for I have nothing to sit on; I only wish I had known it."

"You will find I think, that you will not be considered an interloper."

"Shall I go, father?"

"Yes, if you want to, and Josey and I will trot along home, and I will send back for you towards night."

Charles looked at Lucy, as she was about to alight,—"If Miss Lucy will accept of my assistance just as I am," and he cast his eyes down over his check frock.

"To be sure I shall accept it, and shall expect you to be as polite as when you are in your best dress."

Charles was off his horse in a moment, and Lucy, taking his hand, jumped from the carriage.

"Colonel, you ain't a going? we want you to stop and see the thing on," and the Colonel, without thinking, had given his hand to Slocum.

"Stop, I shan't stop, you've made fuss enough with the thing, as you call it. Don't you never come to me with your pitiful stories again—now I tell you I shan't."

"Stop, Colonel, don't you say it, just forgive me this time, but you see I couldn't keep it from the boys. They kind of smell'd a rat, you know, as soon as they see how Serle acted, and then they remembered about t'other things."

"T'other things? ah! you are a great goose; if you wasn't such a good fellow yourself, I should never do another job for you. But go now, and get your thing on, as you call it, they are all waiting for you. Whoa, Josey."

A slight feeling of the rein, and off again moved the noble beast, apparently prouder than ever, just as though he had entered into the whole scene, and knew well what a heart he carried behind him.

Lucy did not need an introduction to the circle of ladies, that she found herself among as soon as she reached the grove. But they all flocked around her, and seemed ready to devour her with kindness.

"Oh, Miss Lucy, Miss Lucy, how glad we all are that you have come, do come see the table."

"Oh, but my dear," she replied to the pretty girl that had come up, and taken her hand, "I feel ashamed to be among you, for you see when I left home I had no idea of all this. Father merely asked me to take a ride, and see a house moved by oxen. If I had only known about the whole affair, I should have been so glad to have brought my mite."

"Your mite is more than made up by your company," said a very pretty young woman, taking one of Lucy's hands in both of hers, and pressing it warmly.

"Why, Sally Gaines! excuse me, Mrs. Serle, I mean. Oh, how glad I am to see you; how well you look, and Oh, I am so glad for you, what a nice place you are going to have."

The young woman looked at her with an expression of countenance full of feeling, and replied in a very low voice—

"And you know, no doubt, through whose kindness it has been accomplished?"

"I knew nothing, dear, until a few moments since. But

if my father had any hand in it, I shall love him the more for it."

"That is just like you," and imprinting a warm kiss on the fair cheek of Miss Lucy (not fairer than her own, however), she led her to the table. It was a rude construction of boards, and saw-horse block. But its rudeness was concealed by snow-white cloths spread over the whole, and even if the bare boards had been visible, the abundance of great things spread out upon it would have made it a very pleasing sight, especially to a company of hungry young men. There was roast pig, and chicken pie, and boiled ham, and boiled beef, and röast lamb, all cold, and scattered about through the length of the table, with an occasional plate of cold boiled pork, cut into slices, and having a very tempting look. These were the substantials, while mingled among them were plates of fine, large, white biscuit, of wheat bread, and rye; tempting rolls of butter, stamped with various devices. Pies in abundance, of apple and custard, with an endless variety of cake, sweet-meats, pickles, &c., and to crown all, a fire had been kindled, and several kettles were hanging over it, and there was a fragrant odor of tea and coffee, even over all the other good things. How such a variety could have been collected at so short notice, and from voluntary contributions, would have puzzled any one not accustomed to the habits of the country.

"And now, Miss Lucy Johnson, you have got to be the queen of the company, and direct the pouring out of the tea and coffee."

Lucy found it in vain to remonstrate, for there was such a host against her. So with right good glee she took the responsibility, and very soon all necessary arrangements were made to prevent confusion.

With all man's intellectual gifts, it is impossible to conceal the fact that he has strong animal propensities, and that there are times when even his nobler powers are very much under their dominion. A hungry man is not in the best condition to exhibit the good qualities of the species, unless as an exception, the item to be put in, that he is just about to sit down to a board well filled with the right materials.

That, on this occasion, there was no lack of all the good feelings cannot be doubted, for there were sharp appetites, and an abundance to appease them. The work in which they had all been engaged was enough of itself to excite cheerfulness; and if the saying is true, "that if there is any good thing at any time in this world, woman is at one end or the other of it." That additional circumstance must also be reckoned. For woman was there in all the freshness of youth and beauty, and in the fullness of her kind heart. Prettily dressed girls, with smiling faces, were tripping lightly, now here, now there, around the table where sat brothers, cousins, neighbors, and sweethearts. And they were waiting upon them, not figuratively but in reality. Bringing smoking cups of tea and coffee, pushing about sugar-dishes and milk-cups, refilling exhausted plates with fresh heaps of rolls or uncut pies, and sometimes urging some friend a little more bashful than the rest, "to have more of that cake," or pie, or sweet-meats. They felt bold to do so, for the entertainment was of their getting up. At one end of the table, too, sat the queen of the feast, directing her aids in attending upon the empty cups, and there was many a stealthy glance at her, and many a cup of coffee had a double relish imparted from the fact that she herself had noticed the empty cup, and had caught the gentleman's eye, and with her winning smile and graceful sign, had invited him to send it to her.

And now, as though by a sudden impulse all arose, and a very general voice determined that the ladies must be seated, and they would be waiters. There was a little demurring at first, but they soon gave in, and now what a scrambling to get the nicest of every thing, and put it before every one, and what a spilling of the delicious beverage, for hands that could whirl a plough about as if it were a plaything, could not so nicely poise the delicate cup and saucer, and many a pretty lass would turn up her rouguish eye and smile as the cup came trembling down before her.

"You had like to have done it." While another, and may be a whole group, would start from the table, with a scream of delight, because some unlucky wight had made shipwreck of cup, saucer, and all. But the more mishaps there were, the more did the meal appear to relish, for it tended to break up all reserve, and brought those into pleasant contact who had only before been acquaintances at sight.

But the longest and pleasantest day must come to an end, some had a good distance to go, and oxen had stomachs as well as farmers, and must be seen to, and so in straggling companies, the young men departed, but not without many a lingering look behind at the bright faces they were leaving.

CHAPTER VIII.

Charles had become quite attached to Pomp, and Pomp to him, and the idea of having any difficulty in breaking him, or having any such process to go through at all, seemed quite preposterous. But Pomp had a colt's nature about him, however amiable he appeared, and no sooner were the bitts in his mouth, and the reins drawn back, and fastened to the girth, and he found that his head and neck must be held in one position, than he began to show great restlessness, biting on the hard round iron, and throwing his head from side to side, backing, rearing, pawing, sideling, and finally throwing himself down. But all to no purpose, the iron still hurt his mouth, and his head and neck must retain the same contracted arched position. Poor Pomp! this is your first lesson, to teach you that man must be your master. In vain you sidle up to him, and rub your neck against him; he knows that it aches, and he pities you, but how else shall he teach you to obey his will. This torture you must endure until your mouth becomes so sensitive as to feel the gentlest motion of his hand, and you shall be willing to yield to it as quick as thought. And now you are left alone, there is nothing within the enclosure wherewith you can injure yourself, and you must bear, as you can, the trials that have come upon you. Ay, ay, getting angry, are you? What a furious plunge that was! and how the foam flies from your mouth as you toss spitefully from side to side your pinioned head. You will be cooler by the time the day is closing. Poor Pomp, we pity you.

But Pomp was not left alone quite so long as that, for his master, a little anxious about his favorite, came from his work earlier than usual, and when the poor fellow came up quickly to him, bearing no malice, and trying to put his head upon his master's shoulder, the girth was immediately loosened, and the bridle removed, and Pomp led out where he could have a good run, and enjoy himself.

But the great tussle was to come yet, which was to decide the mastership, and it was very doubtful to the lookers on, whose neck would be broken first, the colt or his owner's.

Charles had provided himself with a pair of low wheels, with a long axle, and shafts sufficiently extended, so as to prevent any accident from Pomp's heels, and with this, he resolved to bring the youngster to terms, if there was any such thing.

It required great tact on the part of both brothers to get the frisky creature within the shafts, for he seemed to have a foreboding of evil, if once there. So he flew round from side to side, and every way, until all parties were pretty well excited. He was, however, at last caught between them, and in an instant secured in a manner that precluded the notion of any separation for a trifle.

"And now, old fellow," said Charles, as he sprang into his seat, "you and I don't separate, until one or the other of us is master."

Augustus was not wanting in courage, but when he saw his brother seated behind the furious beast, he began to wish Pomp and they had never met. But he knew his brother's spirit, and how useless it would be to say any thing now. He could only watch with intense interest the fearful contest.

No sooner was Charles in his seat, than Master Pomp was made to feel that he was wanted to go ahead. He therefore chose to do just the opposite, and began running back. Finding this rather a troublesome way of getting along, for more reasons than one, he altered his mind, and all at once gave a spring forward that would have broken any common harness. But nothing gave way, and although the whole concern behind him was lifted bodily, some feet from the ground, they came to the earth again all sound, and as tightly fastened to him as ever. This was followed by a succession of leaps, with an occasional attempt at standing on two legs to the manifest danger, as some thought, of his falling over backwards, and then darting across the road, over the ditch, and up the bank, along the foot-path, and then down again to the opposite side into the duck-pond, frightening the poor paddlers, and causing them to scatter in all directions, and then up an embankment where it seemed impossible for either horse or wheels to keep erect. But Pomp had good command of his legs, and appeared no more to mind the sloping side-hill than a cat or dog. But around he must go, for his master would allow of no stopping until he said whoa, and he had not yet said it, nor did he mean to say it until Master Pomp should be brought under subjection. And now finding that impassible places were of no avail, but the same burden kept fast to him, and the same steady pressure on the bitts continued, when once more in the high-way, he started off to try the effect of a run. This his master expected, and was prepared for it, and he felt now fully assured that the critical moment had come, which would decide the contest.

Charles had procured a pair of bitts of more than usual severity, designing not to exert his strength upon them until absolutely necessary for his own safety, or the good of his horse. The colt started with great speed, and all who witnessed the play of his legs, and the powerful leaps he made, looked on with breathless interest. Augustus was deeply excited, and most heartily wished the colt had never been purchased. Charles, however, seemed perfectly collected, although the fearful rapidity with which he was carried was not calculated to make even the strongest heart quite at ease. He held no tighter rein than he had done, nor by any signs let the beast know that he was not doing just the thing he wanted. The road before him was fair, and for some miles he had nothing to fear; but he had the welfare of his horse in view, as well as his own particular comfort, he only meant to let him get a little tired. Two miles were soon passed over, and there appeared no flagging on the part of Pomp. He now began to gather up the reins until certain that he would have requisite power. He looked to see that his feet were firmly braced, and then calling out, "Whoa," he drew the bitts with great violence once or twice across his mouth, reining him back at the same time with his utmost strength. Pomp threw his head back, made one or two plunges, his pace slackened—a repetition of the first manœuvre with the bitts, and he gave in. He was now white with lather, and as he champed his bitt, and tossed his head, Charles saw that the foam from his mouth was streaked with blood. As there was an open space where he had stopped, which allowed of sufficient room for turning; Charles gave him no breathing time, but as soon as he had fairly brought him to a halt, turned him with his face again towards home. He obeyed with apparent willingness, and when in the road started off on a good round trot, and came back to the astonishment of all with the steadiness of an old horse. Several now called out to Charles to stop, and let the colt go for the day, but he resolved to finish the work he had begun. So he turned and retraced the path he had traveled in such haste, and kept him turning, and trotting, and stopping at his will, until he felt assured there would be no efforts on Pomp's part again to have his own way.

"Poor fellow," said his master, after he had unharnessed him, and was washing his mouth with cold water, "you and I, Pomp, will be better friends after this, than ever. You are my slave now, but you shall find me a kind master." And after Pomp had a good roll, he was led into his snug, warm stall, well littered with straw, and well provided with the substantials for a good supper. It has been a hard day, Pomp, but you and your master will be the happier for many years to come in consequence of it.

"I wouldn't take a hundred dollars for him this minute," said Augustus, as he was rubbing him down with a large wisp of straw.

"And I wouldn't take two hundred, Guss. He will make us a valuable horse for many years; that high spirit will make him more serviceable, when properly subdued, and his courage will prevent him from being frightened. I have no doubt in two months, I will train him so, that if carriage or harness should break, he will not be alarmed."

"Well, he must be your horse, you have had all the trouble with him, and have risked your neck to break him."

"He shall be no more mine than yours, Guss. What do I want of him alone? We can both enjoy him, as we can whatever else we have. That makes me think of the corn, how much is there cribbed up?"

"Three hundred bushels of ears."

"That makes one hundred and fifty bushels of shelled

corn, not a great yield for six acres, to be sure. But we must get the land into better shape by degrees."

"Have you made a calculation, Charley, how we stand compared with our circumstances last spring?"

"I have not, but we can easily do it. Let us go over matters to-night after supper. I am glad you spoke of it."

After supper, Charles took his book, and with Augustus by his side, made out a statement of their concerns. As they had contracted no debts, it was a very simple matter to make out the situation of their affairs.

"You say, Guss, that we have cash on hand,"	$25 00
"Yes, and you have engaged one hundred bushels corn at 80 cents."	80 00
"And we have also engaged, and mostly delivered, 150 bushels of potatoes at 30 cents."	45 00
"Then the buckwheat, Charley, how much is winnowed?"	
"I have counted the bags, there are 40 of them, 2 bushels each, 80 bushels, this the millers take at 50 cents."	40 00
"Well, Charley, we ought to reckon the stock."	
"Yes, there's Pomp, what shall we say for him?"	
"He will bring $100 any day."	
"I wouldn't sell him for double that, but put him down at	80 00
"The cow and calf."	30 00
"And oxen and cart, I bought them cheap, and will put them at cost."	100 00
	$400 00

"Well, we had, you know, Charley, when we began here, two hundred and fifty dollars, we have had our living for six months, and have cleared besides one hundred and fifty dollars."

"But this is not all our gain, for you see, Guss, we have many things laid by for the coming year. Two hogs and corn saved, enough to fatten them, which will find us in pork, and lard, and hams, through the year; we have fifty bushels of potatoes, enough for our use through the year, and to plant next season, and buckwheat enough for ourselves and the hens, and Aunt Casey has laid down butter enough for, as she says, with what we shall make, to last us through the winter. So that, for the coming winter, and even for next spring, we shall have very little to buy, and besides, there will, no doubt, be at least three tons of hay to sell in the spring."

"And that is not all, Charley, don't you think the improvement we have made on our place is worth something? Could not any one afford to give us one hundred dollars more for it, than it was worth last spring? and we shall have more to do with next season; we shall cut more hay, and can keep more stock. For my part I feel that we have got into the right track."

"And then, Guss, we have been our own masters, nobody to drive us, and I am sure we have lived well, almost too well, I have thought sometimes. We have enjoyed our work together—we owe no one any thing, and have been, and now are, as happy as most folks. But, perhaps, Aunt Casey thinks she gets the worst of the bargain?"

Aunt Casey had been listening very attentively to the conversation, for she felt not only a deep interest for them, but she also felt anxious lest they should not be satisfied with their present arrangement. As soon, therefore, as she was appealed to, she lost no time in putting matters to rest so far as she was concerned.

"Oh, the massys, Charley! hŏw you do talk. Did I ever get along as I have this summer? and what trouble is it to do the little cooking that there is to do, and besides having your company, boys, that's worth all the trouble, ten times over. And besides, did I ever do so well for myself? how much do you think now I have laid by since you've been here?"

"How much, Aunty?"

"Hetty, go bring that stocking out of my drawer, it lays in the back corner to the left hand side."

Hetty very soon came smiling back, and laid the stocking, jingling with change, down on the table.

"Why, Aunty, is this all silver?"

"The most on it—there is some coppers, though, for I took the money just as I got it, sometimes more, sometimes less, and put it right in here—for you see I hain't had no use for it—there hain't been nothin' to buy, only some butcher's meat, you know, and the eggs and butter money has bought all that; there it is, I don't rightly myself know, how much, so you better count it." And turning the stocking upside down, such a jumble of small coins rolled out, that the work of counting was no small matter. The boys and Hetty set to work making piles of one dollar each, until they amounted to the sum of twenty-five, and a few over.

"Well done, Aunt Casey!"

The old lady shook her sides heartily.

"It is more money than ever I had afore, and it's all come of your plan of living with me. And now, do you think I count the labor any thing? No, no. If you are only satisfied I am, and I should be an ungrateful creature if I wasn't, as I tell'd Parson Somers to-day. There now. If I didn't like to forget—who do you think has been here to see you to-day? I say you, for I guessed from his conversation that it was more for your sake than mine, that he called. I guess he feels a little puckered about your going to the Episcopals. You know the old gentleman is set in his way, and I guess he means to do right, he is a good man, but he's dreadfully set, and I guess he don't fancy the Episcopals."

"What did he say, Aunty?"

"Well, I guess he didn't say as much as he meant to say. I guess I stumped him a little."

"You did, Aunty! how?"

"Well, he began by saying, "he hadn't seen me for a long time." 'No sir,' said I, 'it ain't been quite so convenient for me, it's a very long walk to the meeting, and the young men seemed to think I hadn't better try to walk so far, and Mr. Jamieson seems a nice man, and preaches such Gospel truth, I thought, may be, seeing the church was so near at hand, I'd better go there, for it is all one, you know, Mr. Somers,' says I. And then the old gentleman bowed two or three times, and didn't seem to know what to say, at last, says he, 'That is all well, Mrs. Casey, but you know we New England folks feel very much afraid of forms and ceremonies; we are afraid lest they should be substituted for pure doctrine, and the graces of the spirit.' 'That's true, no doubt, sir,' says I, 'but may there not be good doctrine and good graces even if they have some forms and ceremonies, I know,' says I, 'it ain't easy getting into their ways, and learning their ups and downs, it kind of confuses one at the first; but after a while, when we learn how to find the place, and what they are going to do, it ain't no wise troublesome, and I kind o' like it. It seems,' says I, 'more as if we all had something to do, and not the minister to do the whole; and then when I'd said that, he colored up, and I began to be frightened, thinks I, the fat's in the fire now, but he did not say no more, only asked about you, and said he would be glad to see you, and I tell'd him you was well, and doin' well, and doin' a world of good."

"Oh, Aunty, what do you mean?"

"Well, I mean just so. Didn't old Colonel Johnson tell me t'other day, and the tears came in his eyes when he said it, 'Mrs. Casey,' said he, 'that Charles Lovell is doing as much good among our young people as the minister himself.'"

"Stop, Aunty, stop now, you have got on the wrong track. Then you parted good friends, you and Mr. Somers?"

"Oh la, yes, but he seemed a little flustered, as I thought."

Charles had, as we have seen, undertaken the charge of teaching a class of young ladies in the Bible with great reluctance. But having commenced, he was resolved to leave nothing undone, that his efforts could accomplish to make it profitable. He studied hard at his leisure hours, and found a great advantage in having before him a definite object upon which to bring all the powers of his mind to bear. Finding, as Mr. Jamieson had told him, that the ladies, although well educated in other respects, were ignorant of many things necessary for a clear and comprehensive understanding of Bible history, he at once put them upon a thorough course, giving them lessons in Jewish rites and ceremonies, ancient, sacred, and profane history, as compiled by Prideaux, and in Eastern manners and customs, as well as Jewish antiquities and geography. His familiar acquaintance with these studies imparted an ease of manner, in guiding others, which at once commanded the respect and confidence of those who had placed themselves under his instruction, and his serious and gentlemanly deportment while conducting the exercises, won such an interest for him in their hearts, that perhaps no one beside their pastor had such power to influence them in their choice of intellectual food and entertainment. The class had held its meetings at the house of Miss Lucy on Sabbath afternoons after the public services of the day had closed, and at first consisted of only a few ladies of the persuasion, where it had originated; but such things in a country town cannot very well be done in a corner. It soon became noised abroad, "what delightful meetings they had," and one and another begged the privilege of attending, until the circle of ladies almost surrounded the large withdrawing-room of the Colonel's. There were many, however, to whom the distance was a serious obstacle—they would come once perhaps—be delighted with the scene, but could only lament that the distance prevented their joining. The number of such at length began to stir up quite a breeze among some of the good people belonging to the Congregational Church, for the question was asked, why they could not have such a class? and whether the Episcopal Church alone could find among its members a man qualified to teach the Bible? These things at length reached the ears of good Mr. Somers, and the old gentleman at once made application to several of his members, both old and young, but found no gentleman to undertake the task of teaching a class after the fashion of that which young Lovell had started. At length, knowing that Charles was still a member of his flock, he resolved to call upon him, and endeavor to persuade him that it was his duty to use what power he had of doing good among those with whom he was more particularly connected. And this was his purpose when he made the call which Aunt Casey alluded to. But Charles had also some business with Mr. Somers, and a few days after that walked to his Parsonage.

The reverend gentleman received him very cordially, for he fondly hoped he had come to apologise for his long absence from his ministrations. Great was his disappointment, therefore, and he could not help showing it in his countenance, when Charles made known his real object, which was: that he might procure a letter of recommendation to the church of Mr. Jamieson.

"But surely, Mr. Lovell, you are not serious in your intention of uniting yourself with the Episcopal Church. I do hope you will think well of such a step before you take it."

"I have thought of the matter, sir, for some time, and so

far as my judgment goes, I feel it my duty to unite in a regular manner with the Christian society where I regularly worship."

"But, my dear young friend, have you thought of the great difference which subsists between the two denominations?"

"There is some difference, sir, I am aware, in forms of worship and church government, but I know of none in such points as are essential."

"That is true, in one sense, I allow, and yet in a very important sense, I should hardly dare assent to it. We may hold the letter, you know, while we reject the spirit of a doctrine—we may hold sound words, while the meaning which those words ought to convey may be so construed as to nullify their power. I know very well that there is much, a good deal that passes well, that looks like religion. But when you come to sift it out from the forms and ceremonies which surround it, there is, I fear, but very little of it to be found."

Charles colored deeply; and was about to say that, perhaps the sifting out of any man's piety from his profession was the peculiar province of Him alone who knows the heart. But he did not say it, he only thought it, and replied in a very calm tone—

"I have not had much experience, sir, except with the society to which I belong, and that with which I have worshipped of late. But I think, I never met with any Christians who give better evidence of true piety than those with whom I now associate."

"Forms, my dear sir, go a great way; they are very pleasing to the natural heart, they tend to lull the conscience, and create a kind of forced piety which has not the real savor to it. You know their doctrine of regeneration, as they hold it up, amounts to nothing more than admission to the church by the rite of baptism."

"I think, sir, that the articles of their church insist upon regeneration, as we understand it. And I am very sure that Mr. Jamieson firmly believes it, and openly preaches it. Are you well acquainted with him, sir?"

"Well, yes, I know Mr. Jamieson, at least I have seen him occsaionally. I have nothing against him."

Charles was silent a moment, for his thoughts troubled him.

Here was a Christian minister, somewhat advanced in life, of high standing, and great influence in all that region, and many were looking up to him as a spiritual guide most safe to follow, and as a pattern of excellence; and within two miles of his house lived a brother clergyman, possessing the faith of Christ, and as Charles knew, most upright and consistent in his walk—lovely in all his deportment, and exhibiting under every circumstance in which he had seen him, the true marks of one who loved the Saviour. And this elder brother could only say concerning him, "I have nothing against him." Was this Christian love? was it Christian courtesy? And why this coldness? He belonged to a different persuasion, he used a few more forms; he felt it to be more consonant with the decency and order of public worship that its services should be prescribed, and of a certain form; he acknowledged one head in matters of church government, instead of the many. And were such considerations sufficient to justify two leaders of the flock of Christ in looking coldly at each other? Charles was about to reply, when a gentleman entered the the room, whom he recognised as one of the officers of Mr. Somer's church.

"Ah, good morning, Mr. Rice, good morning, sir. Mr. Lovell, Deacon Rice, but I believe you are already acquainted." Charles had risen, and given his hand to the gentleman.

"Sit down, gentlemen, I am very glad, Deacon, that you have come in, for I was just talking to Mr. Lovell a little about church matters. He has a notion of uniting with the Episcopal Church, and I wish he may be persuaded to think of the matter a little, before taking such a step. Now, as you have had some little personal experience in the thing, I want you just to tell Mr. Lovell what you know. He is a young man, and I have no doubt wishes to do what is right. Now tell him what you think."

Deacon Rice was doubtless a good man, he had a strong resolution to do just that which he believed right, and not only set his face as a flint against all evil, but did really in his heart abhor it. And he was also a warm-hearted man, although the aspect of his countenance did not favor such an idea in one not very intimate with him. But he was subject to strong prejudices, and allowed them too often to affect his conduct, so that he was by no means a popular man. There were a great many in all, that did not feel any better towards him than they ought, and did not give the good man credit for as much piety, as he doubtless really had. He had been educated from a child, with a distrust of the denomination now in question. He had shunned all intercourse with them. He would not say there was nothing good about them; but there were so many things of a doubtful character, that he preferred just to shake his garments clean of any of their dust. But as Providence often touches us where we are the most sensitive, Deacon Rice had been sorely afflicted by means of this very sect. A son whom he had been educating for the ministry, and who was just about to take his station in the pulpit, and when the father was anticipating the rich pleasure of beholding a child of his standing on the heights of Zion in the midst of his own people, a change came over the mind of the young man. He turned his back upon the denomination in which he, and his father, and his father's father, had been brought up. United with the Episcopal Church, and despising the baptism of his childhood, could not be satisfied until sprinkled anew by what he considered more consecrated hands. It is not to be wondered at, then, if the righteous soul of the good Deacon was grievously vexed; and with his strong prejudices to back him up if he should have gone further in his zeal against what he called the "Church of England" than Christian charity could justify. He threw them all away from the circle of brotherhood, bishops, priests, deacons, prayer-book and all. "He had done with them for ever, they were the offspring of the Scarlet Lady, and too much like her." The Deacon began his address by placing his hand on the top of his head, and smoothing down his foretop, which, by the way, did not need the operation, being already very flat and straight.

"Very glad am I both for your sake, my young friend, as well as the good of our society, that I have dropped in, just so that I may open your eyes a little before you take such a sad step. You are but a young man, Mr. Lovell, and can tell nothing what the feelings of a parent must be to have a grown up son turn his back upon the religion of his parents, count as nothing the solemn act of consecration which his parents made when we offered him at the baptismal altar;

yes, sir, it was not enough that he must leave our worship, but he must, by a public baptism at the hands of a bishop, virtually say, that our ordinances are but a mockery. And I say to you, Mr. Lovell, that a sect which will encourage such things is no better than it ought to be."

Charles listened with great patience, keeping his keen eye fixed in deep attention upon the speaker. Deacon Rice was an old man, and esteemed a wealthy man, and Charles believed him to be a good man. But with all the respect which he felt due from himself to one in the position of Deacon Rice, he could not lose sight of the error into which he had fallen, in his wholsale denunciation of a sect, because some of its members or officers had committed an error, and as soon as the Deacon paused he commenced a reply.

"Perhaps, sir, there may be some wrong among our Episcopal brethren. I will not pretend—"

"Stop, stop, young man, I for one, am not prepared to call them brethren—I—" Just then, Mr. Somers straightened himself in his chair, and putting his hand out—

"So, so, Brother Rice, so, so, we must not carry our feelings quite so far. I would not say so, Brother Rice. And I should like to hear what our young friend has to say."

The Deacon stopped at once, having the most profound respect for his pastor, but his countenance maintained an aspect of much severity.

"I will not pretend to say," Charles resumed, "that there may not be opinions and practices among our brethren of of that order which may be wrong—that they differ from us in some things, I know—but not so far as I am acquainted, in essentials."

"May I ask you, my good sir, what you call essentials? Is not the doctrine of regeneration an essential doctrine?" And the Deacon looked earnestly at him for an answer.

"Certainly, I do, sir, I hold it to be a doctrine taught by our Saviour and his apostles in a very clear manner."

"Yes, and taught, too, as a work wrought by the power of the Holy Spirit upon the heart. Now, how can a sect that holds that the sprinkling of water upon a person regenerates them, hold essential truth? Now answer me that."

Charles looked somewhat surprised, and in rather a low tone answered—

"I should say it was an error, a very radical error. But it has not been my misfortune to hear such a doctrine preached, or in any way promulgated."

"You never have! and yet have attended the Episcopal service for some months!"

"I believe I can answer very decidedly, Deacon Rice, that I have not only never heard such a doctrine preached, but that it is in direct opposition to their articles of faith, and if you will allow me, I will repeat a passage from their 17th article on predestination and election, 'Wherefore they which be endued with so excellent a benefit of God, be called, according to God's purpose, by his spirit working in due season.' And another from the 10th article, 'We have no power to do good works pleasant and acceptable to God without the grace of God by Christ preventing us;' and if you will read all their articles of faith, I think you will agree with me that they do not differ essentially from ours. They hold to the original corruption of man's nature; to justification by faith alone; to the power of the Holy Spirit, and to the necessity of true repentance. Surely with such agreements as these, we ought not to cavil at each other on account of minor differences."

The effect of these remarks, apparently, in no wise altered the views and feelings of the good Deacon, his countenance retaining its stern and incredulous aspect. But upon Mr. Somers were manifested signs of deep interest in the words of young Lovell. He was evidently rising in the estimation of the reverend gentleman. But still he spoke not, and left the Deacon to carry on the argument.

"You will not deny though, Mr. Lovell, that they call those who are baptised in their way, regenerated persons—you can't deny that, and that they think baptism necessary and essential to salvation?"

"I have no doubt, sir, that they consider baptism something more than a mere form, and I think our own article on that head indicates full as much as theirs—we call it 'a sign and seal of union with Christ.' They may use the word regenerated perhaps in a different sense from ourselves. But they do not have any more confidence in the mere ceremony, apart from the working of the Holy Spirit, than we do, at least I think they do not."

"But now, Mr. Lovell, is it not a fact? Do you not know that they *do* feel that their church is the sure place to be saved in. A man once there, and he has a good safe passport to heaven—a little surer and safer than elsewhere, now this you cannot deny."

"I can only answer, sir, so far as I have any knowledge of those of that persuasion, with whom I have been intimate, I have never observed any approach to such a feeling. And all I can say for their church in general is what their articles testify. The 13th article runs thus:

"They also are to be had accursed that presume to say that every man shall be saved by the law, or sect which he professeth, so that he be diligent to frame his life accordingly. For Holy Scripture doth set out unto us only the name of Jesus Christ whereby men must be saved."

"Is that one of the articles of their creed?" And Deacon Rice looked towards Mr. Somers for an answer, as though he feared Mr. Lovell's memory might be at fault. The reverend gentleman was deeply engaged in thought, and did not answer at once. At length he replied—

"Mr. Lovell is doubtless correct, for I see he has taken pains to inform himself, and I think I remember such an article. But it has been my misfortune in early life to come in contact with some distinguished men of that persuasion, who I am sure did not act up to the principles of that article."

"Still, sir," said Charles, "you would judge the church rather by its creed than by the conduct of some of its dignitaries."

"I ought to—I should have done so—that would have been the true course. We should wish thus to be dealt with ourselves."

"Have you never thought, Mr. Somers, that, perhaps in our zeal to avoid resting upon rites and ceremonies, we may have gone to the opposite extreme, and denied to them that spiritual efficacy, which properly belongs to them?"

"Spiritual efficacy! did you say, Mr. Lovell?" And Deacon Rice straightened himself in his chair, and looked with great surprise.

"I believe," and the voice of Lovell had an evident tremor, "that if we could free our minds from all knowledge of the abuse which has been made of the sacraments, and take our ideas from the passages of Scripture which refer to them, we should come to the conclusion that when properly participated, they are to us the vehicles of spiritual nutriment, and that they are infinitely more to us than mere tokens, that we are the disciples of Christ. But I shall very much like to hear the views which Mr. Somers can give us. If I am wrong I wish to be converted."

The Deacon seemed very willing to turn the matter over to his pastor. The subject was leading into deep water, and he did not feel quite able to follow it, so he united in the wish, and Mr. Somers thus appealed to, aroused himself from the deep reverie into which the conversation had thrown him.

"The two sacraments which the great head of the church has appointed are Baptism and the Lord's Supper. The former of these is the initiatory rite by which we are admitted to the church, and to all its privileges."

"Pardon me, my dear sir, you mean the Lord's Supper is the rite by which we enter the church."

"I mean what I said, Deacon Rice, Baptism is the initiatory rite which introduces us to the church and its privileges."

The Deacon looked utterly confounded, things seemed to be growing more and more obscure.

"'Go ye into all the world, preaching the Gospel to every creature, he that believes, and is baptised, shall be saved, and he that believeth not shall be damned.' When on the day of Pentecost the multitude cried out, 'What must we do to be saved?' Peter told them, 'Repent and be baptised every one of you, in the name of the Lord Jesus.' When the eunuch had become a believer, 'Philip went down with him into the water, and baptised him, and he went on his way rejoicing,' and no one can say that he was not entitled to enjoy all the privileges of the church, and to partake of the sacrament as soon and as often as he pleased. So that as an original appointment all who were baptised were considered as members of the Christian church. The practice of baptising infants has led to the necessity of requiring from those who apply for a seat at the Lord's table, an expression of their feelings and views, that a judgment may be formed as to their fitness to be classed as Christians. Although, as baptised persons, there can be no doubt that they are members of the Christian church, and if not subjects of discipline, have a right to the privileges of Christians."

The Deacon now began to wipe his face, and smooth down his hair, and to give evident signs that he was greatly stirred up. He had been young, and was now getting old, but he had never heard such strange doctrine before, verily things began to look misty—he could hold in no longer.

"But does the Reverend say, that our children who are baptised are fit subjects for the communion table? sure am I that some of mine would make strange members, any how, we should soon have more cases of discipline to attend to right off."

"And sure am I, Brother Rice, that it ought not thus to be, and if we parents, and pastors, and deacons, and professing Christians, had acted towards them as we ought to have done, and nurtured them—yes, brother, I say, nurtured them for Christ—had we felt that they were lambs of the flock, and trained them as carefully into obedience to the faith, as we ought, you and I would not now have to mourn in secret over those whom we have by our own act initiated into the church."

The Deacon sank back into his chair, and looked like a man who had reached that point, where the case is hopeless, and the whole concern might as well be given up. He ventured, however, to bring forth in a kind of long sigh, "I can't convert 'em, do my best."

Mr. Somers did not reply, but continued in quite an animated strain.

"These are my views about baptism, as to its first intent and use. And, although we know not how it confers spiritual blessings, yet I think, Deacon Rice, that the very fact that so many of our baptised children, even in spite of our unfaithfulness to them, become the hopeful subjects of grace, is a strong evidence, that in some way the sacred rite has a virtue in it. The difference, Deacon Rice, between us and our Episcopal brother, is, that perhaps they lean a little too much on the sacraments, and we too little."

As the conversation had taken a turn very unexpected to Charles, and as he feared the object of his errand was likely to be forgotten altogether, he took advantage of the first pause to mention it.

"At what time, Mr. Somers, will it be convenient for you to make out the certificate for me?"

"O, ah, yes. Well, brother Rice, you heard me say, that Mr. Lovell was desirous of uniting himself with the Episcopal Church in this place. Of course, there can be no objections to giving him a certificate, however reluctant we may be to part with him."

"Why, I suppose, if he insists upon it, there is no other way. But I do wish that he would think better of it. It seems to me like a quenching of the light that is in him, to send him to such a place, where there is nothing to feed his spirit; nothing but cold formality, not even a prayer to be heard, but what is read from a book."

"I cannot but think, Deacon Rice," said Charles, "that you are mistaken in your views of these brethren, you certainly have seen only some of the worst features of their system."

"I've seen enough, I don't want to see any more."

"Don't you think, sir, that in all our systems some reform might be made for the better. We choose to use no written form in our addresses to the Deity—and how often are we pained in listening to a loose, disjointed petition, in which the same ideas are repeated over and over again, and spun out to a length that is wearisome to the most devout worshipper."

"But just to think—pardon my interruption—just to think that a man cannot go to his room to pray to his God, in secret, but he must take a book with him. What kind of a social meeting must it be where each one has a book before him reading a set form out of it? No, no, my soul! come not thou into their secret."

"Allow me, Deacon Rice, to set you right about that matter. I have enjoyed many precious seasons of social prayer with Mr. Jamieson. I have been with him at the bed-side of the sick and dying, and heard him pour forth most feeling ardent prayer, but no book was used." Mr. Somers now arose and began to walk the room, he was evidently much excited, and Charles continued.

"I have often spent hours with him in converse on the glorious truths of our faith, and often has he at the close of such interviews, proposed that we should unite in prayer, and never have I listened to such melting addresses to the throne of grace."

The voice of Charles was broken, for he was much excited, and the tear started from his eye. Mr. Somers paused, and looked at him a moment, and quickly approaching, grasped his hand.

"Will you go with me, this instant, Mr. Lovell? Brother Rice, I can't stand this; I am a Congregationalist, I know; but I hope also I am a Christian. I know I love my Saviour, and where I see his image, I must love that too; and I shan't have it said another day, no, not another hour, that there is a shade upon my mind towards that Christian brother. What care I for his sect? or whether he prays from a book, or without one, if he has a praying heart? I am going right off to see him, to tell him that I love him, and to ask his forgiveness, that I have not taken pains to be better acquainted with him. And you must excuse me now, Deacon, we will talk over those matters you came to see me about some other time. Good morning. Come, Mr. Lovell, you must go with me."

Charles was so taken by surprise, that he seemed as much astonished as the good Deacon, who sat looking at his minister with an expression that could not easily be mistaken. "Well, well, what will turn up next? What is the world coming to?" How long he continued rocking himself in the chair, after his minister had gone, is not of much consequence. A pleasanter scene awaits us at the study of Mr. Jamieson.

The Rev. William Jamieson, although a single man, and in consequence thereof, free from many cares and anxieties of a worldly nature; had, moreover, as the most of us have sometimes, a dark day, when all the unpleasant things in our lot seem to crowd up in a company together; and two or three heavy sighs escaped, as he sat reclining against the back of his chair, and resting his head upon the arm that was supported by the table.

The first thing that had caused some troublesome feelings was the want of a book, a learned work on some rather difficult points in theology, and which he had seen offered for sale, among the advertisments of his city paper. But the price of the work he knew was more than he could afford to take out of his three hundred dollars salary. This naturally led to his situation and prospects for the future. Three hundred dollars a year would not allow of many family arrangements, and must he never indulge in the sweet sympathy of a loving companion? and this again led off into a train of thought that brought the tinge upon his cheek. There was, no doubt, in that heavenly mind, some earthly weakness to deal with; and then objections began to start up against his remaining in his present situation. His parish was small, and no very great increase to be expected. He was looked upon, he knew, by some of the other denominations, as an intruder; many of its respectable members treated him coldly; he was seldom invited to any of their social scenes; and a respectful bow was the only token of acquaintanceship. But the most unpleasant circumstance in that relation, was the treatment he received from his elder brother in the ministry. He knew that Mr. Somers had the reputation of a man of talent, and of more than ordinary knowledge. He had gathered a large congregation; he was looked up to by the clergy of the neighboring towns. It would have been a comfort for him, a young man, far from any associate of his own persuasion, to have had the intimacy of one so much his elder. He felt willing to learn from his experience, he panted for the society of such an one, from whom he could take practical lessons in the pastor's life. But he had been made to feel that Mr. Somers looked upon him with an evil eye, and yet so conscious was he from what he had learned of that good man, that he was laboring under a wrong impression, and looked upon him not as he really was, but as he thought him to be; that he could feel no resentment, and only mourned in secret that some unhappy circumstance had shut the heart of his brother against him. How he wished for an opportunity to sit beside him, in his little room, and have free converse on those subjects so interesting to them both. He felt sure that not a word of disputation should ever pass between them. And thus his mind was running, and the sad contrast which the reality presented, brought forth one of those deep sighs, of which we have spoken. And just then is mingled with it a rap at the outer door, and he hears his name mentioned, and in a moment more a tap at his own door arouses him from his chair to admit his visitor.

Before he had time to speak, his hand was cordially grasped, and the fine countenance of Mr. Somers was beaming upon him, his lip trembling, his eye bright and piercing in general, now dimmed with tears.

"Brother Jamieson, my dear young brother, forgive me." The speaker paused, evidently from deep excitement, his hand still retaining its grasp, and his eye fixed upon him whom he addressed.

Mr. Jamieson, in his confusion, turned towards young Lovell, who had entered with Mr. Somers, as though seeking an explanation; but Lovell was too much affected himself to make any.

"I have been wrong, Brother Jamieson, but it is only within the last hour that I have been convinced of it; and I am never ashamed, when well convinced of an error, to acknowledge it, and seek forgiveness. I feel that I have neglected you, as a younger Christian brother; that I have been suspicious of you on account of your persuasion; and all I can do now, is to ask for your charity, and your friendship."

Mr. Jamieson could not immediately reply, and he almost feared his imagination had imposed upon him. But the grasp of the hand, the earnest words trembling from the lips of the speaker, soon convinced him that it was a blessed reality; and the heart of the young man was deeply touched, and he could only show by the tears which fell fast and free, and by the warm pressure of his hand, that he had nothing to forgive, and was only too happy to know that now there was no barrier between them.

"I am not going to talk over the past, Brother Jamieson; nor am I wishing to say one word upon any subject, wherein we may hold different views. But I have my reason to believe that our hearts are alike. We both, I trust, 'love Him who first loved us;' we both feel that without his atonement there can be no remission of our sins; and without his grace assisting us, we can do nothing aright. We both believe this, brother?"

"Most firmly and feelingly, I can answer for one of us, Mr. Somers."

"Don't call me Mister; I am much the elder of the two, but not the less your brother, and anxious to be recognised as such. And now step up here, Mr. Lovell."

Charles arose, and stood by him.

"This young man has applied to me for a certificate from the church under my charge, to you, and your pastoral care."

"It was not known by me, sir, that he had any such design. Mr. Lovell will bear me witness, that no such suggestion was ever hinted at by me to him."

Charles was about to speak.

"Mr. Lovell need bear no witness at all, in the matter, Brother Jamieson; I have that opinion of you, that elevates you far above the littleness of proselyting. But, as I said, he has applied to me for a regular passport to your care. And I do it, I believe I can now say, Brother Jamieson, with unfeigned pleasure. Mr. Lovell will understand me, I have no desire, he well knows, to part with a young man who has, by his own efforts, made himself such an efficient member of any religious society. But I have perfect confidence that he will be under good Christian guidance. The lesson I have learned from him, within these few hours past, has well convinced me that he has been familiar with one who understands Christian charity. May he prove to you, and your people, a treasure from the Lord."

Mr. Jamieson took the hand of Charles.

"May the blessing of our covenant God rest upon the relation in which we now stand to each other."

It was a moment of deep interest, and each one felt that an event, thus hallowed by the sweet fruits of Christian love, must be according to the will of Him who dwelleth in love.

"And now, Brother Jamieson, I must leave you for the present, as I have preparation to make for a meeting this evening. It will give me most unfeigned pleasure to see you at my house, and in my study. I may expect you, may I not?"

"Most certainly, sir, I shall come, and, perhaps, so often as to weary you. You can hardly conceive what a desire I have had to be on terms of intimacy with you, and how much this scene appears like a pleasant dream, too pleasant to be real."

"It is a reality, though, my dear brother, depend upon it; and I cannot but hope that it is the beginning of some glorious end. May God bless you abundantly."

"Good bye, Brother Somers. And I may hope to see you here, sometimes, too?"

"No fear of that."

A few moments elapsed after the departure of Mr. Somers, when neither spake. Mr. Jamieson was the first to break silence.

"That man is possessed of a noble mind; his very countenance tells you that he has nothing to conceal. I am sure I feel under great obligations to you for bringing about such a state of things."

"It is not to me that any obligations are due. It has been brought about by an unseen hand; but I hope for great good. Sectarian jealousy, and contests, are the curse which blasts the efforts of the church. Let a spirit of love once get dominion, and the gospel will have a fair opportunity to show its power."

"Right, right! you are right there. I go hand and heart with you in such doctrine, and I mean to follow out my creed at once. Do you know whether Mr. Somers holds his meeting this evening in the Centre School-House?"

"He does."

"Is it a lecture, or properly a social prayer-meeting?"

"He calls it the church prayer-meeting. Mr. Somers takes the lead, and calls upon others to associate with him."

"Will you go with me there?"

"I was designing to go there, and should be delighted to have your company."

Like meetings of the same kind in almost all our churches, the church prayer-meeting at Melton was but poorly attended. The two deacons were there. Some half-a-dozen male members, and perhaps fifteen or twenty females, in a room large enough to accommodate a hundred persons with ease, and out of a church that numbered three hundred communicants.

It was to Mr. Jamieson a matter of surprise to find so small an assembly. He had not yet had much experience in such matters. He entered as unobtrusively as possible, and took a seat among those nearest the door. But scarcely had he sat down, when Mr. Somers arose from his place, and approaching, with a fine glow upon his countenance, took him by the arm, and without scarcely asking, led him to a seat beside himself, upon a raised platform, enclosed by a railing, at one end of the room. Every eye was of course turned towards the visitor, and as all knew Mr. Jamieson by sight, their minds were at once alive with anxious questions as to the meaning of such an apparition. Had the Episcopal minister been converted to Congregationalism, or was he leaning that way? And did Mr. Somers intend to have him take part in the exercises? And would he have out his prayer-book? And many a glance was passed from one to another, and then towards Deacon Rice, who with his brother deacon sat just without the enclosed platform.

The Deacon had not the faculty of keeping his feelings to himself, and no sooner had Mr. Jamieson been seated along side of his pastor than he began to manipulate himself, as the only way he could keep from testifying aloud against such strange proceedings. First he would smooth down the foretop, then the back part of his head, and then he would loosen his neck-cloth, running his finger from the bow in front clear round to the pepper and salt locks that hung in queer little curls just on the edge of his coat-collar.

Mr. Somers commenced the exercises, as usual, with reading a hymn. It was one that all knew, and in which every heart acquainted with Christian sympathy could join,

"Blest be the tie that binds."

For some reason, it seemed peculiarly appropriate. The good pastor read it with evident emotion, and the full chorus, in which both pastor and people united, told most plainly that its sentiments met a hearty response. He then read a short portion of Scripture, and led in prayer. Immediately after this exercise, he commenced, as was his custom, a running comment on the passage of Scripture he had read, dwelling more fully on the closing verse, "The love of Christ constraineth us," &c. The thoughts brought out evidently came from a heart that had drank deeply itself at the holy fountain. As he closed, he spoke a few words, in a low tone, to Mr. Jamieson, who at once arose, and stood before the meeting. It was a moment of deep interest, and every eye was most intently fixed upon the young minister, and a slight flush was evident upon his naturally pale features. He was, in personal appearance, prepossessing; his form, of the full medium height, slender, though of manly build; his countenance strongly marked with intelligence, and of that peculiar cast, that its very expression beamed with seriousness; it might be almost said that a shade of sadness rested upon it. His features were finely proportioned, and whether viewed from the side, or the full front, exhibited the same intellectual finish. His hair, a light brown, lay gracefully back from his forehead, and slightly curling, formed a pleasing background, as it gracefully, yet with a perfectly natural and even careless manner, rested behind his ears.

There was a slight hesitancy, as he commenced speaking, but it lasted only for a moment. At once, he grasped the beautiful idea of a Saviour's love, and in tones plaintive, yet manly, poured forth his gushing thoughts. Charles Lovell was the first to bow his head. He was his bosom friend; he knew well how dear to the heart of the speaker was the theme he dwelt upon, and that the touching thoughts which came forth, with such melting tenderness, were not the mere efforts of the orator; they were the feelings of the firm believer.

But his was not the only head that drooped, for the fire was kindling in every bosom, and soon, as though by some powerful charm, every heart was melted, and the tears fell fast and free. His address was short, and when he paused, while every ear still hung upon his lips, he quietly said,

"Will you accompany me, dear Christian brethren, to the Throne of the heavenly grace?"

More than one paused a moment, to see whether he was about to lead them from a book. But his hands were clasped before him, and his eye, lifted above, was closed, and in beautiful, appropriate language, he was supplicating for such blessings as a company of sinners needed. Deacon Rice had become quiet long before the prayer began; he was a good man, and could no more stand out against such soul-stirring thoughts, than he could wilfully have done an unjust act, and from rubbing his head, he went to wiping away the tears that stole down his rough visage.

As the meeting closed, the good Deacon stepped upon the platform, and, without asking for an introduction, grasped the hand of him, whom, that very morning, he could scarcely bring himself to acknowledge as a Christian brother. He said nothing, nor did Mr. Jamieson attempt to address him, but both seemed perfectly satisfied with the silent salutation.

"And now, Brother Jamieson," said Mr. Somers, "we will go hand in hand to our work; there shall be no my people, and your people; but our business shall be to win souls to our Saviour. Let them then worship in either of our public houses, as they please; I have done with sectarianism; let it go to the winds."

"I respond most heartily, Brother Somers. Let come to me what may, I go with you."

"And I say, Amen, brethren, to the glorious resolution." and the Deacon bowed to the reverend gentlemen, and stepped from the high place to take the hand of young Lovell, whom he saw in waiting at a little distance.

CHAPTER IX.

The bright hues of autumn, like the pleasant things of life, soon fade before us; the earth is strewed with the fallen leaves; they rustle to the passing footstep, and the wind sighs through the barren branches that wave over us.

Charles and his brother had finished their fall work; the barn-yard had been put into a condition to correspond with the new and neat appearance of the barn; a temporary shed had been erected for the comfort of their cattle; and every thing around the premises showed to the passer by that the owners had not only a correct taste, but a just judgment, as to what was for the comfort of the creatures, and those who tended them. And, as the brothers looked over what their hands had accomplished, they felt not only satisfied with what they had done, but surprised that so much progress had been made by them in laying the foundation for their life-work. It was, indeed, but a beginning, but they believed that they had begun at the right end. The house they could do without, at present, and it remained as they had found it, except clearing away the rubbish, which had been for years collecting about it, and setting out some trees for shade, and fruit, on the large plot of green sward in the midst of which it stood. These were as yet merely living, and only served to show that a design was in contemplation at some future time to make this spot a place for inhabitants.

"And now," said Charles, as he and his brother were sitting, one very pleasant day, early in November, on some logs near their barn-yard fence, and talking over their plans, "I don't see but we have done all that we can well do at present; I meant to have had the water from that spring brought to the barn-yard this season, but it is too late to commence it now."

"Especially, if you accept the call you have had."

"I don't know about that, Guss, I don't like to go so far. If I could have a chance to teach in this vicinity, so that I could assist you at times, I should like it; but to leave you with all our winter's work on hand, don't seem to be right."

"There is nothing but what I can do, Charlie, and have all the leisure I want. I should be sorry if I could not get out three hundred rails, and cut all the wood we shall want for the year, and do the chores too. I should go, by all means; you will get one hundred and fifty dollars clear money by teaching the school, and I want you to have it."

"As to that, Guss, it will be no more mine than yours; we go halves, you know, in every thing."

"I shan't touch it, Charlie: you are the eldest, and have improved yourself, and qualified yourself for a teacher; and you will have occasion for money, I guess, sooner than I shall." And Augustus could not repress a smile that some curious thought just then forced upon him.

Charles had been whittling a stick which he picked up from the ground, beneath where they were sitting; he threw it away, and laid his hand on his brother's knee.

"I tell you what it is, Guss; it is my firm intention that you and I shall have no division of interests, at least, for many years to come. When we get married, if we ever do, it will be time enough then, and then perhaps it will be best, that our individual rights should be clearly defined. But until then, we are one; we will pull together, and push together, and I am not afraid but our united efforts will accomplish our independence. If you think my labors in teaching will balance yours at home, I will undertake."

"Well, just as you say; but it seems a most unequal thing. I am sure you have the worst of the bargain."

"It is a pretty good offer, I know; but I am afraid Mr. Somers, in his kindness of heart, has over-estimated my qualifications."

"I guess the old gentleman knows what he is about. But Aunt Casey will be waiting tea for us. If you will walk along, I will be there in a minute, I want to give Pomp his oats."

Charles went on his way along the well-beaten path to the cottage, thinking of the best method of breaking to the old lady the tidings that he was about to leave home for some months.

The offer which Charles had received was indeed, as Augustus had intimated, very favorable, and on many accounts flattering to his feelings. It had come through Mr. Somers, who being extensively known was frequently applied to by committees of schools in neighboring towns, when a teacher of more than ordinary qualifications was wanted. Mr. Somers had taken a near and deep interest in Charles; he saw him more frequently, and had taken pains to ascertain his acquirements, and felt perfectly sure that he could recommend him with safety.

The town of Wellgrove was one of the largest in Connecticut, if we estimate by the number of acres enclosed within its boundaries, extending in length from north to south ten miles, and something like five in breadth. But like a great many towns in that old-fashioned State, it made but little pretension in the way of buildings, or number of inhabitants. Clusters of houses there were in different parts of its territory, but not a large number in any one spot. Scattered at intervals of moderate distance could be seen all over this area of ten by five, snug farm houses comfortable in appearance, but without pretension, ensconced beneath their own beautiful shades, and apparently as independent of the world at large, and as indifferent to its bustle, as the same busy world was of them.

An exception, however, must be made to this state of things in favor of the southern corner of the township. This lay for some distance along the borders of the Sound, and embraced some of the most agreeable scenery which can be found along the shores of that beautiful body of water—fine rolling ridges running out, tongue-like, into its waters, eminences pleasantly divided into rich intervals, and rocky promontories, where the cedar found its sustenance in some mysterious way, coming up through large cracks, and covering spots where to the eye it would seem that nothing but the moss could live. From these eminences, the Sound could be clearly seen, and the rolling of its surf heard among the rocks which lined the shore.

And as the distance to the great city was then but a moderate day's travel, it began to be taken notice of by those who wished to enjoy the retreat of the country, and yet keep fast hold of the ceremonies and amusements of the city. Many fine country-seats, as they were called, had been erected, and every year some new tenement raised its roof from among the many beautiful sites which the locality afforded.

As there was, by degrees, a certain sort of visiting carried on between these migrating inhabitants and the more wealthy families of farmers, there had been a noticeable change wrought in the vicinity. It affected the whole style of living. Their dress, their manners, their carriages, and finally their dwellings, were made conformable to those whom they esteemed superior in such matters; and many a plain, comfortable house was taken down to give place for a stiff, square, unsocial establishment, in imitation of the tasteless fabrics called country-seats, erected by persons from the city. And many a good farm had to bear the burden of a mortgage in order that its owner's sons and daughters might assimilate with those who had money to squander.

Aunt Casey had a good crying spell when Charles announced to her the fact that he had concluded to leave home for the winter; but, as he reasoned with her on its propriety, she wiped her tears away, and went off with one of her laughing turns, as if she was ashamed of her weakness.

The consideration that weighed most heavily on the mind of Charles, was, that he should be obliged to give up the instruction of his Bible class. He had become deeply interested in the work, and it had already exceeded his most sanguine expectations. Besides the lesson on the Sabbath, he devoted one evening in the week to the study of sacred geography, rites and ceremonies of the Jews, and connections of sacred and profane history. The circle of ladies had become quite large, comprising some of the brightest minds from both denominations. His quiet, gentlemanly deportment, free from pedantic stiffness or the nearest approach to lightness, together with his intimate acquaintance with the subjects he taught, all tended to throw around his person as their teacher, a charm that stimulated each individual to earnest application, and seldom was it that one member of the class was not in her place at recitation.

Satisfied, however, that it was his duty to accept the appointment he had received, at the close of one of their meetings, he took occasion to mention his expectation of being absent for the winter. Expressing his regret that he must leave them, he hoped that they would be able to procure some one to take his place, or continue their exercises by appointing, in course, one of their own number to fill it.

A shade of sadness at once passed over every countenance, and scarcely had he reached the door, as about to depart, when Miss Lucy Johnson came out, and arrested him. She was upon such terms of intimacy that she felt free to remonstrate with him.

"Now this is too bad, to leave us in this abrupt manner; you act as though you thought it a matter of small consequence whether the class was broken up or not."

"But I hope you will not allow yourselves to be broken up. You, surely, Miss Lucy, would not permit that, and I am very confident that you are fully competent to teach them; and I have no doubt the class will elect you to do so."

"Then both you and the class think very wrong. I am too well aware of my own deficiencies to venture such a step. Now, you know I never flatter—especially a *friend*. I am in earnest; *must* you go away? or, if so, is it not possible for you to be with us once a fortnight? How far are you going?"

"The distance is probably about seven miles."

"And what is that? I will engage to send our carriage for you; you can spend the night here, and you shall be sent back in the morning; only don't you resign the station you have so well filled. I do not believe the class would be satisfied, even with Mr. Jamieson to take your place."

Charles saw that Lucy was in earnest; her honest, lovely features were all in a glow, and even the tones of her voice had not their usual steadiness. He had no power to refuse her under such circumstances, and after a moment's reflection he replied:

"I have the most perfect confidence that you say to me just what you *feel*, and I certainly am not indifferent to your opinion, nor to the feelings of the other members of the class. I had no idea they felt as you say, and thought that the trial of separation was to be all on my part. I will see to it, that your meetings shall not be broken up, and that without taxing your generosity."

"That is just like yourself. You speak now like Charles Lovell, only in what you say about taxing my generosity. It will be no tax, I assure you."

"I give that up, too. I *know* you will do it with cheerfulness, and, if necessary, occasionally may accept your kindness. Please present my compliments to the ladies, and tell them I will not leave them while they remain so faithful to their part of our engagement together."

The engagement which Charles had determined upon, was to spend his Sabbaths at home. It would, indeed, at times prove inconvenient; but his plan was to have his brother come for him every Saturday afternoon, and take him back early on Monday morning. Pomp had become so much of a horse, that he could accomplish the journey, and to Augustus it would no doubt be gratifying, as he could not only have the satisfaction of driving their common favorite, but also of enjoying their pleasant Sabbaths together.

Charles found upon commencing his duties at Wellgrove, that the old system of providing for the board of a teacher was still in operation, and that it was expected he should migrate from house to house through the winter.

"It will not be expected, however," said the committee-man to him, "to send you to every house—there are a few poor families where you could not be so well accommodated, and provision will be made for you when their turn comes. Your first place, however, will be a pretty stylish one. They are city folks, and keep up considerable of a swell."

"Do they send their children?"

"Not exactly—I believe they have none of their own—there are some young ladies, but I guess they are nieces—they 've done schooling though I'm a thinking—without it is the schooling they 'll get when they are married.

"But the captain has a couple of took-children, a boy and girl—you will have them; I guess it won't be a bad place to go to, not if you like company."

"That depends upon the kind."

"Well, there is a little of all sorts; you will like the old captain, any how. He is a noble-hearted old fellow. But I hope he has got money enough to bear him out, for he must be spending a deal of it. And they say his girls are first-rate girls. If they are as good as they look, they 'll do well enough.

"They 've got fellows enough after them, though; but may be it 's their money they 're after, for they say the girls are both on 'em rich, or like to be. You saw that large house near the school?"

"A little back from the road?"

"Yes, with large elms in front, and fine fixings all about it."

"You will introduce me there?"

"Oh, that will not be necessary. All you have to do is to tell one of the children that you expect to come to Captain Halliday's this evening. They will understand all about it."

Charles felt a little unpleasant at the idea of thus billeting himself upon a family of distinction; but as he saw no way of avoiding the difficulty, resolved to meet it with the best possible grace.

Captain Halliday, the gentleman whose family he was about to introduce himself to, had retired from the sea a few years since, and settled at Wellgrove, for the purpose not only of enjoying on land the sight and smell of salt water, but also, that he might enjoy those comforts, and that independence, which the more expensive habits of the city would not afford from his moderate fortune. It was not his intention to have involved himself, either in the cares or labors of a farm; but overruled by the advice of friends, he had purchased, with his house, a farm of two hundred acres—being assured by his advisers, when remonstrating with them against laying out one-third of his property in this way—"That the place was dog-cheap—that the house could not be built for eight thousand dollars, and that for the ten thousand which the whole was offered for, he could get all his living, and lay up money.

"There is hay and grain for your carriage-horses—grain for your family—poultry, as much as you can stuff—your butter, milk, and eggs and what not. All you will have to lay out money for, will be your clothing and some groceries, and all for seven hundred dollars a year, house-rent and all."

Had it been a matter of building a ship, and rigging her from stem to stern, or providing her with stores for a twelvemonths' voyage, the old captain would have been able to talk understandingly. But he was now off soundings, and had no experience to make any reckonings by—the thing seemed plausible—the location was to his mind, his wife thought well of it, because it was not too far from the city, and the thing was done. He had now been there five years, and many prudent farmers did not hesitate to say that "they hoped he had a long purse—for what between repairs, and new outbuildings, and stone fences, and drains, and improved stock, besides a run of company—there must be a terrible outlay of money."

Mrs. Halliday was even more pleased with the location than she had anticipated. Very social in her feelings, and pleased with company, she found all her wishes in that respect gratified.

Company from the city, through all the summer months, until quite late in the fall, poured in upon her; and she had no stint of praises for the hospitable manner in which she entertained her guests. "Such milk and butter could never be had in the city, money could not buy them; and such fresh air too, and delicious vegetables and fruits, and everything so free and easy, we feel quite at home."

The captain, however, it had been noticed by those most intimate with him, had of late acquired a habit whenever some of his eloquent visitors would be pouring praises upon his "independent style of living," and "the beauty of his situation," of putting his hands down into his pockets, and rattling his change, as though there was a very intimate connection in his mind between the two.

It was not without some trepidation, that Charles found himself walking up the well-shaded avenue to the stately mansion; and when he knocked at the door, and the servant opened it, and looked rather staringly at him, he was almost at a loss as to his proceedings. However, he thought propriety demanded that he should make an introduction of himself at head-quarters.

"Is Mrs. Halliday at home?"

"She is, sir."

"May I see her?"

"Will you please walk in the room, sir? What name shall I give to Mrs. Halliday?"

He was about to say "The teacher of the school," but upon a second thought he merely said, "Mr. Lovell."

He had not to wait long before the lady herself entered. She was neatly dressed in a dark silk, and had a lively, pleasant face, and smiled graciously as she entered. Charles arose, and bowed to her.

"I regret exceedingly, madam, that I am under the necessity of introducing myself to your family, as Mr. Nazro, the committee for the district, thought it would be unnecessary for him to accompany me."

"Oh—ah—You are the teacher then? The children mentioned to me that you was coming, but I did n't expect—please sit down, sir."

The lady was evidently taken by surprise, for the appearance and manners of the young man were altogether at variance with what she had been expecting. The good lady had indulged, it must be confessed, some troublesome thoughts in reference to this teacher, especially at the present time—what, with company on hand, and more expected from the city, should she do with a rough country youth, who would be making her and the girls blush by his awkwardness.

It was, therefore, a very pleasant surprise to her to find the bearing of a true gentleman, where she had expected something in a very different shape. She had, however, some little inward misgivings, lest the pains she had taken to manage matters, so as to keep him one side of the family circle, should affect her character as a lady of true hospitality.

"I am very sorry, Mr. Lovell, that you did not come sooner; we generally take an early tea, and we have all done, and you will be obliged this evening to take your supper alone."

"That will be of no consequence, madam. But I hope you will not put yourself to any trouble on my account. I am used to very simple fare, and in a very plain way, and if you will allow me to give you as little trouble as possible, while I remain here, I shall esteem it a favor."

"It will be no trouble, I assure you, sir, to wait upon you, with the best we have;" and Mrs. Halliday really felt so. "And if you will excuse my giving you your tea alone this evening, and a little one side, I hope, in future, you will be able to be with us. Please excuse me, Mr. Lovell, while I order it for you."

Things had taken a turn, and Charles felt that he had been too hasty in anticipating difficulties.

In a short time, he was led by the servant-maid into a room plainly yet respectably furnished; it was evidently designed as a sort of better kitchen, in which during the warmer months, children and domestics might eat, and be separated from the necessary fires. The windows and outer door opened into a back piazza, and the whole concern had an air about it calculated to make one quite at ease, and at home. Charles felt that if he could be allowed to make this his sitting and eating room while he was there, he would ask nothing further.

A very agreeable supper was provided, and the maid waited upon him with an assiduity quite in contrast with her manner as she first admitted him to the house. As she was about to leave the room, after he had finished, she said to him, curtseying at the same time:

"Mrs. Halliday bid me say to you, sir, when you had done your supper, she would be pleased to see you in the parlor with the family; shall I show you the way, sir?"

"Perhaps Mrs. Halliday will not take it amiss if I absent myself this evening, as I wish to study a little. Shall I be in the way if I take a seat in this room?"

"Oh, la, no, sir, not if it suits your convenience."

It was a failing in Mrs. Halliday, if failing it should be called, to be anxious that her guests should enjoy themselves, and by that she meant that they should be lively. "She disliked," she said, "when folks got together, especially young folks, to see them sitting up stiff, and looking at one another like so many statues, and she never meant to have it so at her house;" and she never did. She was like an uneasy spirit, the moment there seemed to be any pause to the life of the party, and would begin at once to conjure up something to make a stir. As a very necessary assistant at such times, Mrs. Halliday had in general some sprightly young lady of dubious age, and varied talents, who found her house a convenient place to visit, and who was willing to make herself agreeable. At the present time, the person who filled this station was a maiden lady of some years beyond thirty, how many nobody knew, for Miss Hinchdale always laughed very prettily when age was the subject under consideration, and said, "As for her part, she did hope she would soon be out of her teens."

"I don't believe you will, Sally," Mrs. Halliday would reply, "for you grow younger every year."

Now, Sally had a home of her own, or a place she called such, but it was only with relations, not very near, and who were rather "sober folks," as she called them. And as she did not care to work much for her own independence, chose rather to earn a welcome for some months at a time, at such a place as Mrs. Halliday's, by making herself agreeable. She had, when dressed for company, a fresh and showy look, and as she was not very particular about subjects, nor the manner in which she handled them, had always something to say; and as she could play on the piano, and could sing into the bargain, made herself very useful; so much so, that after Sally had been there now for some months, and said something about going home, Mrs. Halliday would by no means hear to it.

"You can't and you shan't go now, Sally Hinchdale, for this is just the time I want you, for there are now so many folks coming up this month, and Julia, you know, is no hand to talk in company, and Adelaide don't fancy company much, so that entertaining them comes all upon me, and you must n't think of leaving me now at any rate."

It was true what Mrs. Halliday said about her nieces; their tastes differed from hers, although for her gratifications they at times entered into her views apparently with a heart interest.

Captain Halliday was heart and soul a sailor, and there is no telling how many nieces and nephews, too, he might have adopted if there had been any who needed his care. The two who made his house their home at present, were without parents, and although not dependent upon him, yet he dealt out to them with as liberal a hand, and cherished them with as much tenderness, as though they were his own children.

And these, whom we have thus briefly noticed, composed the real members of his family, all others being either servants or visitors.

There was a little gathering that evening, as the servant woman had told Mr. Lovell. For besides the gentleman who was a particular attendant upon one of the young ladies, and who boarded at a hotel in the place, he had brought with him what he called an amateur in music, fresh from the city, together with a companion of his own, like himself, a man of wealth, who had seen the unappropriated niece of Captain Halliday, and was, as he said, quite fascinated. Some young ladies from the neighborhood had also stepped in, and the whole made a pretty large circle in the best parlor.

Miss Sally Hinchdale was all curls and ribbons that evening, and whether because there was an amateur present, or a young man of fortune not yet engaged, or that she was in the humor for it, she seemed to be an emblem of vivacity; she was here and there, and nowhere, for two minutes at a time—laughing, and chatting, and tossing back her long ringlets, like any young girl of fourteen.

"Mrs. Halliday" said she, coming up to that lady, who sat slapping her fan upon the little work table, and eyeing her company with some solicitude, "Mrs. Halliday, we must have a dance this evening."

"Well, Sally, anything you say—set them a-going as soon as you like."

So Miss Sally at once stepped, with a very lively air, across the room to one of the gentlemen.

"Mr. Vanderbose, we must have a dance."

"With all my heart."

"Will you arrange the set, while I start off a tune?"

The gentleman was now in his element; he had practiced dancing, and had a pretty foot, that answered such a purpose very well. The other things which Mr. Vanderbose had practiced were not always as innocent, nor as reputable—he had never practiced with either hands, head, or feet, any useful calling. The fortune which his plodding old father had accumulated, and left to him, was ample, and the son thought probably that the father had done work enough for both—his life he meant to make a holiday.

He is a little better dressed, however, than he was when first introduced to my readers, and under more favorable circumstances. His fine house on the point is nearly completed, and he feels very happy, at present, as happy as a man of his desires and habits could very well be; for he has, it is said, at last won the beautiful object he had set his eye upon, and is looking forward to the time when he can claim her as a wife. Poor thing, we pity her, but it will do no good.

She knows, or believes nothing ill of him. Nothing more than a little wildness which most young men are guilty of, especially if tempted by an overstock of money. The fine house, and the fine horses, and the elegant barouche, and the costly trinkets that already sparkle on her heaving breast, and pretty dimpled hand, and fair, rounded arm,—these, the first fruits of the future, cover a multitude of sins—no, of indiscretions, heedlessness, youthful obliquities.

As Mr. Vanderbose commenced his arrangements, the piano was thrown open, and Miss Sally's fingers, in a moment, were flying about the keys, and producing such lively sounds that each one felt their inspiration, and began to strike in and keep step to them. It happened very well that for each young lady a gentleman was in waiting; the couples were even; Mr. Vanderbose had, with great tact, as he seemed to imagine, got the thing into shape, and was just stepping up to take his lady by the hand—when Mrs. Halliday called out:

"But we 've forgot Addie, where is she?"

"Here she is, aunty," said the lovely girl herself, just at that moment entering the room. She was very neatly dressed, and in that respect formed a striking contrast with her equally pretty, and, as most thought, prettier cousin—for the latter was almost arrayed in apparel fitted for a bride, sparkling with jewels, and her face wearing a sunny smile, as though it was indeed the heyday of life with her. The countenance of the other had a smile on it also, just then, but it was only as an accompaniment to her salutation of the company. Which was the loveliest of the two bright stars of the circle it might have been difficult to decide.

Her appearance caused some little confusion; the ceremony of introduction had to be gone through with, for the amateur was a stranger, and then she was an odd one. The gentlemen could not give up their partners, although one of them at least would have been delighted to do so.

"Oh, do; la, I can fix it," said Miss Sally, throwing back her curls. "I can fix it in no time; Mrs. Halliday, you are a first-rate dancer, you be the gentleman for Addie, and all will be straight."

"Oh, do, aunt; I should not desire a better partner; do, aunt, just for the fun of it."

"Oh, no," said Mrs. Halliday, "I have just thought; you

know we have another young gentleman in the house; perhaps I can engage him for Addie."

"Another, aunt! who is it?"

"Another, Mrs. Halliday!" exclaimed several voices at once.

"Why, you know, Sally, the gentleman you had some laugh about at tea to-night—the teacher."

"Has he come? and what does he look like?" exclaimed Miss Sally, clapping her hands, and laughing heartily; and then turning to Mr. Vanderbose, "Don't you think we are highly honored to have a real live Yankee school-master under our roof?"

"Does he carry a tooting weapon?" said the gentleman, clapping his hands in his ecstasy. "By Jupiter, boys and girls, we shall have some fun. Who knows but he's a real Ichabod Crane?"

The laughter that succeeded this classical allusion was very hearty, except on the part of Mrs. Halliday's nieces, whose sense of propriety forbade them to make merry at the expense of any one, especially under their own roof.

"I protest against the young lady's being compelled to dance with any such creature;" and the gentleman who spoke run his hand through his hair, which being very bushy, and rather of a reddish hue, formed a conspicuous part of the person.

"But I am determined to dance with him, if my aunt will introduce him."

"And that I will soon do, if he can be persuaded to it." And Mrs. Halliday at once left the room.

She could not but be a little gratified with the thought that there might be some surprise, when they came to see the subject of their merriment. She heard their loud laughter after having left the room, and had no doubt they were amusing themselves with their idea of a Yankee school-master, associated in their minds with all that was ridiculous and uncouth.

"I hope I may be able to persuade him to come in; the laugh will be against some other folks, if I am not mistaken." This she said to herself, as she entered their common sitting-room, where she expected to find him. To her surprise, he was not there. He could not have gone to his room she knew, for it had not been shown to him. "Perhaps he is in the boys' room," as the room was called adjoining the kitchen, and which has been described. He was there, sure enough; he was busily employed with his book, but arose immediately as she entered.

"I fear, Mr. Lovell, that my servant woman failed to do my errand, that I should be happy to see you among my guests this evening."

Charles slightly blushed.

"I hope, madam, you will excuse me, if I have done wrong in not obeying your summons. The young woman did tell me that you would be happy to see me in the parlor, but having some little work to do I replied to her, that if you would not take it amiss, I could wish to be excused this evening."

"Ah, you are very excusable, but I feared she had not delivered my message, and you would think me very deficient in hospitality. But I have come now to ask a favor of you; our young folks are about to have a little dance. I don't know but you are opposed to dancing; if so, I will not urge you, but if not, it will be quite a favor, for they cannot make out their set for want of a partner for one of the ladies."

"It is some time, madam, since I learned the steps, and I have had but little practice. I fear I shall make but a poor partner. But if you think my presence will add to the pleasure of the company, I submit myself to your command."

"You are very obliging, and I shall feel much indebted to you."

Charles had no apology to make for his appearance, for he had dressed himself in his best; he felt bound to do so our of respect to the strangers among whom he had come, as well as himself. He laid aside his book and at once followed his hostess. The perfect ease of his address and manner made Mrs. Halliday more confident in the surprise his presence would accomplish. And she opened the door, leaning on the arm of young Lovell, and at once led him to the different little groups that were standing about the spacious parlor.

Every sign of merriment was hushed, and each one to whom he was led up, felt called upon to return his easy salutation in the very best manner they could. Whether Miss Adelaide recognized him as one she had ever seen before, we need not say; her eye with its most intense gaze followed him around the circle, and only drooped as her aunt at the last brought him up before her.

"This is the young lady who happens to have no partner. My niece, Miss Adelaide Vincent; Mr. Lovell, Adelaide."

Charles bowed very low, and was evidently much affected, at first blushing deeply, and then losing all color but the fine sunburnt hue, while Miss Adelaide almost forgot her curtsey, and her tongue too, but seemed like one entranced, at first turning deadly pale, and then blushing, as though the rich blood would burst its beautiful cerement. She knew him now, although vastly improved in appearance—the young man at the spring of water! the polite and accomplished host that had so pleasantly entertained her in his humble cottage. But there was no time for inquiry, or apology, or explanation. Charles merely said, as he prepared to lead her out:

"I fear, Miss, you will find me an indifferent partner. I am more accustomed to working than dancing."

"Or taking care of ladies and horses in a thunder-storm? You helped me once; perhaps I can help you now."

None but Mrs. Halliday probably noticed the feeling manifested on the part of her niece, and she, of course, attributed it merely to the effect of surprise.

How Charles went through his part, it would not have been in his power to say. He was conscious of receiving a slight suggestion once from the lovely, artless being, who was moving with him through the mazes of the figure. But she complimented him when they were through. "Only one little mistake, and that no one noticed, for you took my suggestion so quick, and I am so glad of it."

"That I can dance well?"

The earnest look which followed this question, showed a manifest desire to reply, rather to the spirit than the letter of it, and she wished to get the true idea.

"I will answer to that, yes and no. I have some little pride, you know, to gratify in having a partner that moves with ease and grace; that will do for the yes. And as to the no, I rather despise than otherwise a man who would think any the better of himself because he could take a faultless step, and go through the figures of a dance to the admiration of others."

Whether Mr. Vanderbose was very versatile in his humors in general, or for some other cause, there was a marked change in the state of feeling manifested by him before and after the entrance of young Lovell. He doubtless remembered him, although, when his partner suggested the idea that Mr. Lovell and the young man who sheltered them under his roof from the storm, were the same person, he said, "he thought not." Yet a guilty conscience makes a restless mind, and he felt too decidedly uneasy to enjoy the sport longer than through one cotillon, and though he proposed to his partner that they should have some singing, he wanted to hear Murdock.

Julia, in her desire to please, at once carried the request to Miss Sally, and Miss Sally to Mrs. Halliday, and very soon Mr. Vanderbose was urging his friend, at the request of that lady, to favor the company with a popular song.

Mr. Murdock had no objections to exhibiting himself, but being an amateur, it was necessary that his powers, to be properly appreciated, should be brought into contrast with some less skilful performer, and, confident of his own abilities, was desirous that the company should have the best of the entertainment at the last.

"Tell madame that I will do my little part for the entertainment of the ladies, with great pleasure, but I cannot think of letting my voice be heard in precedence of the ladies."

There was such an unnatural and mincing tone to the voice, and such affectation in the manner, that Mrs. Halliday could not help blushing for her guest. But not wishing to dispute the matter with him, she called upon Miss Sally to favor the company with a tune. Miss Sally pouted very prettily, gave her ringlets a toss that sent them somewhere behind her sharp shoulders, touched gently the ivory keys, and at once the company was listening to the song so popular in that day, the far-famed "Legacy."

Miss Sally had a way of her own in singing, and, as though the music of her voice, even with the sweet sounds of the piano, were not sufficient, acted with her expressive eyes, and features, and supple neck, a sort of pantomime, expressive of the varied sentiment of this expressive song. And as my readers doubtless are well acquainted with it, they can realize, without much difficulty, the task which Miss Sally's head and eyes had to perform. As death is the first idea introduced, Miss Sally did the thing as well as could be expected; the head was drooped, the eyes closed, and there was a tendency of the whole careen to come down upon the piano, but before any one could have made any motion for her help, even if they had thought it necessary, her head was up, the curls shaking, and the eyes rolling glorious, and the whole countenance sparkling with "smiles and wine."

It was a wonderful performance, and received by the company with silent applause, at least during its delivery. The amateur did once turn over his perfumed handkerchief upon his lap; that was all—he sat very still, and looked very steadily at her, probably taking a lesson.

The usual meed of approbation awaited Miss Sally, as she gracefully left her seat, and Mr. Murdock, putting his handkerchief in his breast-pocket, and waited upon by his friend, placed himself before the instrument, and facing the company. There was a little buzz as the gentleman took his seat, which soon subsided into perfect stillness; when, throwing himself into the posture of a fancy whip, about to manage a pair of wild horses, he struck the piano with astounding force, and ran his fingers up and down upon the instrument as though it was a play-thing he could do just what he pleased with. The tune, however, was not yet begun, he was merely testing the power of the instrument; and from the motions of his body, which swayed gracefully from side to side, as his outstretched arms followed his flying fingers from the highest tenor to the lowest bass, it was evident that he was preparing for a great effort. Mr. Vanderbose seemed perfectly electrified, and began rubbing his hands, and hunching Miss Julia, who sat beside him, and winking significantly to the gentleman with the bushy-head, and looking round to see how the rest took it.

After awhile the gentleman ceased his manipulations, and assumed a posture for serious work. At this stage of the business he sat very erect; his head was thrown back, his under-jaw, loosened a little from the upper one, was drawn down into the thick folds of a figured neck-cloth, his white teeth just protruding beyond his parted lips, when forthwith there gushed a volume of sound, not unlike a blast from the fireman's trumpet, when his men are getting into danger.

Each person in the room made a slight motion, as though they could not help it; while Mr. Vanderbose fairly jumped from his chair, and stood upright, rubbing his hands, and looking round in ecstasy.

It was the Marseilles hymn that thus broke upon the astonished ears of the audience, and sung in its original language. Miss Sally and the bushy-head looked very knowing, and smiled as occasionally they recognized a word, whose meaning they could Anglicise. They both understood French, a little. Mr. Vanderbose knew nothing about French, and but little of the English; but there was a great noise and violent contortions of the lips, and he felt that it must be a great performance, and a great feather in his cap, that he had introduced an amateur, who could sing in an unknown tongue. He had like to have forgotten the proprieties altogether, and pinched Miss Julia's arm so violently, that she was glad to move a little off.

"Did you ever hear anything like that?" addressing himself to Mrs. Halliday, the moment the last note had exploded.

"I never did," she calmly replied. Another and another song was demanded by the excited Vanderbose, until at length the gentleman abruptly rose from his seat and insisted upon the other gentleman taking his place. Vanderbose could not play, but having taken his full allowance of wine that afternoon, felt just in a state to do something, so he started off in a song, which might have done well enough, perhaps, in the company of his boon companions around the bottle, but as it was, caused the lovely girl by his side to blush more than she could have wished on such an account.

As the other gentleman declined positively having anything to do with the matter, for awhile there was a pause, and Mrs. Halliday began to be weary; so she arose and approaching young Lovell, who, seated by Miss Vincent, was embracing every opportunity for conversation.

"I have no doubt now, Mr. Lovell, that you can give us something more to my mind, than anything we have had this evening. I believe you gentlemen of New England most generally learn to sing;" all this was said in a very low voice.

"Please, madam, excuse me on the present occasion. I have made one desperate experiment this evening."

"And succeeded;" and the pretty speaker, who looked up at him as she thus interrupted his sentence, manifestly seconded the wish of her aunt.

"But you do sing, don't you?" said Mrs. Halliday.

Charles scorned prevarication even in trifling matters.

"I do sing, but only at my own home. I amuse myself there sometimes with my guitar, and in fact have so accustomed myself to its use, that I should not dare to venture my voice without it." Mrs. Halliday was just then interrupted by a question from Miss Sally, who seemed to be also anxious to have something going on.

"I know it, Sally, I know it, and I have been just making a request to Mr. Lovell that he would favor us with a song."

"He will, of course," said Miss Sally. Mrs. Halliday looked to him for a reply when Adelaide, who had stepped from the room but a moment before, entered, and walking up to Mr. Lovell, put a guitar into his hands.

"It may not be as good as the one I saw at your house;" this was said in such a low, confiding tone, and the instrument placed in his hand with such an apparent expectation that he would use it, that he made no reply, but commenced tuning it to the compass of his voice; with some confusion manifest on his fine countenance he turned to Mrs. Halliday:

"I shall not be able to give you anything new or popular. But if you desire it, madam, I will do the best I can."

And without any more ado, immediately started the fine old song,

"Life's like a ship in constant motion,
Sometimes high and sometimes low,
Where every one must brave the ocean,
Whatsoever winds may blow."

Whether Miss Adelaide was alarmed lest her companion, as she had styled him, should not succeed, or for some other cause, she appeared very serious, and had an anxious shade upon her brow. But it lasted only through the first two lines of the song. Evident delight was manifest in the bright sparkle of her eye, and as her aunt, who sat beside her, raised her hand in astonishment and looked at her, Adelaide could not resist the smile of approbation, nor keep back the tear.

Her whole soul seemed melted—the rich tones of his clear, manly voice took hold upon her heart. But who was he? and where had he acquired these accomplishments? She had seen him in his lowly home. She had seen him in his rough attire, and engaged in manual labor; and yet there was a softness and delicacy in his address, equal to anything she had witnessed among those most favorably situated for refinement. She had also been charmed by his powers of conversation. Subjects which young men seldom name were familiar to him, as the common occurrences of the day. Could he have obtained all these under the circumstances in which she had beheld him? But her reveries were suddenly broken in upon, by the opening of a door from an adjoining room, and to the utter surprise of herself and all the company present, the portly form and honest bluff countenance of the good old captain presented themselves. He was neatly dressed, as he always would be, and as he cast his eye round the room made a slight bow, and then fixed his gaze upon the young man, who was sitting with his back in that direction. Adelaide was about to offer him her seat, but he motioned her not to rise, and stepped a little one side that he might have a glimpse of the singer.

He was evidently much excited; his countenance could not well have manifested more earnestness, if he had been, from the deck of his vessel, watching the approach of a severe squall. As the voice of the singer became more firm and animated in the heart-stirring chorus, the captain kept edging along up, and Adelaide thought she saw his lips moving, as though he was about to join in, and he doubtless would, if Charles had continued through the song; but being only acquainted with a few verses of it, stopped before the old captain had got up to a singing pitch.

The moment he ceased, the old gentleman grasped his hand: "That I call—"

"Mr. Halliday," said his good lady, stepping up, "this is Mr. Lovell, the young entleman engaged as our teacher this winter."

"Your most obedient, sir; this I call, as I was going to say, I call singing. Bless my soul, my young fellow, you have called back all my boyish days; I would give more for that song than all the fiddle-de-dums that Sally here squeals out in a year."

"Now, Captain Halliday!" and Miss Sally came up with a very good-natured smile, it must be confessed. "That *is* a compliment; I did n't know that you ever listened to me at all; you always say that you can't bear singing."

"No more I can't; not as they bellow it out now-a-days; you see Mr. Lovell," turning to Charles, whose hand he still held, "I like to hear something that a man's heart can take hold of. In the first place, I want to hear words that have got some meaning to them, and then I want to have them come out as if the one who sung them felt that they had a meaning. But, my dear fellow, you must give us that again or another like it. It is n't often they get me in here, and when they do, I must be paid for it."

"With pleasure, sir, if you think it will afford you any gratification."

"Thank you, sir; that 's off-hand, like a man."

At once Charles dashed off with another sea-song, and it was one that waked up in the old sailor feelings that had been almost quenched by long mingling in land scenes, and perplexing interests. He took his stand immediately in front of Lovell, and fairly started when the brisk and rapid notes first broke forth. But as the bursting sail, the foaming waves, and the bending mast, were portrayed so vividly before him in such stirring notes, he struck his hand with deep emotion on the back of the chair by which he stood, his manly countenance swelled, his eye twinkled rapidly, and an unbidden tear started from its place. The piece was short, and being rapidly performed, to suit its meaning, was soon over, or there is no telling what extravagance he might have been guilty of. Again he grasped Lovell's hand,

"That is almost too good, young man. Ah, it brings back some of the happiest days of my life; thank you, sir, thank you, and when you get tired of the young folks, just come into my room; I want to have a chat with you."

Charles thanked him, and bowing to Mrs. Halliday, "May I ask the liberty of being excused now, Mrs. Halliday?"

"By all means; I feel too much obliged for the exertions you have made for me this evening. But let me show you into a better room."

"Not on my account by any means; if I am not in the way there, I should prefer it."

And making his obeisance to the company, he retired to resume his Euclid. It was getting late, the house-clock had already struck the hour of ten, and Charles was still deeply engaged with his problems, when he heard the gentle steps of a female, passing lightly through the room in which he was sitting. As he turned his head, and caught a glimpse of Miss Adelaide he at once arose. She was apparently about to pass without attracting his notice, but now she paused, and came up to the table by which he had been sitting.

"You must have an interesting book that keeps you up so late?"

"It is somewhat interesting, although the problem I have been at work at is rather difficult. I have mastered it though, I believe."

"You are fond of study?"

"I do not dislike it; there is a pleasure in overcoming difficulties."

"And many things which appear difficult lose that character, when we take hold of them with resolution; as, for instance, our girl has been obliged to go home to-night to wait upon a sick mother, and my aunt has been quite unhappy with the thought how we were going to get breakfast in the morning without a girl. But I have begged her to let me undertake it, and have, therefore, taken the responsibility. I don't fear but I shall be able to do the thing, and am now on my way to make preparations. But you may not fare so well as you otherwise would."

Charles was almost off his guard, and had like to have said that it would be the sweetest meal that he had ever eaten; but his reason came to him in time, he merely replied:

"It must be a poor one, indeed, if I do not relish it."

"Well, you shall see what resolution will do. A pleasant night."

And the lively girl, with a sweet smile, tripped it on her way, and Charles, taking his book, retired to his own room. How much he slept that night it would have been difficult for him to tell. He was awake, however, as the first faint streaks of light were visible in the east, and as he loved the early dawn too heartily not to be abroad to behold its beauty and drink in its freshness, he arose, and descending to the room where he had spent most of the evening, found that no one had yet been there. A thought at once came into his mind how he could assist the lovely handmaid who was to prepare the morning repast. Kindling a fire came very natural to him; he was accustomed to do it at home; the wood-house was at hand, and in a few moments a fine blazing fire crackled upon the large hearth; the tea-kettle was hanging on, and, leaving everything as neat as he found it, he hurried off to enjoy his early walk.

The view from the premises of Captain Halliday was peculiarly fine at the rising of the sun, for a large stretch of the Sound lay spread out before them, and the sun arose as from the bed of waters.

The beauty of the forest had now departed, and no green thing was visible among them, except the dingy pines and cedars. The leaves had done their work, and the naked branches of the trees, like warriors stripped of their needless trappings, were ready for a tussle with the storms of winter.

There was a beauty, however, in the graceful sweep of the long branches of the larger trees, with their necked tendrils hanging in perfect stillness against the clear amber sky. And there was a beauty in the water, that lay stretched like a vast mirror, with the streaks of coming day shining from its surface, and in the mist that covered the meadows, and in the low jutting points of land far—far ahead, and in the white sails that spotted the panorama of water; and there was music in the echo of the boatman's oar as it came in its loneliness upon the still air. And there was in the bosom of Charles a pure and bounding spirit. And he could quaff with delight the freshness of the morning air, and had a taste to enjoy the scene in all its variety. He took his seat upon a clean bare rock, and watched the golden spot in the east, that grew more and more brilliant until its dazzling brightness forbade his gaze, and he cast his eye around upon the hill tops and distant mountains, tinged with a purple crown of glory. But while his eye was taking its fill of loveliness, his mind was no less absorbed with strange and pleasing emotions. What a bundle of inconsistencies is man! To all appearance Charles Lovell was a matter-of-fact person. Taking hold of work with a will that made the thing go, whatever it was—leaving nothing to the chance of fortune—living frugally and paying for everything as he went along—allowing no anticipations of wealth to spoil the enjoyment of what he possessed by the honest labor of his hands. And yet, so far a creature of imagination, that he lived in a poetic world—the gentle breeze that fanned his cheek, the rippled waters of the running brook, the loud roar of the coming tempest, the green earth, the dark blue sky, the trees, the flowers, and the fruits—all had a voice that spoke at once to his heart; a glory shone about them, a charm emanated from them that at times melted him into feelings that he dared not unfold; he did not write them down, nor utter them to another, but was satisfied to enjoy the luxury of his own kindling thoughts in secret. Nor did his imagination spend itself on the material world about him. It took strong hold of his social nature, and its power there was now to be a source of many a severe pang.

The beautiful image which had come across his path, the maiden of the spring and the thunder storm, had been about his path ever since. The object of his waking and sleeping dreams had now been brought near to him, a creature of real flesh and blood, and full as captivating as the one he had been dreaming of, and his heart fluttered with the strong emotion; he has been weaving a golden net-work, but its meshes hold him in a strong embrace. He feels powerless to resist the influence. Reason had often urged the impolicy of his conduct. "How worse than idle, to indulge a thought of one whom he might never meet again;" and now she bids him "pause and reflect upon the vast distance between their positions in life. She, a child favored of fortune, basking in the sunny path, and familiar only with the fairer fruits and flowers—he far down amid its dull realities, toiling for the bread of sustenance." But reason might as well have been quiet, for there he sits upon the rock, and with all the glories of the opening day about him to quicken the inner man, is feasting on the scenes of the past evening, and recalling every word she had spoken to him, and every phase of her beautiful countenance, and every token of her ingenuous heart.

"You rise early, sir! good morning to you."

Charles turned, and beheld the person of Captain Halliday, who had approached him unnoticed. He arose and took the hand which was held out to him.

"Good morning, sir. I usually rise early. Farmers, you know, sir, must make the most of the day."

"Farmers! are you a farmer, young man?"

"I am, sir, in a small way."

"A farmer, ha! Well, all I can say is, I wish you some better trade. I thought they said you was a teacher. Have n't you taken the school here?"

"Oh yes, sir; but that is only for the winter. There is little to occupy me at this season of the year."

"Little to occupy you? then you are more lucky than some other folks. It seems to me that this farming is an everlasting business; there 's no head nor tail to it, one thing laps on to another; it 's enough to worry a man's life and soul out of him; and the worst of all is, there is an everlasting outgo, and the incomes all go into the workmen's pockets and the cattle's bellies. Oh! dear! dear! dear! I 've been a c——d fool; excuse me, sir, for plain speaking, but when a man gets bamboozled into a hornet's nest, and finds all stings and no honey, it 's enough to make a saint swear. But what do you do with your men when you are away? let them eat everything up, and play hocus-pocus with the rest?"

"I am my own man, sir, and have no special trouble on that account."

"Your own man! you don't say you work yourself? You don't look like it; and yet there 's enough of you to strike a manly blow. Give me your hand. Well, it don't feel as if it had been used to handling a marlin-spike, and yet I should n't want a blow from it in a tender spot. But tell me honestly, do you take hold of the plough, and the hoe, and the ox-team yourself?"

"Yes, sir, and the scythe and the pitch-fork too. All the work is done entirely by myself and a brother somewhat younger."

The captain eyed him keenly. "Can you make anything

by it? Do you realize anything from it? any money? anything but what is all swallowed down again by a parcel of hungry cows and hogs?"

Charles was about to reply when the sound of a bell was heard from the back stoop of the house.

"There 's the breakfast-bell, sir; come, you must have an appetite from this morning air; it 's keen, and for my part, I have been pulling and hauling harder than ever I did at a main sheet in a gale of wind, trying to haul out a calf that jumped into the barn-yard well last night."

"In the well! Was it not enclosed, or covered?"

"It ought to have been; but you see, sir, I have had half a dozen Irishmen stoning a well in my yard; it was an old concern, and the stones appeared about to tumble in, so they advised me to take out the stones and relay them, and a pretty sum it will cost me. I 'd better have dug a new one at once. They were a week taking out the old stones, and they have been a week putting them in again; and in the midst of it, one of the blunderheads trips over and down he goes, bucket and all, to the bottom."

"Did it kill him?" said Charles, with much alarm.

"Kill him! no, no danger of such a fellow's dying. He broke his leg, though, and he 'll be laid up three months, probably, and the doctor and all will look to me for expenses. And then the dumb fellows went off to their suppers last night and left the place without the sign of a covering to it, and the first thing I heard this morning when I got out of bed was Patrick jabbering away in the kitchen, and asking them 'to call the captain;' so out I went, and found that a fine English heifer had gone down head first. And so it is from morning to night; it 's nothing but a torment, sir. Sailors are bad enough sometimes; but the laboring men round here seem only sent into the world to eat and plague other people.

The scenes of the past evening had done wonders for Charles, and he had no reason to complain of any want of respect and attention.

A significant glance from the eye of Miss Adelaide, as the captain asked, "How breakfast was had in such good season this morning," assured him that she guessed who had been her assistant; but no allusion further was made to it. The captain, however, was not sparing of praise for his fine cup of coffee.

"I have n't had such a cup of coffee these six months. I should like to know, Sis, where you learned to make it. Give me a girl that can put her hand to anything; don't you say so, Mr. Lovell?"

Mr. Lovell would have replied in the affirmative, but under the circumstances felt rather timid in expressing an opinion. He smiled, but made no reply. Miss Sally, however, was ready with an answer.

"I don't know about that, Captain Halliday. I sometimes think the less ladies know about such matters, the better. I think men ought n't to marry without they can support a decent establishment. Just see the wives of our common farmers; slaves—mere drudges. And what do they look like?"

"I think," replied the captain, "they look as well as the men; they are of a piece."

"You may well say that, Captain Halliday. I do think farming the hatefullest business that a man can pursue; without it is a gentleman farmer. That will do well enough, such as you are, captain; you always keep yourself neatly attired, and your style of living is as genteel as need be; as good as the city any day. But, I mean the real rough-and-tumble farmers. Did you ever see one of them but had great clumsy feet and hands? I would n't marry the best man that ever breathed, if I knew he was a working farmer; would you, girls?" tossing her head, and looking towards the two young ladies, who sat one on each side of Mrs. Halliday, assisting her in waiting upon the table. Adelaide blushed deeply, and warded off a reply by just then taking her uncle's cup to be replenished. But Julia smiling, and looking towards Mr. Lovell, replied:

"Perhaps all farmers are not alike; there must be exceptions. If I am not mistaken, I have seen Mr. Lovell in a farmer's rig, but it seemed to be no hinderance to all the polite address of the gentleman."

It was Charles' turn now to blush; but he managed the matter as well as he could, and making as low an obeisance as the circumstances would permit, he replied:

"It is a compliment I did not expect; but I most highly

prize it, and will remember it for my future encouragement."

"Why, Julia!" said Mrs. Halliday, "where have you ever seen Mr. Lovell?"

"You will remember, aunt, my telling you how well we were sheltered last summer during that great storm."

"I am very glad, then, that we have such an opportunity of making some return to Mr. Lovell for his kind attentions. The girls mentioned it on their coming home. But how is it that neither of you seemed to recognize him last evening?"

Mrs. Halliday had not noticed how much evidence of recognition Adelaide had manifested.

"It is not at all strange, madam," replied Charles. "Dress makes a great difference in any of us."

"But I am not going to permit that charge to lie against me, aunt," and Adelaide, smiling, turned to Mr. Lovell. "I could have introduced Mr. Lovell to *you* had I ever been favored with his name."

"And I felt very sure, aunt," said Julia, also directing her smiling face to Mr. Lovell, "that I knew Mr. Lovell, but I had not so good an opportunity as Addy to form an acquaintance."

"Well, well, well, you are all talking riddles to me. But I tell you what, ladies, and you, my young friend, dress does make a great difference with all of us. I found that out when I went to sea. I never, except in extreme cases, let my men see me dressed like themselves."

Charles, having finished his breakfast, and perhaps glad of an excuse, presented his request to Mrs. Halliday, "as he had an engagement early at the school-room, if he might be permitted to leave?"

"Certainly, sir, if you wish it."

He arose, and making an easy obeisance to the company, left the room.

"Did I ever!" and Miss Sally put up both her hands. "Who would ever have thought of his being a farmer? And does he really work himself?"

As Adelaide was not forward to reply, Julia at once answered Miss Sally's inquiry.

"He was at work when we first saw him—mowing, or something of that kind. Addy wanted a drink of water, and there was a beautiful spring near the road where he was at work; and when he saw what she wanted, he came at once, and helped her to a drink, and I could not but notice him for his ease of manner, and the neatness of his dress. He wore a kind of frock, but it was very clean, and sat well on him, and his shirt collar was as white as snow, and lay turned a little over from his neck; and he had on a neat light-colored beaver, with a low crown, and brim just large enough to keep off the sun; and his teeth looked so white, you know he shows them a little when he smiles, and he spoke so properly, and everything he did was with such an easy, gentlemanly way, that I could not help being struck with him—and so was Addy, too."

"Well, well, well, it takes all sorts of folks to make a world; I must go see to my men, or they will be letting some more of my beasts get down that well. Wife, do you expect those folks from the city to-day?"

"I do, Captain Halliday, and I hope you will do your best to entertain them. You know they are people that live in style, and have been used to the best; and won't you leave me some money, pa? I want to send for some eggs, and our butter is out, and you know the butcher comes this morning."

"Eggs and butter! well done—with all our cows and hens, we can't make out without buying. If we keep on so, I tell you what it is, we shall all have to go to work, and get big hands and big feet, as Sally says."

Sally was not there, she had left the table with the rest.

"I am serious now, wife; this everlasting drain will clear us out, depend upon it. Do you know it costs us more to live than it did in the city; we shall have to sell all out, and I must ship off to sea again."

"Oh, do, husband, stop with your nonsense. You know when you get things once all in order, you will be receiving an income from the farm—it always costs a great deal to begin, you know; and at any rate just now, as the girls are receiving company. Julia will soon be a rich lady, and ride in her carriage—Vanderbose is very rich, no doubt of it; and then Mr. Sampson, who seems to be quite taken with Addy, is worth all of $500,000, Vanderbose says.

"What, that fellow with a red mop on his head?"

"Don't talk so, pa—his hair, to be sure, is red, and a little too thick; but Addy could soon persuade him to have it trimmed, and he is not bad looking otherwise."

"Well, well, you must all work it as you like. But don't you persuade her—money is well enough in its place. I wish I had more of it, but rather than either of those dear girls should be married against their wills, I'd weather the waves and storms as long as I could stand on my legs."

"Not against their wills, certainly, but a good chance should n't be thrown away. It is a very pretty thing, as Aunt Nabby says, 'to live in a fine house, and keep one's carriage, and have servants in plenty, and all that.'"

"Now, wife, don't be telling me what Nabby says. She and I never could hitch horses together, and never will. But how much money do you want?"

"Well, I guess you had better leave me twenty dollars, for Mary wants her wages, her mother is sick, and she has n't been paid these two months."

The captain scraped together the twenty dollars, but he could not help heaving a sigh, as he put his exhausted wallet back again into his pocket, and went out to see to his men.

The expected company arrived that afternoon, and found Captain Halliday's carriage in waiting for them at the hotel, and a small wagon besides to carry the baggage. "A very convenient arrangement," as Charles, the honest coachman, said, "for the company, but very hard for horse flesh, to be lugging back and forth so many folks, with their everlasting heaps of baggage, so far through the sand; it takes a power of oats to keep them up in any decent condition, and he did n't believe the captain would get much thanks for it, after all."

"Well, but the folks seem so clever," said Mary, the cook, to whom he made the remark; "and they are so happy, and they praise our bread and butter so much, and seem so delighted with our beautiful situation. It does one good to hear 'em."

"Yes, yes, you women would work your fingers off, and burn your eyes out, if you can only get a little praise. But I'm a thinking, if the captain aint got a pretty long purse, what between his Irish ditchers, and his Vermont fence-layers, and his York friends, he'll be clean riddled, and he is too clever a man to be so trod upon."

The good captain had been much harassed that day with the blunders of some of his hands, and the wants of others, and had forgotten all about visitors, until, on his approach home near supper-time, when just on the brow of the terraced plot that lay back of his house, he saw a company assembled, and looking round very complacently upon the grounds and scenery. Being too near to retreat in order to save appearances, he made his way towards them.

"Captain Halliday, *how do you do?*" and a gentleman, with a lady leaning on his arm, stepped briskly up and took his hand, and shook it with such cordiality as quite astonished the old captain, and his sailor's heart was just susceptible enough to be touched with such a greeting. So he as cordially returned the salutation.

"Glad to see you, sir; glad to see you; your servant, madam," bowing politely to the lady.

"Mrs. Windham, Captain Halliday." The captain bowed again to the lady, "glad to see you, madam."

"George, jump up here," and a fat, bull-headed young gentleman of about sixteen, sprang up from a rock upon which he was sitting. "Come here, George; captain, this is my son George."

"How do you do, sir; your son looks in good health, sir."

"Well, George does not enjoy good health, sir, and it is mainly on his account we have come into the country so late in the season, just for a change."

"Indeed, madam!"

"There seems to be something the matter with his stomach, captain, and we have tried most everything, and it seems to do no good. So I told Mrs. Windham that I had long wanted to make you a visit up here, as you and I had been old friends, and I have heard so much said about your situation. I thought we would just run up and see how your country bread and butter and fresh air would agree withGeorge."

"Glad to see you, sir; are those the rest of your children?"

"Ah, yes; come here you romps; this is Jane, and here is Susan, and here is Helen; here, nurse, bring the baby—captain, I want to show you a sight. What do you think of that?" taking off a gauze shawl, and exposing to view a little chub of a thing, that looked as though it had been stuffing from the day of its birth. "What do you say to that, captain?"

"Fat child, sir—fat child; city air seems to agree with your children."

"With all but our son George; don't you feel like taking a little bread and milk? You know, mamma, he eat nothing for dinner but that lamb chop—he would n't touch the dessert; I suppose milk you make no account of here, captain?"

"Oh no, sir;" the captain could honestly say that; there was so little came in after the calves had been supplied, that it was not worth thinking of.

"I thought so—nurse, you go in and take the baby; I guess she would like some too; and see that George has stale bread in his milk; I am afraid fresh bread might disagree with him."

"What a glorious life you must have of it here, Captain Halliday! everything within yourself. And this air; ah," taking in a long breath, "it makes one feel ten years younger."

"You have a charming place here, sir," added Mrs. Windham, as the captain made no reply to her husband, his mind being probably absorbed with the thought how Master George was to be supplied with milk, knowing, as he did, that there was scarcely enough for the milk-pitcher. "Such an extended view! such picturesque landscape! and there is such a delightful stillness and quiet withal; it seems as if nothing could ever trouble one here."

"Trouble! my dear wife, they don't know anything about trouble in such a place as this. It must be very delightful for you, captain, after the storms of the ocean to find yourself in such a sunny harbor."

The captain could have told them a different story, but he merely replied:

"Yes, sir—yes, madam, it is so."

There was a very busy company around the supper-table that evening, and there was no lack of praises of the bread, and the butter, and the cream, and the broiled chickens. Plate after plate disappeared, and were as fast replenished. Where they came from the captain hardly knew, and was quite relieved when he found operations ceased, and the operators taking themselves into the parlor.

"And now, I want you, wife," said he, as he arose from

table, "to ask Mr. Lovell to come into my room, after he has done his supper; I want to have a little talk with him this evening."

"Oh, he has had his supper, pa; he has been to tea elsewhere; and what do you think? he came up to me, and says, 'Mrs. Halliday, you have a great many to lodge to-night, and I hope you will allow me to take any place that might be convenient. I can just as well sleep on a settee, or anything of the kind, as not.' And it has happened very well, for now I can take his room for young Windham, as his mother whispered to me that he liked a room to himself."

The captain not being very particular sometimes, let off some rather expressive adjectives, and coupled them all with the fat lubber. But being hushed down by his wife, for whom he had great regard, ended with an eulogy upon Lovell.

"He is a man, every inch of him, and it is a pity he should be turned out of his room for such a—"

"Do—don't, pa. Never mind, you know we have been expecting them, and so we will treat them politely. You go to your room, and I will tell Mr. Lovell you want to see him. How that baby *does* scream! I am afraid it has taken too much of the milk; it was not very fresh, but it was the best I had."

"Good evening, sir, good evening; glad to see you; take a chair. This, you see, is my room; there is such a run of folks, what between my wife's friends, and my nieces' friends, and their friends, that I haul off as soon as decency will permit, and leave them to chat, and dance, and sing by themselves. However, you took me by storm last night. I have n't heard such music this many a day; it made me think of days long gone by. But, sit down, sir, sit down." And Charles, who had been standing out of compliment to his host, took a seat as requested.

"I am right glad you have come in, for I have been longing to have a talk with you ever since our chat this morning, and, in fact, ever since I saw you; for to speak plain, my young friend, you are a kind of nondescript that I can't fathom."

Charles smiled; "I am sorry, sir, if there is anything mysterious about me."

"There is, though, something very mysterious. To look at you, and hear you speak, and see your manners, one would take you for a thorough-bred gentleman, and yet, if I am correctly informed, you are a plain, laboring farmer."

"I hope, sir, the two are not inconsistent with each other."

The old gentleman was going to use a phrase with which he was a little too familiar, but his better sense checked him, so he stammered upon the most expressive words he could muster of a fair character.

"They are very, very much so, sir; as far from each other as heaven and earth, at least in this place."

"I am sorry, sir, that such is your experience."

"Why, sir, only look at it. I have, I believe, a dozen men in my employ, the best I can get, and rather than have them in my house, have put up one for them, where they can eat, and sleep, and drink, and be as dirty as they please. And there is n't one of them that a decent man would want to room with. And just look around our place, at those farmers who live on their own land, and do their own work. They are rough and clownish themselves, and everything about them is of a piece with them; they have n't the manners of a common sailor."

"What you say, sir, is, I fear, too true, from what little I have already seen of this place. But, perhaps, the fault is owing to the peculiarities of this town, rather than to any necessity. So far as I have seen, those who are persons of any consideration here, do not work themselves. Many here are from the city, and their habits of life are the same as they brought with them; and even those who live from the products of their farms, depend upon hired laborers. It is not a proper farming community, and there is too great a distinction between the master and the man. The more respectable laborers have gone to places less exceptionable in this respect, and you are left with the refuse."

The captain looked, with his keen eye, steadily at the young man, and for some time made no reply.

"That is a view of things that has never struck me before. I don't know but you have got the right of the matter. And yet I don't hardly see through the thing, especially in your case. Now, I've seen something of the world, and know something of mankind. I can generally tell a minister, a merchant, a laborer, and a lawyer, only let me have a little talk with them. You was never cut out for a plain, working farmer, my young friend. You can do a great deal better than that. Why, you could make your fortune with that voice of yours, without ever lifting a finger to work, depend upon it; or you could command a handsome salary as clerk."

Charles shook his head, and a glow spread over his countenance, and his eye sparkled with strong emotion.

"I feel myself too much of a man, sir, to do either. I am comparatively poor, I know; I own but a small patrimony, but I am my own master there. I work upon my own soil, I wait upon myself, I am at no man's call; I fear no man's frown, for no man do I owe. I buy no more than I can pay for, I live in a plain yet comfortable home, and with a light heart. I rise in the morning, and go to bed at night. And behind my plough, or with my hoe in my hand, respect myself full as much as I should in bargaining with my fellow men as a merchant, or using the powers of my mind as a lawyer, 'to make wrong appear the better side.'"

The captain took his hand and shook it heartily.

"That 's a man, that 's a man; you have got the right of it, and depend upon it, with such feelings you will make yourself respected. I see through it now. You feel your calling to be an honorable one, and so it is; and you feel yourself equal to any."

"Not exactly, sir. I am, as I have said, comparatively poor. I live in a plainer house than you have erected for your laborers; and I know that many, either wealthy or able to live in some style, are not very careful to place those who are not upon an equality with themselves. I never obtrude myself, but only as circumstances place me endeavor to act my part with self-possession. And while I never court the rich, am not at all abashed in their company."

"Right, that 's right again; you have got it. But you must have been educated. You must have had superior advantages."

"For schooling, I had the advantages which our district schools afford, nothing further. But my father lived long enough to cherish in me a taste for reading, and that of the more solid kind. The few accomplishments which you have been pleased to speak of, I have obtained in a way which is open to any person desirous to make himself agreeable, and who has a taste for the amenities of life. And attention to our personal appearance I hold to be almost a virtue."

Captain Halliday made no reply, but for some time pondered deeply on the words which came with so much earnestness from the lips of young Lovell; at length he asked:

"But I have one more question to put to you. Can you make anything by farming?"

"I cannot expect to make money with the rapidity, nor to to the extent that some do by other employments. But a very little money goes a great way in the country, sir."

The old gentleman now straightened himself to a very erect posture, placed one hand on each knee, and shutting one eye, screwed his face into such a vinegar aspect that Charles had much ado to prevent himself from smiling.

"*A very little money goes a great way in the country!* Young man, I have heard that before; they all preached it to me before I came; but, sir, I find it takes a —— sight of money. I can't help it, sir; it aint often that I swear, but it is more than human nature can stand. It is a great humbug, sir. I believe, sir, as sure as there is a heaven above us, if John Jacob Astor should only go and buy a farm large enough, he 'd sink his millions, sir, in ten years. He 'd be a poor man. Why, sir, just listen to me. I had a handsome little fortune of thirty thousand dollars clear money. Ten thousand I paid for this place, of two hundred acres. Well, at it I went; there were wagons to buy, and ploughs, and oxen, and horses, and what not. One thousand went right slap off for these. Well, what was to be done next? it was spring of the year. I had to buy hay for the cattle, oats for the horses, meal for the pigs; pork, and tea, and butter, and sugar, and molasses. As long a list, sir, as I ever laid in for a voyage to China. Well, they all said, 'Oh, it would all come back again when my crops came in.' But how did it come back? I cut a good crop of hay, but must n't sell any of that; the cattle must eat that, or the farm would run out; so all that came back from that was a hundred dollars paid out for harvesting it. I had ten acres of corn, a fair crop I believe. But I must n't sell that, because the hogs must be fatted, and the cows must have meal in the winter, and the hens could n't live by scratching, when the ground was froze. I had ten acres of oats, but my coachman said the horses had so much to do, the roads were so bad, and the loads so heavy, that if we did n't fill their bellies with oats, they would run down to nothing. And as to milk and butter, we could barely get along with five good cows, and get milk enough to stuff the bellies of the calves and the Irishmen. Not one solitary cent's worth could I sell. And all the time it was call, call, call for money. Why, sir, it has been nothing but dig ditches, build fences, feed creatures, and keep my pocket-book going from morning to night. People talk to me about my beautiful place. It may look very lovely to them, but when a man feels that his life-blood is running away through his pockets, paradise itself would n't give him any pleasure to look at it."

"I fear, sir, you have had bad advisers. A man needs experience on a farm as well as in other business."

"He 'll get it, sir, if he lives on one, no danger of that. It 's all experience from beginning to end. But the great mystery to me is, how they live! and knowing what I do, to be frank with you, Mr. Lovell, I can't bear to think that a fine young fellow, with talents such as you have, should be tied down to such a business; where a man must live upon the cattle's leavings, like a wild Indian, without he has got a pocket with no end to it to draw upon."

Charles saw that the captain was in earnest, and after thanking him for the interest he took in his affairs, in a plain offhand manner unfolded to him his whole situation, the way in which he and his brother managed, and the gains which he had realized thus far, and his prospects for the future.

"And now, sir, when everything around me is in such accordance with my feelings—where such enjoyment attends me in the midst of my occupations, and where every respect is paid to me by those whose society is really to be prized, why should I relinquish my calling, and hazard a certain independence, for the cares, and risks, and vexations of a more enticing profession?"

It was some time before the captain replied; at length he laid his hand on Lovell's arm:

" Mr. Lovell, have you any objections to let me accompany you at some time to your home ?"

" None in the least, sir ; but should be most happy to take your there."

" Done then, it 's a bargain ; and as soon as my good friends here, who have come all the way from the city to see me, have got their fill of broiled chickens, and bread and butter, and so on, I will be ready.

" It is strange to me to hear people, who come from a place where there is everything the earth can produce, right under their noses, talk so much about eating when they get into the country. One would think they came from the midst of war, famine, and pestilence."

CHAPTER X.

Charles had not forgotten his engagement with Captain Halliday, and in about a week after the conversation recorded in the last chapter, Pomp, rigged up to a neat buggy, was standing at the gate, and Captain Halliday, with his great-coat hanging on his arm, in company with Lovell, was opening the gate, and looking with rather a dubious expression at the sprightly creature, as he threw his ears back and forward, and pawed the earth in his impatience.

"You have got a fine horse here, sir, but he looks rather young and gay; I am no great hand at riding, and prefer gentle horses."

"He is under perfect command, sir; as much so as ever your ship was when you had a good helms-man."

"Do you know him?"

"Oh yes, sir, perfectly—he is my own, sir. I have had the breaking of him, and keep him here a little while, so as not to let him lose his good manners."

"Well, well, sir, I trust to what you say; but from his looks I should rather face a hurricane in a good ship, than be behind him alone."

The good beast stood perfectly still until they had got well seated, and then stepped off with a very moderate gait, increasing it to a firm, steady trot.

"He treads firmly, and appears to carry us with great ease; do you say you own him?"

"Yes sir, and have had the pleasure of breaking him to my own mind. He knows my voice, and I believe would obey me if everything should break down, and get against him."

"He is a pretty creature, and I suppose you are very fond of him."

"Almost too much so, for I find it rather hard being separated; but I shall only keep him up here occasionally. My brother must have him part of the time, for he is as fond of him as I am."

"Well, well, I begin to see into things—you make your business your pleasure—you take care of your own things yourself, and you get fond of the employment. I suppose you are your own groom?"

"I am, sir, and I can go in the darkest night, and harness him without the least trouble, for I know where everything is."

Charles felt some little concern about things at home; not that he expected to find everything out of order, or different from the usual course. But not expecting such an addition to their little circle, lest Aunt Casey might not be as well prepared as she would like.

It was quite dark before Charles saw the light from the cottage twinkling through the trees. Pomp winnowed as was his custom, as soon as reined up at the gate, and in a moment Augustus was running out to meet his favorite. A cordial greeting passed between the brothers, and then the captain shook his hand heartily, when Augustus went to caressing Pomp, who by very significant signs was manifesting his delight at being again at his home.

"Aye, aye," said the captain, "you are all of a piece, you boys, I see; love one another, and you aint ashamed to show it; and you love your horse, and he loves you. You will be happy whether you live in a big house, or a little one. May you always keep in the track you have got into."

Augustus jumped into the wagon, and Pomp pranced, and capered away towards the stable, like a boy returning to a loved home, while Charles led his guest through the little grove towards the low light that was shining so cheerfully beyond it.

He opened the door, and at once Captain Halliday was in the place he had so much desired to see, and, for a moment, he stood and contemplated the scene. Just before him, near the centre of the room, stood a table neatly spread for the evening meal, with everything on it glistening in the light of a large glass lamp which stood upon it. The knives, and forks, and plates, and tea set, as highly polished and arranged in as much order as he was accustomed to see at home. While, all around the room, each article seemed to be in its place, and in good condition. All this he saw at a glance, and then advanced to pay his respects to the matronly personage who was seated near the fire in an old-fashioned rocking-chair. One who had known Aunt Casey in former days, would have supposed that she had of late forgotten her widowhood, and "was setting her cap" for a new companion.

Aunt Casey, however, had no such thoughts, but had merely imbibed the spirit of the master of her modest home, and was making the best of what she had. A neat dark calico dress, open at the neck and bosom, and displaying there a very white surplice handkerchief, adorned her person, while a plain cap, with a small lace border, beyond which her light brown hair slightly protruded in its parting above her yet unwrinkled brow, adorned her head. Her chair kept rocking, even after the door had opened, but no sooner did she see Charles than she sprang towards him, and apparently forgetful of the presence of a stranger, caught him round the neck, and gave him a real mother's blessing.

"Aunt Casey, this is Captain Halliday, a gentleman with whom I am staying."

Perhaps a little abashed at the freedom she had been taking, some little confusion was manifested in her reception, and she stepped back and made as good a curtsey as she knew how. But the captain was not satisfied with such a formal greeting. He advanced towards her, and taking her hand, shook it as cordially as if she had been an old friend.

"I am very happy to see you, madam, and wish every young man who has no father nor mother, had as warm-hearted and kind a friend as you seem to be."

"But it aint every young man that is like him, sir; them that know him as I do, can't help loving him."

"I believe you, madam; somehow or other, he seems to have got on the right track. He has made a friend of me already, and I have taken the liberty of coming with him, just to see his home that he seems to love so much."

The old lady now broke into one of her little short laughs.

"Well, sir, it is not much of a place, as you see, but we

try to make the best of it, and may be we are as happy as many who live in grander houses. I know I am; but please take a seat, sir, and make yourself as much at home as you can."

"I will, madam, and with your leave will sit toward your good fire; it feels pleasant, as the air begins to be a little keen, especially riding; but shall I not be in your way?"

"Not in the least, sir, if the smell of the victuals won't be offensive."

"Quite the contrary, madam, I assure you; for the flavor of them, or something else, has given me a sharp appetite. Now don't let me hinder you a moment."

Charles had slipped into the adjoining room, and the old lady watched an opportunity, as soon as she could, to step out and have a word with him.

"How glad I am that you have happened in this evening, for Augustus has killed one of the young turkeys to-day, and I thought I'd make it into a fricasee, you know he is so fond of them; if I'd known it though, dear, I should have had it roasted just for your sake."

"Oh, I shall like it just as well, aunty; I know it will be good. If you could as well as not, give us a cup of coffee."

Aunt Casey had a way of doing things that was so quiet, that one who was in a hurry might have some apprehensions lest she would never get along with the work in hand. But at half-past six, their hour for supper, everything was upon the table, and the little family was standing each at the back of his chair. The captain was too much of a gentleman, even in such a plain establishment, to take his seat before the mistress of the table; therefore did as he saw the others do.

The old lady looked at Charles, to see whether he would think it best, under the circumstances, to do as he was accustomed. But Charles had too strong a sense of duty to Him, whom he acknowledged as the giver of His mercies, to omit his services to Him, even in the presence of one who did not thus acknowledge the gift of God. At once his voice was heard, humbly supplicating a blessing. It was short, but appropriate, and uttered with much feeling. The old lady wiped her eyes, and all settled to the business before them.

"Well, well, well, madam, you call yourselves poor folks, but if this is the way you live, I can tell you there are many rich folks that might be glad to board with you; bless my soul, what a supply have you got here."

"I hope it may prove as good as it looks; but it is all you see, sir, come of our own raisin'."

Taking everything together, it had really a look that was by no means disagreable to a hungry man. For immediately opposite Charles was a large white platter, well filled with the turkey, cut into pieces, and sprinkled with a good supply of light, puffy dumplings. In the centre of the table was a plate heaped up with smoking biscuit, flanked on one side with a dish of baked sweet apples, with large cracks in them, through which the rich juice was forcing its way, and on the other by a bowl of quince sauce. A liberal plate of butter, and a glass saucer of plum sweetmeats, completed the assortment. The latter was, doubtless, together with the cup of coffee, an addition in honor of their guest. The captain made no objection to anything that was handed to him, so that his plate had something the appearance of Jupiter and his satellites; for there stood around it a saucer with the largest apple in it, and a little plate with quince sauce, and a glass saucer of the plums, and his cup of coffee, with the rich cream floating on its top. And the captain went to work with the determination of a man of business. To say nothing of other things, the baked apples, and the coffee, in a particular manner seemed to claim his notice.

"I should like to know, madam," he remarked, as he handed his cup to be filled the third time, "if there is any such thing as my getting a recipe for the making of this coffee. It is the best I ever tasted in my life."

The old lady broke again into a short laugh, the idea of her giving a recipe for anything she prepared, was so ridiculous to her.

"I am glad it suits you, sir; we don't often have it for tea, but Charley told me he thought you might relish it after your ride. I think the cream, sometimes, makes a great difference in coffee, and may be the apples give it a relish."

"And do you keep these young men on such fare all the time?"

Another short laugh.

"Not just the same, sir. Sometimes we will have a chicken, maybe, or a slice of ham, or a little fried pork, or maybe, a little fresh meat, just as it happens. I think a little change is good, and not have the same thing too much. In the country so, where a butcher only comes once in awhile, we make things do that we raise ourselves; and with a little change in the way of cooking them, I don't see but we get along quite comfortable."

"I don't see but you do, madam. I don't doubt you live quite as well as I do, and it costs me, I dare n't say how much, but a deal of money each year."

"Oh, la! Well you see, sir, the things we mostly use, are what we raise. The chickens aint much trouble to raise; it takes a little meal at the first, and a little care, but very soon they do for themselves, and pick up around what they want, and then, when the boys harvest, they fat up. And I had pretty good luck with the turkeys this year; they aint large, but they 're tender and good. And our pork and hams is our own raising; and the boys sell corn and buckwheat enough to buy our wheat; and what with potatoes, and apples, and quinces, and such like, as we have, a body with a little management can make a good variety, without any outgo of money. And what butter and eggs I sell, buys our butcher's meat, so that only our sugar, and tea, and coffee, and molasses, is what we have to buy; and a little family, you know, sir, don't need spend much for them."

The captain made no reply, but his mind was very busy revolving the difference between the apparent wants, and the real comforts of life; and inwardly regretting that he had not, at a much earlier period, taken a meal at Aunt Casey's.

"And now, Captain Halliday," said Charles, "I promised you an opportunity to have your segar; and if you will take this arm-chair in the corner of our big fire-place, I assure you no one will be offended by the smoke."

"A capital place—ah me! Why what a comfortable chair this is; a man might rest in it for the night."

"And if you will excuse me, for a few moments, as I have some things to see to at the barn, I will soon be back."

"By all means; I shall be contented here, you may depend."

Charles stepped into his little room, and was soon out again, arrayed in his working-dress.

"I am fit for rough and tumble now, sir, without the fear of soiling my clothes."

"Bless my soul! Ah, I see you dress according to your business. Well, I don't know, if I was a young girl, but I should fall in love with you as soon in this rig as the other."

Charles smiled, and taking the lantern, he and Augustus left the room.

"He is a man, every inch of him, put on what dress he will."

"Indeed he is, sir; there is few like him."

"And he tells me you all live here as one family."

"Ah, yes, sir. You see the boys was left alone, and they wanted to begin for themselves; and they wanted a home like, and so Charles proposed to me to find all we wanted to use in the family, and for me to take care of them. And a blessed thing it 's been for me, for it makes my poor home so pleasant; it seems like living, now. And then, all my little airnens, now, I can lay up. Why, sir, only to think the last season we counted it up one evening, and what do you think it come to? Twenty-five dollars, clear money, and I 've been making ever since."

The captain could not but meditate a little about the sum, which the old lady thought of such magnitude. How far would twenty-five dollars go in his hands!

"I suppose you have but little company."

"Well, not a great deal, sir; and yet there aint but few evenings when Charles is home, that there aint some one in, sometimes to tea, sometimes just to spend the evening. You see, sir, he is much set by, in this place, both by rich and poor. There 's Parson Jamieson, the Episcopal minister, a lovely man as ever breathed the breath of life, he seems to look upon him as a brother; and then there 's Parson Somers, the Presbyterian minister, he thinks a world of Charles; and then there 's Colonel Johnson, who lives in that large, old-fashioned, nice house, you see on the road, just afore you get here, the old colonel clean doats upon him; and Miss Lucy, his daughter, she is one of the finest young ladies in the place, and she treats him as if he was a brothe.ı. But it 's no wonder they love him. And Parson Somers telled me the other day, that he could go ahead of most of the ministers in the Bible; and it 's no wonder, for he is never idle.

The moment he comes in from his work, off he 'll go and change his dress, and fix himself up nice, and sits right down, looking like any gentleman, and it 's write and read, write and read, all the time. He has got a head full, you may depend on it."

How long the old lady might have gone on, there is no telling, for it was a theme she never got tired of; but the entrance of the young men cautioned her that it was time to stop.

Captain Halliday listened to her with deep attention; he was much interested in her description, and was no doubt moralizing upon it, but a thought just then came into his mind in reference to the lady herself.

"I think Mr. Lovell told me, madam, that your husband died at sea."

"He did so, sir; he died on the voyage to China."

"In what year?"

"Well, it was 18—; he was n't well when he left home, but he said he thought the sea air would revive him, but he did n't get no better."

"Do you remember the name of the ship?"

"It was the Huntress, sir; but the captain's name I can't so well remember; it was Halli something; but it seemed to me it sounded very much like yours, sir; it came into my mind when Charles mentioned your name, sir, that it was like the captain of that ship."

"You are right, madam; your husband's name was John?"

"Oh yes, sir, John Casey."

"The same, madam; the very same; I was the captain of that ship, and well remember the death of your husband."

"Oh dear, sir; can you tell me anything about him? how did he die?"

And the tears began to steal down the old lady's cheek, while Charles and Augustus drew near to the speakers, in their interest for her.

"He died, madam, as I wish I might die, when my turn comes, though I fear I am not making the preparation I ought; I 've got so many things to plague my soul with, about this world's affairs, that I have no chance hardly to think of the next. But I will tell you all about it, madam; John had not been well for some time before we got into the latitude of the Cape, and as we began to feel the chilly winds, as we ran south to double the Cape of Good Hope, he had to take to his berth. I saw he was n't fit for duty, and so made him keep below, and we did what we could for him to make him comfortable, but as we had a stormy time of it, and most of us for days together had to be on deck, John would have fared badly, if it had n't been for a good friend he found in a young Roman Catholic Priest."

Poor Aunt Casey lifted up her hands and eyes, as though horror-stricken.

"Don't be alarmed, my good madam, don't be alarmed; I used to feel towards those fellows as you doubtless do. I am no Catholic, and aint like to be, and I 've seen a good deal of their hocus-pocus work, and I don't fancy them. But this young man, Catholic or no Catholic, was what I call a good Christian man. He kept very much by himself; was civil to every one, and in no way disposed to obtrude his opinions upon any one.

"Sometimes I saw him talking to John; he noticed him probably because he saw that he looked so pale and miserable. But as soon as John took to his berth, down he went, and there you might see him, sometimes talking to him; sometimes giving him some nice thing, which he had got the cook to fix for him; or giving him his medicine, or something or other. I felt afraid, sometimes, lest he might be filling the poor fellow's head full of nonsense, but I did n't like to say anything, because I saw he knew how to take care of a sick person better than any of us; so I let it run on until one day he comes to me, and says he:

"'Poor John is near his end, I believe.'

"So down I went; the sailors seldom have much religion to spare, and I have often felt a very sad heart, I assure you, because when standing by the dying bed of some of my men I had n't a word to say to the poor fellows, that might direct them on their long and unknown journey. But somehow I felt as if I must say something to John; I feared he had been made to believe that the Virgin, or some saint or other, would take charge of him, and see him safe to Heaven; now I knew that all of them together would be of no more use at such a time, than an umbrella in a Typhoon. So I was determined to find out what the poor fellow thought about the matter. 'Well,' said I 'John, you seem to be drawing near to port.'

"'I am, sir; I am near my end, captain; and I thank you for all your kindness to me.'

"'That's neither here nor there, John,' said I; 'you was faithful at your post, when you was well, and it's no more than my duty to see that you are as well provided for, as circumstances will permit. A ship's steerage is a poor place to be sick in, anyhow; but John,' said I, 'how is it with you about other matters; you are not long for this world you know.'

"'I am not, sir; but I have no fears on that account.'

"'But you know, John,' said I, 'we sailors don't generally keep so good a look-out for the next world, as we do for the shoals and breakers of the port we are nearing.'

"'I know it, sir, it's too true; but I lay my trust in one that is mighty to save."

The captain's voice now trembled so as scarcely to enable him to get out the sentence.

"'Whom do you mean, John?' said I.

"'I mean,' he said, with his eyes bright and gazing full upon me, 'I mean the Lord Jesus Christ, the Saviour of sinners. I have been a poor sinner, but he came to save sinners, and he has said, "Whosoever cometh to me I will in nowise cast out," and I have gone to Him, and my soul is full of peace.'"

Aunt Casey could restrain herself no longer, but, leaning back in her chair, burst out into a flood of tears, while each one present, not excepting the old captain, silently joined with her. As soon as the violence of her feelings had somewhat subsided, she gave vent in words to her feelings of gratitude.

"The Lord be praised for his mercies to my poor husband. Bless the Lord, oh my soul."

"I say amen for you, madam, with all my heart."

"But how did it come about, sir? who instructed him? how did he learn such precious truths?"

"You shall hear, madam. I have told you that my suspicions had been excited lest the young priest had put wrong notions in his head, but when I heard him express his firm trust in one—" the captain's voice again faltered, "I felt a load from my mind. 'John,' said I, 'I am glad to hear you speak so. I was afraid that the young man who has been so kind to you, might have been putting some wrong notions in your head, teaching you to put your trust in some saint or other. You know he is a Roman Catholic.'

"'I don't know, sir,' said John, 'what persuasion he holds to. I never asked him. Only I know that he has been a good friend to one that was a stranger to him, and that he has said precious prayers for me, and has tried to make me feel that if I would confess all my sins, and believe on the Lord Jesus Christ, I should be saved; and do you think that was wrong?'

"'No, John,' said I, 'and may God bless him for it.' So you see, madam, your husband was enabled to die in peace through the kind offices of a Roman Catholic."

"May the Lord bless him, wherever he is on the face of the earth."

"I say amen to that too, madam. And now, Mr. Lovell, what do you say for a start toward home?"

"The horse is ready, sir, when you say the word."

"Well, madam," rising and taking the old lady by the hand, "I came to see you out of curiosity, and I have been highly gratified with my visit. I see that happiness and good order, and all the decencies of life, can be enjoyed under a very humble roof, and that it would be a great deal better for us all to think less of show and more of such things as really contribute to our happiness. Good-bye, madam; this is not the last time, I hope, that I shall see you."

"Oh I hope not, sir; you have told me that, sir, which has made me almost too happy. I aint got anything now to ask for more."

CHAPTER XI.

As the letter which Margaret Simmons had placed in the hands of Charles Lovell will now be of use in the progress of our story, it may as well, perhaps, be given to the reader, without further comment.

"Mr. Charles Lovell:

"As I have ever had a sincere respect for you, since we were children together, and as I know you are now much thought of and respected by most people, and as you have not, like many others since I have grown up, passed me by unnoticed, because fallen into poverty, and especially since, in an hour of heart-breaking agony, you acted such a kind and generous part, I cannot bear the thought of leaving the world without letting you know the cause of that suffering, nor can I bear the thought that *you* should think of me, even after I am dead, worse than I deserve. I have been vain, I know, and light, and fond of such things as our circumstances could not afford; I have had a fondness for the gayer things of life; I wanted to break away from my poor condition and take a stand with those who live in the higher walks of life. Oh, I have had foolish, foolish thoughts about such things. But they have gone now, the bubble has burst, my folly has come upon me, bitterly do I suffer, and hope is gone.

"A young man, among others that frequented our lone house for the purpose of fishing, took particular pains to be agreeable. I heard accidentally that he was very rich. He was not attractive in his appearance, but he dressed finely, and seemed to have money to squander; he was at first very kind to me; I had no adviser; my poor mother, you know, she had no suspicions. I associated with him. He seemed honest and honorable, and offered to marry me, only wished that it might be secretly done, as his father, who was a very old and queer man, might disinherit him, if he knew he had married a poor girl; he could not live long, he said, as he was then far gone with a cancer, and as soon as he was dead I should be taken to the city and live in style. Ah, how could I think a *man* could want to deceive one whom he seemed to love, and who was alone and unprotected, as he knew me to be. I had some fears, but in an evil hour I yielded to his views and accompanied him to one he said was a clergyman, in another State, and was married. I took no certificate, I had no witnesses. For some time all seemed to be well, although my fears began to arise. All at once the whole truth was told me, and by whom! by him in whom I had trusted. On that sad evening, when in my misery you found me, he revealed to me the terrible fact that our marriage was only a counterfeit, that the ceremony was performed by a companion of his own who for the time assumed the character of a clergyman, and who had left the country to be gone many years. In my misery I pleaded with him, but he merely offered me a purse of gold. The rest you know. I shall soon be in eternity, and would not add to my guilt by telling you an untruth. I have reason to think that he never gave me his right name, from the fact that I find on this ring, which he took one evening from his finger and put upon mine, that it has the initials of quite another name engraven on the inside. I commit it to you. I wish no revenge; but oh, if you should ever meet him and find some other as foolish as myself in danger from him, alarm her in season, save her as you would from the fangs of a deadly serpent. May God bless you for your kindness to a poor, unhappy, lost girl.

"MARGARET SIMMONS."

Margaret Simmons was dead, but Charles believed he had indeed met with the wretch, who was to all intents her murderer. He could not tell why, but he had always in his own mind associated the muffled horsemen, whom he had occasionally seen pass his cottage, with the one whom he saw ill-treat that poor girl; and also, with the man who was sheltered under his roof, and the attendant upon those lovely females during that summer storm. He had, as we have seen, again met him; he has heard his name—has been introduced, and is at times an occupant of the same habitation. The ring Charles still retained, and the initial letters engraved on its interior were V. D. H. He had, as opportunity offered, examined the gentleman's hand; it had never labored, was delicate as many a lady's. Why Mr. Vanderbose should treat him with such marked incivility he could not imagine, unless suspicious that the eye of Lovell had been upon him in his secret visits to the region where he lived. But for his incivility, Charles cared not. The injunction of the wretched Margaret bore upon his mind. He feared not, indeed, that the miserable coward would dare venture to trifle with one situated as this young lady was; but how could he bear the thought that virtue and loveliness should be in the power of such an one, although shielded by all the defence and protection of the most sure marriage.

Charles had probably never read the instructive history of the hero of La Mancha. Nor had he experience enough of worldly matters to have learned the lesson—that there are a great many evils which cannot very well be righted here. He felt sure that one of those bright and sunny beings who flitted about in his presence, as emblems of innocence and love, was in danger of throwing away her young and happy life by connection with a man without virtue, without honor, without even the common feelings of humanity, and his spirit was troubled within him, and he resolved to do what he could to prevent it.

A few days after the visit recorded in the last chapter, Captain Halliday requested him to take a walk to his barns, and see some of his fine stock. It was late in the afternoon, just after his return from school, and the last day that Charles expected to remain at the house where he had been treated so kindly.

"I know that you are a good judge of horseflesh, Mr. Lovell. I want to see if you know anything about cows. You know, I suppose, that I have a fine stock of foreign cattle?"

"I have heard you had, sir; I should very much like to look at them."

"Come along then. I take some pleasure in showing them, and that is pretty much all the good they have done me as yet."

"Are they not profitable, sir, as milkers? I have heard great stories of the quantity of milk and butter such creatures yield."

"Well, it 's pretty much like the rest of the story I 've told you about my farm; everything seems to end like the battle between the Kilkenny cats—there is nothing left worth mentioning. The cows, you see, in the first place, cost a thundering sight of money. I dare not tell you how much, for fear you will think me a greater fool than I really am. Well, since I gave so much for them, why of course they must have extra care taken of them, and so I have hired an Englishman who professes to know all about such matters. I give him fifteen dollars a month, and ground enough to raise what he wants for his own family, and to pasture a cow; one hundred and eighty dollars a year, money out of pocket, besides other things."

"I suppose, sir, you sell milk and butter enough to ballance that?"

"Sell milk and butter! Why, Mr. Lovell, I have bought more than half my butter since I have been here."

As they were walking together, Charles turned towards the captain a look of great astonishment.

"You may well look astonished, my young friend, for it 's been a matter of great wonderment to me; and sometimes —but it does no good, I know—but I can 't help it; it makes me swear. People say to me, 'Captain Halliday, how independent you must live; your own milk, and butter, and all that.' But, sir, I tell you how it is; you see they have calves; well, if it was common stock, why they would be fatted in a short time, and then go off to the butcher, and we should have the milk. But these calves are too pretty to sell; all 'ring-streaked, speckled and spotted;' that fellow will say to me, 'Captain Halliday, you would n't think of parting with that calf; it 's a picture of a creature,' and then go on with a long lingo, showing me its fine points, and all that; and so, fool-like, I let him have his way. And then the calf is so fine, that he must have the best of keeping—all the cow's milk, and more too, if he can drink it."

"But I suppose you sell them sometimes, sir, after they are somewhat grown; such stock bring high prices in our country."

"There, too, is another tail to the end of that kite. Whenever I talk of selling some of the larger creatures, they all join in a cry against it. Why, Captain Halliday! if you sell your stock what will become of the farm—it will all run out; the more stock a man can keep the better for the farm. So you see, sir, how it is—the hay, and corn, and oats can't be sold, because the cattle want them, and the cattle can't be sold, because the farm will go to ruin without *them;* and what the ——, Mr. Lovell, I don't like to say bad words before you—but what under heaven is to be left for me? Don't you see, sir, nothing but to pay the clown's wages, stuff their bellies, and provide for my family as I can."

They had stopped by the bars, and the captain was standing, with one hand hold of the post, and with the other making such significant gestures as the excitement of the occasion demanded, for he had worked himself up, as he always did, when upon this subject.

"And that aint all, Mr. Lovell. I like hospitality, sir—I like to receive it abroad, and I like to exercise it at home. But, sir, I tell you," he spoke now in a whisper; "between you and me, and this post, this entertaining of folks, who come and throw themselves upon you, as if you was common property—folks, too, that have no more claim than mere passing acquaintance, who would n't put their hands in their pocket for a York sixpence to save me from limbo, and who seem to feel that they lay me under obligations by praising my fine situation, and all that; I tell you, sir, it aint the thing—I 'm tired of it. But come, let 's get over the bars, and see the stock."

Charles was too much of a farmer not to be able to appreciate the beautiful creatures, and soon showed that he was no novice, by at once pointing out here and there an animal that exhibited the right marks. One especially he singled out as the most perfect of its kind, and was very warm in his praises.

"Aha! I see, sir," said the dairyman; "the young man is no fool about the matter—he 's picked out Daisy among the whole herd. Ah, sir, she 's a picture—what delicate horns, and such a slim neck, and look along her back, Captain Halliday, as straight as an arrow, and so broad across the hips; and what a fine yellow bag, and the teats large and well set; and her legs, sir—did you ever see straighter limbs on a race horse? Ah, sir, she 's a beauty—I 've often told you."

The captain had indeed heard the story often before—he knew it pretty well by heart.

"And how much milk do you say she gives, Mr. Bronson?"

"Milk, sir! oh, there 's no telling how much, but there 's a power of it, sir; you see, sir, I lets the calf take as much as he wants, and then I milks her, and feeds the two other calves; so you see with that, sir—so that with the help of a little oil cake, the other two are as sleek as any mole, sir, you ever see."

"Show us the calf, Bronson; where is it? I want Mr. Lovell to see her calf."

"That I will, sir; and if he or any other man ever saw a finer, then my name aint Bronson McGaw, that 's all."

And so Mr. Bronson McGaw sprang into the stable, and in a moment more out he jumped again, with the calf behind his heels, jumping and kicking, and in high glee, with the sight of its dam.

"I never saw a more beautiful creature, sir—spotted, too, exactly like its mother. How old is it, sir?"

"That is more than I know—old enough to kill, and fat enough too, I should think."

"Aha, Captain Halliday, you would n't think of such a thing, to sell Daisy's calf, and a heifer too—it would be like cutting your own throat, sir, indeed it would."

"Such a calf as that, sir, with the fine qualities of the mother, should not be killed, sir. I agree with Mr. Bronson there."

"You fancy it then, do you?" said the captain, eyeing Charles with a slight smile playing at the corners of his mouth.

"I do indeed think, sir, that I never saw its equal; and how old did you say it was?" turning to Mr. McGaw.

"Just six weeks and a day old, sir."

"It is very large, indeed, for one of that age; I should not have been surprised if you had said three months, instead of six weeks."

"Mr. Lovell, step round here, will you?" Charles followed the captain to some little distance, while the man let the calf get at its mother, still holding the end of the rope in his hand, and muttering to himself something about the wickedness of slaying a creature of the like of that. When the captain had got far enough to be out of hearing, he turned to Charles.

"Mr. Lovell, it aint often that I have met with a man, young or old, that I have taken the fancy to that I have to you; nor one from whom I have learned so many things, that might have been profitable to me, and may yet be. But that aint to the purpose. That calf, I agree with you, is too good to kill. If I should try to sell him, ten chances to one they would n't give me one quarter what it is worth. Now, if you will accept of it, as a present from a friend," taking the hand of Charles, and giving it a hearty grasp, "you shall have it."

Charles was utterly confounded. It was, indeed, in his circumstances, a most valuable gift; but he felt a great delicacy in accepting it, lest it should be like taking advantage of a noble heart.

"Captain Halliday, I thank you most heartily for the kind feelings you are pleased to express towards me. You have treated me with unexpected attention since I have been with you, and both yourself and family have laid me under obligations that I cannot well express. From our relative positions, I had no right to expect anything beyond mere civility. I have received nothing but courtesy and kindness." Charles blushed deeply, for he was much excited.

"I understand, sir, what you mean by our 'relative positions in society.' I have seen too much of the world to be affected by such matters. Your conduct, while with us, has been that of a gentleman, and your manliness in upholding your own calling, although one that demands hearty toil, has won my sincere respect; and I am glad of this opportunity to acknowledge it. The trifling gift I offer is merely that you may have some memento of one who values your friendship."

"I cannot, under such circumstances, refuse to take what would be to me of great value; but I hope, sir, the friendship which you have been pleased to offer me will not need such a token of remembrance."

"I hope not, sir; but the creature is yours, and I will send my man with it any day that you say. Young Daisy will be in good hands. Ah, that old woman! Some may look down upon her, but I tell you, young man, she has a warm heart; and I hope you will stick to her, so long as she has a pulse to beat."

"Never fear that, sir; I should as soon think now of deserting a parent."

"I believe you. But don't you say a word to that Englishman what kind of a bargain we have made for that calf; if he thought it was going for nothing, as he would call it, he would be almost tempted to poison it. And now, come, let 's home again; and when you get through with the ladies to-night, just give me a call in my room."

Charles was very glad of the invitation, as he had made up his mind to reveal some things which he knew, and which he rightly thought, concerned the future happiness of one, at least, of those in whom the good-hearted old gentleman was deeply interested. How he should introduce the subject, or what he might or ought to say, were matters which he left as occasion might demand, or an opportunity offer.

It was some time, however, before any such opportunity offered, until at length the captain happened to ask him if he had ever seen the new house on Roder's Point.

"Only at a distance, sir?"

"Well, it 's a costly building, and a fine view from it, although not just to my mind. I hope, however, the poor thing will be happy in it."

"Then it is decided, is it, Captain Halliday, that Miss Julia is to be married to Mr. Vanderbose?"

"Pretty much so, I suppose."

"Do you know him, sir? that is, have you been long acquainted with him?"

"Bless your heart, I don't know much about him. All I know is this, if he don't treat her handsomely, like a gentleman and a husband should, I 'll wring his neck; I 'll wring any man's neck who should treat either of those dear girls ill. You see, Mr. Lovell, they are both my nieces; one of them, Julia, is the niece of my wife, and the other is my own sister's daughter; but that make no difference to me. My wife and I are one, and her relations are my relations. I don't know any difference, and never mean to. I love them both alike, and they both love me, and I should like to see the man living that should dare to treat them otherwise than kindly."

"There would be little danger, sir, that any man who deserves the name could do otherwise. But, sir, ladies with the fine feelings which your nieces seem to possess, and who have been nourished so affectionately, may suffer untold agony from one to whom they might be united, who had no heart to give them in return."

"That is very true; but men don't carry hearts now a-days; and if girls are willing to take them without, how is it to be helped?"

As Charles could not say, he was obliged to be silent; it was a phase of the case he had not thought of.

"You see, Mr. Lovell, I'll tell you how it is; when these two girls came under my care, they were little bits of things, and I took them and did by them just as if they were my own, and always meant to. Well, they grew up, and between you and me, not very bad looking; spry, lively, good, honest-hearted, handsome girls. Well, as they began to go out into the world, and folks began to crowd round them, and it was seen that they were going to be something more than common, Aunt Nabby—you have heard them speak of her?"

"I have not, sir."

"Well, I must tell you then; they have got an Aunt Nabby; she is my sister, and that's all; I can't say that we are much alike; we never hitch horses together, at any rate. But you see, she is rich; she is her own boss—a widow; she lives in the city, keeps her carriage, liveried servants, and all that, and is just as fond of making a show as ever a peacock was of spreading his fine feathers out to the sun. Well, it struck Aunt Nabby that it would be a fine thing for her to have the girls in her big house, to fill it up a little, and bring company to it; and a fine thing for them to have such a chance as she could give them, to introduce them among what she calls the first company; and, to make a long story short, in fine, she was to make them her heirs. So you see, they are heiresses to a pretty considerable estate, that is, if they ever get it; and here's the rub, they have got to do as she says—you understand?"

Mr. Lovell assented that he did.

"Now, my sister thinks that money is the first and the

last of all earthly good, and an angel from heaven would be nothing to her if he had no bonds and mortgages, or stocks, or houses and lots in the city; he 'd stand no chance at all; he would n't have even a hearing. I 'm afraid this segar smoke troubles you—you look pale, I 'll throw it away."

"By no means, sir; it is not at all offensive."

"Well, now you know well enough, or I hope you do, that I am not just of a mind with Aunt Nabby about this. But what was I to do? I must either say no—they shall never be under her influence, and be taught that money is the God to be worshipped, and so cut off all expectations for them from her—or I must give in, and let her do by them as she has promised, and let them take their chance. You see, my young friend, I have told you a little how *confusedly* things have gone with me up here, and I don't see but I must pull up stakes, and off to sea again; now in that case, you see, it would be better they should be in the good graces of one who can do well by them, and she does the thing that 's handsome; you see, she is proud of them, and well she may be. But I must say she does well by them."

It was some time before Charles could find anything to say in reply; the revelation made to him had shut up all his ideas, and brought a sort of faintness over his heart. In a little while, the captain having lighted another segar, after being again assured by Charles that it was not disagreeable to him, resumed the subject.

"You asked me, Mr. Lovell, if I knew this Vanderbose; I knew his old father, a little chunky German—he used to keep a corner grocery. I 've seen him many a time behind the counter, with his tow apron on, dealing out liquor to the darkies, that used to sit in gangs around his door. How he made so much money is a mystery to me. But he is done selling drams now, and has gone where he could n't take his money with him, and this son of his is the only heir.

"I don't know so much about him as I could wish. He is one of Aunt Nabby's 'respectable society,' as she calls the circle she gathers about her, and the match I suppose is pretty much of her making.

"And that chum of his is another—the chap with the red hair. They say he is fishing for Addy. I let them alone—let them work it as they think best. If girls will have money, and choose to take men without brains, or hearts either, they must do so; all I do is to say to them, 'don't you marry by the persuasion of man or woman—make up your own minds, and when you want your old uncle's advice, or his care or protection, you shall have it while I can stand on my legs, or raise my arm.'"

Charles felt that to volunteer advice, under such circumstance, would be worse than idle; and his first attempt to right some of the wrongs of life has only resulted in blasting the fond hopes he had been cherishing, and scattering into confusion some of the beautiful fancies which he has often and long indulged.

CHAPTER XII.

The wall of partition which had been so happily broken down between the two pastors at Milton, was to both a matter of continued thankfulness. A pleasant interchange of visits at each other's study was weekly enjoyed by them, and generally on the day immediately succeeding the Sabbath. They could there compare the subjects which each mind had been led to dwell upon, and their trains of thought. They could ask counsel one of another, and sympathize in difficulties each had to encounter, and by converse on their duties, and trials, and encouragements, and glorious hopes, strengthen each other for the work to which each was assigned in the vineyard of their Master.

"But I have been thinking," said Mr. Jamieson to his elder brother on one of these occasions, "since I find so much advantage in the enjoyment of your long experience in the ministry, whether we might not embrace in our circle the young man who labors in our vicinity among the Methodists. Do you know him, brother Somers?"

"I must confess with shame, that I do not. I cannot say that I have ever seen him. There is a good deal of prejudice in the minds of my people against that persuasion, and from what I occasionally hear, I suppose the same evil exists among them; they are prejudiced against us."

"Such things ought not so to be; and yet, constituted as we all are, we must expect this hinderance to the power of the gospel. What a pity we can't exercise our belief, and pursue our great work, in the spirit of an enlarged charity for others, who differ on some non-essential points."

"It is indeed to be lamented. And so far as in us lies, we should each of us, each Christian minister and Christian man, free himself from all such feelings as would hinder the full flow of heavenly charity. You asked me if I was acquainted with Mr. Foster—his name is Foster, is it not?"

"It is, sir."

"I have never seen him, to my knowledge; but I cannot say that I have not heard of him; for he is engaged to be married to a very lovely young lady, who is often at my house; and if he is worthy of her, and at all fit to be her companion, he must be a man of some excellence."

"What do you think, brother Somers, of making him a call; perhaps he may take it kindly?"

"With all my heart; it certainly can do no harm, and who knows what may come out of it. Do you know where he lives?"

"I believe I do, sir, and if agreeable to you will appoint to-morrow morning for the visit."

"I will be ready."

As the distance to the dwelling of Mr. Foster was rather too far a walk from the house of Mr. Somers, Mr. Jamieson had procured a conveyance, and was on his way to the latter, when his eye was attraced by a traveller on foot, walking in the path by the fence, and going in the direction of his own place of residence. As it might be one of his own people about to call on him, he slackened his pace, and as they drew near, so that he could recognize the countenance, turned his horse's head towards the fence, drove up to the foot-path and jumped out.

"Brother Foster, how do you do this morning? I am glad that we have met, for I was just on my way to your house."

The person addressed was a young man, a few years the junior of Mr. Jamieson. He was of rather a delicate frame, his countenance agreeable, though somewhat pale, and with an eye of peculiar softness, giving an impression of deep and tender feeling.

He was evidently much surprised at the salutation, for his cheek flushed, and he put out his hand and received the cordial grasp, and returned it as heartily, without speaking, until Mr. Jamieson had again said that he was about to call upon him.

"I am very happy then, sir, to have met you, for I was on my way to see you. I was wishing to thank you, Mr. Jamieson, for your attention to that afflicted family during my absence."

"You mean where the young woman died? I felt delicate at first about going in to see them, as they did not belong to my charge particularly, but being in the neighborhood, and hearing that you were away, and that the young woman was very low, I ventured to call."

"And you were enabled to afford great consolation, not only to the dying one, but to all the family; and I felt that I could not do less than call upon you, and acknowledge your kindness, although I have never had the pleasure of an introduction."

"I believe we shall not need that formality now; and as I am on my way to the house of Mr. Somers, who was to accompany me in my visit to you, will you not jump in with me and ride there?"

As the young man hesitated, Mr. Jamieson resumed:

"If you have an engagement that demands attention, I will not urge you, and we can all meet at some other time."

"I have no engagement that need prevent; nor is it because it would not be most grateful to my feelings; but you know, Mr. Jamieson, that Mr. Somers is a much older man than myself; he has been long the established minister in this region; he stands very high in the community, and—and—perhaps does not feel friendly to our persuasion, and—"

"Stop, brother Foster, stop, and just let me say to you, dismiss all such ideas at once. Mr. Somers stands high, I know, and deservedly so; he has commanding talents, and a strong hold of the respect and affection of the community. But he has a noble spirit, above all sectarian prejudice; or, if he has been influenced by it, is ready to break the fetters, and embrace every true-hearted minister or Christian, with affection. I will guarantee you a cordial reception."

Without further hesitancy, Mr. Foster entered the carriage, and in a short time both gentlemen were seated in the pleasant study of Mr. Somers, and admiring the order in which everything was arranged, and the valuable collection of works that extended over the entire surface of two sides of the room.

The reverend gentleman soon made his appearance, and as he entered both of the young men arose.

"I have the pleasure of introducing to you our brother, whom we had designed to call upon this morning. Brother Foster, Mr. Somers."

Mr. Somers took the hand of the young man, and for a moment was silent; he was evidently much affected.

"This is the Lord's doing, and it is marvellous in our eyes. Brother, you will pardon me that I have suffered you so long to be laboring near me, and have taken no more pains to become acquainted with you, and to sustain you in your work."

"And I take this opportunity, also, brother Foster," said Mr. Jamieson "to acknowledge my deficiencies in this respect; but, I assure you, it has not been from any feeling of opposition; but rather from a suspicion that you cared not for the fellowship of one of my persuasion."

As Mr. Foster replied, a tear fell upon his pale cheek, and his words came forth in trembling accents.

"And I, brethren, have also pardon to ask of each of you, for the same cause and for the same reason which Mr. Jamieson has just mentioned. I have kept away from you; I have indulged wrong suspicions; I am young; I am poor; I am obliged to labor hard some days in the week in order to gain my daily bread; and I felt—I know now it was wrong—but I felt that you—that you—"

"Looked down upon you? Not just so, brother Foster, not just so, I do assure you, and I can speak for brother Jamieson also: we have not looked down upon you; and especially could we not do so on account of your poverty, for we are ourselves not over-burdened with this world's goods."

"Perhaps not, brethren; I know that very few of those who preach the gospel, of any denomination, have much to spare from their yearly allowance. But when I say that I am poor, it is a poverty that can be felt. You, probably, have no idea how small a stipend I receive; only one hundred dollars."

"One hundred dollars a year!!!" exclaimed both the listeners at once.

"That is all, brethren."

"And how, my dear brother, can you sustain yourself? how can you clothe yourself? how can you provide yourself with the books which are almost a necessary of life?"

st want, Mr. Somers, I have suffered from most

keenly; for, although I pretend to no great scholarship, yet my mind has a longing for more intellectual food than I have ever yet been able to supply it with, and especially for that knowledge which would enable me better to fulfil my ministry. And I must confess to you, that as I have passed your house occasionally, my eye has turned towards this pleasant study, and the books which line these walls; and I fear I have indulged, on such occasions, too much of a feeling allied to envy, for I contrasted it with my own narrow closet, and my few old volumes."

"Perhaps, my dear young brother, that closet you speak of can testify to more ardent prayers, and richer communings with your Saviour, than my better room. But one thing you must promise me, that you will come to my house, and make free use of whatever my library affords. Let us be no longer strangers to each other's wants. But how is it that you can live on your salary? You surely have no one but yourself to support?"

"I have an aged mother dependent on me. The salary I receive is deemed by our society sufficient for a single man; and whatever it may fall short of supplying, must be made up in some way by my own exertions, either by labor in the shop, or field, or in teaching school. My health has not allowed of the confinement of the latter employment, and I have therefore resorted to labor in the field. But I often think it would be much better for my hearers, as well as pleasanter for myself, if it could be otherwise. Perhaps, though, the toil is needed, and the self-denial I am obliged to practice, a wholesome discipline."

"Well, well, I find I am not too old to learn, and I hope I am not too old to profit. But let us understand one another for the future. We are ministers of Christ, thrown together, by the providence of God, in a part of his vineyard. Some of our views on some points differ. Now, we want to have an understanding together as to some essential points, on which we can heartily agree. And as Brother Jamieson and I were about to call upon you this morning, I have thought the matter over to see if there was not a basis on which we three could stand together, and go hand in hand to the work."

"I have no doubt there is," said Mr. Foster; "and I should

be very glad, for one, to have you, sir, make out such a platform."

"And so should I," responded Mr. Jamieson.

"Well, brethren, here it is; the creed is a very short one:

"1. That we are all lost sinners; and that our only hope for salvation is in and through the blood and merits of our Lord and Saviour Jesus Christ.

"2. That our union to Him can only be accomplished by repentance for our sins, and faith in his atoning blood. And that these must be wrought in us by the power of the Holy Spirit.

"Can you subscribe to these, brethren?"

"With all our heart," replied each of the young men.

"Then, here let us stand, brethren. It is a glorious platform, based on an everlasting rock."

"Glory to God," shouted out the young Methodist. His heart was overflowing, and he had thus been accustomed to let out his feelings.

"Amen," said Mr. Jamieson, his eye sparkling with unusual emotion.

"On this platform, brethren, we can labor shoulder to shoulder. We will try to win souls to the Saviour. We will cherish a spirit of love among all our people. We will show to the world, that although we may have different opinions about forms of worship, and forms of government, and even about some of the doctrines of our faith, yet upon those which are essential to us as Christians, we are agreed, heart and soul."

"Amen—Glory to God," again burst from the lips of the excited youth.

"And so say I, too, my dear brother, Glory to God;" and the good old man sat down, overcome by the strong emotions of his heart, and covered his face.

For some time each sat in silence pondering on the happy relation which had now been established between them. At length Mr. Somers again opened the conversation, by proposing a plan for action that might have a tendency to create harmony and kind feeling, and a Christian sympathy between their different denominations, without interfering with the particular and stated duties of each pastor, in his appointed place.

"My proposition, brethren, is this: that at some central point we hold a union meeting once a month, and invite our several congregations to attend. What think you of it?"

"Good, good," was the ready response of both the young men.

"The most central spot which I can now think of, is the large room lately fitted up for public meetings, of a secular kind—perhaps that fact may prove objectionable to you, brother Jamieson?"

Mr. Jamieson reflected a moment.

"Perhaps, brother, I differ from you in my views of the sacredness of the place consecrated to religious worship. I should be very unwilling to see the house which has been set apart most solemnly for the express purpose of worship, made use of for anything that was not strictly such. But I can see no reason why we may not make use of any place, not notoriously desecrated by improper uses, to proclaim the gospel, or for prayer. Our Saviour gathered the multitudes around him in the market places, and Paul preached in the Areopagus, and in the Roman theatre. I can see no reason why we should be afraid to gather our people in a room, which as yet has only been used for civil and proper purposes."

"If you are agreed, then, we will give notices from our pulpits the next Lord's day, that a union meeting will be held in the new Town Hall, a fortnight from this evening. It may not succeed; many may be startled by the announcement, and some offended. But I cannot but hope good will come of it."

Both the young ministers acquiesced in the arrangement, and with kindly greetings left the study of Mr. Somers for their respective homes.

As Mr. Somers had anticipated, the notice from his pulpit produced much excitement for a few days; but as they knew that their pastor was not easily to be turned aside, and as Deacon Rice, the most influential among them, was very still about the matter, all was hushed up, and most of the people soon became anxious for the evening to come, that they might see how the thing would work.

In Mr. Jamieson's church things assumed a serious aspect; many old ladies were much alarmed, and disgusted, and so busy were they in stirring up a breeze, that it was thought prudent to send two of their leading men to speak with the reverend gentleman on the subject, and see what could be done to stop the proceedings.

The two gentlemen selected were our friends, old Col. Johnson and Esquire Jones.

The colonel we know pretty well, and will need no introduction; Esquire Jones was a well-meaning man—not very fond of argument, and generally ready, if the thing was n't too bad, to let the point go rather than be obliged to talk too much about it.

Mr. Jamieson received the gentlemen with all that kindness of manner which was so habitual to him.

"Esquire Jones and myself have called upon you, this morning, sir, to talk over matters and things concerning our church.

"It seems that some of our good people have been much stirred up about the—the notice you gave out on the last Sabbath. I hear that some feel afraid that you are breaking the rules of our church, and others that you are turning Methodist or Presbyterian, or something or other of that kind; and they say that you even pray sometimes without a book, and are about to do away with the necessity of a consecrated church, by countenancing religious worship in places where such things ought not to be.

"Now, sir, I tell you what they say, and we are ready to hear your story on the other side."

The colonel had assumed a very serious air, and looked steadily at Mr. Jamieson all the time he was speaking, while Esquire Jones sat twisting his thumbs together, and looking at the colonel.

Mr. Jamieson, in a very ready manner, opened the whole matter before them, by giving an account of his proceedings hitherto, and of the commencement and design of the present plan. The colonel listened very attentively, turning his eye occasionally towards Esquire Jones, who, at such times, looked towards him, and by winking significantly, manifested that he comprehended the thing.

The colonel waited until Mr. Jamieson had made a full explanation, before he attempted a reply.

"Then it seems, sir, that all you design, and those connected with you, is merely to get us together in a kind of Christian manner, just by way of getting us a little used to one another's ways before we get to heaven; and to try to get up a little of that sort of feeling which we have every reason to believe will be most current there. Not a bad idea, it strikes me, sir—not a bad idea. What do you think, squire?"

"I think so too."

"It has always seemed to me, squire, and you, reverend sir, rather a puzzler how we are all going to get along when we come to be thrust, Episcopalians, Presbyterians, Baptists, Methodists, Quakers, and what not, all together in that blessed world, where there is to be no jarring, nor confusion of any kind, and so bitter as some of us are against those that differ from us. I say it 's been a puzzler to me how the thing was to be managed. Now, this seems to me a little like making the right kind of preparation. What do you think, squire?"

"I think so too."

"And we may then tell the good folks, Mr. Jamieson, that you have no designs whatever against our particular creed, or forms, or regulations; and that they need n't be afraid of being taken up and dipped bodily in the water during this cold weather, nor of being knocked down and converted by a Methodist. And as to the prayer-book, and the impropriety of using a place for prayer that was n't consecrated to that purpose, I shall ask them, shall I? if they ever read of Jonah in the whale's belly, and whether he did n't say a prayer in there? and he must have done it without a book. Don't you think so, squire?"

"He must in fact."

"So you see, reverend sir, you can just go on with your plan of trying to get things put a little into something of a Christian shape. And it 's my candid belief, sir, if the thing could be done, and you, and your brother ministers, could just get us all together, if we did n't do anything more than just to shake hands, and say how do you do to one another, it will be a great deal better than to have us all go on as we have, fighting, and scratching, and scolding, and snarling with one another, to the very gate of heaven. We shall have to be civil if we get there, and the great question with me is, and it 's a puzzler too, how we are going to mend our manners so quick ?

" ' As the tree falls so it lies.' What do you say, squire?"

" I should think it would."

" Colonel Johnson, I think you have expressed a great truth, although you have used some hard figures. Charity is to be the grace that will distinguish the children of God, when Faith and Hope shall have accomplished their work. Without it, there can be no heaven for us in the presence of God, for God is love. I fear we have too long forgotten this glorious truth. Without cultivating, and practising the grace here, we can hardly be said to be educating for heaven."

The old colonel arose and grasped the hand of his young minister, and cordially shook it.

" You have got the marrow of the thing now, sir; and have expressed the beautiful idea in more becoming language than I have done, I must confess. I have not long to stay in this world, I know; but I should like, before I die, to see something done by way of breaking down this hateful wall of partition between those who no doubt in heart mean to do right. Go on, sir, go on, and you shall have my most cordial support; and tell your brother ministers, that whatever old colonel Johnson can do to help on with the great object, shall be done with a right good will."

" I shall be most happy to do so."

" Well, Squire Jones, if we have nothing further to say to our minister, we may as well be going."

" Nothing further, sir. I think we had better be going. All very satisfactory."

CHAPTER XIII.

Those who have never made the country their home through all seasons of the year, have often very erroneous ideas concerning its winters. The shivering citizen, muffled in his cloak, and battling with the searching winds that sweep between the high ranks of brick walls, longs to reach his dwelling; and as he bolts the door behind him, and hastens to his parlor fire-side, blesses his stars that he does not live in the naked country, where winds and snows beat around the lone dwelling, and where nought is to be seen abroad but Nature in her most desolate form. Little does he think that what pinches him, and sends him shivering to his corner, but warms the blood and animates the spirit of the sons of storm and sunshine. The bleak wind moaning through the leafless trees—the snow flakes whirling in giddy mazes through the air—the rain pattering on the long, low roof, bring but music to his ear, and beauty to his sight. And even the keen and cutting frost, that clasps with its iron bands the streamlet and the river, makes fairy pictures for him, even from the breath which he expires, and from the dew that steals in silence on the earth and trees.

Who thinks of shrinking from the frosty air, when all abroad is sparkling with the brightness of ten thousand diamonds? or from the driving snow, when the merry bells are jingling, and fair ones are wrapped beneath the ample fur and nestling by your side?

Winter brings no sorrow to the country. No homeless, houseless wretches, shivering in want and misery, and huddled in promiscuous masses, within cold, cheerless dens, can there be found. Few princely mansions rear their proud turrets to proclaim their owner's wealth; but fewer still, the humble cots where plenty does not dwell. There have been days of toil, and strong arms have wielded the heavy axe, and little hands have gathered in the falling chips, and the treasures from the garden and the field have been garnered, and the spinning-wheel has been buzzing, and light fingers have been plying the needle. All have done something against the time of need.

And when the cold blast comes, the fire crackles on the hearth, and the table bears its full supply of homely fare, and the warm garment protects against the frost and the rain; and the winter, with its storm and cold, is shorn of its terrors.

There had been some days of stormy weather at Wellgrove, and the adjoining town, Milton. First, a light, drizzling rain, and, as the night came on, snow began to mingle with the increasing drops, and both together froze where they fell. And then the rain was turned to hail, and it could be heard by those who happened to turn upon their pillows through the night, pattering quietly against the window-pane; and finally, as morning came, the air was filled with the dense snow, silently speeding to the earth, and covering all the barrenness of nature with a white and beautiful robe. And through the day and coming night, the work went on, and farmers rested by their warm firesides, and thought how easy it would be to take their logs to mill, and gather at their sheds the next year's wood. And young men and maidens laughed in the lightness of their hearts, and planned the merry sleigh-rides, or prepared for social visits.

Charles Lovell had spent the time allotted to him at Captain Halliday's, and had taken up his abode elsewhere. He had been pressed by the kind-hearted captain and his lady to remain longer, but had respectfully declined, promising, however, to be a frequent visitor.

Winter had diminished the family circle there; visitors ceased to flock from the city; Miss Julia had gone to spend the season with her Aunt Nabby, in New York, very much to the gratification of her suitor, who could enjoy the dissipation which he loved, and the society of the girl whom he was seeking to marry.

Mr. Sampson lingered but a few days after his friend Vanderbose had left. He either found the country too lonely, or was discouraged at the small progress which he made in winning an interest in the lovely girl he had set his eye upon. She had not refused him, for he had not ventured yet to ask her hand. With all the confidence with which his wealth inspired him, he could not gather resolution enough to make any proposals. He did all he could to persuade her to spend the winter in the city, but in vain. So he departed with no stronger hopes of success than when he came.

Just as the storm had cleared away, and the bright sun shone out upon the clear white snow, and the merry bells were jingling on the teams that had turned out to break the pathways through the village, Charles was handed a letter from the post-office. He opened it with joy, for he knew by the direction that it was from his friend, Mr. Jamieson. An extract from it will suffice to explain its purport.

"You will remember my telling you of an appointment which had been made some time since for a union meeting. It took place, as you know, and was highly successful, and, contrary to our first plan, that it should be held once a month, has been, by the urgent solicitations of those who attended, held weekly. The result you are also in some measure acquainted with. Glorious has been the work which for some time has been going on. But where true love is kindled in the heart, its fruits will be manifest, and the meeting I have named to you, at Mr. Foster's, is so evidently of the right kind that I rejoice in it, as well on that account as for the comfort it may afford that worthy man. Perhaps you do not know that he has been for some time engaged to a lovely girl; but from the straitened circumstances in which he is placed dares not, for the present, think of marriage.

"The plan has been started among our more wealthy folks of the Presbyterian and Episcopal persuasions, to meet at his house and take their offerings with them, and if possible place him a little above-board. I know you will rejoice in such a project, and would wish to be there."

"That I will," said Charles to himself; "I will go and help what I can in such a noble work." And the thought at once occurred to him, "How I should like to ask Miss Adelaide to accompany me. But—" and his heart sank within him, because of all the objections that might be raised by herself or others. But the thing itself was so enchanting; there would be a bright moon; a beautiful snow-path; and such a companion by his side. He almost trembled at the mere anticipation.

The appointment was for the next evening, and whatever arrangements he made must be attended to at once. He sat down to his supper, but he made a very light meal of it, and as soon as he could, left the table. A few additions to his toilet, and he was on his way to the mansion of Captain Halliday. He feared it would be in vain, but still, as though impelled by a power he could not resist, on he walked at a rapid pace. He reached the stoop, and his knees faltered under him as he ascended, and he was obliged to raise the heavy knocker with both hands to give a steady stroke. Adelaide was alone in the parlor, and his reception was as pleasant as he could have asked for. But his own mind was in such a state of commotion, that, in spite of all the freedom with which she conversed, and her frank and confiding manner, he could only get out short sentences, and even at times only answered by a monosyllable.

Her eye was more than once turned towards him with a gaze that manifested a desire to pry into the cause for conduct so unusual with him. At length she asked, with evident interest:

"Are you not well this evening?"

The question startled him, but it brought him to the point.

"Oh yes, certainly, very well I thank you; but I was just thinking of a letter I received to-day, from my friend Mr. Jamieson; you have heard me speak of him?"

"Oh, yes. I hope nothing has happened at your home."

The truly ingenuous manner in which this was said, and the interest manifested by the lovely, artless girl, enabled him at once to break through his restraint, and he told her the purport of the letter.

"And I have taken the liberty, Miss Vincent, of asking the pleasure of your company; the sleighing will be beautiful, and we shall have a full moon."

He had never seen Adelaide, but on one other occasion, blush so deeply. She was evidently taken by surprise; and her confusion alarmed him; he wished he could recall what he had said.

"You are very kind; I don't know. I should delight to

have a sleigh-ride, and by moonlight, too. How far do you say it is?"

"About six miles from here.

"Six miles! If you will excuse me a few moments, I will ask my aunt what she thinks of it."

"Oh, certainly," and Charles arose, as she left the room, and listened until her light step died away, and then, throwing himself upon the chair, endeavored, by every possible means, to quiet his agitation.

But there is little use in reasoning when one is in love, and placed just at the balancing point between hope and fear; it is about as well to give up thinking for the time, for thinking throws no light on that about which we are most concerned, and generally makes matters worse,

It seemed a very long time that she was gone, and yet, when he heard her step approaching the door, he almost wished she had not come so soon.

"I am sorry, Mr. Lovell, to have kept you waiting so long. But you see, after talking with my aunt I thought I would go and see uncle, too. And he, you know, does not like to say right off what he thinks; he must have a long argument first. However, they do not object, seeing the invitation has come from you, so you must keep in mind that you are in their good graces."

"Then I may expect the pleasure of your company."

"If you think it will be proper for me, a stranger, to go to such a meeting. You see, I trust to your sense of the proprieties," smiling, and coloring a little, as she said it.

"I will see that you are not introduced where you will not be most heartily welcome. I will call at five to morrow evening."

And precisely at five o'clock, on the next afternoon, Charles reined up his sprightly horse before the gate; and all his fears of disappointment were at once put to rest, for the door immediately opened, and, well muffled up in furs, and smiling sweetly to his respectful salutation, came tripping out the lovely object for which his heart had been in a flutter all day. Her uncle was by her side.

"I tell you what it is, young man; if you don't bring back this girl safe and sound, woe be to you."

"No fear of me, uncle;" and the lively girl, assisted by her kind relative, sprang into the sleigh.

"No danger, sir, I will do my best to return her safe and sound. Please, Miss Adelaide," this was the first time Charles had used such a familiar term, "please place your feet upon that box, it will keep them warm."

"Why, what in the world have you got here?" and the old captain fumbled at the bottom of the sleigh. "Bless my soul, how nice this is. Why, sis, how comfortable this will be for you. Well, I see, Mr. Charles, you understand how to treat the ladies' feet, as well as the gentlemen's palates—I have n't forgot that supper yet. Well, a pleasant ride to you. And this buffalo goes before, ha! Well, you need n't fear Jack Frost now. Take care of that horse, he looks as if he wanted to break things. Good-bye to you."

"Good-bye, uncle."

Charles bowed as best he could, for Pomp was very impatient.

"Come, Pomp!" and, with the spring of a deer, the beautiful creature started off, and the merry bells jingled to a lively measure.

Six miles, with Pomp feeling as he then did, were soon passed over. The moon, however, had time to rise, and just throw her cold beams across the pure white snow. She was in the full, and her red round face, as it rose from the water, which could be clearly seen by the long streak of light upon its bosom, was an object of pleasing interest. And the hearts of the youthful pair were just in a state to enjoy any beauty that nature might present.

Never, perhaps, before, if the whole truth could be known, did the moon look so strangely agreeable. It was almost a fairy scene; and the dark woods, against which her light fell, looked beautiful too, and every common object made a picture of its own.

And now they rise a gentle eminence, and all at once Pomp is reined into the deep snow; a team heavily laden is in the path.

"Whoa, haw, whoop! Hillo, Lovell, is that you? ha! ha! ha!"

The well-known voice caused Charles to hold up, just as he was about passing a heavily-loaded sled, with two yoke of oxen.

"I guess I shall be there in time, ha! ha! ha! Lovell how are you? going to the gathering?"

"Ah, Slocum, what in the world! have you left your trade, and turned teamster."

"Ha! ha! ha! not exactly; but you see the old colonel wanted me just to go and pick out the boards and shingles, to see that they should be of the best. We are going to have a tight roof over his head, and all things fixed up to a T. Glorious times, I tell you; never see the like afore; and the colonel says it is all your doings, ha! ha! ha! But I won't keep you. Whoa, haw, come along, haw, whoop!" and the teamster fell back beside his oxen, cracking his long whip over them, and Pomp, no longer restrained, pranced on his way.

"A strange fellow that, but one of the kindest hearts that ever beat."

"He seems to know you pretty well."

"He knows us all, and we all know him. He is our boss carpenter in these parts. He is now, however, on a labor of love. The few words he has said, have let out the whole matter to me. Colonel Johnson, of whom I have told you some anecdotes, has sent him to purchase that load of lumber as a present to the young minister; and this man has given his time and labor to bring it over, and he will, no doubt, give many good days' work in fixing up the house. He is as happy now as he wants to be."

"He must have a noble spirit under that rough covering he had on. How much more the heart yields its respect to such a man, than to the gaudy outside with a selfish spirit."

Charles was about to say how rejoiced he was to hear her express such a sentiment, when their attention was attracted to a scene close at hand, and he exclaimed:

"There is to be a gathering indeed."

For some distance now, on each side of the road, could be seen horses and sleighs, of all varieties, fastened to the fence, while several were discharging their loads opposite a small gate. A dwelling of some kind was there, but it was not easy to distinguish it from the dark shadow of the trees which surrounded it.

Adelaide felt some delicacy in entering a place crowded as it was with perfect strangers to her. But Miss Lucy Johnson was at the door, and Charles had only to introduce his fair charge to her, and in a few moments all feeling of restraint was gone; for every one seemed happy, and ready to give a hearty welcome to all they met. She soon found, too, that her companion, however retiring and unobtrusive he had borne himself at the house of her uncle, was here a person of distinction. At once he was surrounded by old and young—every one was ready to greet him—young ladies seemed to court his notice, and gentlemen with powdered heads singled him out, and shook him cordially by the hand.

Lucy led Adelaide to a seat in one corner of the room, as she requested to be placed where she could observe what was going on without being herself brought into notice.

"And now, dear, I must leave you for a short time, as I have some arrangements to complete for the supper."

"Oh, I shall do well enough—don't let me detain you."

"We will endeavor to entertain the young lady," said two or three smiling girls, who were seated near her; and Lucy, in her peculiarly graceful manner, glided through the throng, and was out of sight in a moment.

It could easily be perceived that the company assembled was composed of very different classes in society, for although all present were decently arrayed, yet the style of dress and peculiarity of manner were quite dissimilar.

But the kindly spirit that was so manifest, and which seemed the pervading feeling, made all other distinctions of little account. Seats were arranged along the walls of the room, and were mostly filled, but they seemed only designed as occasional resting-places. Most of the company was in motion; gathered in little knots, conversing awhile, and then breaking up, and mingling with other circles, going out and in of the room, shaking hands with new comers, or recognizing acquaintances already there.

The house was not large, and was a very plain one even for the country, and the furniture of an order very different from anything Adelaide had ever seen before. There was no carpet on the floor, and the walls were white-washed, and all the woodwork without any paint. But there was an aspect of neatness over the whole.

Adelaide found her companions very ready to answer any

questions, or give her any information about persons or things.

There was, however, little need for asking—they were so wide awake upon all subjects, so full of the spirit of the scene, and so communicative, that it was not possible to be within hearing distance and remain ignorant of anything about the premises.

"I do wish supper was ready, Jane—have you seen the table?" Jane nodded from somewhere near at hand; "Is n't it beautiful; I guess there never was so much cake here before. But I 'm glad of it. I wonder if they have brought much of other things."

"I guess you 'd think so, Mary Ann, if you 'd been out in the buttery; there 's enough there to feed a family a whole year, I should think. They 've got Charles Lovell there taking down an account of everything as it comes in, and I should think he 'd be crazy."

"You would a good deal rather he was here, would n't you, Liz?"

"Me! now, Mary Ann, you hush—you think as much of Charley Lovell as I do, I guess. Yes, I wish he was here. But catch him to come and sit down among the girls. It 's as much as one can do to get a bow from him. But there he comes—don't he look finely to-night; and there 's Parson Jamieson, the Episcopal minister, and there 's Mr. Somers, too. Now I guess we are going to have something or other. Just look, Mary Ann, just look at Mr. Somers; his good old face fairly shines; you can see he is happy now—there is n't a single wrinkle to be seen. I don't care, I do love ministers anyhow."

"When they are the kind of ministers we have here. How fond they seem to be of one another; and see how Mr. Foster's black eyes sparkle to-night? I wonder if Fanny Pearl is here yet?"

"Why, certainly—there she is, don't you see her; as true as the world, she is sitting close by Mrs. Somers! how sweet she looks. It is too bad they can't be married; I do think people ought n't to ask a man to preach if they can't just give him enough to live on—I do think Fanny Pearl is beautiful, but her father is poor, and Mr. Foster is poor, and so you see they can't keep house, nor nothing."

"How do you know, Mary Ann, but there will be so much brought here this evening, that it will keep them for one year, at any rate, and that is far enough to look ahead, aint it?"

"I wish they would get married, for I know we girls shall be at the wedding, and I have n't been at a wedding in a great while."

The lively conversation of the young ladies was broken in upon by the sound of the clear, full voice of Mr. Somers, and the house was at once hushed to silence.

"Beloved friends! you have come here this evening, to testify your respect and affection for this, my young brother;" and the good old gentleman laid his hand kindly upon the shoulder of Mr. Foster, who was seated beside Mrs. Somers, and near to her who had just been the object of such special interest with our young friends; Miss Fanny Pearl. "And I know it will be very gratifying to you all to learn something of the events of the evening; and how far the object has been accomplished for which we have come together. Our reverend brother Jamieson will now read off some of the items."

Mr. Somers then took a seat beside Mr. Foster, and Mr. Jamieson, who remained standing, unrolled a small paper and read as follows:

Four barrels of flour from four different individuals.

Sugar from various sources, about eighty pounds; tea, in all ten pounds.

Molasses, one barrel from a member of the Episcopal church.

Cheese, in all about sixty pounds.

Butter, estimated at one hundred pounds.

Pork, one half barrel from a member of the Presbyterian church.

Four yards superfine black cloth from some young men of the Episcopal church.

One piece fine cotton shirting.

One piece cotton sheeting.

One light-colored silk dress from the young ladies of the Episcopal church.

At the mention of this there was a general buzz of approbation, and Miss Fanny Pearl began to fan herself quite rapidly.

Five thousand shingles and two thousand feet of clear seasoned boards, to be used in making a tight roof over the head of the Reverend Mr. Foster, and in putting his house in neat and comfortable repair; from a friend.

A voice called out from the back room "That 's from the old colonel; Colonel Johnson, God bless him." Some clapped, some called out amen; and for a few moments nothing could be heard but words of admiration at the timely and generous gift.

Charles Lovell colored deeply; he had no idea before, who the donor was, until Slocum, for it was he that let out the secret, called the name; and perhaps there was a little pride mingling with his feelings of joy. Lucy had finished her duties about the table, and taken a seat by Adelaide; she was listening with deep attention, and a heart full of interest, when her father's name was called out thus unexpectedly; she looked a moment as if overcome with surprise, and then yielded to her feelings. It was as new to her, as to any one in the room; as she supposed his offering had been brought by herself. Oh, how her heart blessed him, and what a shower of kisses she meditated so soon as she got home.

As this closed the list in Mr. Jamieson's hands, Mr. Somers arose and stated to the assembly, that he had one more communication to make. It was a short one.

"I hold in my hand a list of ten names, members of my own pastoral charge, who have subscribed the amount of two hundred dollars a year, for two years, to be paid to the Rev. Mr. Foster, as an addition to his salary. It is given as a token of brotherly feeling towards the Methodist persuasion. And, brethren—" Mr. Somers raised his hand, as in the act of speaking, but his feelings were too deeply excited. Every eye was fixed upon him, and when they saw his lips quivering, and the tear gathering, the power of sympathy, like an electric shock, at once swept over them. There was a moment of silence, and then a rush towards the place where Mr. Foster was seated. He had done his best to keep within bounds the strong emotions which the scene had excited. The whole to him had been a surprise; but when Mr. Somers, in his feeling manner, proclaimed this additional testimony of kindness, and he felt the warm grasp of congratulation from the hands eager to embrace him, how could he do less than give vent to his excited feelings? Ah! let those tears fall, dear Christian brother, for far too seldom are they wrung forth by such a cause. Heaven's own light is reflecting from them, brighter than any sparkle from the costliest gem. Such tears would scarcely be unsightly where the angels dwell.

But it is time for supper, and the word is passed that "all is ready." Charles had not forgotten his fair charge, although not wishing to be thought by her officious in his gallantry. But he felt called upon to wait upon her to the table. It had been spread in the kitchen of the house, a long, low room, with an immense fire-place, and doors opening into it from all directions. Had any one looked at the walls and the furniture, it would have been very manifest as a plain apartment; but no one thought of such things. A large blazing fire threw its warmth around, and the long table, covered with piles of all the good things which the country at that season of the year so readily produced, with lights blazing in all directions, formed too agreeable a sight for the eye to be directed to things of minor consequence. All present had helped to furnish it, and so they all felt welcome; each one had done something towards the enjoyment of the evening, and felt a right to be happy. It was no splendid pageant got up for the gratification of vanity, but a feast of love, where the heart could enjoy its holy sympathies, and let out its full feelings. But, like all pleasant things on earth, it could only last for a limited space. The good things had been partaken of to the full, the kind words had all been spoken, the hearty laugh had been freely indulged, and the hour had arrived when they must separate. Once more the voice of good Mr. Somers was heard giving out the lines of a parting hymn. All joined heartily in the song of Zion, and then came the bustle of preparation for departure.

And now for home, and a ride upon the pure white snow, with the silvery light of the fair round moon.

Charles had not obtruded himself upon Adelaide through the evening. He well knew that she had not accompanied him for the purpose of being exhibited as one to whom he was particularly attentive, and he had too much good sense to be officious. Perhaps he carried the matter a little too far.

"And now, Miss Adelaide, shall we prepare to return?" She smiled very pleasantly as she replied :

"Just as *you* say ; you know I am under your direction this evening."

There was a strange emphasis on the little word you, that made a singular impression upon his sensitive feelings, and at once he began to rebuke himself for being over-nice in his sense of propriety ; and all the time he was getting Pomp ready, that word kept sounding in his ear ; and then, when he came to conduct her to the sleigh, the readiness with which she took his arm, and the confiding manner in which she rested upon him for support, as they walked along the hard-beaten snow-path, affected him, he could not tell why ; but it all seemed like a pleasing dream. The conclusions which he dared to indulge were too enchanting to be real. Oh, could that walk have been extended through the six miles they were to ride, it would have been too short even then. But here is Pomp close at hand, and impatient to be loosened and on his way ; and the arm must be withdrawn, for there is considerable fixing to do, as the fair one with his help takes her seat upon the thick furs.

"But, oh dear, how is this!" and Adelaide stooped, and felt the flat stone, upon which, with the most delicate care, Charles had placed those little feet ; "has this stone retained its warmth so long? Now, I do believe you have had it by the fire."

"I think it will keep warm until we get home."

"You are very kind ; but what is to be done now?"

"This shawl appears to be a supernumerary, and by wrapping it round in this manner, I think, with the buffalo before us, you will not suffer from the cold."

And, without making the least objection, she permitted him to fix things to his own notion. It was a delicate operation, to be sure, and his hands were none the steadiest just then. He managed, however, to do the thing skilfully, and then, with the same delicate handling, arranged the outer robe, so that if the cold got in it must be by some round-about way.

"How comfortably you have fixed me! but all this while you are standing in the snow *yourself*."

"Oh, I don't mind it. I am not the least cold. I am used to it."

That was true, Master Charley! You could brave most storms that rage in our climate. But you are not used to such delicate operations as you have just been performing, nor to the sound of such a sweet voice, speaking, in all simplicity, the guileless feelings of a pure heart, words of interest for you. And your blood is coursing so swiftly through your veins that the cold of Nova Zembla could scarce affect you now. It was true, indeed, you were not cold, and when you took your seat beside that precious bundle you had been wrapping up so tenderly, you were not cold; we all believe you. Now say the word, and let Pomp go, for he has been prancing long enough. Gingle, gingle, gingle; how swiftly the runners cut through the crust of the deep snow as Pomp tears his way to the beaten track, and then, as though borne upon the air, the gliding vehicle smoothly slips along.

"What a lovely evening it is!" and Adelaide, as she said it, threw her veil aside, that she might see more clearly all its beauties.

Charles saw her bright eye gazing at the lovely moon, and be looked up there too. It was a sight worth looking at, to be sure; it always is; that silver ball hanging on nothing in the dark blue sky. But now her rays seem to sink into his soul, and wake up visions of beauty and happiness too rich to be interrupted by his own words. He did not reply, but kept gazing at the moon.

Awhile the sound of other gingling bells are about them, before and behind; but the distance was short that supplied them with company, for their path home lay in a direction different from that of any who had been with them that evening. It was a lone road, but they turned into it without any apparent feeling that the loss of companions would diminish aught of the pleasantness of their ride.

Dear reader, have you ever lived in the country? Have you ever rode through the pure, white snow, when the moon was in her brightness; so bright that every delicate curve in the wreathed and feathery mantle could be distinctly seen; when every sweeping branch lay pencilled in shadow by your side; when the frost upon the low bushes threw off sparkles of silver light; and the mist that marked the windings of the living stream, just rose above the earth, and, like a delicate veil, screened the rough, bare alders from your view; when, through the huge forest trees, the moon-beams came down aslant upon their gnarled, black trunks; and, as you looked into their depths, strange shapes appeared, and Fancy fashioned them to suit her taste; and at such a time were you so fastened to the common, stale routine of life, so much a creature of reality, that you could not cut yourself adrift, and float awhile upon the fairy stream, and enjoy the world of silvery sweetness that was spread around? Could you not? Then you are not fitted to be a dweller where Nature spreads her beauties. The lighted streets, the flaring windows, the bustling crowd, and the din of Babel, are doubtless more pleasing to your taste. Take the enjoyment they can give. You doubtless have no sympathy with these young hearts. Farewell.

Come, Pomp, we turn to you. Why do you arch your neck, and shake your bells so lazily, and lift your feet so high, and make no faster progress? have you entered into the feelings of your master, and wish to make the journey last as long as may be? or perhaps it is some trick which he has taught you, and it is his hand that tells you "there is no haste, only keep moving." But why are those long pauses? have all subjects of conversation been exhausted? and why does Adelaide still keep her veil thrown back? Is it that she may see the moon? or that there may not be even a silken gauze to deaden communion with that manly heart that sits beside her? There is no telling. But so it was, that often as Charles turned to ask "if she was comfortable?" or "what she thought of this or that?" he met the soft, sweet gaze of those bright eyes, fixed as in fullest confidence; and that sweet smile, which went like fire to his heart, and kindled up such thoughts, that for some time again he would be silent. Ah, those thoughts! how strangely did they work! how bold they were sometimes! almost ready to break forth in words, and then they would be hushed. No; he would not now—now that she was all alone, and in his care, and by his special invitation. No; he would not do anything that should give her cause to think he had a selfish end in view. No. If he ever told her of his love, it should be when on her own "vantage ground," and under no obligations for his care and protection.

Ah, Charles! there is a right time for every daring act; a

time when the circumstances are at their "full conjunction of preparedness." But we respect your motives, and we would not soil the brightness of your honorable feelings by one wish of ours; only—

But the lone road is passed, and dwellings begin to thicken, and at last Pomp curves from the track, and stands steadily at the gate, from whence at first began this happy scene.

And now the shawl is to be unwrapped, and the buffalo thrown aside; and again, she rests upon his arm.

As they stood upon the platform of her uncle's stoop, and about to separate, she said:

"Now what shall I say for my pleasant ride? shall I say, thank you?"

"Please do not; the obligation, I assure you, rests all upon me." And Charles looked most serious as he said it; and the countenance of Adelaide, just tinged as it had been with a smile, settled at once into that cast so peculiar to her in moments of earnestness, when the shade of sadness just rested above the soft gaze of her bright eye. Long, long did Charles remember it.

"But you *will* let me say, that it has been the pleasantest ride I ever enjoyed."

He took her hand, bowed very low, and almost touched it with his lips; ah, he could have gone upon his knee, and blessed her for those words, and vowed a life of constancy and love; but he forbore. He could not reply; his heart was too full for that; and as the servant opened the door, he made a silent obeisance and departed.

CHAPTER XIV.

"OH, Miss Adelaide!" and the servant maid whispered as she spoke, "who do you think has come? Your Aunt Nabby!"

Adelaide had just entered the hall, and the door had scarcely closed, when she heard this announcement. She turned very pale, and could scarcely bring out the simple reply:

"Has she?"

"Yes, she has come, and she has been sitting up a purpose to see you. Your uncle and aunt have gone to bed, but she said she could not go to rest till you came home, and she seems in a great pucker about something or another; and if I was you, I 'd slip off to bed, for you look pale and tired."

"Oh no, thank you, Mary. I had better see my aunt, if she has been sitting up for me."

The mention of Aunt Nabby's name immediately brought to the mind of Adelaide an "idea" of something wrong, something that did not suit, of frowns, and surmises, and hard expressions, and an overbearing manner. But as she had been waiting to see her, and as her conscience accused her of naught, she at once resolved to go into the back parlor, where the maid informed her that her aunt was seated, "rocking herself in the big chair, as if she would rack it to pieces."

As Adelaide entered the room, her aunt immediately arose.

"How do you do, aunt?"

"I am pretty well, Adelaide."

Adelaide had kissed her aunt, and was taking off her bonnet and furs, at the same time asking questions about members of the family in the city. Her aunt having at once resumed her seat, commenced rocking.

"The family in the city are well, and doing well; and I wish I could have the same assurance, that *all* its members were pursuing a proper course."

Adelaide had by this time disrobed herself, and taking a seat in the corner, fixed her eye in all honesty and simple-heartedness upon the face of her relation; and as she did not exactly comprehend to whom the exception in her aunt's remark had reference, very likely looked somewhat in doubt.

"Adelaide! Adelaide! don't look at me in that hypocritical manner, as though you did not understand my allusion; that it is for *you* my anxieties are aroused, and my heart pained, and my pride—yes, I may say it—my pride greatly humbled." And then having delivered herself, she rocked faster than ever.

Adelaide was perfectly astonished, and knew not what to say. Deeply affected, her beautiful countenance was suffused with a burning blush, but her bright eye was still fixed upon her aunt.

"I had heard, indeed, that your conduct of late had been, to say the least, very extraordinary; but little did I imagine that I should ever live to be a witness to the degradation of my own flesh and blood."

Adelaide could remain silent no longer.

"As you say that you allude to me, aunt, may I know wherein I have acted so as to merit such strong expressions of disapprobation? What have I done? do tell me, aunt, I beg of you."

The lady stopped rocking, and rose from her seat. Her countenance was deadly pale, and she shook her finger, with pointed earnestness, at her almost affrighted niece.

"What have you done! Can you sit there, Adelaide, and calmly ask me such a question? What have you done! Have you not lowered yourself, and put a stain upon the respectability of our family, by allowing attentions from one who is far below you in the world? Have you not even, in the presence of gentlemen of respectability, shown a decided preference for one who is far down among the menials of life? Have you not even degraded yourself by going off alone on an evening ride? Oh, Adelaide!" and the excited lady clasped her hands in agony, "that I ever should have it to say of my own sister's daughter!" And almost exhausted with the violence of her feelings, she sank again into her chair, and began to rock.

"I am very sorry, aunt, if my going away this evening is

not approved by you. I had the consent of my uncle and Aunt Halliday. And the gentleman with whom I went is much respected by them both."

"Gentleman! gentleman! a pretty gentleman! A plain working farmer, a mere clod-hopper. I suppose he waited upon you with his tow frock on, and his cow-hide boots; you must have felt highly honored by his company. And I suppose he took the same liberty with you that he has been in the habit of doing with his mates, the milk-maids; how many times did he kiss you on the road?"

"Aunt Nabby, you are very unjust;" and Adelaide, unable to endure any longer the torture of her feelings, burst into a flood of tears.

"Yes, Adelaide," her voice had softened considerably, "ah, yes, that is always the way; I am unjust merely because I am desirous of having my own sister's child keep in mind that she has a standing a little above the common herd. What would your father have thought, when himself the first gentleman in the assembly-room, with his gold knee-buckles, and silk stockings, and his silver-mounted dress-sword by his side, and the first people in the city for his companions; what would he have thought, if one had told him that a daughter of his should one day accept the attentions of a day-laborer? Unjust indeed! Is that, Adelaide, the return I am to receive for all my interest for you? Have I not already, from the circle of my visitors, been so happy as to introduce your cousin Julia to one who can and will make a lady of her? Yes, Julia will soon ride in her coach. And so may you, Adelaide, or so you might, but I don't know that you will ever recover from the fall you have made. Mr. Sampson, I must tell you, Adelaide, however much he admires you, would never for an instant think of you, did he know—"

"I have not the least desire, aunt, for Mr. Sampson's attentions or regard. But I do not wish to be unjust towards you—you must forgive my hasty expressions. But you do not know Mr. Lovell, or you would never have spoken of him as you did."

"Lovell! Lovell! who is he?"

"Why, the young gentleman who waited upon me this evening; and I must not allow injustice to him on my account. I must say, aunt, that I have never been treated with more true politeness by any gentleman. His behavior towards me, whether alone or in company, has been the most delicate; his manners are refined, and his principles, I believe, to be most pure and manly."

"Well, well, well, say no more, Adelaide; my work is done—I see my work is done. All my regard for you, and for the honor of our family, is looked upon as a matter of no moment. I suppose you are engaged to him—I feared it; but have come on to see if my past services for you all, my interest for the good of our family, my authority as your mother's only sister, could not yet avail to turn you from your purpose, and save you yet."

"Your fears on my account, aunt, are very groundless. Mr. Lovell has never, probably, had the most distant thought of such a thing. He certainly has never hinted it to me."

Mrs. Abigail Ratoon was silent; she felt a great burden taken from her mind, for she had construed Adelaide's remarks in favor of Mr. Lovell as sure evidence of an interest in him.

You have relieved my mind greatly, Adelaide. Then you have no interest in him after all? you do not love him?"

Oh, that blush! how it has come, like the meteor's flash, and spread all over that delicate cheek, and over those beating temples, and even upon that fair, smooth forehead. Speak quickly, Adelaide, for the eye of your aunt is fixed upon you—she has asked you a home question.

"You don't suppose, aunt, that I should yield my affections to one who has never asked me for them?"

"I hope not—and I am greatly rejoiced at what you say, for I did look upon you as lost. And now you must not lay too much to heart the earnest expressions I have dropped. You know, my child—you must know that you are the object of my greatest solicitude; your cousin, Julia, I have befriended on your Aunt Halliday's account, as well as because she is so subservient to my wishes. But you are my only blood relation—the only one to inherit when I am gone. Your poor brother, you know, is lost—lost to his friends and the world—gone we know not where, and—the least we say of him the better. But on you my interest centres—and now I wish you to return with me, and at my house you will have an opportunity to see the world. This is no place for you. My brother, I know, has a very kind heart, and so has sister Halliday; but the advantages here are not just as you need, now coming into society. With me you can be introduced to a large circle, a coach to ride in at your pleasure, servants at command, and the means of coming out in a way becoming my niece; and to leave you shut up here in this humdrum place—it will never do; I should consider myself deficient in duty towards you to allow it."

Adelaide had too many conflicting thoughts to manage just then to enable her to make any reply. She dared not at once say No! to her aunt's proposal, for fear of another outbreak of passion, and yet her repugnance to it was too sincere to allow her to acquiesce.

"Another thing I must tell you, Adelaide, but I tell you in great confidence. Your Uncle Halliday is quite embarrassed in his means; he has a good heart, and feels very kindly to you, but I know that he ought not to be at any more expense for his family than is absolutely necessary. To me you must look—you shall want for nothing; and when I am gone, who is then to inherit my property but yourself? You see, then, that everything conspires to make you an object of no common interest. I want you to appreciate yourself as you ought. Many a fine girl throws herself away, merely from this fact. But you cannot think, my child, what a load is taken from my mind, now that you tell me that you have no interest in that Lovell. And now, Adelaide, you had better retire, as you will want to be up very early, for your things must all be ready by 9 o'clock."

Adelaide was too full of feeling, and too desirous of being alone, to say aught that might prolong the intercourse, and so they parted for the night.

Adelaide shut her door, and placing the lamp in a corner, took her seat by the window, and looked out upon the bright moon. There was something in that beautiful luminary now that made her appear a confidant, and the scenes of the evening came back in all their freshness. The smiling faces she had seen around her, the kind words she had heard, the power of sympathy under whose spell she had sat with so much delight, the heaven-born thoughts that had been expressed in language that thrilled both speaker and hearers,—the whole of that feast of love passed again before her, and then the unpresuming politeness of him who had been her companion. So full of kindness, and so marked with respect and delicacy, the agreeable conversation, the strange beauty of the scenery, the long pauses that seemed to tell of feelings that were too sacred for utterance, the parting at her uncle's door, his last look. Ah; she will remember it long. The emotions it conveyed she dare not shape into their true meaning, even in thought. And yet her mind would hang around that point, as if a charm was in it. And then the morrow. Must she bid adieu to these simple pleasures? Must she leave the beauties which at the earliest dawn and at the closing day her mind had feasted on? She had always loved the country. Now it seemed dearer to her than ever.

And must she leave so suddenly? What would *he* think to learn that she had gone, perhaps to return no more? What a marked token of indifference after all his delicate attention! and yet how could she make it known?

Adelaide was at the breakfast-table in season the next morning, but her part in the repast was soon finished. And, asking leave of her Aunt Halliday to retire, the three relations were left to enjoy a private interview.

"I tell you what it is, Nabby," said the captain, "I don't believe Addy wants to go away; and, although I think myself it must be lonesome for her here, yet I don't like to have her baulked; she is too good not to have her own way."

"That is just as much, brother, as you men know about things which concern young ladies. They don't know what they want themselves. I know Adelaide is a good girl, and she has a bright mind; but, at her age, girls are very apt to have romantic notions about life, which we, who are older, know to be very foolish. They have nonsensical ideas about love and affection, and all that; but how they are to be provided for, and how they are to keep up their standing in society, never comes into their head. Now, we know that love without the elegances of life about one, is like a balloon with a rent in it, just good for nothing at all."

"I don't know about that, Nabby; money is a very necessary article, and the elegances of life are very well in their way, but the— Nabby, you don't mean to say that there is no true love or happiness upon earth but among the rich."

"How can people be happy, brother, when their circumstances are straitened? Would you try to make me believe that, when I pass by one of these rude cottages you have around you in the country, and see the man hard at work, toiling for his daily bread, that he has any idea beyond getting enough to eat and drink?"

"That is the main chance, I know, Nabby; but if my guess is right, there aint much loftier ideas in the minds of many who don't toil, as you call it. We are never too old to learn, Nabby; and I must tell you that I have learned some new lessons in life, which make me feel that if I had learned them earlier, I might have enjoyed a world of comfort and happiness with a very small part of the means I have spent in trying to live according to the notions your head is full of. What would you say, if I was to tell you that I had seen persons living with all the comforts of life about them, and with all the refinement of polite manners, and the enjoyment of intelligent intercourse, in a plain, rough cottage, no better than the one my hired laborers inhabit? You may shake your head, but seeing is believing." Then turning to his wife, "I do wish Lovell would just step in now, that Aunt Nabby might see a sample; could n't you send for him?"

"Oh, my dear, I am afraid Mr. Lovell would think strange of it."

Mrs. Halliday had an inward dread of exciting Aunt Nabby.

"Well, then, you just tell sister Nabby all about him, in and out."

"Oh, well, I must say Mr. Lovell has shown himself to be a gentleman; he certainly behaved with great propriety while he stayed here."

"Stayed here! and do I understand, then, that this young man Lovell, has been staying under this roof, and associating with my niece?" Aunt Nabby knew it all before, but it suited her turn to profess ignorance.

"He has been, Nabby, and a finer fellow never came under my roof, nor yours either. He is a gentleman, as I call it, of the first water. A man with a heart and soul in him. None of your dandy-jacks, with gold chains and fine coats, and no more brains than enough to enable them to drive tandem."

"Brother, you have said enough. I don't want to hear any more. But I just tell you once for all, that if you care no more for the respectability of our family, than to introduce a man, a common day-laborer, as I understand, in summer, and a common Yankee schoolmaster in winter, to a niece of mine, and keep him under your roof in such dangerous contiguity to a simple-hearted girl as Adelaide, it is high time she went away. That is all I have to say."

The old captain's face was red almost to a purple hue, and the honest indignation that burned within was ready to explode with a fury that would have made Aunt Nabby glad to have been back within her own establishment. But his reason told him it would answer no good end. He loved Adelaide dearly. He knew his own circumstances, and felt the sad truth that he might be obliged to cast her upon the care of his sister. He would not throw an obstacle in her way of being well provided for. And yet he must do something.

"I shall make no objections, Nabby, to your taking Addy, and doing well for her. But I can tell you, if your plan is to try to make up a match for her with that milk-sop with a red head, that has been up here bothering round her, you had better let her go and learn a trade, and take care of herself."

"Mr. Sampson, brother, is a young man highly connected, and he has a very handsome property in his own right. I think it would be a very great thing for Adelaide, if such a match could be made up as you call it."

"I know all about his connexions; his old father made his money by selling drams; nothing very respectable in that, although I take one occasionally myself. The fellow has money, no doubt; but what else has he got? His head would make a very good mop, and I guess that is all it's good for. But have your own way; only remember Addy shall have no compulsion. I would work before the mast as I begun, before any of those ruff-scuffs with plenty of money in their pockets shall have her without her own consent. And more than this, if what I hear of Vanderbose is true, I am sadly afraid our poor Julia will rue the day you ever introduced her to that num-scull."

The captain having "said his say," arose from the table

and went out, his heart full of indignation. But blaming himself most of all, that he had not managed more wisely and kept himself in circumstances of independence.

The handsome covered sleigh of Mrs. Abigail Ratoon was at the door by the time appointed, and Adelaide, as a victim to the destiny she knew not how to avoid, was in readiness to accompany her. When she left the table, she had retired to her room, so long a place of pleasantness and peace, in order to compose her mind for the hour of separation. She took her prayer-book, and read from the Psaltery some of those delightful passages so well calculated to impress upon the mind the safety and happiness of those who cast themselves and their interests upon the care of God. A dark shadow had come over her heart. It had come suddenly, and without warning; and she could only trust for help from Him by whose mandate it had come. A knock at the door.

"Our time is near, Adelaide; are you ready?" It was Aunt Nabby.

"I will be down in a moment, aunt." She could have gone then, but some tell-tale tears must be dried first.

No sooner had Aunt Nabby retired, than she heard the step of her kind old uncle approaching; the door was at once opened.

"Well, Addy, I am glad to see you don't part with your old uncle and your old home with a smile. I had rather see those tears than not. I could shed some myself if it would do any good. Be a good girl, and don't let any one persuade you to any act your own heart does not approve. And while I live, remember you shan't want for a father's hand and a father's heart." Bursting into a full flood of tears, and throwing her arms around his neck:

"Dear, dear uncle, I could live and die with you; but only let me say one word to you. Cannot I remain here with you? My Aunt Nabby tells me that you are not as well off as you once was; cannot I remain, and help Aunt Halliday and you, to get along; I know I can do a great deal to comfort you; I will work for you and help aunt to save."

The good old captain could stand a great deal, before his feelings should be manifested; but when he saw the earnest look of that dear young creature, her eyes swimming in tears, and heard her soft words trembling with the ardor of her feelings towards him, he had to let nature take its course.

"I did n't think, Addy, that I should ever shed tears again. I have never wept since I stood by my mother's grave and that is a long, long time ago. No, my dear, you had better go with your aunt; she has her strange ways, but she will do well for you, no doubt. I shall not probably remain in this place long. I must sell out, Addy, and go to work again. But don't let that grieve you. There, now, dry your eyes, and don't let Aunt Nabby think that you dislike to go with her. Maybe good will come of it all yet."

That was a wise thought, and a happy expression to close the parting interview. It was in keeping with the good words Adelaide had been reading, and at once she was greatly composed. It was a stream of light from behind the dark cloud. "Maybe good will come of it."

CHAPTER XV.

Dear reader, were you ever in love? We mean hopefully so. If not, we pity you. But if you have been, you can save us a great deal of labor in our efforts to describe the feelings of young Lovell, as he awoke to the new breaking day; for you can tell, or rather you can feel with what peculiar charms familiar objects had arrayed themselves. Hope shone brightly on that low streak of cloud just gilded with coming day, and upon those bare branches that hung between him and the amber sky; and upon the white smoke that curled up so gracefully from the chimney top, and upon every object that his eye beheld. And every sound, too, came in melodious measure to his ear. The clarion notes of chanticleer, the soft cooing of the doves, the smothered lowing of the cattle, and the well-known pawing of Pomp, impatient for his feed, all somehow seemed linked to the past evening; all seemed to respond pleasantly to the elasticity of his own feelings.

Only those who have lived in villages can realize how quickly news spreads from house to house. To such it will not seem strange that when Charles sat down with the family, where he was residing, to their early meal, he was startled with the question:

"Did you see the great lady from the city at the captain's last evening? They say the great lady, or the rich lady, I suppose it means the same thing, Captain Halliday's sister, has come, and that Miss Adelaide is going to the city with her. I thought she would n't stay long after the beaux had gone."

Charles was conscious of something like cold creeping about his heart. Not that he had any confidence in the report, but so sensitive had he become, that the least shadow cast upon a name so dear to him, or even the careless mention of her name by those who knew not of her excellences, seemed almost like sacrilege. He must, however, say something in reply, and he did it in a very quiet, unconcerned manner.

"I was there only a few moments, but I heard no mention of the lady."

"It is true though, for Betsey Cook called in here a little while since to ask if I was going to the quilting this afternoon, at Squire Pierce's; and she up and told me all about it. She said that Captain Halliday's boy was over to their house to buy some butter, and he said they must have some whether or no, for the captain's sister was there from the city, and that she was going away at 9 o'clock, and that Miss Addy was going with her, and that their Mary said that she was n't coming back this winter, if she ever did."

Charles did not feel bound to stop eating all the while this young lady was delivering her budget, for the address was not in particular pointed at him, but seemed to be rattled off for the benefit of all the family. It being one of those little communities which are found in the country, as well as city occasionally, where a little news, especially neighborhood news, is the most interesting subject that can be introduced. Charles was not just in his element. As he had but little to say to them in general, it was not wondered at that he took but little notice of what was said, and kept in a quiet way handling his knife and fork.

"I wonder if it is true that Miss Vincent is going to be married to that red-headed fellow that has been round her so long. I guess she is though, or she would n't be in such a hurry to be off to the city. I'll bet anything her aunt has come up to take her down to get her wedding-clothes. Well, I guess there 'll be great doings, for they say he is very rich. He is richer, they say, than Vanderbose."

Various replies were made by members of the family, but Charles took not the least interest in what was said from anything that could be seen, but kept steadily at work until he had finished, and then asked leave to retire.

All things now wore a sombre aspect; the halo that surrounded them on his waking that morning had vanished. A strange deadness had come over all his feelings, and he could have settled down upon his chair, and left the world to take care of itself. Well for him that he had duties which must be attended to; and, smothering his feelings as he best could, to them he applied himself with his usual promptness. Some days passed before he again made a call at the house, where his heart had found so much to interest it. He was received with marked kindness, by both the captain and his lady.

"Quiet times now, Mr. Lovell; the young folks have all cleared out—gone into winter quarters. I miss our girls though, I must say. If a body could have them alone without so many trampers after them. But they will enjoy themselves better in the city, no doubt, except Addy. I don't believe but Addy would have been just as happy here as she will be there."

"Why, I don't know, my dear husband; Addy tries to make the best of things, let her be where she will. But you know there is but little company here in the winter, and young folks like to be where there is a good deal stirring. At any rate, Aunt Nabby would have it so, whether or no."

"You see," said the captain, turning towards Charles, "my sister, Mrs. Abigail Ratoon, Aunt Nabby, as we call her, having plenty of money, and nothing else to do, has taken it into her head to be god-mother to our nieces. She coaxes them, and scolds them, and plagues and worries them, until they give in, and let her have her own way. They must dress, and behave, and marry, just as she says, and I'm afraid she'll make a dreadful muss of it yet."

"Well, we must say, Mr. Halliday, that she takes a great deal of pains for their good; she certainly gives them a good chance to do well."

"That's just as it will turn out; we have got to wait and see. She is determined that they shall marry rich, and I suppose she will bring it about some way, for when a woman sets her mind upon accomplishing a point she is very apt to carry it through."

"But you see, Mr. Lovell, I want you to understand me. I am no despiser of money, nor do I think any less of a man for having a good long purse. But when a man calculates that his wealth will make up for every other deficiency, and only regards it as a means to gratify every low desire, and has neither a sound head, nor a sound heart, and very little of either,—I say his money ought not to be held out as a lure to a good, honest-hearted, whole-soul girl, and it grinds my very soul to think of it."

Charles could say nothing in reply. He had no wealth of his own, and therefore did not wish to carp at those who had. He had already informed Captain Halliday what he believed to be true about Vanderbose, and had done all that he thought was his duty.

Mrs. Halliday, anxious to get her husband upon some other subject, presented another topic for conversation, and the names of the young ladies were not mentioned again during the whole evening.

Charles had learned nothing by his visit that gave him any satisfaction. He had no doubt, now, that every influence would be used to persuade Adelaide to receive the attentions of Mr. Sampson. It would be a sacrifice, he knew, and his heart sickened at the thought. A sacrifice of all that was lovely to meanness, and weakness, and vice.

The winter had nearly passed, and the time was at hand for the closing of his school, and he was glad at the prospect of a return to his labors, and his home. He had learned much of life during his sojourn at Wellgrove. He was much wiser than when he came there, if not so happy. He had, indeed, enjoyed some taste of exquisite happiness, but he had suffered, also, those acute pangs to which a sensitive heart is exposed. He had learned to feel that, after all, he was not quite the independent being he had imagined himself to be; and, with a chastened view of life, he prepared to enter again upon the track he had marked out for the future.

It was the last week of his stay at Wellgrove, when a letter was put into his hands by the post-boy. He saw by the mark that it was from the city, and the hand-writing that of a lady's. He did not dare to open it until he reached his room, and then, bursting the seal, turned his eye at once to the signature. He pressed it to his lips, and then, as calmly as he could, commenced to read its contents. They were as follows:

"Mr. Charles Lovell:

"I know not that your nice sense of propriety will approve my present act. But circumstances sometimes require us to step over the conventional boundaries of social intercourse. I feel myself called upon to do so now.

"You must have thought my conduct very singular, after the agreeable intercourse we had enjoyed, that I should have left thus suddenly, and without apprizing you of my intention to go away. I assure you it was as unexpected to me as it must have been to you, that our parting on my uncle's stoop was in all probability to be a final one.

"I cannot explain to you all the causes for the occurrence; and can only trust that you will have confidence enough in my sense of propriety, as well as in my feelings of friendship, to believe that the causes were beyond my control.

"Now I can say 'good-bye' in peace, and record my best wishes for your happiness, and shall not feel ashamed to meet you, should we ever cross each other's track again.

"I subscribe myself your friend,

"Adelaide Vincent.

"P. S.—You need not feel yourself obligated to answer this, as all I designed will have been accomplished when you have read it."

Again and again did Charles peruse the precious document. At first it revived his most ardent hopes; but as he studied it more closely, those hopes grew more faint. He saw that, after all, there was the same mystery about it that had involved all his intercourse with Adelaide. It was just like herself; frank, generous, and kind. She was not ashamed to acknowledge her friendship, but beyond that his hopes as a lover could find no ground for encouragement.

He cherished the precious document, though, as a choice legacy from one whose place in his heart was as unbroken as ever. If he loved too strongly, he felt assured that his affections were bound to one who was worthy of them; and the future, that mist upon the path of life into which he could not penetrate, he would leave with Him who ordereth all things well.

Home is a sacred name. It may be a humble one. No external adornings may distinguish it; there may be nothing to gratify the pride, nor much to please the taste. But if love dwells there; if warm hearts are ready to greet us, and mingle the fulness of their sympathies with ours; we should be thankful for it, we should prize it as a gift from heaven.

How Aunt Casey chuckled with delight as Charles took his seat again at the head of their little table! and with what alacrity she stirred about her household duties! The first thing, however, she must show him, was the pet she had been tending so faithfully all winter. It was evening when Charles reached his home, and as supper was ready, that pleasant meal must first be enjoyed. No sooner, however, was it fairly finished, than the old lady seized the lantern.

"Now, darling, you must just come with me and see Daisy."

"But you are not going to the barn, aunty!"

"Oh, but she aint in the barn. You see, I thought the barn would be too far off, and in stormy weather it might n't be so easy for me to get there; so I got Guss to make a pen for her just back of the little wood-house."

Charles followed the old lady, eagerly anxious to see the valuable gift he had received.

"Here, Daisy, Daisy!" At her call the pretty creature quietly arose from her straw bed, and stretching herself out, came up, and began to lick her hand.

"Why, aunty, what have you done with her? she has grown so. I should scarcely have known it was the same calf. Why she is fat enough to kill."

"Don't speak the word, dear; I would n't have her killed for twice my year's earnings."

"Nor I, aunty, for all mine. If for nothing else, on account of the kind friend who gave her to me, and the interest you have taken in her."

"Bless your kind heart for that."

"But how is it, aunty, that she has thrived so."

"Well, you see, darling, in the first place I made Gussy give the old cow plenty of the turnips you raised, and she gave us most as much milk as in pasture; so I had enough, besides making our butter, to give Daisy a good bellyfull twice a day, by mixing a little warm water with it."

"But you don't tell me that this calf has grown so on skim milk, and that watered, too?"

"It 's truth, darling; but, then, I did n't depend altogether on that. You see, I got Gussy to have a little corn ground, and I made a little supawn for her, and put a little of that in the milk as she could bear it, and so by degrees a little more; and then, after a little while, we had a little rye ground, bran and all together, and so I threw a little of that in the bottom of the pail, dry-like, and so I got her off from the milk, and now she takes a handful or two, night and morning, and drinks clear water, and eats hay like anything. But don't she look sleek?"

"She does look beautifully."

"Well, I am so glad you are pleased with her."

Augustus had not the rapidity of action that distinguished Charles. He took things moderately, but he kept steadily attending to whatever he had to do; and had, through the winter, accomplished even more than either he or Charles had expected. He had cut up all the wood they needed for the next winter; and piled in the wood-house, besides, a large heap of brush for summer use, neatly thrown together at a convenient distance for Aunt Casey to collect for her fire. He had split out and holed one hundred posts, and drawn three hundred rails from a few miles distance, where Charles had purchased them; besides attending faithfully to the chores, and making the most of their materials for enriching their ground the coming season.

"Well, Guss," said Charles, after seeing all he had done, "you have earned good wages at home this winter; you must have kept pretty busy."

"I have n't hurried myself; I have taken my own time, and had leisure enough, too, and have studied a little, too, into the bargain."

"Well, I am glad to be home again, I assure you. Everything looks in first-rate order. I must go to work now, and scratch hard, for I have been laying out considerable to do. But, first of all, I must go and see old Duncan, and get leave to have our lime landed at the old mill; I have laid out one hundred dollars on lime for the farm."

"A hundred dollars of your winter's earnings for lime! that 's too bad, Charley."

"Well, Guss, how could I lay it out better? Our land once enriched, what better capital do we want?"

"That is true, I know; but it seems hard to take your money that you have worked so hard for, and lay it out so."

"No harder, Guss, than for you to be cutting wood and holing posts, while I have been part of the time playing gentlemen. And forty dollars more I shall lay out for fish."

"Fish! what to do with them?"

"To place in the land, to be sure, and raise potatoes."

"That is a wild notion, Charley, depend upon it. I hope you have not engaged them too. You know, just think for one moment, of what use would potatoes be to you in any quantities? Last year, we happened to sell what we raised because many failed in raising them; but in general, they will not sell here; we should have to cart them ten miles to market."

"But I expect, Guss, to have a thousand bushels."

Augustus sat down upon a heap of posts and began to whittle, and made no reply, while Charles, amused by the very serious countenance of his brother, burst out into a hearty fit of laughter.

"If you aint wild, Charley, you are pretty near it."

"Why, one thousand bushels is no great yield, Guss, for six acres."

"Nothing extraordinary to be sure; but that 's not the thing. What are you to do with them? It will take all of six weeks to cart them, do our best."

"Yes; but I have not told you all yet. A captain of a sloop, who makes a business of picking up loads, has offered to come and take them from our landing at the mill, and will either buy them at the market price, or sell them for us."

"Can you depend on him?"

"Yes, with great certainty."

"Well, that might answer. I know that fish makes good manure for potatoes. But I hate to have you take all your money and run such a risk with it.

"No more risk, Guss, than anybody has to run, who invests capital in business; nor so much. If we miss a crop, the manure will still be in the ground, at any rate. If we don't venture anything to gain a crop, we ought not to expect any great return; for my part, I had rather trust our money to the keeping of the soil, than to the keeping of some people."

"We shall have to scratch for it then, if you are going to plant so much. Shan't we want more help?"

"I think not. I feel just like work myself, and I know you will do your part; and by managing a little, and taking things in time, I think we shall keep ahead of our work."

"Well, let 's at it; what had we better do first?"

"We will go to sharpening rails right off; and this evening I will go and see Duncan, for the lime will be here next week."

The old mill to which Charles had alluded was but a short distance from their house. It was situated on one of the small creeks that ran through the long stretch of marsh, and was what is called a tide-mill. It was an old shingled edifice, which had never been painted, and had seen its best days. It stood "all alone in its glory," with the exception of a long, low dwelling, at a short distance from it, on what was termed the main land. This was the miller's home, and between these two localities, old Duncan might be seen, morning, noon, and night, going and returning to his meals and labors. When we think of millers in general, we are apt to imagine a good round face, with a bright merry eye, and a full, well-fed body, ready with a joke, and a long yarn, and smiling at his customers as though the toll well paid him for powdering their grain.

But Mr. Duncan was a tall, lantern-jawed man, who never seemed to improve by all the provender that passed through his hands. He had a grim, sour look, as though the world and he were not on very good terms, and should n't be if he could help it. He was somewhat bent at the shoulders, no doubt owing to the heavy loads they were obliged to bear; and he appeared to make no effort to straighten up. He was, however, not so morose as he appeared. The mill had, in former days, done considerable business. Sloops came there loaded with grain, and departed with cargoes of rye and Indian meal, for the West Indies, or our own southern ports. But none came there now, and all its custom was derived from the few farmers in the vicinity, who found it more convenient to carry their grists there, than to the more thickly-settled part of the town.

In one corner of the mill was a small room partitioned off, with an old stove in it. A large, well-worn, rush-bottom arm-chair, a little rickety desk, one or two blocks sawed off from the end of a log, as extra seats, and a very various collection of fish-poles, guns, traps, old coats, bags, and broken cogs, some in the corner, some on nails, and some peeping out from a shelf that ran round quite high upon two sides of the room. Cobwebs, like mantles of charity, covered most of the articles, and the stray dust from the mill lay in undisturbed repose wherever it might find a resting-place, except on the old arm chair, that was clean as constant use could make it.

The old, low, broad wheel went round very much as if it was tired of going, and the cogs and wheels inside kept up a very moderate easy jog, and the mill-stones went round as if nobody was waiting for them.

As it was not yet the turning of the tide, when Charles reached the mill, he found Mr. Duncan sitting in his arm-chair, with his long legs stretched out against the hearth of the stove, his elbows resting upon the arms of his chair, and his head, which always had a little, low-crowned white hat on, bent over upon his chest, in a position that looked very much like dosing. Charles, as he entered, felt dubious about speaking, thinking that the good man was doubtless enjoying a nap, until he noticed that a pipe protruded from beneath the head, and seemed to be in operation; and almost immediately the head was raised, and the broad staring eyes of its owner were fastened upon him.

"Good evening, Mr. Duncan."

The pipe was slowly taken down, but no reply was made to this salutation, nor any motion of the body attempted for some moments. Mr. Duncan was doubtless endeavoring to make up his mind whose grist was wanted, and whether that particular grist was done. Not finding, however, any record among his mental statistics that gave him any light, he simply said:

"Your servant, sir."

"Good evening, Mr. Duncan."

"Oh, ah, yes; it's you, is it? How do you do to-night, Mr. Lovell. Take a seat."

And Charles took a seat on one of the blocks.

"It was all so still here, Mr. Duncan, that I feared you were not in."

"Well, you see it wants ten minutes to the turning," taking out an old silver watch, and holding its face towards Charles, "and I thought I mought as well be resting here as resting to the house," (some said he had n't much rest there,) "and then I can keep a look-out for the drowners."

"Drowners! Mr. Duncan."

"Why, sir, there aint nobody that gits drowned but they must come here to do it; walk right off into the race, or go splashing into the dam, or right among the sedges back of the mill; if there 's a hole to git into they 're sure to find it."

"It is rather a bad night to be round here, I must say, and I walked rather carefully myself; the fog is very thick."

"That 's it; you see they are crazy with their eeling, and crabbing, and there aint one on 'em that can swim, or they don't; they go right down, and its about clean shook my wits. There 's been no less than three juries here the last year; you see when the tide 's in we have deep water here."

"Sloops come up here with ease, I understand, Mr. Duncan."

"Time was, Mr. Lovell," and Mr. Duncan made a hitch in his chair, and turned round to face his visitor; "time *was*, when three sloops have laid side by side at the old dock here, and night and day hands was at work loading and unloading, and barrels of meal a-rolling out, and bags of corn a-coming in, and three run o' stone could n't go fast enough. Time *was* when I 've seen all that."

"How many run of stone have you now, Mr. Duncan?"

"Only one, only one. Times is changed. You see the trade fell off, and they set up the new mill on the mile-run, and things did n't go right, and they 've been going wrong now a good while, and I guess they 'll keep so. When things once git a-going wrong in this world, Mr. Lovell, they 're apt to keep a-going; it seems natural for 'em;" and with that the old man commenced puffing again at his pipe, as though there might possibly be some comfort in that; if there was, he meant to have it.

"I have come to see you this evening, Mr. Duncan, to ask the favor of you to permit a few hundred bushels of lime to be landed on your dock, until we can cart it off. The sloop will be along with it next week."

"Entirely welcome, entirely welcome. Time *was* when

you would have had to watch your chance, but there aint much danger of your being disturbed now. But I must go hoist the gate, and let the stone be a turning, for they 'll be here by break-o'-day, hallooing for their grist."

And thus saying, Mr. Duncan gathered his legs in, and by the help of his hands on the arms of his chair, arrived at an erect position.

"Just sit still, Mr. Lovell, and I 'll be back to rights;" and with both hands pressing against the small of his back, and a groan or two, he shuffled out of the room.

Scarcely had he started when Charles thought he heard a call for help; and, listening attentively, it was repeated with great earnestness. Charles rushed into the mill.

"Mr. Duncan, Mr. Duncan, stop, stop! there is some one calling for help."

The miller had his hand upon the lever and was in the act of raising his arm. Charles caught his arm.

"There is some one calling for help; you had better not start your wheel."

Duncan made no reply, but with his lower jaw dropped down, and his eyes staring wildly, stood perfectly still in the act of listening. In an instant more he heard his name distinctly called, and apparently from under the wheel.

"Gosh! there 's another," and he ran to the other door. "Where are you? who are you? what is it?" The last sentence coming out at the top of his voice.

"It 's me—bring a light here; I 've got in and can't get out."

Duncan ran into the little room, caught down the lantern, and was out in an instant; he seemed to have forgotten all his ailments, and was evidently under great excitement. The night had become very dark—a dense fog having settled all over the salt marsh.

With great care, and trembling with the apprehension of some terrible calamity, Duncan stepped along to the edge of the race-way, calling out continually, "Where are you? who are you?"

"Here I am—bring your light this way."

The sound came apparently from under the wheel.

"Are you in the water? or where are you?

"I don't know where I am, but I am fast into some part of your mill, and I can't get out."

Duncan stepped carefully along, muttering some terrible oaths,—he was very apt to do so when frightened,—until he came almost in contact with the slimy paddles of his big wheel, when he suddenly exclaimed:

"Oh, gosh!" Charles stepped up beside him and looked at the object which had excited Mr. Duncan's astonishment. An old rickety skiff lay just beneath, with its bow fast in between the paddles of the wheel, while in its stern sat a man dressed in a sailor's garb, and his countenance manifesting great alarm.

"You good for nothing imp of Satan, what do you mean by poking about with your old skiff such a dark night; one-half minute more and you 'd been a dead man—you 'd been smashed to atoms."

The man seemed rather surprised at the harsh language of the miller, but made no reply. He merely stepped to the front part of his boat, and began pushing against the wheel, endeavoring to extricate himself from his unpleasant position; but the boat was too securely locked in, he could not move her.

"Will you please, Mr. Duncan, to step down and help me to push my boat off?"

But Mr. Duncan had no idea of venturing his carcass into such a peril, for besides the boat looking rather small for two, he was conscious that his gate was none of the strongest, and in case of any accident to that, with a full head of water pouring upon his wheel, the boat and its contents would have been of small consideration. It was no trifling distance between the boat and the platform on which he stood. He was, however, extremely anxious to get the man out of danger; he had become very sensitive on the subject of drowning; so, giving the lantern to Charles, he laid himself flat down, and stretched out his arm towards the man.

"Take hold of my hand and try to climb up." The man, however, had no idea of leaving his boat, but taking no notice of the hand kept working against the old wheel."

"I tell you what it is, mister, do you take hold of my hand and git out, just as quick as you can. My gate aint none of the strongest, and the tide is full in—your life aint safe a minute."

Thus urged the man arose, and taking the offered hand,

put his feet into the logs, and was soon on the platform. Duncan was greatly relieved. He drew a long breath—his under-jaw dropped, and the vials of his wrath were immediately poured forth.

"Never mind, Mr. Duncan, swearing won't help the matter—only let me have a boat-hook, for if my boat should be broken, how can I get back to my family to-night?"

The boat-hook was produced along with a whole batch of curses, to which no reply was made. It was no easy matter, however, with their united strength to get the skiff out of its peril. It was at length accomplished, and the eager boatman, so soon as it was free again, sprang in. At which Duncan seemed fired with rage, and running into the mill, hoisted his gate, and in an instant more the water was boiling and tearing through the race-way, carrying the boat along in the rapid current. Charles was truly alarmed, but the boatman seemed to know what to do; he let the skiff glide out to the still water, and then made her fast. Immediately he sprang ashore and entered the mill, and advanced to where Mr. Duncan was busy emptying bags into his hopper. Charles could not hear what passed between them, for the cogs were rattling and the stones buzzing, and the whole concern more or less making some peculiar noise of its own—even to the plates of the old stove. The miller, however, took a bag which the man handed to him, and proceeded to a bin, near where Charles was standing, and began to ladle in some fine flour; when the bag was about half full, he stopped and asked:

"How much do you want?"

The man turned very pale, and his voice trembled as he spoke.

"Well, just as much as you think you can spare me. You know what I said to you about it?"

"I did n't hear nothing you said, only you wanted some meal. How much do you want?"

"I told you, you know, Mr. Duncan, that I could n't pay for it now; but you shall have it the first fish we haul."

"I'll see the old mill turned bottom upwards into the creek first. Here do you come, poking around such a night as this, and running into my wheel, and a little more would have been pounded to death in it; and then the whole town a-coming here, and asking me how it is that people drown *here* so, and a coroner's jury a-sitting and swearing, everybody making a great fuss, just as if I can help folks drowning themselves. And then into the bargain you want me to trust you meal. I shan't do it; the people on the island owe me enough already." And then turning to Charles, "Folks seems to think a miller's grain never costs nothing, just as if it was rained down from heaven on to him."

Charles had watched the pale and agonized countenance of the boatman with deep interest. At first from curiosity, as it was a face so peculiarly arranged that he could not make up his mind whether its owner was a youth, like himself, or a man of middle age. His spry, elastic motion, the smoothness of his cheeks and upper lip, contrasted strangely to his mind with a stiff, thick red beard that covered his neck, and the long, coarse yellowish hair that hung down over his brow and ears. And what to him appeared singular, also, was the darkness of his eyebrows, in contrast with his hair and whiskers. But his feelings of curiosity almost immediately gave place to that of pity. The man was evidently not accustomed to beg, or ask favors; and the look of anguish with which he saw the miller empty back the contents of the bag into his bin, was too much for Charles. He at once stepped up.

"Mr. Duncan, you can let the man have the flour. Fill the bag, sir, I will pay for it."

Duncan looked at Charles in great wonder, hardly comprehending what he said.

"Fill the bag, I said, Mr. Duncan; I will give you the money for it." And then turning to the astonished boatman, in whose eye he saw the tear gathering:

"You live on Oyster Island, sir, and follow fishing?"

"I do, sir."

"Step this way, sir;" and the man followed him into the little room.

"I was going to the island in the morning in pursuit of some one from whom I could get a quantity of fish; I want it for my land."

"I have no seine of my own, sir; but others have, and I assist them. I should not fear but we can supply you."

"Do the fish run yet?"

"Not for a fortnight or three weeks."

"And if I come to the island, I can no doubt make an arrangement for what I want?"

"You can without doubt, sir. My name, sir, is McDougall."

Charles thought he colored a little, and there was a slight hesitancy in his utterance of the name.

"Your kindness to a stranger, sir, has been very singular; but I hope you will not have to repent it. My necessity, and the need of those dependent upon me, alone could have compelled me to come here at such a time; and if I had been obliged to return empty-handed, it would have been a sad journey home. May I ask the name of one who has thus laid me under obligations?"

Charles gave his name, and assisted the boatman in carrying his bag to the skiff; and as the little boat glided off into the deep water, and the sound of his oars alone gave token of the lonely voyage, Charles pondered on the scene. He thought how well it was that he happened there at the time; and how sad might have been the heart of that stranger on his gloomy track to his home.

And the light from his own cottage looked brighter as he approached it; and his head lay upon his pillow that night in a sweeter rest even than usual.

Besides enriching his land, and making preparation for a larger profit than the last year had afforded, Charles kept an eye upon his future home. He had his own fancy about a home. He did not think of it merely, as a house with so many rooms in it; a place to eat, and to sleep in; but to his mind there must be the idea of permanency about. Trees for fruit that would be plucked by those of another generation; trees for ornament and shade; under whose wide-spreading branches he and his might often enjoy the cooling breeze, when the sun was in his strength, and whose noble proportions might captivate his eye for years to come, and that might link the days when his step would be tottering, and his arm weak, with those of his youth and manhood; and he wished them to be clustered around his dwelling, as though their fruits and shade were for its benefit.

"I think," said Augustus to him one day, as he was planning where to place some trees, "first of all, I would cut down that large apple tree which stands just north of the house; apple trees are not very ornamental."

"Not for the world, Guss, that is a fine tree. Its fruit, indeed, is not so valuable as some others; but the tree is thrifty and well formed; and it has such a domestic look. Oh, no! Guss, we must let that stand, and the old oak off in the corner there, and that walnut too. I think we shall yet enlarge the yard, so as to take them in; and by setting out our trees irregularly, the whole will appear more easy. I don't fancy a house surrounded by trees set in rows like ranks of soldiers, it is too unnatural; and I think we had better scatter them, so that they may appear to belong to those already standing about."

Augustus smiled. "Well, just as you say; only tell me where to dig, for if you or I are going to have any benefit from them, they ought to be growing as quick as possible."

"They will be growing, Guss, while you and I are sleeping, and busy about other things; and we shall every once in awhile be glad to notice their progress. And then, if we should live, how pleasant it will be for us to look away up into their large branches, and admire their stately forms, and think of all the happiness we are now enjoying, and of all we may have enjoyed for many years in our snug home."

"In the old stone house?"

"Yes, in the old stone house. You may laugh, Guss; I don't wonder that you do. But I have a plan in my head by which, for a little expense, we may make this old house the nucleus to a comfortable, convenient, pretty home for us."

"You have given a right name to it, Charley. It will be the nucleus, if it 's any part of a house. It is strong enough to bear a load on the top of it, up as high as you like. But I think you are taking a pretty long look ahead, Charley."

"Well, there is no harm in that, Guss, if we don't let it interfere with present duty; and besides, it takes a pretty long look to see the large branches of this tree I am holding, but I can see them; I mean in fancy, Guss. But that makes me think of our cattle-shed. You know we merely put on a temporary roof of boards. It ought to be shingled, and then it would correspond with the barn, and the whole establishment would have an uniform, snug appearance."

"How much would it cost?"

"It would take more than I should dare to spend. We must lay in some things for the summer, and we shall both need a few articles of clothing. And then we ought to keep some money on hand, in case some necessary article should be wanted, which we do not now think of; and I don't like the feeling of being out of money."

"Billings would trust you, Charley, in a minute. He has told me several times, that anything we wanted in his line we could have at cash price, and he 'd trust us six months. He has a lumber yard, you know, as well as a store."

Charles looked at his brother, with every token of alarm in his countenance.

"You have not purchased anything there, I hope, Guss, without paying for it?"

"Not a cent's worth, Charley."

"Nor anywhere else?"

"No, not a cent's worth."

"You gave me a real start, Guss, to hear you talk so lightly about getting trusted. Mr. Billings is very kind, but remember, Guss, *I will not buy on credit;* remember that, and let us keep to it. We shall then know that what we have is our own. We shall feel under obligations to no man. We shall keep our hearts light, and we shall not grow gray before our time."

"Agreed, Charley. I should not have mentioned it, if I had thought it was going to work you up so. Agreed, I say, and let us stick to it. But why can't you sell the old hay? the cattle are now in pasture. There is all of three tons in the bottom of the bay."

"You think so?"

"There is more than two tons, I know."

"You must have been very prudent, then, Guss; and they don't look as if they had been starved."

"I gave them all they would eat, but I did n't let them waste it. I saw enough of wasting hay at Clawson's."

It turned out that Augustus had guessed right about the hay, and two tons could be spared, besides leaving enough on hand as occasion might require.

"And now, Guss," said Charles, as he came back with his team, after carrying the second load, "we have got the money in our hands, we can talk more certainly about our shingles. Slocum will be here to-morrow, so we must arrange everything to-day, and have the shingles on hand. And the day after, if possible, I must go to Oyster Island, and see about the fish."

Slocum was always glad of a chance to work for the Lovells. He said "he liked Aunt Casey's cooking so much, he wished they would give him a six months' job."

"You will have it one of these days, I guess, Mr. Slocum, when Charley begins at the old stone house."

"We will blow her up, Guss, ha! ha! ha! Blow her up with powder; that will be the quickest way to get it out of the way. A sledge-hammer won't touch it."

"Oh, but he don't want it taken down; he is going to make a house of it—a home, he calls it."

"How you talk, Guss! ha! ha! ha! Charley don't though? and that 's what all these trees are for? Nation! he' ll have a woods about him one of these days. I tell you what, Charley looks a long way ahead, and now just see, Guss, how the thing is fixed. The barn, and shed, and the yard, and all; when this spot comes to be all fenced in, and these trees get a-growing, it will look nice, I tell you; and it all looks as if it was going to be together, of a piece; and that made him so set about having the shed just fixed as it is. I wanted him to put it on t 'other side, but no. You see he has got a plan in his head, and when he does anything about the place, why he makes it jibe with other things that he is going to do. It 's a grand way, Guss, if a man has a head long enough to do it. But the old house! ha! ha! ha!"

"We shall have to wait and see what is to be done with that."

Oyster Island could be distinctly seen from the old mill, or from any spot commanding a view of the marsh. But it only appeared, in the distance, as a more elevated spot, on which a few trees were growing. It was, however, surrounded entirely by water, the main creek parting and running on each side of it, before uniting with the Sound.

It was a small tract of land, not perfectly barren, and yet with very little soil upon it that seemed adapted to cultivation. Some low cedars, and a few scrub oaks, formed a little clump of wood, that served as a shelter from the storms of winter, exposed as the island was to the full sweep of the winds from the open Sound.

Charles had never visited it, and began to fear lest he might have difficulty in finding the location of McDougall, but he saw a beaten footpath near where he tied his boat, and following a short distance through the cedars, came suddenly upon a small, mean cottage, built of logs and boards roughly put together, and thatched with straw. It was near the water, and, recognizing the little skiff, he was about to enter the dwelling, when the man he was in quest of appeared, turning a corner of his rude habitation. He walked quickly up and grasped the hand of Charles with great earnestess.

"Ah, sir, how rejoiced I am to see you. It is but a poor place we have to live in, as you see; all we can do is to bid you a hearty welcome." With that he advanced to the door and walked in, followed by Lovell.

"This is the gentleman, Margaret, who treated me so kindly at the mill, the other evening."

The woman made a slight curtsey, and then advanced and took his offered hand. She could not speak, but her look was enough to have made full compensation to Charles, if he had desired any. Nor did *he* say much; for his mind was fully occupied with the strange contrast between the pair he had thus become introduced to, and the circumstances in which they lived. The appearance of the man, his language, and at times his manner, had attracted his notice from the first; and now much more was he astonished, as he looked at the pale and somewhat emaciated, but handsome face of his wife.

That she had never been brought up under their present circumstances, he needed not to ask. And that the little fellow by her side, who was hanging to her dress and looking up with some alarm at the stranger, was not the child of those who had been low born or bred, he was well assured. His heart was enlisted at once, and, without inquiring into their past history, without asking them whether crime or misfortune had brought them to their present condition, he would have been ready, had he possessed abundant means, to have lifted them up, and carried them into the civilization and refinement which he felt confident they had been accustomed to. Thus he felt from merely the first impression which had been made upon him.

"I believe I understood your name aright, sir? Lovell, was it not?"

"Yes sir, my name is Lovell."

This seemed to have been said by McDougall, as a gentle hint to his wife that she had as yet said nothing, not even spoken the name of their visitor. Her pale cheek slightly flushed as she said:

"Mr. Lovell's name will not be easily forgotten by us, and it is a great pleasure to be able personally to express our feelings, although we can in no other way just now show our gratitude."

Charles begged that neither of them would mention the matter again, and that he himself could hardly feel grateful enough, that he had been so fortunately there at the time.

"And now," said McDougall, "if you will accompany me, Mr. Lovell, I think you can make such a bargain for your fish as will satisfy you."

The huts occupied by the other inhabitants were at some little distance, almost the whole of them on the opposite side of the island, and on their way Charles ventured to make some inquiries as to the means which could be found here for a living, and even once rather hinted at the advantages which a person might have to obtain the comforts of life nearer to a more densely-populated place, and where all were not poor. But no reply was made, and the subject of conversation changed.

The man, however, told him by way of apology for his present straitened condition, that during a great storm in the winter his seine had been carried off, and his inability to procure another rendered him dependent upon others for work, as they happened to need assistance.

"Then if you had a seine, you might probably supply all I should need, and have all the profits to yourself."

"That is true, sir; it has been a great loss, but I must do the best I can."

"How much would it cost?"

"I can procure one for five dollars—it is not a new one, but will answer me well."

Charles stopped. "Mr. McDougall, I should much prefer that you should have what little gain you can make out of it; I want to lay out about fifty dollars for fish, and if you think you can supply me, I will advance the money for you to purchase the seine."

"You are very kind, sir; I am but a stranger to you, and surely have no such claim upon your generosity. It would indeed be a great thing for me."

"We need go no further then, sir; I will advance you the money, to be returned in fish."

"And if my life is spared it shall be returned with your other favor."

"I have no fears of that, sir."

"You will partake of some refreshment, such as we can give you, before your return? My wife will expect you, and no doubt have some little things ready." Charles had just then no objections to something of the kind, and he had also a strong desire to see more of this strange family. He, therefore, as the request appeared to be sincere, did not hesitate to follow his host.

A small table was set already, covered with a clean white cloth, and a broiled fish, with some bread-cakes newly made, constituted the only articles upon it. Nothing was said by way of apology; but, as they took their seats around the simple meal, the lady—we must call her so, in spite of all the rude materials which surrounded her—looked expressively at Charles a moment.

"Perhaps Mr. Lovell will ask a blessing?"

But little was said during the meal; Charles was in no mood for conversation, and both the man and his wife appeared somewhat embarrassed by his presence. They seeming to prefer subjects quite foreign to their own condition and circumstances, and Charles was too much absorbed by the strange anomally to enter heartily into other matters. Their simple repast was soon finished, and he at once prepared to take his leave.

"I hope," said Mrs. McDougall, as she gave him her hand, "this will not be the last time we shall see Mr. Lovell; it would be a great pleasure occasionally to see one who—"

"Oh, I shall see Mr. Lovell soon, and perhaps he may like to sail down here occasionally in pleasant weather."

"We so seldom—I may say never, see any one."

"But my dear," again interrupting his wife, "remember we are but poor folks; and although we should be very happy to see Mr. Lovell, who has been so kind to us, we can offer but poor inducement to any one to come out of their way to visit us, and our neighbors here are very kind."

Charles knew not exactly how to reply. He ventured, however, to say:

"I hope this may not be the last interview we shall have. I have but little leisure, but if I can be of any service to you at any time, I shall esteem it a favor that you would let me know it."

"Oh, thank you, sir," said the wife, and her lip trembled as she uttered the word "good-bye," while her look betrayed feelings of deep emotion.

Having completed all needful arrangements for the fish, Charles parted with his new, and to him strange acquaintance, fully resolved in his own mind to know more about them, if the thing could be accomplished without rudeness.

The business of spreading the lime was indeed the most tedious operation the young men had yet passed through.

"There, now, Guss," and Charles threw his shovel into the cart as he spoke, "that is the last of it; and when you have harrowed this ridge, the field will be ready for planting."

"It is a good job, now it is done; planting and hoeing will only be play after this. But somehow, it seems too bad to think that your hundred dollars, you worked so hard for last winter, should be sprinkled over the ground in this manner, and put out of sight so soon. It requires some faith to believe that you are going to get it back again."

"I don't feel at all uneasy about that, Guss; our experiment last year satisfied me fully, and even if we should not get repaid this year, we shall feel the benefit of it for years to come."

"Well, I am satisfied, if you are. But who is that driving so furiously this way?"

"It is Ben Blarcom; here he comes, right through the bars, and across the ploughed ground, lime and all, whip-it-a-cut."

"Hurra, boys, how are you? Why, Charley Lovell, how you look! what have you been doing? turned miller? you have n't bought old Duncan out, have you? I wish you would. How are you, Guss?"

"Well and hearty."

"That 's the sort. Well, boys, I 'm upon the run this

morning. I 've got more than twenty places to go to. We are going to have a crow-hunt, and we want every fellow that can handle a gun to join us. We shall meet at Foster's, to morrow morning, and then in the evening the old fellow is to prepare a supper for us. We shall have glorious times, I tell you; and the fellows said I must make you and Guss come, at any rate."

"I don't know how Guss will feel about it, he is much more expert with a gun than I am; but I tell you what it is, Ben, we have got so much to do that I dare not leave my work a single hour; we have laid out enough for three men, and scratch hard too."

"And so have I. But where 's the use, Charley, of strapping to it like a slave; a holiday once in awhile is good for a fellow, and I mean to have it, and let the work take care of itself."

"If it would only do that, Ben. But you know that farmers' work has to be done in the season for it, or we miss our chance."

"Yes, I know that; but all you have to do is to work the harder next day; do two days' work in one."

"I have n't got the knack of that, Ben. I wish I had; it would come very handy just now."

"Well, I tell you how I do, Charley. When I want to go off on a spree, I get some of the fellows to exchange work with me, and so we go at it, 'hurra boys,' and work like distraction, and then when they want a lift, I go and help them."

"But when you work like distraction, as you call it, how do you feel next day, Ben?"

"Ha! ha! ha! Charley, you 've got me there; don't talk about it. I don't know but you 're right about that. But we must have this crow-hunt; and then, the supper at night, you know. What do you say to it, Guss?"

"Is Charley going?"

"He says you are the best shot."

"I guess he can kill a crow, if he tries. Are you going, Charley?"

"I don't feel that I can spare the time; but if you would like to go, I 'll do the ploughing."

"I shan't go without you do, anyhow; but I should think we 'd get pinched for it, by-and-bye."

"Well, boys, I can't wait, but you had better think of it; meet us at Foster's, and let the work whistle for one day; good morning to you." And off he drove again, Jehu-like.

"Ben will spend all this day getting ready for to-morrow, and then he will be so tired the next day after the hunt, that he will lose another day in getting rest."

"I guess we shall feel as happy to be jogging along with our work; and as to the supper, I enjoy mine well enough every night; and besides, I find by keeping steady along, we get through more work in a week than one would think for, and don't get very tired either."

"That 's it, Guss; a steady pull, a strong pull, and a pull together and it 's got to go, if there is any go to it."

CHAPTER XVI.

It is a very pleasant thing to live in a nice house, even in a city; to have all the luxuries of life about one; a carriage at command to saunter in through a splendid promenade, on fine sunny days, and servants to wait upon every want; and, doubtless, many who passed the very respectable establishment of Mrs. Abigail Ratoon, in Park place, and saw a very handsome young lady come down its steps, and enter the fine roomy coach by which a liveried waiter stood, holding open its door for her; and beheld the prancing steeds bear off the lovely passenger; thought within themselves, "what a nice time she must have of it; how happy she must be." And the young lady herself had no objections, whatever, to all these arrangements, in themselves considered; they were all well enough; but could any of those who perhaps envied her position, have known that this same young lady had a mind of her own on some matters of more consequence than the conveniences that were at her disposal; and that it was fully expected of her, that for their consideration she was to yield up all her own peculiar views and feelings; they might perhaps have come to a different conclusion as to the happiness of her condition. At least the young lady herself had come to such a conclusion; and at this very time is on her way to consult with a friend, in whom she can confide, and if possible make some arrangement for a change in her life. The carriage awhile rolled along through the beautiful thoroughfare of Broadway, and then turned into a cross street, and stopped before a small, plain looking house, on which was a little tin sign, "Mrs. Willis, dress-maker."

At once the door of the carriage was opened, and the waiter as before stood by it, and the sprightly girl sprang to the pavement and entered the house.

A lady of middle age, with a very mild and winning countenance, sat alone in the room, busily employed on a dress; and as her door opened, she turned and put out her hand.

"Good morning, dear, how do you do? How is your aunt this morning?"

"All well, I thank you, Mrs. Willis. You are busy with Aunt Nabby's dress, I see."

"Yes, and I have just finished it; in a minute I will have it ready. I have worked almost all night upon it, for you know I promised it to your aunt this morning, and she don't take it well to be disappointed."

"Well, I am glad, for your sake, that you have succeeded, although it must be very hard for you to work so much at nights."

"There is no help for it, my dear, not if I remain in the city. And sometimes I think that it would be much better for me to try to get some place in the country, where rent would be cheap, and living cheap, and a body could feel a little free; it 's hard work here to make the two ends meet. But I have a letter for you, dear, at last. I dare not, you know, send it round to you, and I thought maybe you would be along in here to-day."

And so saying, she arose, and opening a drawer, placed the letter in the hand of her visitor. She then resumed her work, and both were silent for a time.

"Well, Mrs. Willis, it is a bargain. She has accepted my offer."

"You don't say so!"

"She has, with one curious proviso; 'if my personal appearance and manners shall correspond with her expectations.' Curious, is it not?"

"I think it is; but you need not fear on that account, dear. She can't but like your looks and behavior, anyhow. But it is a very queer item for the principal of a seminary to put in; but people all have their notions. There, now, this dress is complete, I believe; and I will just pin it up, and put it in the carriage when you go. And now, dear, I want to talk with you a little about this matter of your going away. Have you thought it all well over, dear Miss Adelaide?"

"I have, Mrs. Willis. I have thought of it every way I can."

"You have not told your aunt about it yet?"

"No, but I shall inform her of it this very day."

"I am afraid you don't know your aunt, Adelaide. She is very set in her way. I am afraid she will turn you off altogether."

"I can hardly think she can do that, Mrs. Willis, when I tell her all my reasons. And I think some things have happened of late, that will cause her to feel that I am not so wrong. She knows that I have no one now on whom I can depend. Uncle Halliday has gone, you know; and surely she cannot blame me very much, for wishing to learn how to take care of myself."

"Well, I don't know, dear. She has queer ways, and set ways, and unforgiving ways; when she once takes a notion against a thing, or a person, it is hard turning her. And I am so afraid that maybe she might just take it in her head to cast you off altogether; and, oh dear, it 's a dreadful thing to be cast on the world alone, especially for one like your self. Everything is so different with one; everybody seems to feel so different when one is dependent for a living, or have full and plenty around them."

"Well, you know, Mrs. Willis, I will see first how Aunt Nabby feels. I directed my letter to be sent to your care, so that her name might not be implicated. I shall try not to offend her. But I do want to feel a little as if I could act as my own feelings and judgment dictate, and not be obliged to submit like an automaton to the complete guidance of another."

"Well, dear, I hope it may turn out well, and that you may be guided in a right way. It is a great thing in this world to do right."

The bundle is handed to the footman, to deposit within the carriage; and, bidding a pleasant good morning to Mrs. Willis, the young lady again takes her seat, and is whirled off to her home.

Adelaide had made Mrs. Willis, whom she knew to be a good woman, and true in her friendly feelings towards her, a confidant, only in some few particulars, of the trials which she suffered from her aunt; and she had done this because she must have some place where letters could be directed to her. She knew how much opposed her aunt was to have her "stoop" to do anything for her own maintenance; and feared that she would not only consider her own name contaminated, but would take measures that might effectually hinder whatever plans might be in progress for that object. The time had come, however, when the strength of her purpose must be tested, and the plans she had in view unfolded. And an opportunity was afforded her soon after.

She had returned from the errand upon which she had gone out that morning, partly for her aunt, and partly, as we have seen, on her own account. Mrs. Abigail Ratoon had examined the dress which Adelaide brought for her, and was just about to hang it up in her wardrobe, when, with a pleasant smile upon her face, she turned towards her niece:

"Who do you think has been here?"

Adelaide mentioned one or two names

"Yes, they have both called, but only think, Mr. Sampson has been here again! and I really felt glad to see him, for I have been afraid, ever since the evening of the party, and young De Luce hung round you so, and seemed to absorb all your attention, that Sampson had taken a miff."

Adelaide would have replied, "that she would have no objections had such an event occurred," but she was too much excited just then to say anything.

"But he came in as pleasant as ever, and seemed quite disappointed not to see you. I do think he has a very amiable disposition. And what do you think! he said he has been buying a span of grays, and he is going to-morrow to drive up to see Julia and Vanderbose, and try his horses, and he said it would give him great pleasure to have your company. And I told him I thought you would no doubt be happy to have such an opportunity to visit your cousin."

"I am sorry, aunt, that you gave him any encouragement."

"And why so, Adelaide?"

And Mrs. Ratoon took her seat in a large arm-chair, as though the matter to be attended to was a very serious one, and requested her niece to lay down her hat, and sit down; "she wanted to talk with her."

"And why not, Adelaide?"

Adelaide endeavored to command her feelings, and to say nothing that might give her aunt unnecessary pain.

"To-morrow, you know, aunt, is the Sabbath. You probably did not think of it at the time."

"Ah, yes, I know it is. But then it will not be like riding out of town and back again, merely for pleasure; we should not do that, you know. No respectable family does that. You would be off immediately in the country, you know; and it is very common for friends to ride fifteen or twenty miles to visit connexions; you would not go to a tavern or anything of that kind."

"It would appear to me, aunt, all the time like a violation of the Sabbath. You know Uncle Halliday was always particular himself about the Sabbath, and has so trained both Julia and myself in that respect, that I am sure we shall neither of us ever be happy in its violation."

"And how would the Sabbath be violated, Adelaide, by your merely going off in a quiet way, disturbing nobody, mingling in no crowd, and visiting your relation, one that you love and with whom you have been brought up. If you have both been so *religiously* educated, you surely need not fear each other's society on the Sabbath."

"We should not, aunt; dear cousin Julia and myself have often enjoyed many sacred Sabbaths together, but Julia is not now her own mistress."

"What do you mean by that, Adelaide? do you mean that Julia has a master over her, one who tyrannizes over her and oppresses her? Not her own mistress! has she not a splendid establishment entirely under her command? Has she a want that cannot be gratified? I wish you would tell me what you mean, Adelaide, by intimating what you do?"

"I mean, aunt, and if you do not already know it, I must tell you. Julia has no doubt plenty of money in her purse, plenty of servants at her command, and everything around her that might gratify her vanity, if she took delight in mere show. But her husband takes pleasure in things which she cannot sympathize in. He has associates whom she utterly despises; her evenings are no longer scenes of pleasant social intercourse, and her Sabbaths are no longer days of sacred rest; he has companions with whom he spends his evenings, and sometimes a great part of the night, such as Julia can have no communion with. And I am very sorry to say it, but—"

"*But*," and her aunt interrupted her with an angry tone. "I don't want to hear any of your *buts*, Adelaide. You have always been strangely prejudiced against Vanderbose; you never seemed to fancy the idea of your cousin being raised to such an elevated position. I don't want to hear servants' stories repeated in my presence."

She well knew they were not merely "servants' stories;" but her pride was wounded by hearing aught that might condemn the choice she had made for her niece.

"I am afraid, Adelaide, that you merely make your pretended regard for the Sabbath a cloak to cover your want of obedience to my will. If the truth was known, it is not so much the Sabbath as it is your foolish prejudice against Mr. Sampson."

"I acknowledge, aunt, that if it was not on the Sabbath, the idea of a ride with Mr. Sampson, and alone too, is very unpleasant to me, and I should not be willing to accept his invitation, was it made for any other day."

"And after I have told him that you would be glad to go!"

"I regret exceedingly, aunt, that you told him so."

"You regret exceedingly! Adelaide you *shall* go!" and her aunt arose, and repeated the fiat with great violence of manner.

"You *shall* go. I will see who is to be mistress here—remember, miss, you are under my thumb now—you have no Uncle Halliday to run to with your pitiful stories; and upon me you are dependent for the clothes on your back, and the bread that you eat. You *shall* go—you *shall* go—you shall—you shall go—" and screaming the last sentence out at the top of her voice, she went off into a hysteric spasm, screaming and tearing her hair, and flying about the room like a mad person.

At once the household of servants rushed into the room, and her confidential waiting-maid flew to her, and catching her in her arms, began saying all manner of soothing things, while the others flocked around Adelaide, eagerly inquiring into the cause of the calamity. The screams continued for some time, until Mrs. Betsey Snuffle, the waiting-maid aforesaid, very prudently hinted to her the danger "that the neighbors might hear and be coming in, and how disgraceful it would be." When suddenly there was a hushing up of the storm, a few heavy groans, a few long-drawn sighs, a little weak sling, with great difficulty gulped down, and a rolling out of soft and flattering words by Mrs. Betsey, at length terminated the hubbub. The servants, one by one, went off again to their duties—only Mrs. Betsey; she stayed until things were all "put to rights," and then, as she left too, stepped along by where Adelaide still sat in the chair, where her aunt had first ordered her to sit, and whispered loud enough though to be heard through the room:

"Miss Adelaide, you 'll be the death of your aunt, if you don't give in to her demands."

It may seem surprising that Adelaide had not exhibited more alarm, or taken more pains to quiet the distracted feelings of her relation. But Adelaide was acting under a strong sense of duty; she was fully resolved as to the step she was about to take; she had done no wrong, and she well knew that all interference on her part would only aggravate the unpleasant symptoms. She, therefore, quietly retained her seat, although her mind was tossed as the ship when winds and waves are contrary. The only way by which she could retain her own self-possession, was to keep steadily in view the simple idea,—

"That it was her duty to release herself from a bondage that she had never voluntarily sought, and which imposed upon her sacrifices inconsistent with her obligations to God, and the finer feelings of her nature."

It took Mrs. Abigail some time to recover fully. But as soon as she did so, it was very evident that the storm had not cleansed the atmosphere. Awhile she walked the room, probably expecting her niece to begin the conversation, and in a more humble strain. She waited in vain, however, and finally again resumed the seat in her arm-chair.

"I see it is high time, Adelaide, that you fully understood your position. You are in some sense alone in the world. You have been unfortunate in some of your connections."

Adelaide colored deeply, and fixed her bright eye full upon her aunt.

"I mean, you know, in regard to your brother. He is dead to you, you know, and to the world, if he is not really so."

"Aunt Ratoon, you are the only one who has ever been unkind enough to taunt me with a calamity beyond my power to have foreseen or prevented. But I say to you now that there are very strong doubts against the charge under which my poor brother has been suffering, and for which he is held to be guilty; and I have supposed, aunt, that you had given him the benefit of your charity, at least. But, I believe, Aunt Ratoon, that Charles is innocent, and I *will* believe it."

"Oh, well! Adelaide, we will let that go; it matters not—he is, we know not where—nor in what condition; at any rate, you have no dependence from that source. Your Uncle Halliday has made almost a wreck of his fortune, and has gone to China again, and you have no dependence there; on my care alone are you cast, and from my fortune alone can you ever have any expectations. But I tell you now, once for all, my will must be obeyed; and I shall not be unreasonable with you. I have indeed told Mr. Sampson that you would doubtless accompany him to-morrow. We will waive that; I will not ask you to violate, as you call it, the Sabbath. You may keep it as quietly as you please. But I shall propose to Mr. Sampson to defer his visit until Monday, and then, Adelaide, I shall insist upon it that you accompany him."

"I hope, aunt, that you will think better of it, before you see that gentleman. I have told you that it would be very unpleasant for me to be placed in any such situation with Mr. Sampson."

"It was not very unpleasant, Adelaide, for you to ride off alone, and at night, too, with a plain country clown. I may say at the very risk of your reputation."

Adelaide was too full of indignation to reply, and she knew it would be of no avail; it would be impossible to disabuse her aunt's mind of its strong prejudice, so she sat silently composing her feelings, and preparing herself for the accomplishment of her determined purpose.

"No; I am resolved, Adelaide, that my will must be obeyed. I ask nothing unreasonable. Mr. Sampson is a gentleman of respectability—of high standing. There can be no possible objection to his waiting upon you, on a visit to your cousin. I shall expect you to comply with my wish, without any more words on either side."

Her aunt was about to leave her, having risen from her

seat, and was walking towards the door, when Adelaide, with a very trembling tone, spoke:

"Aunt Ratoon!"

The lady stopped and looked towards her, with evident complacency. She felt, doubtless, from the whole manner of her niece, that the great end had been accomplished, and her own triumph was complete.

"Aunt Ratoon, I wish to say a few words to you, and I want you patiently to listen to me." Her aunt's countenance again resumed its stern cast. "I do not wish to be a cause of trial to you, and have endeavored, so far as I could, to avoid either disobedience to your requests, or even an unwilling compliance. But the matter which you urge upon me now is one that comes so directly in conflict with my feelings, and is so repugnant to my heart, that I cannot comply with it. I can never, by any act of mine, encourage the attentions of one whom no earthly considerations could induce me to accept for a husband. And since you have spoken so positively, I cannot expect you to retract. Therefore, I think we had better separate. I had rather earn my living, aunt, than submit to a sacrifice of all I hold dear. If my presence will not be offensive to you, I would ask the privilege of remaining under your roof until the first of next week."

"Earn your living! And how, pray, are you to do that? Do you design to bring all your connexions to disgrace by engaging in some menial service?"

Her aunt was evidently alarmed.

"I have no intention, aunt, of engaging in any service which is not of itself respectable. I can get employment as a teacher."

"As a teacher! as a teacher! Oh, Adelaide!" And Mrs. Abigail Ratoon clasped her hands together, and threw herself again into her chair. "And has it come to this! my own sister's daughter a hired teacher? Oh! oh! oh! Little did I think—but no matter. One thing I tell you, Adelaide; I want you to hear me, and to remember. *If* you leave my house, and engage yourself to any such employment, even if you do it for a single week, *I will never leave you one cent.* And more than that, you shall in such case never again put your foot within my doors. I would spurn you from it as I would a filthy beggar."

Adelaide arose, and assuming a dignity not usual with her, her beautiful countenance glowing with excitement:

"I shall not wait, then, aunt, to have you put to such a necessity. I will relieve you of my presence at once."

Her aunt sat very erect, putting out her hand, and bending forward her body as she spoke:

"The sooner the better; but remember, when your feet once cross the threshold, it will be too late to turn back; they must never step again within this house; no, not even to attend my funeral. I shall disinherit and disown you."

Adelaide immediately left the room, and retired to her own apartment to prepare for her departure. She had a variety of rich dresses, which had been supplied by her aunt, but as she felt that they would not be suitable for the future situation she would most likely occupy, she left them all hanging in the handsome wardrobe, and gathered together only such articles as had been given to her by her kind old uncle. The rich jewels from her hands she also laid aside, leaving them to her who had bestowed them; and then locking her trunk, left it standing in the room she had occupied. She knew that it would answer no good purpose again to see her aunt. Her last farewell of her had been taken; she therefore took leave of the servants, and making no explanation, merely requested that her trunk might be brought down and delivered to whomsoever she might send for it. And then she walked forth into the street, and felt that she had no longer a home on earth.

CHAPTER XVII.

Deacon Rice, as has been said, was a man of property. He was called rich for the country; he had a valuable farm, that brought him yearly a handsome income; and had some few thousands at interest. His eldest son having a taste for city life, and a mercantile business, his father, when he was arrived at age, had given him a snug capital, and the young man had used it so advantageously, that it was said hundreds of thousands passed annually through his hands; "that he was getting rich, and could buy out his good old father any day." He had not as yet taken a partner, from the fact that the old gentleman had always steadily objected to any such arrangement; and as the young man was still dependent upon his father's name for a considerable sum at the Melton Bank, it was necessary for him to yield a point on which the old gentleman was very strenuous.

"One young man," the deacon said, "might be kept within bounds; but it was doubling the risk to get two together."

However, as Frank Rice felt the necessity of having a partner, because of his inability to attend to all parts of his business, he again, on a visit to his native place, proposed the subject to his father. But the old gentleman found some objections, arising in his own mind, to all whom his son named, until, in the course of conversation, some reference was made to Charles Lovell.

"By the way, Frank, if you could get such a young man as that, I don't know but it would be the best thing you could do."

"Charley is a fine fellow, father; a noble fellow."

"Yes, and he is a business man too; everything goes on at his little place there as systematic as clock work; and he understands matters, too, which one would not think a farmer could."

The truth was, that the deacon had become, for various reasons, a warm admirer of Charles; all his old prejudices had melted away. Two of his daughters were members of his Bible class, and by them he was constantly hearing him spoken of in terms of unlimited admiration. He also had an opportunity for becoming acquainted with his prompt business habits, by his being associated with him in the management of some town affairs; and the old gentleman lost no opportunity of speaking loudly in his praise. "He was a young man," he said, "who would be a credit to himself, and to the place where he lived."

It was a very sultry day, the air dry and hot, and the ground was parched by a drought, that had now lasted for some time.

Charles and his brother were busily employed with their hoes, although the potatoes they were hilling gave but small promise of a remunerating crop. The dry and dusty earth, and the hot atmosphere, combined to make it one of those seasons of labor, when even the most resolute would be languid, and glad to see the sun reaching the point which marked the hour for rest.

"There comes Frank Rice, down the road, in his fine gig. I guess Frank is right glad that he has no hoeing to do now-a-days. They say Frank is doing a great business, and will soon be richer than the old man."

As Augustus said this, he stopped his hoe a moment, to take a view of the handsome establishment.

Charles made no reply; he merely turned his eye in the direction Augustus was looking, and kept on with his work. It was one of those days in which Charles was quite sober.

As the gig approached that part of the field in which the young men were at work, its progress was retarded until at length it stopped, and the gentleman sprang out and began to fasten his horse.

"He is coming to see us, Charley."

"Well, I shall be glad to see him. He is rather a clever fellow, I think."

"Well, boys, hard at work; it 's a hot day, aint it?"

"Pretty warm," said Charles, advancing to give his hand, "and very sultry—the most unpleasant weather, it seems to me, I ever felt."

The young man greeted the brothers with his old cordiality. Frank was, in fact, a noble-minded, generous youth.

"It is hot hoeing to-day, I know, but perhaps you don't feel the heat so much as those who are not in the field?"

"I believe it is as cool here as anywhere, but I for one shall have no objections to see the sun a little lower. If ever I felt lazy, I do now."

"Well, Charley, suppose you throw down your hoe and walk a little way with me. I want to talk with you awhile."

Charles at once buried his hoe in the dusty soil, and leaving it in an erect position, walked off with his visitor towards an apple tree, whose thickly-branched top offered an agreeable protection. They both seated themselves upon the cool grass.

"I have called to-day, Charley, not only to say 'how do you do?' but to see you about a matter of business, and when business is on the carpet, my motto is 'attend to it right off.'"

He then at once unfolded to Charles the circumstances in which he was placed, and his desire to obtain a suitable partner, and that it was his desire and also the wish of his father, that Charles would consent to relinquish his present occupation and take an interest in his concern.

"I am doing a large business; my sales last year amounted to one hundred thousand dollars, and my profits were at least twelve thousand dollars, and I offer you to engage with me for five years. The first two years to have one-quarter of the profits, and the remaining three to have one-third; now what say you to pulling up stakes, and linking our fates together."

"I cannot but thank you, Frank, for your proposal. It is certainly a very generous one; and I feel deeply this testimony of your confidence. But I have no capital, and I have no knowledge of business."

"Capital I don't expect; I cannot say I don't want it, for you know the more we have to do with, the more business, in general, we can do. As to the knowledge of business, you have got all the knowledge requisite at present. You are, in the first place, known to be a driving, go-ahead fellow; you are accustomed to application—to close application; you attend to your business promptly in the time of it; you are a good writer, and a good arithmetician, and you know how to address people in a gentlemanly way; your manners are easy, and, above all, I can trust to your honor. And all I want to ask of you is, not to decide right off; think of it, and come up this evening and see me, and we will have a good talk about it. And you can talk with my father too, and see how he feels about it. What do you say to that? will you come?"

Charles could not but accept his invitation to call and converse about it, and to take the subject into serious consideration.

"That 's the sort, Charley, and now I 'm off; you need not say anything about this matter, except to your brother, or to some friend whom you may wish to consult."

"I keep but few things from Augustus. I have no other friend that I should wish to consult."

Charles accompanied him to the place where his horse stood, and waited until Frank drove off with his fine establishment, and then turned and walked back towards the place where his hoe stood, in all its loneliness. It looked very common-place, and the potato bells, with their dry and spindling tops, looked rather prosy; and if anytning, the heat was more oppressive. He went to work, however, in good earnest, for Augustus had gone through his own row, and was returning on his.

As soon as they met, they both concluded, as the afternoon was so far gone, they would allow it to pass for a day's work.

"Well, Guss, what do you think?"

"I think how Aunt Casey's cup of tea will relish to-night, with some of that fresh rye bread she is baking, with a slice or two of cold ham."

"It will be good, won't it, after such a hard day? But what else do you think?"

"I think, then, how pleasant it will be on our own little back stoop. The moon will rise soon after the sun sets, and I think how nice it will be to sit there with my fiddle in the cool air, and see the long streak of moon-light on the water, and the shadow of the distant headlands, and the lights twinkling from them."

"Well done, Guss; you are getting quite romantic."

"I don't know as to that, but I enjoy myself better on an evening, on that old stoop, than anywhere else; it pays one for all the labors of the day."

"I am glad to hear you say so, Guss. It is a good thing to be satisfied with our home. But what do you think Frank Rice wanted of me?"

"Why, I suppose, to invite you to the deacon's. I'll bet anything the girls have put him up to it."

"I am invited there, that's true, but not to see the girls. Frank has been making proposals to me to join him in his business."

"What! to be a partner?"

"Yes, for five years. The two first years he offers me one-quarter, and the other three one-third. He is doing a large business, and he don't ask me to bring any capital."

"It is very liberal in Frank, aint it? You accepted, did n't you? You are a lucky fellow, Charley; that has come of the girls, I know it has."

"I told him I would think about it. It is a serious matter, you know, to change one's business and habits of life."

"You won't have to change your habits much, Charley. You are always, you know, busy at something. You never fiddle away your time, as I do."

"I am to go this evening, and see Frank, and he is to tell me all about his business. I shan't make up my mind, Guss, without thinking well about it."

"I know that; but it seems to me a great offer."

The reception of Charles by the family of Deacon Rice was very marked. The old gentleman gave him a cordial grasp of the hand, and the young ladies were not at all backward in manifesting their satisfaction with the proposed arrangement.

After passing a few civilities with the family, Frank proposed to Charles that they should adjourn to his father's office, where they could converse freely, and without interruption.

"You know," said Frank, after they had got seated, "I am always for hurrying matters up, and so I shall begin my story right off. In the first place, my father, as you know, started me with five thousand dollars in cash; this you know, would go but a little way in the dry-goods business. I had to go along very slow, I assure you, for a year or two. Then he got courage enough to let me have his name for five thousand more; on this I raised the money at the Melton Bank, and that, with some credit I had made for myself, and the names of some friends who exchanged paper with me for five thousand more, gave me a good lift. And last year, as I have said, my sales amounted to one hundred thousand dollars; and I have now, by my last balance-sheet, twenty thousand dollars to my credit."

"That is, you are now worth twenty thousand dollars?"

"Yes, yes—that is, there may be some bad debts. A man can hardly be said to have realized much until the whole concern is wound up. But that is the balance my books show; you see we must sell on credit, there is no help for it—some risk, no doubt; but we must look out and sell to safe names, if we can; and that is the reason I want a partner. I want to be out of doors more, and finding out about people; and then our money matters are no trifle to get along with, and I want some one to consult with, and help me to manage all straight."

"I should think it would keep *one* person pretty busy."

"Busy! there is no mistake about that. Farmers sometimes talk as though they had a slavish life of it. But I have worked harder for myself than ever I did for my father. And that aint all; there is a world of anxiety; but you know, in order to accomplish anything, we must buckle to it—nothing venture, nothing gained."

"That is true, if one does not venture too far."

"True, likewise, Charles, and that is another reason why I want you to join me. My father has great confidence in your prudence and judgment; and two heads, you know, are better than one. I know, Charles, with you to attend especially to our books, and arranging of money matters, and myself at liberty to see to customers, and buying goods, we shall do a swimming business. I would n't thank any one to insure us sales for the coming year of two hundred thousand dollars."

"But there is something, Frank, which I do not quite comprehend. You say you sell on credit; you must, with your amount of sales, have a large amount standing out, besides what you have invested in stock. How do you manage? You must buy a great deal on credit too."

"Pretty much all—that 's the thing of it. I could n't do so large a business if I did n't."

"But what if those you sell to should not be able to meet their payments to you? yours must be met."

"That they must, there is no go by to them, and that 's the thing of it again, you see, Charley; that makes the rub sometimes. I tell you what, it is no child's play. I have seen nights in which I have not slept a wink, thinking how I should contrive to meet my payments the next day. But that is only once in awhile, when everything seems to get out of kelter. Why, in general, I think nothing of having to meet twenty thousand dollars in one week, and very little on hand to begin with. You will soon get used to that, Charley. Here is a case in hand; four days from now, I have got ten thousand dollars to pay. I was in hopes to have got a lift from our bank here, but they are 'tight up,' they say, and can't let me have a dollar."

"How will you do then?"

"Do! why, if I can't do any better, I must skin it awhile."

"What 's that?"

"Why, did you never skin it, Charley? go borrow from Peter to pay Paul, and then borrow of Timothy to pay Peter again, and so keep it going until times come round right again. You have borrowed money from some of the fellows before now, have n't you?"

"I never borrowed a cent in my life."

"Why, don't you owe anybody?"

"Not a cent."

Frank Rice looked at him with a very serious air.

"You dress well, Charley, as well as any gentleman in the country needs to; do you never get anything on tick? not even at old Chubback's?"

"Not a cent."

"Then it makes no matter to you who is pleased or displeased; you fear no man's frown, and you ask no man's favor?"

"Not because I owe them anything."

"You must be a happy fellow, Charley, you sleep well, don't you?"

Charles smiled.

"Generally I have no trouble about that."

"Well, I tell you what it is, Charley, I want just such a fellow as you are along side of me to keep me in check. And you must not be frightened at all. I have told you—you know I hate any deception—I have told you the worst, and you will find out the better side after awhile. I have good hopes of making a fortune, and there are a good many things about a large business in the city that are pleasant. We live pretty well. A good deal of money passes through one's hands, and we can make a respectable show at any rate, and then there are great chances for speculations. All a man wants is to have his wits about him; and I tell you honestly what I think, that with your prudence and ability, and my run of business, and both our heads together, a fortune will be sure to us. I tell you what it is, when the old gentleman hears that you don't owe a cent, he will cling to you with both hands, for to tell you the truth, he thought it very likely, seeing what improvements you have been making, that you must have gone in debt; and lest you should be unwilling to go away on that account, he told me that I might say to you he would advance the money to pay them off."

"I feel deeply, I can assure you, Frank, the confidence reposed in me. I shall treat your proposal with all that candor and fairness it deserves. And my decision shall be given to you just as soon as justice to you and myself may require."

Frank arose and took his hand.

"That is you, Charley; and all I hope is that you may decide in the affirmative."

Never before had Charles Lovell such cause for the exercise of his reason and judgment, and he was fully aware of the responsibility that rested upon him. The present dispensation of Providence was so peculiar, so unexpected, so unlike anything in his experience hitherto, that he could recall nothing from the past to be a direction to the decision he was called upon to make. He was a firm believer in the guiding hand of Providence. Was this a call, intimating the propriety of relinquishing his present designs? or intended to establish him more firmly in their prosecution?

When Charles retired at his usual hour that night, it was not to enjoy his wonted rest. His thoughts were too busy to allow of that sweet repose which a day of steady toil had never failed to bring. Strange as it may seem, he had a strong inclination to accept the proposal made to him, and that from the first moment he heard it. Not that he had become tired of his present calling, or had lost his taste for the simple pleasures of the country. But his mind was fascinated with the idea of a large business, and even the difficulties which were connected with it had a charm about them. They were such as would demand ceaseless energy; but the more intense the struggle, the more joyous would be a final triumph.

There was also a sly thought that he hardly dared to own as his, and yet it kept intruding its claims with great pertinacity, and no little effect. How much more favorably would he be situated for the accomplishment of the great desire of his heart. How much more likely his chance to obtain the object upon which his affections had become so decidedly fixed. With how much greater assurance could he offer his hand to the beautiful and accomplished Adelaide Vincent, as Charles Lovell, the enterprising merchant, than as Charles Lovell, the owner merely of a small farm? And his ready imagination brought up fair visions of what might be in a few years of successful trade. The luxuries of life at his command; a splendid mansion furnished with every elegance to please the taste, and the fair mistress of his heart leaning upon his arm as he walked through his own stately halls, and smiling upon him in her own sweet way, and looking up to him as the lord of the mansion whose energy, and taste, and generous love had provided such a rare retreat.

At times, some darker views would present themselves in strong contrast with these bright scenes, but he had a strange unwillingness to give them a steady look; his heart was too much under the influence of hope and strong desire, to allow his reason her legitimate scope of action.

And thus he passed the night, a sleepless night. And for the first time, Charles arose to pursue his daily labors, unrefreshed by that blessed cordial which gives to toiling man new life and vigor for the coming day.

The first object that attracted his notice, was the beautiful creature which Aunt Casey had tended with so much care the past winter. It came running up to him to receive its morning allowance of some light grain, which he was still in the habit of affording it. He could not but admire its fair form, and delicately spotted skin, and its lively action as it frisked about in expectation of the coming treat. But somehow he took not that satisfaction in thinking of its progress to maturity as heretofore.

As he approached the stable, the well-known neigh of Pomp accosted him, and on opening the door, the bright eye of his noble young horse was fixed upon him, and every limb was in motion, as if capering for joy at his master's presence. He patted him on the neck, rubbed his hand down his sleek round back, poured out his grain into the manger, and left him to attend to other chores; he seemed almost afraid to trust himself long with Pomp.

Augustus perceived that his brother was deeply engaged in thought, and through the day troubled him with but few questions. It was rather a still day between them. That evening Charles was engaged at the Rice's. A party was to be given in honor of Frank, and all the choice ones of Melton would be there. With more than usual care he dressed himself for the evening. Aunt Casey had taken especial pains with his ruffles, for she knew his taste for a fine plait; and, as he arrayed himself, and thought of her motherly care, a deep sigh escaped him. He had not yet intimated to her the possibility of their being separated.

The evening passed as most evenings of the kind do; there was no lack of good things. There was lively conversation, and pleasant music, and bright smiles, and much apparent, and no doubt much real happiness. Charles Lovell was the undoubted star among the gentlemen. Very particular attention was paid to him, especially by the members of the family, and his singing was the treat of the evening. Miss Julia Rice stood near to him, and seemed to drink in his rich strains as though she could not be satisfied. The new prospects before the young farmer had apparently enlightened her as to some excellences which she had never so distinctly observed before.

Lucy Johnson, who as usual had been waited upon by Charles, could not but notice the attention which her favorite received, and was highly gratified. She could not, however, help observing the change in his manner and appearance. A settled seriousness had been manifest upon his countenance through all the joyous scenes of the evening, and if a smile came over it, almost immediately it passed completely away. His manner, too, was stiff and restrained, and there was nothing of that light and playful demeanor so usual with him amid such scenes.

The weather being warm, the company was not confined to the room; some stood upon the piazza, and in the broad hall, and on the smooth green lawn in the bright moonlight. Other groups wandered down the garden path, and seated themselves on the benches of the arbor.

Charles had withdrawn from the circle in the parlor, and was looking through the window at the lively scene without, when a well-known voice spoke close beside him.

"You are dull to-night; are you not well?"

He turned and saw the kind eye of her who had been so long his well-tried friend, beaming with interest upon him. There was something in her look, or in his own feelings at the time, that deeply affected him, and it was with difficulty he replied:

"Ah, Miss Lucy!"

"Can you never lay aside that Miss? or must I retaliate by always addressing you as Mr. Lovell?"

"Please don't; I will try to meet your wishes, for I am sure every token of intimacy you allow, is too dear to me to be thrown away."

"There you are again, with that serious air; what ails you to-night, cousin?" (sometimes she used this familiar title.) "Are you not well?"

"Oh yes, perfectly so; do I appear so serious?"

"Decidedly so; perhaps a little walk may enliven you? What say you?"

"With all my heart."

Lucy led him designedly where they might not be overheard.

"Now, Cousin Charles, you have got to tell me what is the matter. There is a riddle going on that I cannot guess out. You are evidently the distinguished guest of the evening, and yet you have hardly graciousness enough about you to be even polite. How could you sit so long and keep Miss Julia, standing by as your humble servant, even after you had done singing?"

"Did I?"

"Certainly you did; now come tell me one thing, you have not fallen in love again?"

"You know all my heart about such matters. I am no changeling."

"There now, I have wounded you, and I did not mean it; forgive my trifling with your feelings, and I will forgive your hard reply."

"I did not mean to speak hard. I am very unhappy, dear Lucy."

"I thought so; and may *I* not know the cause?"

"Yes, you shall know it; I will tell you all, but I cannot now. I will tell you on our way home."

Charles had not designed to communicate with any one until he had made up his own mind. But Lucy took him by surprise, and she kept him to his word, for, as soon as the party had broken up and they were on their way home, she reminded him of his promise. He hesitated not, but at once revealed to her the singular proposal which had been made to him. She listened with fixed attention, although evidently with a sad heart, until he had told her the whole story. For some moments after he had finished not a word was spoken by either. At length Charles, with much earnestness, said:

"Lucy, can you tell me what I shall do?"

"I am not a proper person, Charles, to advise you about such an important step, for two reasons: First, I should feel sad to have you go away, on my own account, and on account of many who feel attached to you here, and who will miss your presence very, very much. And the second reason is, because my judgment as a lady, in reference to business matters, would be of no account. So that my feelings on one side, and my ignorance on the other, forbid that I should say a word. You must be your own counsellor, Charles. I see now why it was that you put on such a serious air, and I do not wonder at it; for the decision you will make may have a most important bearing on the future happiness and usefulness of your life. I suppose I am a little peculiar in my views, but it seems to me, if I were a man, I should ask myself, Whether my calling was a useful one, and allowed my mind freedom for the indulgence of its nobler feelings? It does not seem to me that any amount of money can repay, if all the energies of the soul must be engaged in its accumulation."

Charles made no reply. They had reached her home. He walked up the front yard with her, and stood beside her on the ample stoop. As the servant was coming, she gave him her hand:

"Good night. You know where to go for counsel; and may you have His blessing, whether you—"

She could say no more. Charles saw her emotion, and his own feelings were too tender to trust a word from his lips. He turned as the door opened, and went on his way.

As Charles was about to pass the old stone building, he turned and looked at it, in the full beams of the moonlight, for a moment, and then walked up and seated himself on some timber that lay piled up beside it. He had of late taken a peculiar interest in that old house. He had spent hours in all, looking at it, and planning how he could make additions to it, until, in his own mind, there was already engraven a picture as it was to be. A neat, commodious home, with those little trees now scattered in various clusters here and there, spreading their branches in all directions, and shooting their tops far above its roof, and equalling in beauty those already grown. And now, in all its freshness, this picture spreads its charms before him. This home, with treasures richer than the mines contain; where all his heart desired was enclosed; gathered through years of faithful care and manly toil; unfolds its every line of beauty to his view. It was a calm, still hour—such an one as the mind unspoiled by vice or avarice loves, and in which it enjoys its clearest views.

And here upon this spot, and amid the sweet silence of nature's resting hour, he resolved to decide the question that involved his weal or woe for life. One solemn aspiration he raised to Him, on whose blessing and guidance he most frequently depended. And then, with all the fairness of a truth-loving mind, he placed before his view the advantages and disadvantages of each calling that laid claim to his preference. And thus he reasoned:

"My present business affords me no great scope for enterprise. With my limited capital, a few hundreds a year are all that I can calculate upon at present. A wise treatment of my land will, of course, in time increase its value. It can be made to produce many fold its present returns. But years must be consumed in patient labor. I must bear the heat and drought of summer. I must exercise patience, frugality, judgment, and perseverance.

"In the new business to which I am called, no capital on my part is required, except that which my head and hands may be able to yield. But their efforts must be exerted to the extent of my ability. I shall assume vast responsibilities. I shall be, probably, for many years, under obligations to my fellow men. I shall be obliged to ask favors. I shall have a heavy amount of debts due to me, and a large amount of indebtedness from me to others, which must be promptly met, and at all hazards. I shall be subject to reverses in the course of general trade; to times of commercial embarrassment; and whether in prosperous or adverse currents, I must apply all the energies of my mind to the one single idea—that of making gain, and of preserving it from being swept away.

"The highest object I shall have attained after many years of intense devotion to my business, will be an independence for the rest of my life. Of this, however, the chances against me will be ten to one; this is the estimate of sober-minded, knowing men. But one in ten of those who start in the race for fortune, gain the prize; and even of that small number, many are obliged in their race to become bankrupt, and although cleared by law from the obligations which they are unable to meet, go down to old age and to their graves largely indebted to their fellow-men.

"In my present business I have no care to harass my mind. I can leave my work in the field with a light heart. I can enjoy the rich feasts which highly-cultivated minds afford, either from books or from social intercourse. I can enjoy in all their fulness the beauties of nature which I so much love. I can lie down at night with no distracting care to disturb my rest, and when I awake in the morning my heart is light and ready to drink in the freshness of the new day. I can, without a doubt, provide for myself a home, such as my heart aspires after. And my living is as sure as anything earthly can be. I can stretch my thoughts to others, and use what influence I have to the utmost. I have found no hinderance hitherto, but am treated with kindness and respect by all. *I owe no man anything*, and never need to do so. And I am an independent *man*."

Charles started to his feet. The last thought came with a quickening power to his mind. He fairly shook his arms as though they had been shackled, and he felt the fetters snap.

"Yes, I am a free man in its fullest sense. My bread is sweet; it comes from honest labor, and at no man's cost. And a free man I will ever be, so help me God."

Light as a bird let loose, that chirps and swings away upon the buoyant air, the mind of Charles arose and soared in freedom. He had no more doubts. His path lay bright and clear before him. The dear old spot on which he stood was radiant with beauty. A hearty thanksgiving at once arose to Heaven, and a fervent prayer that he might be strengthened to walk steadily and with a single purpose in the way which from the first had been his choice. Sweet was his sleep that night, and with a light heart he hailed the morning dawn. Pomp and his other pets were tended and caressed, as friends with whom he meant to sojourn, and be as happy as he could.

According to appointment he met Frank the next morning, and in a clear and decided manner made known his reasons for declining the offer he had received.

"In my present business I find great pleasure. Its duties are not burdensome to me. It allows me the free enjoyment of my better feelings. Nature, with its simple beauties, has perpetual charms for me, and no distracting care disturbs my mind; no sense of obligation weighs down my spirit. I wish to be a free man, so long as I live."

Frank took his hand.

"I am sorry, Charley, that you and I cannot be together. But your reasons are satisfactory, perfectly so. And I am almost ready to wish that I too had never left the country. But I am in for it, and must push ahead, sink or swim. I hope to succeed, and when I am able, you may depend upon seeing me somewhere near you, and I hope we may yet spend many happy days up here in company."

"I hope so," responded Charles, cordially shaking his hand, "with all my heart."

They parted better friends than ever; each to pursue his chosen path for life, and reap the fruits which they might find therein.

CHAPTER XVIII.

THAT Lucy Johnson loved the Reverend Charles Jamieson, she never attempted to deny. "Yes, I do love him," she would say to any of her companions who rallied her on the subject. "I love him just as much as any of you, and I believe more, too; for I never get drowsy under his preaching, and that is more than many of my friends can say."

"No, but I don't mean as a preacher; you love him one side of that," said Julia Rice, one day to her.

"That I do, Julia; he is a most excellent pastor; his visits are well-timed, and his instructions and counsels most edifying. I am always profited by his visits."

"No, no, but I don't mean preaching or pastoral visits, or anything of that kind; you are not going to get round me that way; don't you love him as a man? Now tell me that."

"I do, most certainly. He is a gentlemen of highly-refined manners; his mind is richly stored, and he has powers of conversation that enable him to bring them forth with great ease. He is a most delightful companion; don't you think so yourself, Julia, from what you have seen of him?"

"Oh, well, but that is another thing; everybody admires him, and to tell you the truth, if it would do any good, we could all fall in love with him together. But we all know pretty well whom *he* loves; and I for one don't blame him. You are just the one for a minister, Lucy, everybody says."

"I cannot tell as to that, Julia; it will be time enough to think what kind of a minister's wife I should make, when there is any prospect of my becoming such."

This conversation took place between these young ladies, as they were sitting by themselves in one corner of a very large room in the house of Deacon Rice, where was assembled a score of ladies from the different denominations, all busily employed with their needles in making preparations for the marriage of the Rev. Mr. Foster. His house had been nicely refitted by the means which were contributed at the donation party during the winter. And now, the ladies, who all felt deeply interested in Fanny Pearl, were making up sundry articles in the house-keeping line, and for arraying the beautiful bride.

It was very true that Lucy had not yet had the opportunity of deciding whether she was a suitable person for a minister's wife. She had never yet been asked to become such. That she loved Mr. Jamieson as a gifted and brilliant preacher, as a faithful and wise pastor, and as an accomplished gentleman, she candidly confessed. And in the same way she was not ashamed to own that she loved Charles Lovell. He was an engaging young man, of pure and generous feelings, whose mind was improved far beyond what was usual for his years. He had a confiding disposition, and made her the depository of his joys and trials. Although by many looked upon as beneath her in station, such an idea had no weight with Lucy. He was her chosen companion when she needed one on any excursion from home. She had a sincere affection for Charles, and was not ashamed to have it known. But there was a depth in Lucy's love that could not be fathomed by common minds, and when she was rallied by her companions as to her feelings for either of these gentlemen, she received it pleasantly and gave her answer according to their ideas of love and not her own. She was no prude, nor coquette; the attention she showed to both these gentlemen they fully understood; to one she was a source of great happiness, and he found in her the kindness and faithfulness of a sister, and to the other she was all that he could reasonably expect, but nothing that his heart could lay hold upon to satisfy its strong emotions towards her.

Charles Jamieson was now in his thirty-first year. He was still living as when first introduced to our notice. The people over whom he was placed were strongly united to him; his congregation had indeed increased in numbers, and his church on the Sabbath was well filled. But those who had been added brought no additional strength, so far as pecuniary matters were concerned; and his salary was still paid by those who had provided for it from the first. It was enough for him in his present condition, but not sufficient to allow him to think of establishing himself as the head of a family. Of this he never thought as a cause of complaint. At times, indeed, his mind would dwell upon the idea of a happy home with one he loved, but the thought never produced restlessness, nor a desire for change. His sphere of labor was not so large as that of many less gifted than himself, but he always found work to do. A considerable number of his people were poor, and some of them lived remote from the place of worship, and were not able to attend regularly on the Sabbath. To these he carried the gospel, holding frequent meetings among them, visiting from house to house, and bearing about the whole of his parish in his beautiful deportment, those graces which emanate from the pure Christian as visibly as light from a burning torch. He, therefore, did not repine because the field assigned to him was no larger. He only felt anxious to do his work well.

But that rich flow of feeling with which he had been endowed, although a gift of great value, which mellowed his character, and made a way for him to every heart, was like every other precious inheritance, subject to its attendant trials.

Few, indeed, would be the hearts in this strange world, whose sympathies could unite and beat in beautiful harmony with his. But to such his strong affections would cling with a power the common heart knows nothing of. And such an one he had met in Lucy Johnson. Nor could he any more control that subtile influence which communion with her wrapped about his heart, than he could have driven from the air around the rose its precious perfume. He did not ask himself the serious question, Whether a corresponding emotion affected her? No sign had he ever discovered—no word, or look had reached him that gave the least assurance of her love. For reasons all sufficient, he had refrained from indulging in visions of bliss which could only tend to unfit him for his work. And yet he had thoughts of her, as one whom he loved, and whom he had no power or wish to banish from his heart.

Nothing had ever been said to him about the smallness of

his salary. His people knew how limited it was, and they knew better than he what they could afford to give him. He labored not for hire, he loved his work; and he well knew that the Master whom he served, had all hearts and all possessions at disposal, and there he left himself.

It was one of the loveliest days of summer, about the middle of the afternoon; he was sitting by the window of his pleasant study enjoying the cool shade of the large weeping willow, whose sweeping branches hung nearly within his reach, when a visitor was announced, and on rising to receive him, he met the friendly grasp of the old colonel.

"How *are* you, my dear sir?"

"Colonel Johnson, I am extremely happy to see you here."

"And I am very happy to be here, for you have got such a charming, cool box of a room here; but it is something of a walk; heigh ho! I am getting old, I do believe; I can't stand it as I used to; and that hussey has gone off with Josey to see about this wedding that 's coming off in a few days; but she is to call for me as she goes home."

All this was said while he was taking possession of the large, easy, study chair, which his young pastor had placed for him in the most airy situation.

"Neat as a pin, neat as a pin, everything in order," and the old gentleman cast his eyes around upon the shelves of books, and on the spotless green cover of his desk, and the bright polish of his furniture. "You are as snug here as a man need to be; I mean a young man without a family; snug enough; but you know, my dear sir, that I am a meddlesome sort of a man, always dipping into other folks' affairs. I suppose it is because I have not a great deal of my own to see to."

"I believe, sir, your friends never complain of your interference."

"Well, I believe, in the main, I don't mean to harm them. But I sometimes think that we are, in general, too apt to let one another alone; and many a fine fellow has to suffer a good deal because no one asks him, in right good earnest, and with a meaning to it, 'How dost thou do?' and it is for this purpose I have taken the liberty of calling on you this afternoon. I don't come as an officer of the church, but as a friend that feels, to say the least, very kindly towards you, just to ask you, how do you do? how do you get along?"

"I have not the shadow of a doubt, my dear sir, as to your kind feelings. You have manifested them in too many ways. I thank you for your kind inquiry, and am happy to say, in reference to all personal matters, I have great cause for gratitude."

"That is all well enough; it is well to be grateful even for small favors. But you certainly could have no objections to receiving an addition to your causes for gratitude; you have made a little go a good way."

"I have endeavored, sir, to make the most of my means, and have limited my desires to what my ability allowed."

"A very wise arrangement. It would be a deal better for all your parishioners if they could be induced to adopt your practice; but to make the matter short, Mr. Jamieson, a few of us have been talking the matter over a little, and we think something ought to be done by way of giving you a chance, if you feel so disposed, to—to—to settle down—that is, if you feel so disposed, you know—" at the same time putting his hand upon the shoulder of his young minister; "you may, like other young men, wish to take to yourself a wife—you understand me."

The young man smiled, and at the same time his fair countenance was suffused with a blush that would not have done discredit to the cheek of a delicate maiden.

"Ah, I see how it is; you feel a little shy; well, that's a good sign; a young man that can talk about such a matter as marriage, without being a little put out of sorts at the first brush, why, you see, he don't show just the right feeling on the subject. But you must understand me, my dear sir, I have not come to pry into any of your secrets—to know who it is you are to be linked to, or anything about that—that's your look-out, only wishing you the utmost happiness, and just as good a partner as we think you deserve. The fact is just here; it has been hinted around of late, and I suppose I can guess how it has come, that you are engaged to a lady out of town, that it is a matter that has been on the carpet now for some time, and I for one feel, such being the case, that you ought to have an increase to your salary. Now, I have been frank with you, and I want you to be so with me.

You know that there are not many among us that can give very liberally, but we mean to do the thing that is right. If you are engaged to a lady that has an income of her own, or friends that are able to give her one, why, perhaps, in that case, you would not need so large an addition as if she had nothing. And I tell you, my dear sir," again patting him on the shoulder, "we are not going to keep you among us to be pinched out of your manliness by keeping you on beggar's fare; no, no, we have called you to be our spiritual guide, and we shall sustain you in respectability and comfort, if we have to make a common concern of it, and share our own incomes with you. Make your mind easy on that score, and now just let out the whole truth, as you would to a father."

It was impossible for one possessed of any sensibility not to have been touched by this paternal address. Mr. Jamieson was so overcome, that for some time he could only grasp in silence the hand of his kind-hearted friend. But there were some things in his address which required, on his part, a decided answer, and as soon as he could speak with composure, he replied:

"I will not attempt to thank you, my dear sir, for the token you now give me of your own kind feelings and those of this people; such unlooked-for generosity demands more than I can now embody in words. But will you please say to those who have united with you in this act, that I hope each of them may enjoy the reward of the liberal soul. As to what you say, Colonel Johnson, about my private arrangements, I must correct the error into which my friends have fallen. I am not, sir, nor have ever been on terms of such intimacy with any lady; nor have I ever yet sought such a favor; my circumstances hitherto have forbidden me the privilege. But, sir, I frankly acknowledge to you, that nothing but my limited means could have prevented me long ere this from seeking the affections of one whom I most ardently love."

"There need be no hinderance now, I assure you, my young friend; I pledge you a good support; I am authorized so to do. Just go to work, then, as quick as you can."

Mr. Jamieson was much excited, and for some moments was silent, merely answering in a rather oblivious manner to some questions of the colonel on parish matters. At length with a tremulous voice he began:

"I have always conceived it right and proper, sir, that any attempt to gain the affections of a lady, must, if she have parents, be through their approbation. I lay my suit, therefore, sir, at your feet, humbly asking your permission to gain if I can your daughter's heart."

The old gentleman had been sitting before him, and looking with intense interest. He kept his mouth going as though he had something there very hard to chew; and as the full idea was unfolded, his countenance assumed a cast of most unfeigned surprise. At length, pushing his chair back a little:

"Handsomely done, sir—handsomely done; I little thought, sir—I trust you will credit me, sir—that things were to take such a turn as this. Well, well, well," pushing his chair each time as he spoke, "I see a man never knows when he begins to meddle with such matters, where or what the end will be; I am sure I did n't. You have gone a little faster to work than my calculations. My Lucy! well, I can't say you have made a bad choice; and so far as I am concerned you shall have no obstacle in your way. I don't know the gentleman I should be able to commit her to with so much confidence. But, body-a-me! what a predicament I have placed myself in!"

"By no means, sir, regret what has taken place. It was as far, sir, from my intention to have made this declaration to you at this time, as it was unexpected by yourself, sir. But I could not allow you, sir, to take an active part in advancing my interests under such circumstances."

"That is true; you are right. Body-a-me! how it would have looked! Well, well, you know better than I do what chance you have for success. My best wishes are on your side, at any rate. And here comes Josey."

At a fine flowing pace, the noble horse came along the smooth road, bearing the neat and roomy carriage behind him; while the fair hands of his young mistress merely held the reins as a kind of ceremony. It seemed by no means a matter of necessity, for at the first sound of her gentle voice the obedient creature stopped, with so easy and graceful a motion, as if he feared too sudden a halt might discompose the fair one whom he carried.

"Whoa, Josey, whoa." The old gentleman seemed to be in a great hurry to be off. He sprang in quite nimbly, and as soon as he touched the reins Josey became restless, tossing his head, and pawing the ground, and looking back to see if all was ready.

"Whoa, Josey; good morning, sir—good afternoon—I mean good day, sir."

The two young folks had barely time to pass a slight salutation, before Josey tripped away with his load, as if supper-time was drawing near, and he must be there by the hour.

Whether Lucy was able to define to herself, or to anybody else, exactly in what way she loved William Jamieson besides as a minister, a pastor, and a gentleman, it will not be worth while to inquire. Neither will it be best to draw the veil and see how the reverend gentleman made her to understand the difference between a pastoral visit and that of a lover Somehow or other the thing *was* managed, and not very long either after the scene recorded above.

The old gentleman probably suspected what was the business on hand, for, contrary to his usual custom, he left the young people to entertain themselves as they best could, and retired to his own room. It was adjoining the parlor, a fine, spacious, cheerful apartment, with windows reaching to the floor, and opening upon a wide piazza, surrounded with shrubs and flowers, and from which you entered immediately into a highly-cultivated garden.

Seated by one of the long open windows, in his large, leathern-bottomed chair, his hair frizzled and powdered, his shoes highly polished, his knee-buckles shining like new silver, and with his book in hand, he might have passed for a good personification of dignified repose. And everything about the room corresponded to its master. The furniture was of the most substantial kind, of an ancient fashion, when mahogany was cheap, and money plenty. Large square bottomed chairs, with high, pointed backs, and heavy legs, resting on broad lion's feet curiously carved. Tables that seemed made to be stationary, or only moved on special occasions; with a high secretary or book-case reaching almost to the heavy cornice on the ceiling. Every chair conveyed the idea of repose, and told of days when there was time enough to lean back and take one's ease; when men, and women too, had some leisure in this bustling world, and knew how to enjoy it. When they could form the social ring about the blazing hearth, and with the fragrant cup in their hand, and the plate upon their knee, pass round the sparkling wit and the hearty laugh, and make the atmosphere about them jovial with their cheer.

The twilight had come on, and the little birds were singing their last notes, ere they closed their eyes upon their swinging perch; and there the good old man sat, indulging in those thoughts which so become the evening hour, and the silvery age, when his door was gently opened, and William Jamieson, with Lucy leaning on his arm, came in. As they approached he rose to meet them. Not a word was spoken until Lucy, as she leaned her head upon his bosom, in a calm, clear tone, simply said:

"Your blessing, father."

He put his arm about her, and fondly pressed her to him.

"May you prove as rich a blessing to him upon whose arm you lean, as you have to me, my dear, dear Lucy. May God bless you both."

He took the hand of Mr. Jamieson, and pressing it cordially:

"I commit to you my dearest treasure; and I thank God that I can do it with the utmost confidence, without a fear but you will prove all that you seem to be. And now, Lucy, I wish you just to leave your friend a little while with me; I want to have a talk with him."

And Lucy, taking a good hearty kiss as her father released her from his embrace, tripped lightly away, and the two gentlemen were once more alone together.

"And now, sir, will you please to come and sit down here by me, for I want to finish that business you and I were upon the other day, when things took such a strange turn, and knocked all my plans in the head—those chairs were never made to lift, just drag it along; and now first of all I must say to you that I am hereafter not going to make any stranger of you. You have of your own free will taken my Lucy, and whoever gets her must be my son whether or no."

"No hard condition, I assure you, sir."

"You can't tell yet what the conditions may be; but first of all you must have an increase to your salary, and as I am not now going to run round to see about that matter, I shall take the liberty of adding to it what I think will be sufficient to make a pair of young folks comfortable. I shall to-morrow morning settle upon Lucy three hundred dollars a year; it is no great sum, but with your income will make what I call a good beginning for young folks."

Mr. Jamieson was much moved, and about to express his gratitude, but the old colonel, putting his hand upon his arm:

"No matter now, not a word, if you please. I am not a rich man, as many suppose, but I have got enough; my gift to you and Lucy will still leave me a thousand a year more than I shall want for myself. But there is another thing you will be obliged to submit to. I have a large house here, and I call it a very comfortable one too. I shall want you and Lucy to take possession of it. My apartments I shall keep just as I have done; the rest shall be yours and Lucy's. You shall be your own master and mistress. I shall be with you as much as I please, and when I wish I can be alone; but Lucy and I must be under the same roof. Not a word, just keep quiet. Our old servants are used to their young mistress, and everything can go on just as it always has; so you see, you will have no need to depend upon the people to get you up a parsonage, and all that. And last of all, you will have Josey at your command to go about just when you please; and I don't see why we can't be as happy as—at any rate as we deserve. Not a word; I know how you feel; thank the Lord as much as you please; but I am consulting just my own happiness. You can go now and tell Lucy how it is all fixed; and I shall say to our good friends who have wanted to raise your salary, 'Raise away as much as you please, but I shall have nothing to do with it.' Now, not a word. God bless you. Just go and see Lucy."

CHAPTER XIX.

THE Institution in which Adelaide Vincent had received an appointment, that is, provided, upon inspection, she should suit the views of the Lady Principal, was in that day a "celebrated Institution." It was under the charge of Miss Martinett, probably a very accomplished lady. She was tolerably well versed in the several branches which she professed to teach, and had several assistants to aid her in the various classes; a little Frenchman instructed the pupils in music and dancing, and two young ladies assisted in hearing the recitations in history, rhetoric, moral and political science, natural and mental philosophy, and several other things of like necessary attainment. One peculiarity which Miss Martinett had adopted, and which answered her turn very well, was, that the books used at this "celebrated school" should be all prepared with questions and answers, so that no matter how abstruse the subject, neither teachers nor scholars could at any time be put to any very great trouble in accomplishing their several tasks. It was a happy expedient. The teachers could never be at a loss, with the book before them, and the scholars would be sure to graduate with eclat; that is, if they had tolerably good memories.

It did indeed, at times, to some of the pupils whose minds were more grasping than the rest, seem to be a very "humdrum" way of spending their time and some who had graduated with high honors, were bold to say, after they had left school for a few months, that it was difficult for them to imagine that they had learned anything; but that was a matter of no moment. Miss Martinett's school was a "celebrated Institution;" all the first people sent their daughters there; and if the first people approved of it, why, surely the more moderate portion of the community ought to be satisfied.

But, although Miss Martinett was so very particular in confining her teachers to the question and answer system, as they found it in the books, she was, herself, very much given to lecturing, not indeed on the sciences, but on the manners, and customs, and proprieties of genteel life. She had a great idea of the manners of the "old school," as she understood them. That was, great stiffness in dress, very erect postures, very regular motions, very long garments, and great shyness towards young men. As to the latter item, it may have been all well enough. Young men need watching; they always have been, and perhaps always will be, meddling with young girls, to the infinite distress of prudish old aunts, and maiden principals of "popular Institutions."

She had, also, a great regard for the complexion, and was very sensitive as to any tendency in her pupils to grossness of form, and had an exalted idea of an attenuated diet, as helping to give true lady-like delicacy to both.

"High living," she said, "ought never to be indulged in by those who made any pretensions to gentility; and I shall never, depend upon it, young ladies, be charged by you, in after life, with having contributed to a gross and vulgar form."

And, so far as diet was concerned, there was little probability that any such sin would be laid by them at her door. Rice was her favorite comestible, and many were the varieties in which this innocent grain was served up. The most famous, however, and those which were most likely to be remembered by them, was paupau and chick*ee*; the latter being what is commonly known as devil'd chicken. That being, however, a vulgar name, Miss Martinett had given it a much more simple term. Chick*ee* certainly has a better sound.

What the first dish consisted of, besides boiled rice and a little dash of strong butter, it would have been difficult for one, not in the secret of its preparation, to determine. But Miss Martinett called it "paupau," an East Indian dish, and as paupau they eat it—all they could. The chick*ee* was rice, also, with a scattering of chicken meat sprinkled through it, and so mixed up that with a very little of the chicken, a great deal of the rice had of necessity to be forked up. The chick*ee* was, however, the favorite dish. It had some flavor to it, was always smoking hot, and once in a while one might happen to get almost a good mouthful of chicken. This created an expectation that more would be coming, and thus they may have been said to have " eaten it in hope."

Miss Martinett was also very precise in all her arrangements. Every young lady was obliged, immediately on coming from her room in the morning, to present herself in what Miss Martinett was pleased to call the " ante-room," a small apartment adjoining the one in which the paupau and chickee were to be eaten. There, seated in a large chair, was the Lady Principal, holding herself very erect, a matter of necessity to all appearance; for from the frill that lay around the crown of her head to the flounce at the bottom of the long dress, everything was so very stiff with starch, or something else, that there could not possibly be anything like bending.

" That is pretty well for you, Miss Ketchum; your hair has not been quite drawn up as tight as it should be." The poor girl looked already as though every hair was being pulled the wrong way.

" Your hair is well enough, Miss Shawn; but of all sights! you must have forgotten your stays this morning, miss."

" No, ma'am—Miss Marsh drew them for me as tight as she could." She was a fine wholesome-looking girl, and appeared to have been well fed at home.

" I fear you will never get into shape. I do my best for you while you are under my care, but the long vacation spoils it all. If you *will* stuff so, there is not much use in my strict attention to you while you are here. But I must try what can be done this term. You are really a fright; you must be put upon paupau and nothing else; ah, here comes a grace."

Enter a young slender creature, naturally pretty, but so distorted by dress that she appeared more like a bandaged corpse than a living girl of sixteen. Hair exceedingly smooth behind, and lying over very far on the foretop, arms down, waist straight and long, and nothing to speak of in circumference; dress sweeping the floor. With measured step she stalked before the lady inspectress, and really seemed proud of the approbation which was bestowed upon her.

" You can eat freely of chickee, my dear, it won't hurt *you*."

"Nor me either," said Miss Shawn, in a whisper to one of her companions.

"Whispering! whispering! in my presence too! who is it?"

But it seemed to be nobody, for all looked round very innocently at one another to see who had done the naughty thing.

Tingle, tingle, tingle! That was as much as to say, 'The paupau is ready." No one appeared in any haste. The lady arose, and in a very stately manner made motions, which were perfectly understood, and passing again in review, they proceeded in a solemn manner into the adjoining room, and, taking their seats, sat like so many statues, until the lady had taken her station at the head of the table.

The table was quite a long one, for it was a very "celebrated institution," and there was no want of pupils. Plates of bread cut very square, and in small pieces, were distributed throughout its length; and an occasional plate of butter, a few scattering dishes of dried beef cut very thin, with a full supply of smoking paupau, made up the variety of eatables. To each young lady was distributed a cup of tea, made as tea ought to be made for young ladies with weak nerves. As everything went by rule in this celebrated establishment, it was of great consequence that those concerned in the matter should do what was to be done in the way of eating with all possible expedition; for the moment the lady principal had accomplished her task of supplying her own precious casket with as much paupau as she thought expedient, her little bell sounded a gentle alarm, and all must cease operations, and the paupau, and bread, and butter, and beef, if any was left, were to remain in statu quo. This was the law of the table, and it was well understood; and by several, Miss Shawn in particular, was generally anticipated by using great diligence in the work before them; the last-named young lady making no scruples of putting down her bread and butter double, besides making rapid movements with her paupau spoon.

In general, most of the business was acomplished by the time the bell tinkled; for what with their heads strained up, and their bodies strained in, and their want of relish for the food, a very few mouthfuls answered all purposes.

But the most trying of all the duties which the lady principal had to perform, was in guarding her precious charge during their daily walks in pleasant weather.

It happened that not very far from this noted establishment for young ladies, there was a school for boys. They were wicked boys, all of them, as the lady principal assured her pupils; and, under terrible threats for disobedience, they were forbidden to speak to, or even look at them. Now, it was a matter of daily occurrence, that while the lady would be marching along in great state, with her long line of the graces in her rear, these naughty boys would use all manner of contrivances to pass a sly word to some little favorite in the group, or to thrust into their hands a paper of peanuts, or sugar-kisses, or maybe a bundle of round hearts. It was very wicked for them to do so; but the girls, some of them, had such little witching smiles, and such pretty roguish black eyes, and took the little gifts in such a delightfully sly manner, and tucked them out of sight with such evident good will, that the boys were really not so much to blame after all. It was very trying to the lady principal, and she did what she could to remedy the evil. It would not do for one in her station to turn round, and in a commanding tone order off the vagrants. All she could possibly do in person was to frown at them indignantly. But the boys were such hardened little wretches, that it was said they were seen to smile when she did so. Her assistants in the school, although able to hear recitations when the questions and answers were all before them in plain print, were not just such as she wished to parade before the public. One of them had such a careless manner of walking, and made such sad work with her heels, that the lady principal feared she might be taken for some very common person; and the other had an unfortunate twist to her nose, which might not only make her too conspicuous to passers-by, but might possibly excite the ridicule of those wicked boys, and so only make matters worse.

These untoward circumstances may seem very trifling in themselves, but it so happened that they were helpful towards the completion of an engagement with Miss Adelaide Vincent.

When Adelaide left the house of her aunt, she at once repaired to the house of Mrs. Willis, and after spending the Sabbath there, started early on Monday morning in the public stage for the town of ———, on the banks of the North River. As there was still some uncertainty whether she would be able to make an arrangement with Miss Martinett, that lady declining to say anything positive before seeing the person who wished to be employed, Adelaide entered the institution with rather a trembling heart. She was not long, however, doomed to a state of uncertainty, for no sooner did the lady principal look upon her beautiful countenance, and perceive that her form was a perfect model of symmetry, and that her carriage was marked with gentility and grace, than she resolved to engage her. She did it, too, upon her own terms, for Adelaide was in no condition to bargain. All she wished was a situation of respectability, where she could use the talents she possessed in providing for her own independence. She little thought another woman could be found as unjust, as arbitrary, and as tyrannical as the one she had been under, and, with little regard to her own advantage in the contract yielded to the fair words that were addressed to her, and, in fact, threw herself upon the generosity of Miss Martinett.

After all arrangements had been completed, and she had left the presence for her own room, the lady could not help ejaculating, "What an acquisition!"

And this was very true; an acquisition indeed was she in a place where young and loving hearts were thrown under the deadening influence of pride and selfishness.

The assistants whom Miss Martinett had hitherto engaged were neither very ill-natured nor remarkably selfish. But they had no very fixed character, either for good or evil. They knew but little, were very poor, and although the compensation they received was small, yet it was object enough for them to command an obsequious obedience to the rules of their employer. The tender and guileless hearts of the pupils found no sympathy from them; and they had every reason to look upon them as mere spies upon their few hours of freedom.

Adelaide's first appearance among the girls was like a ray of sunshine after a season of dark and lowering weather. Bright smiles met her salutation on every side, for she smiled upon them. The lady principal never smiled, and her assistants did as they saw her do.

"Oh, I do hope she will hear our class," said one.

"And I hope she will be the monitor in our sleeping-room," said another.

"It makes me hungry to look at her," said Miss Shawn; "I 'll bet anything she has got cakes in her pocket."

Miss Martinett heard nothing of these sly remarks, and appointed Miss Vincent to a class according to her own excellent judgment. She selected some of the dullest scholars, or those she esteemed such, and placed them under the charge of the new assistant. Miss Shawn was one of them. She dared not laugh, so she had to "make-believe-cry;" tears did absolutely come; how she got them is of no consequence.

"Here are the young ladies whose recitations you will attend to, Miss Vincent; and you will feel yourself especially bound to watch over them, and see that in all things they conform to the printed rules. You will also find your bed in their room, and for all their delinquences I look to you as responsible." Adelaide colored deeply. "The rules are to be observed, you will understand, Miss Vincent, without deviation, and without the least abridgment."

The stately lady stepped off to another part of the room, and left Adelaide to her task.

The hearing of their recitations was a very easy matter; but it occurred to the mind of Adelaide, that it might add some interest to the tedious routine if she should, after having gone over the lesson according to the prescribed rule, review it by varying her questions and adding a few explanations of her own. At first, this was such a novel procedure, that but few of them could give a correct reply to even the simplest question that was not down on the book. But by degrees they became much interested. They listened with strict attention to her explanations. They liked to hear her voice, and to look at the pleasant features that beamed upon them so kindly. They began to love their studies the more they comprehended of them, and their hour of recitations became at length the most pleasant of all the twenty-four, excepting that which brought them all together, and alone with their sweet teacher in their sleeping apartment. The tying up of the hair in the morning had been to them a very unpleasant matter, but Miss Vincent had such a soft and easy way of doing it, and had so many expressions of tenderness for them while under the operation, that they bore it with as little complaining as possible.

"All very well," said the lady principal at the morning review, "all except Miss Shawn; she seems to me to grow more out of shape, do all I can."

Adelaide looked at Miss Shawn, but saw nothing out of shape except what was caused by the measures used to compress her round full form to the *beau ideal* of Miss Martinett.

"I believe I shall even have to deny her the paupau."

As the paupau was a new dish to Adelaide, she could form no opinion of the propriety of Miss Martinett's suggestion.

"You will prepare yourself, Miss Vincent, to accompany me in my walk with my pupils this afternoon. You will remember that we allow no familiarity with our pupils by any persons foreign to the institution; and if you are annoyed in any such way, you must show by your looks, at once, that speaking to the pupils is not allowed."

As soon as it was known that Miss Vincent was to accompany them in their walk, there was a general rush towards her on the first opportunity afforded by the absence of the lady principal.

"*Do*, Miss Vincent, walk in our division;" and "Do, Miss Vincent, walk in ours;" and "Do, Miss Vincent, let me take your arm."

Adelaide smiled. She could not yet comprehend why her presence was of so much consequence. She could not realize that their young hearts, separated from the loves of home, were panting for tokens of the sympathy they had been accustomed to there.

Whether it was that those wicked boys were deterred by beholding one who had the bearing of a real lady, in company with those they fancied, or that there was some secret understanding with those little witches, certain it was, Adelaide had no occasions for making up a hard face, even if she could have done the thing. The only annoyance experienced was from a fine-looking youth, who bowed very respectfully as he passed, and in a sly way slipped a parcel into the hand of Miss Shawn, and then continued on his way. Where the young lady disposed of it would be idle to inquire; but that evening there was great doings in their private room; cakes were in abundance, and pieces of candy, and pea-nuts, and sugar-almonds. And Adelaide found a heap of good things lying on the top of her own bed.

"Do taste them, Miss Vincent; you don't know how good they are."

It would have done no good for her to refuse, for they all put in their plea; and when she had gratified them in this, Miss Shawn was so delighted that she ran up and kissed her. And as they saw that no offence was taken, but Miss Vincent kissed the kind-hearted girl in return, they all came up for a like favor.

"Oh, dear, how good it is to have some one that a body can love. You are going to stay here a long time, aint you, Miss Vincent?" said Miss Shawn. Every one in the room, at the same time, turned an inquiring look at Adelaide.

"I cannot say, my dear, how long. Perhaps Miss Martinett may not be satisfied with me."

"Where is your home, Miss Vincent?"

Adelaide colored deeply, and hesitated a moment.

"This is my home, for the present."

The idea of such a place being home to any one, seemed to be something they could not comprehend. Home, to them, was a place where there was neither paupau nor chick*ee*. Where there were no arbitrary rules, and stiff processions, and hard looks and bells to tell them when they must stop eating. Home was a place of smiles, and kisses, and kind words, and freedom, and happy evenings, and bright mornings. To speak of the institution as home, they could not quite comprehend it.

"Oh yes, you stay here at present, and we hope you will stay a long while; but what I mean is, where is your home?"

"I believe I understand you, dear, but—" Adelaide's lip trembled, "I have no other home at present."

"No other home!" and the sweet girl threw herself upon her breast and burst into tears. Adelaide pressed her fondly to her, and kissing her, replied:

"If I am faithful to discharge my duty, and trust in God, He will provide for me. He will make kind friends for me, just as you are, dear, and when I cannot stay here any longer, there will be some other place, no doubt, where I can earn my support."

"I know what I mean to do then; I mean to study hard,

and behave myself, and mind all the rules, and be just as good and particular as I can be, just so Miss Martinett will like you and want to keep you."

"And so will I."

"And so will I."

"And so will we all."

Blesings on your guileless hearts! ye are yet unspoiled by contact with a selfish world. *All* you would love if they would let you. How little do you think that your kind designs will work the evil that you so much dread, and that she whose interests you are designing to further, will but find that your love for her has made even this poor resting-place a refuge no longer.

CHAPTER XX.

THE neat carriage of Colonel Johnson had been standing for some time before the gate, and Josey was getting restless, and, as he had tried tossing his head and pawing with his feet, he gave a loud neigh. Just then his old master came forth from his front door, dressed with more than usual care. He was in his suit of brown, his court dress, as he called it, and with his black silk hose, his largest silver buckles, his well-powdered hair, and large brimmed beaver, he made, indeed a very respectable appearance. Dressed, likewise, in a neat suit, becoming his profession, the Rev. Mr. Jamieson came immediately after him.

"Well, well, I hear you ; I suppose you are tired waiting for me, Josey ; but we are ready now. Whoa, Josey."

"I suppose you will be the driver, sir ?" said Mr. Jamieson, as he stood by the side of the carriage, waiting respectfully for the Colonel to step in.

"I am not going to do any such thing. A son of your age ought to drive his father, and I want you to learn Josey's ways."

"I will, sir, with great pleasure ; I am fond of driving a good horse."

The old gentleman stepped in and took his seat on the broad, well-stuffed cushion, and was immediately followed by his intended son-in-law.

"Whoa, Josey, whoa, sir."

Josey had started off at a tremendous rate, and was increasing his speed every moment, shaking his head violently, and showing signs of being in a very bad state of feeling.

"Whoa, Josey ; don't pull on the reins, sir, don't pull ; it only makes matters worse ; slack them up quick ; there now, you see, whoa, Josey, you see now, he wont bear it. He will mind when he is spoken to, if you don't speak too hard. He won't bear scolding, and he won't bear pulling; just hold the reins with a gentle hand, so that his mouth can feel your guidance, that is all you want. Now you see how he has cooled down. He is something like his master, easily guided and checked by gentleness and a kind word, but only made perverse and headstrong by pulling tight on the reins and hallooing at him. He don't know what a stroke of the whip means. There, you see how beautiful he goes; and no matter what happens behind him or before him, only speak gently and in a soothing manner, and he will fear nothing."

"It is certainly a great pleasure to drive such an animal. He must have cost you a large sum."

"By no means; you see I got him when a colt and made him very tame and fond of me, so that he always seemed to know that I was his friend. I had a little trouble in breaking him. It required, indeed, a great deal of care, but I have been richly repaid; no money could buy him now. Away with you, Josey."

And along the pleasant winding road, amid all the variety with which the fields were loaded, rolled the easy vehicle, borne at a good free pace by the noble horse, with apparently as little effort as though travelling in the open field, with no burden behind him. It was a bright afternoon, and not warm for the season, and the journey they were upon was of a nature to inspire kind and pleasant feelings. They were to meet a concourse of neighbors and townsmen at the house of Mr. Foster, to celebrate his marriage with the lovely Fanny Pearl.

As they drove up, and the old gentleman was about to alight, "I wish," said he, "you would just drive Josey under the shade of that tree, and there let him stand, but don't attempt to fasten him—he won't bear to be tied."

It was a small house of only one story in front, but with a gable roof; there was abundant space in the attic for rooms; and, therefore, on both ends of the building were windows above, corresponding with those below. A small back building projected from the rear, containing a summer kitchen and wood-house, and adding greatly to the appearance of the place as to convenience and comfort. The house had never been painted, and of course the clapboards now were well browned, and quite in contrast with its newly-shingled roof. But to one who understood country matters, it had a very pleasant aspect, for the reason that every part which was essential to comfort externally had been repaired, and gave it a thrifty, substantial appearance. Even the old picket fence in front, and at the sides, was all straightened, with its gates swinging freely, the paths cleared of every weed, and as hard as a boarded floor; old apple-trees and cherry-trees clustered around; and one tall pear-tree, well loaded with fruit, hung its branches so near to the south window, that one might easily pluck them from thence.

The curb around the well, with its long sweep and dangling bucket, appeared also to have been thoroughly attended to, and gave promise of many a refreshing draught.

The old colonel cast his eye around with a satisfied air, and, turning to his companion:

"It looks well—it looks in order—it looks as though, other things being right, there might be a deal of comfort enjoyed here. That Slocum knows how to fix things."

At the door they were met by Mr. Somers:

"Col. Johnson, you are the very man I have been wishing to see. I have been looking over the premises, and it does one's heart good to think what a nice, snug box the dear young couple are going to have."

"Glad to hear it, sir," shaking Mr. Somers very cordially by the hand; "glad to hear it; and, to tell you the truth, I have come along a little before the time just to take a peep myself. The young folks I understand will be here at four o'clock."

"But how is it, brother Jamieson, that you are not in your canonicals? You are to marry them, are you not?

"My canonicals are on hand, brother Somers," lifting up a leather portmanteau; "I think too much of them, and of the ceremony too, not to have everything done in the best style. But I don't fancy riding in them."

The parents of Fanny Pearl were poor, and their house too small to accommodate the numbers who had been invited. It was, therefore, concluded that all the young friends should, in company with the bridegroom, go to her house, and attend her and her parents to the new home, where the marriage ceremony was to be performed. Lucy Johnson and Julia

Rice had been selected as bride's-maids, from the Episcopal and Congregational societies, and a young lady from the society to which the Rev. Mr. Foster belonged. The same order had been agreed upon for groom's-men. Fanny Pearl being a member of Mr. Jamieson's church, of course he had been invited to perform the ceremony, while the Rev. Mr. Somers was to ask the blessing on their new abode.

"There is nothing here, you see, Col. Johnson, that would be thought much of by those who have been accustomed to the show of a city establishment."

"And what of that, my dear sir? Do you think there is a couple about to be linked together in the great city, that has a better prospect of happiness? Everything indeed is plain, but it has a comfortable look. That carpet is home-made, but one does not feel afraid to tread on it; and those chairs have neither mahogany nor gilding about them, but they are very easy to sit in; and that table may be of cherry, possibly, but it has a fine polish on it; and I doubt not those who sit around it will feel that they have great cause for gratitude."

"I doubt it not—but step in here, colonel."

"Well, well, well, this does one's heart good; what a snug box of a kitchen, and what a pleasant view from those windows, and all so conveniently arranged; that door, I suppose, leads into their bedroom, and that one into their keeping-room, and that one, I suppose, leads into their buttery?"

"Yes, sir—and well stocked it is, too. I should think they would not be obliged to lay out any money for food for a year to come."

"Have you been into Mr. Foster's study, brother Somers?" said Mr. Jamieson, who had followed them through the rooms;" I am not quite so much an amateur of kitchens and butteries as you two gentlemen; my experience in that way being all to come. But I profess to know when I get into a snug and convenient place for books, and the pen."

The two gentlemen followed him to the north side of the house, where, separated by a passage from the other rooms, was the place selected for the peculiar use of the young minister. It was about twelve by eighteen feet in size, lighted by three windows opening to the south and west, and from each a pretty view met the eye,—green grass, and flowering shrubs, and trees scattered here and there, and through their openings the blue waters of the distant Sound. The interior of the room had few adornments; one end of it was fitted with shelves and plain glass frames, within which was stored a handsome collection of books recently presented to him, and near one of the windows was an oblong table neatly covered with fine green cloth. Upon it lay a portfolio, a stand for ink and pens, and a Bible of convenient size for common use. A large easy-chair, well cushioned, stood by the table, presenting a very inviting appearance. The old colonel, at the suggestion of Mr. Somers, placed himself in it.

"I dont feel that this is quite the place for me, although I must say that I would a little rather be in the shoes or the chair of that young man, than in that of many who would stand a good deal higher in the estimation of the world."

"That you might well say, sir, and I have no doubt could the walls of this little room speak, they would tell of many ardent prayers put up for us all here; for this has always been his study, although its present appearance is owing to the effort we made last winter. And I think no one of us will ever have to regret that step. It was indeed a blessed sight to behold here so many of different persuasions, all uniting in harmony and love to do an act of kindness. You were not here, Colonel Johnson, but your name was blessed by many lips, and I have no doubt many an ardent prayer ascended for blessings on your head."

"I aint a-going to stay here if you talk so. I don't care how much they pray, but I don't want to hear about it."

And the old colonel arose, but Mr. Somers seized his hand.

"You and I, colonel, have known each other a great many years, and I believe you will do me the justice to acknowledge that I was never given to flattery."

"I never thought you was."

"And I know you too well, sir, not to feel that you are far above desiring your own praise. But I know that you like to see your fellows happy, and you also like to know that when you design a benefit, it has accomplished its end."

"No doubt, sir, no doubt; that is natural enough. But all I try to do in my small way is just to give them a lift, just to help them, so that they can begin to help themselves, and it don't take much in most cases to do that."

"I cannot tell, my dear sir, how much you have expended in this way, but I know that there are many who freely own that you have helped them to independence."

"Tut, tut, tut, they talk a great deal more than there is any need of; but just sit down, my good sir, here by the side of me. We shall have a little time to spare before the young folks are along. I suppose Mr. Jamieson has gone to put on his regimentals, to be ready for service. And now what I tell you is for two reasons. The first, that you may not give me credit for what I do not deserve. And the second, that you may be able to instruct some of your rich men how to do a great deal of good without materially injuring their own capital. You say, sir, and it is true, I do not deny it, that I have helped a great many people who are now standing on their own foundation, independent men. Well, sir, it is true what I tell you, I am not out of pocket, by all I have done, over one thousand dollars."

"Colonel Johnson, you utterly surprise me."

"I thought I should. But this is the way I have managed. I have no great property, much less than many suppose, but enough for all my purposes. I have always kept a little loose money on hand for the special purpose of being ready on an emergency to give a helping hand at the right time. Well, sir, I have a friend, a queer sort of fellow sometimes, but his heart is big enough to fill a dozen common men. You know him. He belongs to your church, Slocum."

"Aye, a good man that; much better than he tries to appear."

"He is a noble fellow, sir; he ought to have a monument of brass erected to his memory. Well, sir, Slocum you see, knows everybody and everything, for he has his nose into everybody's business, and they all take it in good part because they know he don't mean any harm. Well, Slocum will come to me and say: 'Colonel, there is a young fellow that 's been rather wild, and he has got into bad company, and he has run a little into debt, and he is getting clear discouraged, and I 'm afraid if something aint done for him, he 'll stick fast and go to the dogs; and I do believe, if he could just be encouraged a bit, and feel that he is a free man, he would cut loose of bad habits and make a first-rate man. And then again he 'll come with a long story about some other fellow that has got a family, and is somewhat in debt;

and some who are impatient are about to lay hold of his property and break him up, and maybe break down all his resolution into the bargain. And then, maybe there is another who has been struggling to get along with a young family, but can't get ahead because it takes all his earnings to pay rent. A small place is offered him very cheap; if he could only be helped to buy it he would raise enough on it to support his family and keep a cow, and all that. Well, sir, I I run the risk, one hundred here, two hundred there, and maybe five hundred elsewhere, or even as high sometimes as one thousand dollars; let it go, and see how it turns out. When I help, I help. I take no interest. I tell them all the interest I want is to know that it has done them any good. If they get along, they may pay me when they are able. There, sir, you see, 'is the thing of it.' The help I give them is without security; it raises them, you see, right up on their feet. It gives them a fair chance. It puts *hope* in their heart." And the old gentleman very significantly clapped his hand on the arm of Mr. Somers. "It gives him *hope*, sir. It takes off his burden. He goes to work with a right good will, and a light heart; depend upon it, sir, there is many a poor fellow obliged to tug along through life under a burden that he cannot throw off himself. A little help at the right time might take the wrinkles from his brow, and throw sunlight on his dreary path."

Mr. Somers looked at the old man with intense interest, as he thus let out not only his secret of doing good, but also the warm glow of his kind heart.

"And you say, you are only one thousand dollars out of pocket by all you have done?"

"I'll explain to you, sir, how that is. Some men, you know, who have a little loose money to spare, will take, say five or six thousand dollars, and use it in a speculation. That sum, they say, they will risk. If they make by it, well and good; if they lose, it will be but the six thousand dollars; they shall not risk any more than that sum. Well, sir, I thought I would try how the thing would work as a kind of speculation. Not that I cared to make anything by it; but somehow it seemed to me that I could get a greater amount of happiness, and confer a greater amount of happiness, by just setting apart five thousand dollars for the purpose of using in the way I have told you. Some of it I keep out at interest, and some I keep on hand, ready for a call. Well, that which is at interest helps to keep the other good, as I add the interest to the principal."

"And do you get any that you thus lend, back again?"

"Almost invariably. I never ask for it. But, sir, you know that most men would feel, under all these circumstances, very anxious to repay. The help afforded them has given them such a start, that they soon get above-board. But what if I should lose sometimes? Don't men in any speculation lose sometimes?"

"Yes, colonel, but yours is a certain gain either way. A rich enjoyment for your heart here, and a treasure laid up above."

"Don't, sir, don't talk so, I beg of you; don't talk about my laying up anything anywhere. I get full pay here, and more than pay *up there*, sir;" and the old man raised his hand. "All I hope for is of free grace."

Mr. Somers grasped his hand, and shook it fervently.

"Colonel Johnson, you and I have long been on speaking terms; but, sir, you must let me look upon you hereafter as a bosom friend."

"With all my heart, sir, and proud shall I be to call you so."

"I have learned a lesson this afternoon that I shall try to profit by."

"You won't mention names!"

"Not if you forbid me."

"I do; unless—unless, your judgment tells you that you can do some good by it. But here comes our reverend, all fixed up for the ceremony. Do you know that I and your brother here, as you call him, have been telling one another some secrets?"

Mr. Jamieson, to whom the latter part of the address was made, seemed somewhat confused. A slight blush tinged his cheek, as he looked first at one, and then at the other of the gentlemen.

"Don't be alarmed, Brother Jamieson, our secrets have had no reference to you."

"Not as yet; but as Mr. Somers and I have been forming a sort of a league of friendship, it is but right that he should know all about matters and things in particular, for I mean that he shall perform the ceremony, when you and Lucy are made one."

Mr. Somers eagerly grasped the hand of Mr. Jamieson:

"My dear brother, I can almost say, 'Now let thy servant depart in peace.' What could I have asked more for you, as my best friend, than such a treasure as that young lady? I hope your prospect of earthly happiness will not cool your heavenly zeal."

"I'll see to that, my dear sir," said the colonel clapping his hand on the shoulder of Mr. Somers. "I'll see to that. He has got to take me, you know, into the bargain; I'll be a thorn in his side; I'll see to it that he aint too happy."

The tidings, "They are coming," now were heard, and all, at once, prepared to receive them. It was a beautiful sight to witness such a long cavalcade of youth; all dressed in their best, and their smiling faces in such unison with the bright sky and the green earth. As speedily as possible, they alighted, and without forming a regular procession came arm in arm following the happy pair. The bride was very tastefully dressed, but few seemed to think of that or of their own display. They loved her, for she had been among them as the beauteous lily, never seeking to be noticed, but shedding around her quiet path the sweet fragrance of a loving spirit. And all were happy, because she was; all rejoiced in the pleasant prospect before her, and were heartily glad that Fanny Pearl was about to have such a pleasant home.

The bridal party was arrayed, the impressive ceremony performed by Mr. Jamieson was soon over, and those who had long loved were pronounced to be, for good or ill, one until death.

The Reverend Mr. Somers then arose; his eye sparkled with delight, as he looked around upon the assemblage of happy faces:

"May heaven's best blessings rest upon these two beloved youth, who have now thus solemnly pledged their troth to each other. We all rejoice in their happy union; we rejoice in all the mercies that meet them in this home, provided for them by the kindness of their covenant God. And now in their name and at their request, I rise to consecrate it to the service of Him, for whom they wish to live, and to implore His blessing on it, and on them."

The bridal party knelt before the man of God, as his uplifted hands arose towards heaven. Hushed in breathless silence, the whole assembly listened to the outpouring of his short, but ardent supplication; and when he closed, amen resounded audibly from many, whose hearts, with unaffected interest, united in every wish that had been sent on high.

Happy pair! you have commenced with God. Yourselves, your home, your service, your basket, and your store, you hold as His. Arise and take the cup of bliss which your Heavenly Father holds out for you. Take it freely, for He gives in love, and safely rest upon His arm, who has the fulness of the earth at His disposal.

CHAPTER XXI.

FROM the happy scenes of a bridal hour, and the cheerful home of the newly-married pair, to the "celebrated institution" of Miss Martinett, if not an agreeable change, is, however, a very necessary one, in the progress of our story.

Time passes quickly away when in the constant discharge of duty. Adelaide had now for some months faithfully pursued her daily course. The little circle of girls assigned to her had become so essential to her happiness, that she looked forward to the hour of separation with a sad heart. The term had nearly expired, and the girls were counting the days which would intervene before they would be released from the tedious ceremonials of Miss Martinett's rule, to the freedom and happiness of home. Adelaide was too unselfish not to sympathize with them, and would often listen with deep interest to the free expressions of delight which they indulged, when, together with them in their room, they felt at liberty to let out their feelings.

"I do wish," said Caroline Shawn to her, one evening, after they had been thus talking together of all that they should see and do; "I do wish you could just see what a time there will be when I get home. The first thing I shall meet will be Hector, old Hector, the watch-dog. First he will begin to bark, and then as soon as he knows me he will begin to sneeze and wriggle himself about, and then he will jump on me, and caper round, and make such a fuss; and father and mother will be running out on the stoop and down on the lawn; and then Judy, the cook, she will run up from the kitchen, and take me right into the buttery and show me all the nice things she has made ready for me, and then she will cut me a nice large slice of pie, and stuff my hand full of cakes. Oh dear! how I wish you could go with me!"

"I am very glad, my dear, that you have such a home to think of, and I hope you may enjoy all your anticipations. But I hope, my dear, you will not forget what we have talked about, but will remember that all your blessings demand from you a very grateful heart."

"Oh, I hope I shall not forget," and the affectionate girl leaned her head on the shoulder of Adelaide, and threw her arms around her neck. "Oh, I do wish you would go with me. I know I shall feel better, and do better, if you are with me; it seems so easy to be good where you are."

Adelaide felt that it would not do for her to foster such an idea, and after endeavoring to impress upon her the importance of acting rightly, independent of the presence or countenance of friends, turned the subject of conversation. Caroline Shawn, however, was a girl of strong feelings, and not easily turned aside when her mind was fixed on an object; so, without saying a word of her design, at once wrote home, stating her wishes, and requesting leave to invite the teacher who had been so kind to her, and whom she so much loved, to spend the vacation at her own home in company with her. In a few days an answer was received; a letter came to her enclosing one for Miss Vincent, from both her parents, urging her in the most cordial manner, and adding that their own carriage should be sent to convey them.

The letter came at a time when they were all convened in the "ante-room" preparatory to breakfast. Miss Shawn had no sooner opened her letter and found one for Miss Vincent, than she ran up to her and placed it in her hands:

"Do read it quick, I know it 's an invitation; do read it."

"Miss Shawn, Miss Shawn," said the hard voice of the lady principal, "you forget your manners. Where are you?"

The happy girl was immediately silent; but the severe look which Miss Vincent received from Miss Martinett manifested that her displeasure was excited. Adelaide calmly put the letter in her pocket, and stood ready for marching orders. But there was a severer scowl than usual on the brow of the lady, and more than one noticed that the little bell sounded some minutes sooner that morning than common. Poor Caroline Shawn, with all her despatch, declared "she had n't got half down what she wanted to."

"And, oh dear Miss Vincent, you *will* go now, won't you? Oh we shall have such nice times; we can have such beautiful walks all alone with Hector, and Aunt Judy will fix us such nice lunches, and you shall ride Janet, my pony, whenever you like. And, oh—"

There is no telling how long Caroline would have gone on enumerating the many fine things in prospect, had she not been interrupted by the sound of footsteps near the door.

"I wonder who that is?" said Caroline. "I have heard it several times when we get alone."

"Oh, I presume it is some of the girls, my dear, walking in the passage."

"Shall I go see?"

"Oh no, dear; if they wish anything they will come in, no doubt; but what makes you look so anxious? you are not afraid?"

"Oh no; but I should like to see who it is, for the girls say that Miss Sharpe goes round listening at the doors."

"Perhaps that is unjust, my dear. You know we ought not to think evil, and we ought always so to conduct as not to fear being overheard."

"Yes, I know; but Miss Sharpe don't like you, I know she don't, and—"

"Hush, hush, dear Caroline; let us always endeavor conscientiously to discharge our duty, and not be anxious about the love of others."

"I don't believe Miss Sharpe loves any one."

"Let us drop her name, my dear, and talk about our journey. I have made up my mind, since you desire it so much, to accept the kind invitation of your parents."

"Oh dear," and the warm-hearted girl threw her arms round the neck of her teacher, and kissed her again and again, in the fulness of her joy. Adelaide had used no art thus to gain the love of her pupils. She had been faithfnl in reproving their faults. She had required perfect lessons and strict attention to the rules of the school. But she had taken pains to enlarge upon the subject she was teaching, and had endeavored to give them an understanding of it. This had excited their minds to study, and increased their respect for her. Her manners, also, had ever been dignified, whether at recitations or in their private rooms, although so blended with kindness that they felt under no painful restraint; and beyond all this she had endeavored to instill into their minds the principles of religion. She nightly read to them a portion of Scripture from her prayer-book, and then knelt down with them, and in the beautiful petitions there provided, commended herself and them to God.

All this had thrown a charm about her to their young minds. They could confide in her; they could not help loving her, for they were sure that she loved them.

Miss Sharpe, the elder assistant of Miss Martinett, had, for some cause not worth inquiring into, begun to look upon Adelaide Vincent with an eye of jealousy. Miss Sharpe was also famous for finding out things, and on that account was more dreaded in the institution than any other individual, except Miss Martinett herself. She was always going about with a noiseless step, and many wondered what her business was that carried her into so many different parts of the establishment. She had a great way of entering rooms suddenly, where she had no particular supervision; stepping in and looking round a moment, and then apologizing for having come into the wrong room. Two or three girls could never get together to exchange secrets, but all at once they would find Miss Sharpe fumbling about after something very near to them, paying no particular attention to them, but never finding the thing looked for. The girls said—but what will not boarding-school girls say sometimes—that "Miss Martinett kept her for a spy." It was naughty and dangerous for them to say so. But so many little things that they said, came to the ears of Miss Martinett, that they could not help charging some one as an informer; and as Miss Sharpe was not very popular, they charged it to her.

It was a very common occurrence for Miss Sharpe to be summoned to a private interview with the lady principal, and therefore she was not at all surprised, after the little affair in the "ante-room" that morning, on receiving, after the exercises of the day were over, a command to attend Miss Martinett in her private room.

"I am glad that you have been so ready to obey my summons, Miss Sharpe; you are my oldest assistant, and I feel that I can rely upon you in carrying out my plans for the proper subordination of the school. Things seem to be getting into a very loose way. I have never allowed liberties in my presence, and I never will. How is it that the youngest assistant I have gains such attention, not only from those she teaches, but also from all the other scholars. She is indeed, I perceive, the chief star among you all."

"Indeed, Miss Martinett, it is not for me to say, ma'am. I always try to do your bidding, and to see that all keep the rules. But I know what I know, ma'am, and I have been thinking this blessed day, ma'am, if there was n't something done, I for one would have to give up. It is n't in human nature to have one's own class all the time a-listening to another teacher, and running after her, and showing such favoritism. But it aint done without means, ma'am."

"Means! what means do you refer to?"

"Well, ma'am, there are great means used, more than I should dare to tell of."

"And why should you not dare to tell? is anybody here to be feared besides me?"

"Ah, no ma'am, surely not, but how could I know that it was not all done with the approbation of Miss Martinett."

"My approbation goes with the observance of my rules, and not otherwise."

"Then it is not your will, that all the time of the class should be taken up with talking to them, instead of hearing them recite from the books?"

"By no means; and who dares to deviate thus from my positive instructions?"

"Oh, well ma'am, I did n't know but you had given liberty to Miss Vincent to do so, as she spends so much time at it."

"And is that so?"

"Indeed it is ma'am, and that aint all; there is a great familiarity going on with the scholars; sometimes they will get on her lap, and put their arms round her neck, just as if she was n't your assistant and bound to keep them at a distance; but I'm afraid that aint the worst of it."

"Let me know the whole truth, Miss Sharpe. I am the principal, and ought to know everything that is going wrong."

"That is what I think, ma'am. I don't know if you will think it wrong, but your other assistants have n't thought it right for them to be teaching any kind of religion to the scholars. You know, you have said to me that my duty was to hear the lessons, and see to the rules, and not to be teaching my religion to the scholars; and it seems to me a right thing, for I don't think the parents would all like to have their children made Catholics or Episcopalians, which is pretty much the same thing."

"And is this done?"

"Well, ma'am, I think if you could know what I do, you would think it was so; for I have seen it, and anybody can see it that should happen to go into Miss Vincent's room about the bed hour."

"What have you seen?"

"Well, ma'am, I have seen them all on their knees round her, just as if she was some saint or other, and she reading from a book, a prayer or something of the kind. If they aint all Catholics, then I miss my guess; and that 's the way they are so won over, so that Miss Vincent is invited to their homes, and all that."

"To their homes! who has invited her?"

"Well, it is Miss Shawn. You know her father is called a very rich man, and lives in great style, and his carriage is to be sent for her, just as if she was some great lady like yourself, ma'am."

"Well, well, it is so, is it? I shall see about it; I shall teach all my assistants that I am not to be undermined. You can go, Miss Sharpe."

Miss Sharpe curtseyed very low as she left the room, and Miss Martinett again rang the bell, saying to herself, as she resumed her seat:

"We shall see."

A young woman soon answered the summons.

"Is Miss Vincent in her room, Margaret?"

"She has gone, with ever so many of the girls after her, down the garden, ma'am."

"Call her to me, Margaret."

The manner of the mistress at once assured the servant that something was wrong, and, taking the same tone in which she had been addressed, called aloud to Miss Vincent, even before she came up to the group of young ladies:

"The mistress wants you, Miss Vincent, right away in her room."

Adelaide colored, but immediately prepared to obey; while

the girls, looking indignantly at the servant, exclaimed to each other :

"What can it mean? Dear Miss Vincent, what is the matter?"

"Oh, nothing of consequence, I presume."

While Caroline Shawn, clinging to her arm until they had gotten a little way from the group, whispered :

"I'm afraid it's the letter. Oh dear, I am so sorry I did not wait until we were alone."

"You did nothing wrong, my dear; then do not fear the consequences. The servant may have been out of humor for some cause of her own."

But Adelaide soon perceived, on coming into the room, that Miss Martinett was much excited.

"You seem to have made no great haste, Miss Vincent, to obey my summons."

"I believe I made no delay, madam, after I received your message."

"I expect prompt and implicit obedience to my requests, and to all my rules, and I must and will have it. I believe, Miss Vincent, you perfectly understand that you are here yet on probation."

"That was the understanding when I engaged, Miss Martinett; but I had hoped my term of probation was past, and that my services met your demands, and were satisfactory."

"No term was specified. Of course it cannot be expected in an institution like this, whose reputation is world-wide, that teachers can be permanently engaged without a long and severe trial. Six months, at least, I require."

"I believe it is nearly that period since I came."

"It is so, and therefore I have thought proper to let you know that your services will be no longer required. You are at liberty to go now at any moment."

Adelaide was confounded, and would fain have inquired "why it was?" but no opportunity was afforded her so to do. She merely said :

"Then I may consider that my engagement is at an end?"

"Your probation is at an end, and I shall have no further need for your services."

Adelaide arose, but stood a moment, as though she expected something further would be said. She could hardly think that Miss Martinett would suffer a separation, so harsh in its manner, and so cruel to one who had depended upon her sense of justice for remuneration, to take place without the offer of some compensation. But the cold, stern gaze of the unfeeling woman soon told her that all hope of mercy or justice from her was vain. She made her obeisance, and at once retired to her own room. For a few moments she gave way to her over-burdened feelings, and then, calming her spirits by the thought that the Father of the fatherless knew all the honesty of her intentions, she sat down and reviewed her course since she had been in her present situation. She saw nothing to charge herself with; nothing to regret; nothing that she would have done otherwise, could she have foreseen the consequences which had befallen her.

But the review of the past finished, the future with all its realities was now to be encountered, and into its dark mist she tried to penetrate. She must leave her present abode, but for what other shelter? Her aunt had solemnly forbidden her ever again to pass her threshold. Her kind old uncle was far away, and her Aunt Halliday was among relatives in a distant State. She had some acquaintances, apparent friends, who might be glad to see her under different circumstances. To cast herself upon any that she knew, and tell them she was in need of a shelter, was too much like beggary; the thought was abhorrent to her sensitive spirit. Almost in despair, she rose and paced the room. It was, indeed, a wide, wide world upon which she was thrown. At times, in her agony, she was almost tempted to go down and tell that stern, selfish woman all the desolateness of her situation, and ask her in charity to keep her until some place should offer. But that dark, cold gaze would immediately come back, in all its forbidding power. No, death itself would be better than such a step.

At length the thought occurred, that in the great city some situation as teacher in a private family might be found. And she remembered the humble home of Mrs. Willis, to which she had once in her extremity fled, and who had been, in former years, under great obligations to her Uncle Halliday. She had to think quick and act with promptness, for she even feared at any moment a messenger might be sent to order her from the house. She went to her trunk, and took out her little purse, and, with a trembling hand, counted its contents. Five dollars alone remained to her, with which to venture abroad into the crowded avenues of life, where money alone could be her security for even a lodging for the night.

She closed her purse, and, placing it in her pocket, commenced packing her trunk. Just then there was a gentle knock at the door. She opened it, and Caroline Shawn, with noiseless step, entered.

"Oh, what is it? what is it, dear Miss Vincent? Do tell me."

"I am going away, my dear."

"Oh, but you shan't go. I won't stay here if you do." At the same time clasping her arms around Adelaide, burst into tears Deeply affected at this token of her love, Adelaid wept freely with her.

"But where are you going?"

"I can hardly tell, my dear; but—"

"You shall go to my home; you *shall* go there, and I will go with you. I will go this minute; nobody shall hinder me."

"Stop, stop, Caroline, be calm. I am sorry that I have given way to my feelings; only stop and think one moment. You know Miss Martinett; you are under her power at present. She would not allow you to leave this house; and if she should know how you feel, you might be made to suffer a great deal. Mind what I tell you now. You know that I love you, and I am very sure that you love me; but let no one see that you grieve because I am gone. You have some weeks yet to stay before your vacation. I dread to think how you may be made to suffer in that time; be a good girl."

It was with great difficulty, however, that Adelaide could calm the excited girl, and not until she had promised to write to her, and let her know what school she was in.

"For I know that my papa will let me go anywhere where you are a teacher."

As soon as Adelaide had packed her trunk, she went out and sought a person to carry it to one of the sloops, as she knew that one or more sailed that evening for the city. Another fond embrace, not only from Miss Shawn, but from each one of her class that was fortunate enough to see her, and then she walked away and sought the boat that was to carry her from a place where she had enjoyed and suffered so much, to new and untried scenes.

Adelaide had never before been upon the Hudson, but she had no heart to enjoy its enchanting scenery. The dark and rugged highlands, shutting in the prospect and enclosing her within their massive ramparts, were too much like the present circumstances in which she was so strangely placed. And yet her eye would fasten on them as though there was a charm in their dreariness.

It was not until the afternoon of the next day, that she found herself gliding, behind a moderate breeze, along the outskirts of New York. It had no welcome for her; no friends awaited her, a fugitive and a stranger. She watched the clustering houses and the long streets as they passed, only as tokens that she had reached the place where she must supplicate a few days shelter as an act of friendship.

"Where, Miss, shall your trunk be sent?"

Adelaide was much confused, as the captain, having fastened his sloop to the dock, came up to her and put this question.

"Perhaps, if it would not be inconvenient to you, I should be glad to let it remain awhile."

"Just as you please."

And, accepting his assistance to reach the dock, she quickly walked on her way amid carts, and packages of goods, and rolling casks, and rough, boisterous men, and dirty, forbidding women and children. It was some distance to the house of Mrs. Willis, and the afternoon was already far advanced. So, threading her way as rapidly as she could, into one of the less crowded thoroughfares, she hastened to make sure at least of a shelter before the evening should be upon her.

At length she reached the house, and hurried up the steps, and with a trembling hand rung the bell. Again and again she pulled the little brass knob, but no sign was returned that she was heard. Her heart began to beat violently; again she pulled the bell with greater force. She could hear it echo through the house, but no footstep approached to give her entrance, nor could she hear a sound that gave token of any living being within. She looked at the windows; they were closed, and her attention was attracted by a written notice on the side of the house, "This House to Let." A cold chill ran over her, and she felt her limbs failing; just then a voice from behind called out:

"I guess you need n't ring there, there aint no one in; they 're all gone."

She turned, and her eye met a dirty looking object, in the shape of a woman. She had a pail in her hand from which she had just thrown some slops into the street. Adelaide stepped down to her.

"Do you know if Mrs. Willis still lives here, good woman?"

"I know she don't, they moved away more than a week ago."

"Do you know where she has removed to?"

"It 's what I don't; but their servant woman told me they were going into the country somewhere; that times was too hard in the city; and that 's all I know about it."

The effort to question the woman had, for the moment, diverted her mind, and the weakness of her frame passed off. Without waiting any longer, she at once began to retrace her steps. The signs of evening were now evident, and already the men, with little ladders on their shoulders, were hurrying along to light their lamps for the night. All she met seemed to be hastening to their homes. A deadly weight pressed upon her heart as she glanced at the passers-by, with the desperate hope of seeing some face that she knew. It soon grew dark in the city, and some means she must at once devise, to avoid the horrible dilemma of finding herself, late at night, a wanderer through the streets.

Should she return to the boat and ask a lodging there? But she remembered that the captain and his hands were rough, profane men; and all the passengers left when she did.

Should she go to a public house? But ignorant as she was of all establishments of the kind, she might find herself in full as rude company.

As she thought, she still walked on down the crowded passage of Broadway, until at length she found herself in the midst of a multitude of lights, scattered about in different directions, and people of all ages and conditions walking to and fro, and jostling each other in their haste to get along. She had never before noticed it at night, although often had she passed by the old Oswego Market—*Swager*, as it was usually called—by day-light, in her aunt's carriage. Those who may be able to remember that nuisance at the junction of Maiden Lane and Broadway, can well imagine the feelings of Miss Vincent, when she found herself in the midst of the old rookery itself, and its kindred buildings on each side of the street. She stood a moment and watched the bustling throng, and listened to the babel sounds that filled the air. Dried-up old women, wrapped in dirty cloaks and hoods, were busy around their different clusters of baskets; some measuring out small quantities of vegetables; some talking loudly in their earnest bargaining; some seated at their ease, and refreshing their wearied frames with a nut-cake and a bowl of tea, and some laughing merrily, and apparently as joyous as though the rude materials around, and the rough nature, of their occupation, had as much to excite the merriment of the heart as if housed beneath a gilded ceiling and surrounded by the fineries of life; and doubtless, to them, it was so.

Adelaide saw that all were busy, too busy to notice her; and more than once she was thrust aside by some, who having purchased their supplies, were hurrying with baskets on their arms away for home. And all at once she remembered that it was the last evening of the week, and the morrow was the Sabbath. And where should she spend it? She passed out of the crowd, and then paused, if possible to to make some decision as to whither she should direct her steps. The lights from the windows shone full upon her, and more than one glanced a second look at her as they passed, as though wondering why one like her should be there, and alone. A young woman plainly dressed, just tripped by her at a sprightly gait, and gave the poor trembling girl a hasty glance, and then another, and then she paused, and turning round, watched her a moment, and then with a slow step, as though not well assured of the propriety of what she was about to do, came up and looked her full in the face.

“ Have you lost your way, Miss?”

There was something so quickening to the heart of Adelaide, in the kind tone and look of the speaker, that the tears started as she replied:

“ C[illegible] you tell me where I can find lodgings for the night?”

"Are you a stranger here?"

Adelaide was too excited to reply.

"Will you please step a little one side, Miss, until I can speak to you, where there is not such a crowd."

Adelaide followed her, and then in as few words as possible explained enough of her situation to excite the deep interest of the stranger.

"I am not acquainted enough with any public house that I could take you to, but if you will go with me, I can give you a room, though it may not be so good as you have been accustomed to."

"Oh! can you? Any place will be good enough in a decent family."

"I am a poor girl, and work for my living with my needle, and board out myself; but you will find the house clean and decent, and maybe you will be much safer than in a large place. Have you any trunk?"

And when Adelaide had told her, she replied:

"Then we will go right down and get a boy to carry it."

"Oh, you are very good; but it is giving you a great deal of trouble."

"Oh, I don't mind the trouble, for I should n't have slept a wink to night, if I had gone on after I saw how sorrowful you looked. I knew you must be a stranger and in trouble, and I know what it is to be a stranger in such a large place as this, where every one is only thinking of themselves. When I came here from the country I did n't know a living soul in this great city. Oh, it is a terrible thing to be a stranger in the city. It aint like the country, where every one's house is open, and all are ready to do you a kindness. May I be bold enough to ask what part of the country you came from?"

"My home has been at Wellgrove."

"Oh dear! and that is the next town to Melton, and I am from Melton. Oh, I am so glad I have happened to come across you."

They talked as they were walking, and soon reached the pier where the sloop lay. The young woman showed that she understood the ways of the city, by bargaining with the boy before he touched the trunk, and then kept looking back continually to see that he was close behind them. It was not far they had to go, for she turned down Ann street, and at a small low frame building she told the boy to put down the trunk, and his shilling being paid, he went whistling on his way back.

"Now," said she, "I don't want you to say what is n't true, but I must make as though you was a neighbor of mine from the country, for the old lady lives all alone; there is only us two, and she is very particular who she takes into her house. May I ask your name?"

"Adelaide Vincent."

"And if I call you Miss Adelaide, you won't take offence?" Adelaide assured her she would not, and that she could leave out the Miss.

"And my name is Margaret Leslie—be sure and call me Margaret."

The little knocker was then raised, and an elderly woman cleanly dressed, with her spectacles thrown up on her cap, opened the door, and stood holding it in her hand, as though somewhat amazed at seeing a stranger.

"Don't be frightened, Aunt Polly; this is a young lady from my part of the country, that I have brought to spend the Sabbath. She is alone in the city, and I don't like to have her go to a public house."

"Ah, well, come in;" and Margaret seizing the trunk, would carry it in spite of Adelaide's efforts to assist.

"You aint been used to carrying trunks, I know, and I am."

It was a small house, to be sure, and very plainly furnished, but everything was clean and in order.

"I could n't think," said the old lady, after they were all seated, "what made you so late to-night; and I began to be uneasy, for the city is getting so big, and there is so many different kinds of people getting in it, that it aint safe to be out much a-nights, as when I was young."

Adelaide enjoyed the simple fare on their little tea-table, and laid her down to rest in the plain, clean room, with a sense of obligation for God's great mercy to her, which she had never before experienced.

The Sabbath had passed, and Adelaide arose early from a sleepless bed, in order to prepare herself for the work which lay before her. She thought before the close of the day, that the old lady had manifested signs of uneasiness, and after retiring she heard quite a loud and earnest conversation between her and the young woman, and the idea suggested itself that she was the subject of it. Sensitive by reason of her late experience, her mind became to much agitated to allow of repose. She dressed herself, and sat by the little window that looked out into a small yard. Tall houses reared their rough walls all around, and every object wore that bleak and cheerless aspect which a cloudy winter-day presents in the city. All without was but too true a picture of her own desolate path. Away from earth she turned her thoughts towards Him who "comforteth them that are cast down," and there she tried to rest for support and direction.

"Will you come to breakfast, Miss?" said the trembling voice of Margaret, and as Adelaide looked at her she saw that she had been weeping. There was no opportunity then to ask any questions, so Adelaide immediately arose and followed to the table. As she came into the room and pleasantly saluted the old lady, she received but a cold nod of the head in return. It was a short and silent meal, and immediately after Adelaide had returned to her room, Margaret came to her:

"I don't know but you will think me very rude, but may I ask you, Miss, what you are going to do? It may be none of my business, but Mrs. Strong, the lady who keeps the house, has taken a notion against you, and, say what I can, she says you shan't stay here no longer."

"I am sure I am very sorry if I have done anything to displease her, and if I knew what it was I would tell her so. Shall I go and see her, Margaret?"

"It would n't do the least good, Miss. She is very set in her way. She is deaf, you know, too, and it is hard making her understand. I tried to tell her all I knew. But she said it was n't very likely that a young lady dressed as well as you was, would come here all alone, and be in such a fix. And she said a great many things I should n't like to repeat. But if you have any friends anywhere, please do go back to them; for what *will* you do in this wicked city, and all alone too. And she threatens me if I have anything more to do with you, she won't let me stay in this house another day. And indeed, Miss, I have to work hard with my needle every day just to keep myself in a decent place."

"You shall not be troubled, I assure you, Margaret, on my account. I will go away immediately. My trunk, perhaps, may remain until I find a place to board."

And the good-hearted Margaret sat down, and burst into tears. Adelaide did what she could at once to soothe her.

"Oh, I am so sorry, after all your kindness, to have caused you so much trouble."

"It is not for myself, Miss, that I feel. But what if you should n't find a place to stay? Oh, you don't know what it is to be alone in the city, and one like yourself, You don't know how shy people are, I mean the decent sort; and then you are so likely to get among them that aint what they ought to be. If you was only a working-girl, and wanted a service-place, that might be got in a day or two. But any one that looks on you knows you aint fit for no such thing."

Adelaide felt the terrible reality which the honest girl pictured to her, and the difficulties which surrounded her were such as she could never have imagined. She felt now what it was to brave the world, without having first been prepared for the encounter. Her situation was one of extremity, that must be met at once. She could stay no longer where she was, and therefore, first of all, went to settle for what expense she had incurred. The old lady was very moderate in her charge, but the trifling sum she took left merely a pittance in her purse; a few shillings alone remained.

With a heart fluttering with weakness, she returned to her room, and tried to collect her thoughts. Money she must have at the sacrifice of anything which she could possibly do without; and the only article which she possessed that might be available for that purpose, was her watch. It had been a present from her uncle, and she valued it on that account. But her feelings must now give way to her necessities. She went to her trunk, and withdrew the little treasure from its casket, and at once left the room to go forth and seek for a purchaser. As she was going through the passage, the old lady met her:

"I want to say a word to you before you go. You ought to go right home to your friends, where you came from; now I tell you so. You did very wrong in coming away so, all start alone. And folks can't see into it; and it aint reputable for a young gal like you to be prowling about the streets of a great city, without any friends or kin to take care of you. You aint brought up to work and take care of yourself, and you aint nowise fit to be alone. So I tell you go right home, and behave yourself, and stay there before folks talk more about you than they do."

Adelaide was too much confounded to reply, even if it would have done any good; and, therefore, with this addition to her misery, she left the house and went on her way. Her steps were directed towards Broadway, where she knew some of the largest jewellers' shops were located. With much trepidation in her manner, she offered her little treasure. It was a splendid establishment, several persons were in attendance behind the counter; one of them took it from her trembling hand, opened it, looked at its contents, shut it up again, and examined the outside, occasionally looking at the pale and anxious girl. At length he handed it back, and merely said: "We don't wish to purchase," and walked along towards some customers who just then came in.

Adelaide turned, and went on her way. And so at each place she passed, where watches were hung out for sale, she called, and at each received the same cold answer. One, indeed, apparently more frank than the rest, told her that they did not like to purchase such articles from strangers; that they had run risks enough that way.

"But it is my own property," she replied.

"Very likely, Miss, but we don't want it."

And thus rebuffed, she walked along, her limbs growing more and more feeble, from the extreme agitation of her mind. She passed the great park, and then on and on, until all signs of those shops where jewelry was sold were gone, and few stores of any kind were to be seen, except at the corners of the streets. At length she thought she spied a large watch hung over the sidewalk as a sign, and she hastened towards it. It proved to be a watchmaker's; a small, unpretending place. Once more, with a deeply agitated mind, she made the attempt to dispose of her treasure. She saw but one person, and he was seated before the window, with an eye-glass over one eye, examining the inside of a large and costly watch. She waited until he very leisurely took the glass from his eye, and laid down his work, and arose and stood ready to wait upon her.

"I want, sir, to sell this," handing him her watch. The man looked fixedly at her a moment. "I want to sell it very much, and will part with it much below its value."

The man opened it and examined its works, and then closing it, laid the watch down on the glass case before her.

"It seems to be a fair article, but to tell you the truth I dare not buy from a stranger anything of this kind; I have already suffered by it."

For a little time Adelaide said nothing. It was the death-blow to her hopes; she took it up, and, about to depart, asked in tones so broken, as scarcely to be understood:

"Then you cannot give me anything for it?"

The man did not answer, for just then a gentleman, whom Adelaide had not before noticed, came from the back part of the store, and walking up behind the counter looked at her in a very scrutinizing manner. He was a gentleman of middle age, portly in his make, well dressed, and with a fine open countenance. He had a newspaper in his hand, which he had doubtless been reading.

"Will you let me see your watch, Miss? it is your own property, you say?"

"It is sir, truly."

"Have you tried to sell it elsewhere."

"I have, sir, at almost all the jewellers, but they all decline to purchase."

"The trouble is this; there are so many tricks played upon them by persons offering such articles for sale, that have not been honestly come by, they fear to purchase from strangers."

Adelaide was about to speak, but he interrupted her.

"You need say nothing as to that; I believe you are the rightful owner of the watch. I tell you what I will do. I do not want to purchase the watch, but I will give you twenty dollars on account of it, and you can leave it here with this gentleman to dispose of; and whatever he gets more for it, you shall have; or if you should wish to redeem it, in three or four months, you can do so. Will that answer you?"

"It will, sir; it will be a great favor to me." And, as the gentleman looked at her, he saw that her eyes were filled with tears. He took out the money and handed it to her, and then walked to the back part of the store again.

The other took the watch, and asking what name he should put down, she opened her purse and handed him a small card. As soon as she had left, the gentleman who had so promptly assisted her, again came behind the counter, and made an apology for thus interfering in the way of business.

"I have no doubt, now, that is a case of real distress. Did you ever see a more beautiful countenance? Poor young thing, I should like to know more about her. Did she leave any name?"

The shopman, who was about resuming his work, opened a small drawer, where lay the little watch, and taking the card laid it down on the case. The gentleman had to put on his spectacles, for the writing was in a very fine hand.

"What is this? Ade-laide—Ade-laide Vin-cent—Adelaide Vincent—Adelaide Vincent—that name is familiar—let me think. My heavens! Mr. Grinnel, which way did she go?" and running back to get his hat and cane, stopped as he was about to leave the store:

"I will call for my watch by-and-bye; what time will it be done?"

"At four o'clock."

"Did that young lady say anything about her place of residence—where she stayed?"

"No sir; I say no, but it strikes me I heard her say something about Ann street; but I paid no particular attention to what she was saying, as I had no idea of purchasing the watch."

"You heard no number?"

"Not that I remember."

"You say she went down street?"

"Yes sir. But I think there is another gentleman in pursuit of her."

"Another! who?"

"Why you know, probably, the character of Bob ———. I saw him dodging back and forth the window, while she stood here, and the moment she was off he was off too. Bob is never after much good."

"The scoundrel!" and with a rapid step the gentleman left the shop, shaking his cane, and muttering some hard things to himself.

CHAPTER XXII.

Old Colonel Johnson was sitting in his snug room; a fire was blazing on the hearth; it was not quite the time for fires, but the old gentleman, as the latter part of the fall approached, would have one, at least in the morning and evening.

He was now sitting before it with his newspaper, which he had just received, held open to be thoroughly dried, preparatory to his enjoyment of its contents, when a visitor was announced, and, turning to receive him, sprang from his seat with the agility of a young man.

"My good fellow, how are you? But I don't know but I ought to give you a good scolding. It is all of two weeks that you have not had your feet in this house. Come, sit down, Master Charles, and give an account of yourself."

"I have been unusually busy, sir, of late, getting off my crops to market."

"Ay, ay, yes, yes, I heard you was sending off a boat-load of potatoes. A great man you are getting to be! I thought the old landing would never be used again, in my day. And I understand you have persuaded old Duncan, the miller, to repair his kilns again, for drying corn-meal, and we shall have vessels here, I suppose, loading for the West Indies and all that. A pretty upstart of a fellow! But tell me candidly, what is the truth about it?"

"Well, sir, I have been putting my potatoes on board a sloop. It does not quite load her, to be sure, but there were enough to induce the captain to run up here, from Wellgrove, and take them in."

"And that is the reason why you went so largely into the potato line. Ay, ay, I see you know not only how to work but how to manage; if you had been obliged to cart them all to market it would have cost you about half you would get for them."

"It would have been a very serious undertaking, sir, to have carried seven hundred bushels of potatoes so many miles."

"And have you sold them out-and-out?"

"Yes sir. I suppose I might, possibly, have done better by sending them on my own account; but the captain offered me forty-three cents per bushel, cash, and I thought I had better accept of it."

"You are right. Why, you will get three hundred dollars for your potato crop?"

"Yes sir; not quite what I expected, but the drought injured them somewhat. I am well satisfied, however."

"And how did your corn turn out? Did the lime answer well?"

"I think it has, sir. We have sold one hundred and fifty bushels, besides reserving what we need for ourselves. But I have been buying; I laid out two hundred and fifty dollars of the money, which I received for my potatoes, in corn."

"And have had it kiln-dried?"

"Yes sir; and have cleared, altogether, fifty dollars on the operation."

"And that, added to your own crop of corn, and your potatoes, gives you five hundred dollars for your summer's work. A pretty good operation; and your land in a better state in the bargain. Well, well, that will do."

"We feel well paid for our labor, and have now a little capital to work upon. A few hundred dollars loose money we find of great advantage."

"Yes, it is a great advantage if one knows how to use it. A man wants a clear head in farming, as well as strong hands. And may I ask, what you are going to do with your money this winter?"

"We do not intend to let it lie idle. We have cut quite a crop of hay this season, which, with all our other provender, will enable us to keep much more stock than we have on hand. And as I wish to teach my brother to lean upon his own judgment, I have concluded to let him take two hundred dollars, and go north about fifty miles from here, where they have a short crop of hay, and are selling young cattle very low. I think he can invest it to advantage, and very safely, too."

"Ay, ay; I see you keep your eyes looking in all directions. That will be a fine thing for your farm next summer."

"That is what I thought; and if we have more than we can pasture in the spring, we can easily get them kept in the mountains for a small charge."

"So you can, that is true. But to change the subject a moment; Lucy has been telling me a strange story about a family down on Oyster Island. What is it about them?"

"Well, sir, to tell you the truth, it was with reference to them that I have called to see you. I feel quite concerned for their condition."

"What is the matter with them? Are they suffering? Who are they?"

"That I do not know, sir; there is some great mystery about them. They are not suffering at present. They have probably provision enough to subsist on through the winter. But the hovel they live in is not a fit habitation for human beings, in our country, in the winter months. It is a fixture I should think the man had put up himself with boards and straw."

"Bless my soul, how you talk!"

"And that is not all, sir; there is something strange about the family."

"Well, do tell what it is; you are getting as bad as Slocum; tell right off, what the trouble is."

"Well, sir, they are evidently persons far superior to their condition. The man, with a rough exterior, betrays occasionally, by his language and feelings, a refinement that I have never before met with in like circumstances. His wife is a lovely woman, quite young, and manifestly does not belong to the class with which they are now associated. I have been several times to see them, and feel more interested for them each time. The man seems, at times, very sad, almost like one who was broken-hearted; but he makes no complaint, and rather avoids any reference to their condition, as though he feared they might be thought objects of charity. He seems peculiarly fond of his wife and child, and I should judge, from what little I have occasionally seen, that on their account his mind at times is in great agony. But she tries to put on a cheerful air, and makes the best of things. But it pains me to think that she should be thus compelled to live, while possessed of those sensitive feelings which must have been nourished in some superior situation."

The old gentleman had arisen and thrown down his paper, and was walking about as was his custom when under any excitement. He stopped, however, before Charles closed, and looked steadily at him.

"It pains you, indeed! and so it ought. I tell you what it is, neighbor, this world is sadly out of joint. How it has got so, aint worth quarrelling about. But how things are ever going to be all righted, is more than *I* can see through. I have tried, Mr. Lovell, in my small way, to straighten them a little, but what does it amount to? As fast as one is up, there is another crying out for help. I am glad of one thing, though, that I don't live in a city, where poverty and distress exhibit their misery whenever a man sticks his head out of the door. I should n't dare to go out, nor to stay in. But what can be done for these folks? You 'd better go right off and see Slocum, and get some kind of a thing put up for them. Body-a-me, what a world it is! and the season is getting so late, too, and they are such a ways off!"

The colonel began to move about again, and to hitch up his small-clothes, and to manifest so much restlessness, that Charles had to do his best to keep from smiling, and dared not attempt to speak.

"Come, Master Charles, you are quick enough about your own business, and smart enough, too. Can't you think of something? Had n't you better go right off and get Slocum?"

"I have been thinking that perhaps some better plan could be devised, to get them off the island."

"Well, well, what is it? Anything to get them out of that hovel."

"Well, sir, you know the old house that has been standing empty for three or four months, down in the hollow near the end of your meadow lot; I don't know to whom it belongs, but it might be hired probably, and with a little fixing would be, in comparison with their present place, quite comfortable."

"I don't know what you may please to call comfortable, if such a place as that can be made so. Why, man, I bought that old rookery lately just to keep people out of it. Old Munson owned it, and as long as he could get any miserable wretches to give him five dollars a-year for it, he would let them in. It aint decent for any human being to live in, and I was going to pull it down as a nuisance."

"I know, sir, it has been a bad place, and that bad people have generally lived in it. But the timbers are sound, and most of the roof is good; with a few shingles to patch the roof, and a few boards to cover the broken places in the clapboards, and some hinges for the doors, and some glass for the windows, and all well cleaned out, and white-washed, it might be made quite comfortable. I am sure it would be infinitely better than the place they are now in."

"Well, if you can make that place decent with a few shingles, and boards, and hinges, and so on, I don't know what you can't do. But somehow you have made a picture of it already, that makes me think better of the place; I am glad I did n't pull it down. I'll never pull down anything after this that has got three legs to stand on, until I let you go and see it. But there is one thing, perhaps, you have n't thought about. How are they going to live when they get there?"

"I have thought of that, sir. The man is able to work, and I think very willing. In winter he can earn good wages by going into the woods, and at other seasons, there is little need for a man to be idle; there are enough to employ him."

"True enough; and now do you go right straight off and see Slocum, and tell him for me to go right away and fix that place according to your directions. You ought to be made captain-general over all old rookeries that want fixing up; you would make them quite comfortable places. Come, go right off, for I am in a hurry to see the thing fixed; and stop one minute—when you and Slocum have worked it into shape and whitewashed it, so that it is decent for a Christian man to go in, just let me know; and then there is another thing—do you tell Lucy to go into our garret, and pick out of her stores there of old tables, carpets chairs, and what not, such things as you and she may think will add to their comfort, and we will have them put in; and here, stop—don't go yet." The old gentleman had him fast by a button of his coat.

"Don't you say a word to the family about it, nor to any

living soul, what we are fixing the old house for; and then, when all is done, I will have you and Lucy go over to the island, and break it to them, and we will have them brought right over, bag and baggage, and clap them right in their 'nice comfortable' home; and maybe we will have a few things put into their buttery, a little pork, and molasses, and tea, and sugar, and such trifles, to make them feel a little easy like; and you can say to the man that as soon as he is ready, I have some chopping and sawing to do."

Slocum had, as usual, a job on hand, but the old colonel must be attended to whether or no, and he and Charles were soon working with a right good will at the old building.

"It 's a pretty hard case this, Lovell, ha! ha! ha! but I guess we 'll make her tight and trim before we 've done."

In a very few days there was quite a new face on things. The roof was somewhat speckled, the new shingles here and there, and everywhere, all over it, made a pepper and salt appearance; but it stood the test of a hard rain to the full satisfaction of Slocum, who was a great friend to tight roofs. He often said, "if a man had a tight roof over his head, and plenty of pork in the barrel, it was n't much matter how things looked." But Charles had a great idea of looks, and as he felt that his credit with the old colonel was somewhat at stake in the matter, determined to make "the old thing," as Slocum called it, look as well as circumstances would permit. So he went to work at straightening things on the outside, righting the fences, and hanging the gate, and clearing away old rubbish; and finally, after the inside was whitewashed, he made a composition that would stand the weather, and gave the clapboards two good coats of it. Slocum laughed at him a good deal at first, but, when he saw how much more finished it looked:

"I tell you what, Lovell, ha! ha! ha! you are the best hand to make the most out of an old thing I ever saw. The colonel won't know his old crow's nest."

And then Charles and Lucy went to work rummaging in the upper loft, among the cast-off things, that had been accumulating for many years; and it was wonderful to them how much they found that Charles said would help to make them comfortable; and when they put them in the building, and spread down an old carpet, which, after Lucy's mending, looked "most as good as new," and set the wooden-chairs around, and an old cherry-table, and even a rocking-chair to which Lucy had fixed a cushion, and some andirons, with little brass knobs on the top, and shovel and tongs to match, it really looked, as Charles said, "quite comfortable," and Lucy was so struck by it herself that she could not help saying:

"How much better this is, than to keep these things up in our garret lying useless. I mean to give away everything up there, if I can find any one that can make use of them."

The little bed-room, too, was fitted up with a plain bedstead, with bed and bedding, and such things as Lucy knew would tend to give it a snug look. The old colonel took the charge of the buttery stores upon himself, and Josey was sent down with the lumber-wagon pretty well loaded; and from his lively manner, seemed to understand that he was upon an errand of love, and bore the wagon along, as if there was no weight to it at all. It was, however, quite a load, for there was not only a fair supply of lighter articles, but the colonel had filled all the spare room with potatoes, and turnips, and cabbages, and even some heads of his choice celery.

Old Duncan did not like the idea of loaning his boat, when he found upon what errand Charles was bound.

"There were poor folks," he said, "enough round the mill already, without bringing any more. The first thing they would do, would be to run to him for meal to fill their bellies, and no money to pay for it. But I'm getting to be a big fool, and can't say any more that my soul is my own. Yes, you may take it, but there aint another man living in the town should have it for such a purpose. I'd stave her bottom in first."

It proved a pleasant day for the season; and Lucy, well wrapped up, enjoyed the bracing air on the water, and the errand on which she was bound. She was going to carry good tidings to a weary soul. To tell to the lonely and desolate that there were yet loving hearts in the world; hearts that fed on angel's fare, whose richest enjoyments sprang from the warm sympathy which bound them to their kind.

At Charles' request, Frank, the colonel's gardener, and his brother Augustus, had accompanied them, and when they reached the island, remained in the boat, while he and Lucy walked on, and apprized the family of their object. Lucy had never seen much of poverty. The form in which it had been presented to her in her native town was far from being repulsive. Charles had endeavored to give her a description of the place, but she had formed no true idea of it; for when they had passed through the cedars, and were at once in full view of the little low, straw-covered hut, she stopped, and clasping her hands, exclaimed:

"And human beings live there!"

"Let us be silent, and appear as little as possible to notice things. I feared you had formed no conception of the truth."

Just as they were about to enter, McDougall came from a side of the building, against which he had apparently been casting up an embankment of earth. He had a shovel in his hand, which, as soon as he saw them, he laid down; and with a look of surprise, but still with a welcome air, extended his hand.

"I did not expect this pleasure, sir, so late in the season."

"I had a little errand to you, sir; and being a pleasant day, have taken the liberty of bringing a lady with me, as I thought Mrs. McDougall might be glad to see one of whom I have often spoken to her. Miss Johnson, Mr. McDougall."

His bow was with a grace that utterly confounded Lucy; and it was evidently the result rather of instinct or habit, which had its way before he had time to reflect, for he immediately assumed rather a clownish air, and there was a marked change in his language as he addressed Lucy.

"We are rather poor folks, you know, and things be rather helter skelter; but my woman will be glad to see the lady, no doubt."

He opened the door, remaining without himself, and permitted his guests to enter. If Lucy had been affected by a sight of the dwelling, and surprised at the strange contrast in the man, her wonder was at its height when, on entering the small apartment, she beheld a beautiful female, apparently not much beyond her own age; although her head was covered with a cap tied under her chin, and which concealed almost the whole of her hair, and gave to a casual observer, at the first glance, an idea of a middle-aged matron. She was dressed in a very plain manner; that is, the materials of her dress was of a very cheap kind, but it fitted snugly to her person, and Lucy noticed at once that her form was of the most graceful mould. With a bright smile she arose, and with great ease of manner approached to welcome her visitors. And, giving her hand to Mr. Lovell:

"Oh, sir, how glad I am to see you once again, before our long and dreary winter has set in. And this must be your sister?"

"I am quite willing to own the title, ma'am," said Lucy, smiling, and looking archly at Charles.

"I dare not quite claim so high an honor, madam; this is Miss Johnson, of whom you have heard me speak, and this is Mrs. McDougall; pardon me for not having made the introduction sooner."

"I am very happy to see you, Miss Johnson; your name is quite familiar to me through Mr. Lovell. I presume he waives the privilege of calling you sister, for the sake of a dearer title."

"By no means, ma'am; if he will not own me as a sister, he shall claim no relation to me whatever. But he is a good boy, and I shall love him whether or no."

"I believe that all must do so, that know him. Take this seat, Miss Johnson. Our accommodations are not designed for visitors such as yourself," offering her the only apology for a chair that was to be seen.

"Oh no, I like this bench quite well; and is that your boy?"

A fine, manly little fellow, of four years of age, came up, at once to Lucy, and held out his hand. She parted his dark locks from his fair forehead, and gave him a kiss; wondering both at the beauty and polite bearing of the boy. The whole was, indeed, to Lucy a vision of romance.

"Miss Johnson has a little business with you, Mrs. McDougall, while I spend a few moments with your husband; our stay must, of necessity, be short."

It had thus been arranged between them, that Lucy should unfold the plan to the wife, while Charles arranged matters with the husband.

It will be unnecessary to detail all the arguments which Charles made use of to overcome the reluctance of the man to make any change in his location. And it was not until he ventured to urge the propriety of his removal, by reference to the trials his wife and child must be exposed to during the severity of winter, that he seemed at all disposed to yield. He was, indeed, deeply moved. He sat down upon a log, and covering his face with his hands for some time, appeared to be agonizing under a severe struggle. At length he arose, and grasped the hand of Charles, while the big tears rolled down his manly face:

"You have touched a tender chord, sir. Hardships I can endure myself, but I must confess to you, that the thought of keeping my dear wife and child under the circumstances they now are in, is a trial I should not wish my bitterest enemy to endure. I thank you, from my inmost soul, for all your kind and generous treatment of me. You have a heart that will make your path through life a blessing; and may the blessing of the stranger, the suffering, and the deeply wronged, rest upon you and yours forever. I accept your generous offer, and only hope I may be able to prove my gratitude."

Charles could only press more cordially the hand he held. He was now convinced that the being before him was far removed from the class in which circumstances had placed him. A man of education and refinement in the garb of a rough fisherman.

McDougall now, as though anxious to communicate with his wife, entered the house, and Charles followed. At once she sprang towards him, and he fondly embraced her:

"We will go, Agnes."

"For our boy's sake, Robert."

Although they spoke to each other scarcely above a whisper, Charles heard the name by which she addressed her husband. He had always been known as Jacob McDougall. In the excitement of the moment she had breathed into his ear that name which was dearest to her love.

"And now, Mr. McDougall," said Charles, "we have no time to lose; our days are short, and the sooner we are getting ready the better. I have a boat large enough to carry us all, and such things as you may wish to take, and help enough to assist in carrying them."

"You are very generous and thoughtful, sir, but we shall need but little aid in taking our few necessaries."

While the men were busy removing the things, Mrs. McDougall ran to the neighboring dwellings to say farewell to those who had treated her with much kindness; and in less than an hour from the time they had decided to remove, the boat, with its little cargo, was winding along up the creek towards the old mill.

Lucy and Charles, thinking it would be more delicate for them not to be present on their first entering the house, parted from them for the night, leaving Frank to assist in carrying their things, and to show them the way.

The old colonel had been quite restless all the afternoon, getting up frequently and peering through the windows for signs of Lucy's return. At length her light step was heard in the hall, and the happy girl was soon giving him a hearty kiss.

"Back safe, are you, darling? and what kind of a time have you had?"

"Oh, delightful, father; we have brought them along, bag and baggage. But oh, father, what a place they have been living in! and such strange people! or rather, so strange is it that they should be in such circumstances."

"And what did they say to their new place?"

"Oh, we can very easily realize that, father; but Charles and I thought it would be better to leave them to enjoy it, without our presence; so we sent Frank to show them the way, and we came straight home."

"Hut, tut, tut; but I should have thought you would have wanted to see how they liked things. But I see Frank is coming."

Frank and his employer had been many years together; a pretty good sign for both. As he passed through the hall, the old colonel called him into his sitting-room.

"Well, sir, you have brought them all safe back."

"In faith I have, sir. The good luck has been with us."

"Strange sort of folks they say they are?"

"Indeed, and its not far from the truth."

"Very poor, they say."

"Poor! well they are not like any poor folks as ever I see. Poor, indeed! no, no."

"But Lucy tells me that they lived in a wretched hovel, and all that"

"That is true enough; it was not the place for decent people of any sort, and it's like enough they have not the wherewith to help themselves. But, sir, they 're as careful of manners as yourself, or Miss Lucy, or Mr. Charley, either one. I've seen poor folks, and am well acquent with their ways. But—," and Master Frank carried out the rest of the idea by shaking his head.

"You don't think they are impostors!"

"Not in the least, your honor, no imposture about it; but it's the queerest upshot of luck, or misfortune, or whatever ye call it, that has happened to the folks; take my warrant for it. You see, sir, Miss Lucy bid me just show them the way to the new biggin, and I was fain glad to do it, for having myself a little curiosity in that way. So I walks along a little on the head, and the boy he comes and takes me by the hand. The man himself had a large bundle on his back, and another in his hand, and his woman was fain to help him with one or the other, but deuce a bit would he let her touch a finger's weight. Thinks I, if ye were like other poor folks, ye would e'en let the woman bear her share of the bargain; help and help alike.

"And then, at the rising of the hill—you know it 's a little steep like, your honor—what does he do but drop his weights, and make her lean upon his arm, until the top was gained, and then back he goes in a trice for his bundles; no, no, sir, they are no poor folks, depend on it."

"And maybe they did n't care much about the house after all?"

"Aha, your honor, ye should have seen 'em; it would have done your heart good. You know, sir, that as you get to the top of the hill the house is close to the hand. Well, sir, I'm a-thinking Miss Lucy and Mr. Charley had n't been very forward in speaking of the place, for no sooner did I point my finger towards it, than they both stood stock still, as if they had been shotted. And then I see the tears a-coming, as the woman's hands was raised up, as if imploring heaven's mercy on you. Your honor ought to have seen that look, it would have been worth ten years of your life."

The colonel saw it as much as was necessary, for his face began to swell, and he could n't have told Frank to go on if Frank had been at all disposed to stop.

" And it 's no wonder, your honor, for a nice bit of a place it is. That Charley Lovell is a dabster at making ould things new. Gin I wanted a house I 'd buy an ould shanty and put it into his hands to fix; it would be better than to build one span new. But the half aint told your honor yet. Thinks I, if your hearts warm so at the sight of the shell, what will ye do when ye get into the nut itself. So I hands the box I carried to the side of the door, and bids them good even. And they turned and looked at me. It was all the thanks I wanted. I saw from their looks, there was no spaking to be done; so I makes as if I would throw up the wood a little that Charley Lovell had brought there, just for pretence-like to be hanging around. And a peep was no hard to be got through the little window in the room. But, ah me, such a sight!"

" Were they pleased, do you think?"

" Pleased, were they! Ah, well; it brought the heart to my mouth, your honor. They jist fell into one another's arms, with the boy between them. Oh *dear*! oh dear! And then down on their knees to thank the Lord, and your honor, no doubt, and maybe all the rest of us. Ah, sir, I doubt not they are true Catholics."

" Catholics! Catholics! what do you mean by that, sir?"

" I mean in respect to their praying, sir."

" Why, don't you think any but Catholics pray?"

" It 's like they do, sir, in their churches on Sundays; but I 've been in many a family that calls themselves *Protestants*, but de'l a bit of praying was there, but maybe a little bit over their dinner, to season it like."

The old colonel was silent, and Frank, thinking that he had no further occasion for him, made his obeisance and withdrew.

" He is a blunt fellow, that Frank; but he is honest, and I don't know but he is right about our Christian manners; perhaps we keep things a little too secret."

CHAPTER XXIII.

Adelaide left the shop with a much lighter heart than she entered it. She had now some means of command, to sustain her for a few weeks. She had also met with unexpected kindness from a stranger, and that encouraged her. And now the great question with her was—where she should find a resting place? Without thinking why, she went back again towards the house where she had as yet found a refuge; perhaps with some faint expectation that she might be permitted to make explanations that would satisfy the old lady. But what was her surprise, on reaching the house, to find that her trunk was standing on the stoop. She felt that such treatment was rather cruel, but was determined to avoid giving, if possible, any further trouble to the old lady. Margaret had directed her to a family in the upper part of the city where she might possibly obtain board, and thither she immediately went. She found, on making inquiries, that the kind-hearted girl had been there before her, and made such a statement of what she knew and thought in reference to the stranger, that all difficulties were removed. It was a plain establishment, but neat, and apparently respectable.

Her next care was to return and get some one to carry her trunk from its exposed situation to her new place of abode; and with a lighter heart than she had enjoyed for many days, she tripped along, unconscious of evil, and thinking only of the pleasure of having, if only for a few weeks, a resting-place—a spot on earth where she could feel that she was not barely on sufferance.

Her trunk still remained as she had last left it, and she began at once to look round for some one who would be likely to carry it for her. And just then, a young man rather fashionably dressed, and who appeared to be walking very much at his leisure, passed by her—looked at her, and then at the trunk. He bowed respectfully to her.

"Can I be of any assistance to you, Miss? Are you in want of a porter?"

She thanked him for his politeness, but said she would not trouble him, as there would doubtless be one along soon.

"It would be no kind of trouble to me, Miss. As this street is not much of a business place, you may have to wait for some time. Allow me to step into the next street and call one."

The offer was made in such a civil manner, that Adelaide thought it might be deemed prudery in her to refuse. She thanked him, therefore, for his kindness, and consented. He was about to depart, and had advanced a few steps, when turning round and again addressing her:

"May I take the liberty to ask if you accompany your trunk? and if it is any distance? If so, had I not better procure you a hack; the charge will be the same, probably, unless you prefer walking."

She was conscious of being somewhat fatigued. It was some distance, and for a moment she hesitated.

"Allow me then to do so. I know an excellent fellow that will carry you safely, and will have him here in a moment."

Thinking of no real objection, as the cost would be the same, and yet with a faint idea of some danger, she, without absolutely saying that he might, still allowed him to go and do as he wished. Alas! poor girl! She little thought that through all her wanderings that day, an evil eye had been upon her. The "lurker in secret places" had followed—had kept her in view amid the multitude, "waiting at the corners of the streets;" unseen or unnoticed he had tracked her, and at last he has got his coil about her innocent steps, and she will soon be in the net, as thoughtless of harm as the sweet bird that sits and sings upon the bough, and then flies into the snare where lies the tempting bait.

The gentleman who had been so kind to Adelaide that morning, and had left the jeweller's shop in such haste to overtake her, found, as many do in a large city, that it is not worth while to be in a hurry, that is, if one has many acquaintances and only an occasional visitor. The gentleman in question had, moreover, a well-filled purse, and was extensively known in the money market. And it was utterly out of the question for him to resist the hearty salutations he received, or the kind inquiries concerning his family and his farm. Nor could he break away as he wished to, from some proposals made to him for investments, or questions and answers about stocks, or the all-absorbing topic of our foreign relations, and the prospects of a commercial crisis. It was, indeed, rather an exciting time just then, for such as had much to lose. He released himself, however, from each as soon as politeness would allow; but in all, much time was consumed. At length he reached Ann street, and walked leisurely along on its narrow, broken sidewalks, crossing the street occasionally, and looking up at the windows, and strictly scrutinizing the faces of such ladies as he met. At length the trunk standing on the stoop attracted his notice, and he crossed over and looked up at the house, and into the windows as far as he could, and finally took the liberty of stooping down to see whether there was a name on the trunk. He had to stoop, because the platform on which it rested was nearly level with the pavement.

The only direction upon it was in two capital letters on the top, formed by brass nails, A. V. He thought a moment, "It must be the same;" he stepped up and knocked at the door; the old lady, after two or three alarms had been given, opened the door.

"I wish to inquire, madam, whether the owner of this trunk lives here?" She did not, probably, hear what he said, but as he pointed to the trunk, took something of his meaning, and answered very short:

"No, no, I knows nothing about it," and without much ceremony closed the door. He stepped off from the stoop, more confounded than ever, but firmly resolved, if possible, to find the owner—the conduct of the old woman increasing the interest he already felt. For awhile he lingered round, and then, having some business in a neighboring street, he concluded to walk there, and after he had attended to it, return, and in some way watch until the trunk was called for. The business detained him longer than he expected, and it was past two o'clock when he again entered Ann street. He walked with a quick step, and as he approached the house saw that the trunk was gone, but a young woman was standing in the door, and wringing her hands, and manifesting signs of deep emotion. He stepped up and asked:

"If the trunk, which had been standing on the stoop, was owned by a young lady, Miss Vincent?"

"Oh dear, yes; but I am most out of my senses for her; for, just as I was coming I see her getting into a carriage, and a young man, after he had shut the door, stepped to the driver—so that woman told me on the next stoop—and handed him a bank-bill, and the driver cut up his horses, and went like everything; and then I see the young man myself run round the corner, and jump into a handsome gig with a negro fellow in it, and he drove off too, just as fast as he could; and they tell me he 's a dreadful bad man."

"Is that the carriage?"

"Yes sir, that 's it, away up there; oh, its turning now, it will be out of sight. Oh dear, dear, I am afraid she 's lost."

The gentleman called loudly to a hack just passing:

"Are you engaged?"

"I am, sir."

"I will give you ten dollars for an hour's drive. Did you see that carriage just turn into Nassau street?"

"With one white horse?"

"Yes, the same—bring me up with it, or keep it in sight until it stops; I will give you ten dollars an hour if you come up with it."

"I will do my best, sir; but you must be quick—jump in."

The carriage was now out of sight, but the driver guessed that it was probably making for Chatham and the Bowery, or one of the low streets forking off from Chatham, and the great thing was to get a view of it before leaving the last-named street. Urged by such a fee in prospect, but little regard was paid to the city regulations against fast driving, and many a one who had come near being injured by the furious speed, turned and uttered various curses, and shook their canes. But had they known what need there was for that reckless haste, they would have urged him with their shouts of encouragement, and joined in the race themselves.

When Adelaide found herself really in the carriage, and received the polite bow of the young man, as the driver closed the door, she could not but feel grateful for his attentions, and wondered at the strange turn which her affairs had taken, when kindnesses were thus unexpectedly meted out to her. As Nassau and Chatham streets were in the direction she wished to go, of course she felt that all was right. The only thing which at all disturbed her, was the unusual rapidity with which she was driven; but this she accounted for, by supposing that probably the hackman had an appointment, and wished to get this job accomplished as soon as possible. So setting her mind at rest, she amused herself with watching the multitude of human beings as they jostled each other in the crowded sidewalks.

It was not until she had proceeded some distance up the Bowery, that she noticed even that the carriage had taken that route; she thought it could not possibly be the nearest, but still she hesitated to speak to the driver, especially as she would be obliged to put her head out of the window to do so, there being no other means of communication with him.

In those days, dwelling-houses were only scattered at intervals beyond the Bull's Head, in that now densely-populated avenue, and all east of it was an open country. Lanes, or unpaved streets, ran off from it towards the East river, but they were not built upon, and only served to point out how that region of the city was to be laid out. Here and there, amid the extended fields, could be seen a mansion, erected as the summer residence of some wealthy citizen; but there were not many of these. A few moments would, therefore, suffice to pass from the crowd into the stillness of an open country; and, before Adelaide could make up her mind to arrest the progress of the driver, she found herself whirled into a lane, and beheld on each side the plain post and rail fences, and the extended fields that she had been so long accustomed to. However agreeable such a prospect might have been to her under other circumstances, it now filled her with terrible fears, and she endeavored at once to lower the sash of the door that she might speak to the driver, or call for help; but to her dismay, she found the strap had been removed on each sash, and also that there was no knob within whereby the bolt of the doors could be turned. She called aloud to the hackman, but he either did not hear, or paid no regard to her call, and she thought the speed of the horses was increased. A distressing faintness oppressed her, and her whole frame was in a violent tremor. She felt her strength departing. Terrible thoughts came rushing upon her; all she had ever heard of the sad victims to the satanic stratagems of abandoned men, came fresh to mind. Again she made an effort to raise the glass, but it refused to stir. They were now near a clump of cedars, a swamp lay on one side, and a field covered with large rocks and wild briers on the other. No signs of a habitation but at a great distance, too far to be of any benefit to her. She seized her small parasol, which had been lying on the seat before her, and with one blow shivered the glass, and, at the imminent hazard of injury to her person, thrust out her arm and turned the fastening of the door. The driver at once reined up, and in a boisterous manner, accompanied with profanity, demanded the reason for her conduct. She stopped not to argue or explain, but sprang in the instant from her dreaded prison. It was, however, only to meet worse evils, for, almost as she alighted on the ground, the young man who had been so polite to her was by her side. She saw him spring from his gig, which was also reined up just behind the carriage. He approached her with the same polite bow, and begged her not to be alarmed:

"It is a mere ruse of mine, as I saw you was a stranger in town. My house is close at hand; you shall have every attention that hospitality can afford you. I beg you not to be in the least alarmed."

The effort Adelaide had made to release herself from the carriage had driven off her faintness, and she was fully sensible of the terrible necessity for all the command of her mind. The house the wretch had spoken of she saw now indeed close at hand, near the cedars already mentioned. She threw a hasty glance around, and perceived that it was a low place, and even the road by which she had come there was hidden, except for a short distance, by a declivity, at the foot of which they then were. She felt that to make an alarm could be of no avail; she therefore answered, with as much composure as possible:

"I am sorry, sir, since you believed me to be a stranger, that you should thus have brought me out of my way; but, if you will order the driver to deliver my trunk at the place he was to have left me, I will find my way there, without giving you any further trouble."

The driver, however, feeling that he had performed his part of the contract, had already cast the trunk upon the ground, and, springing to his seat, drove off on a different road from that which he came, and at a rapid rate. At the same moment the unfeeling wretch, who had thus ensnared her, grasped her arm, as he perceived she was about to go on her way. No longer able to command herself, and seeing the servant, at his master's command, about to aid him in compelling her to enter the house, she uttered a loud scream. At that instant a carriage was seen descending the declivity, the horses at their full speed, and two men seated on the driver's box. At once she was hurried within the gate and up the path. She knew not whether friends or foes were in that carriage, for it suddenly stopped, and in a moment her eye fell upon the portly form of him who had befriended her that morning:

"Oh, save me, save me, dear sir."

One blow from his hand laid the servant prostrate on the earth, while his heavy cane, wielded by an arm nerved almost with frantic fury, flew against the vile wretch, his master. He staggered, but did not fall, the blood gushing from amid his hair and running in streams down his face, now distorted by rage, pain, and disappointment, into the aspect of a fiend. In an instant he drew a dirk from his bosom and sprang towards his assailant, but the weapon flew into the air, and his arm, broken by the blow, fell helpless by his side. It was but the work of an instant more to bear the weeping, trembling girl back to the carriage.

"Fear nothing now, dear; you are in the hands of a friend. I am the father of Caroline Shawn; and, if I am not mistaken, you was but a few days since her teacher."

"I was; and oh, are you her father?" And, overcome with the excitement she had passed through, and the sudden change from the hands of a dreaded foe to those of a trustful friend, she fell helpless into his arms. Mr. Shawn waited not to use means for her restoration, but taking her with him into the carraige, ordered the driver to pick up her trunk, and hasten back.

"That fellow is howling like a maniac, and there will probably be more of his gang upon us."

And, scarcely were his words uttered, when two, at least, were seen rushing from the house towards them. The carriage, however, was off, and at good speed on its way, by the direction of Mr. Shawn, to the City Hotel.

The streets were being lighted when the carriage stopped at the more private entrance of the hotel. Mr. Shawn had done all that was in his power to calm the excitement into which Adelaide had been thrown; but she was still so weak, as to need his assistance to mount the steps. He led her into a private parlor, where sat a lady of fine appearance, and much younger than the gentleman.

"My dear, I introduce you to Miss Adelaide Vincent, the young lady we have heard so much about, and who was so rudely dismissed from Miss Martinett's institution."

Mrs. Shawn embraced her affectionately, and Adelaide wept for joy.

Mr. Shawn took her hand, and soothingly said:

"Be as calm as you can; you are with friends now, who are able and ready to protect you. Mamma," addressing Mrs. Shawn, "I have a long story to tell you of the scenes of this day; but we will leave it until after supper, which you may order in our room here, as quickly as possible."

It was the intention of Mr. Shawn to have made complaint against the vile creature who had caused so much suffering. But believing that he had, for the present at least, received something of a chastisement, and knowing that a public prosecution would be attended by many trying things for the young lady, he concluded to let it drop.

The kind attentions of Mrs. Shawn, and her assurance that Adelaide was to return home with them, and that Caroline was to be at once sent for, and to be placed under her instruction; and that she was to look upon their house as her own home, was, indeed, like the oil of gladness to a wounded heart. Light and joy had suddenly broken upon her path, so lately surrounded with darkness and sorrow. She had trusted in the Lord; she had tried to discharge her duty; she had looked to Him to be her guide, and she had found her deliverance. The girl who had manifested such a kind spirit was not forgotten. Mrs. Shawn went to see her, and, liking her appearance, engaged her, for handsome wages, to become a member of her family, and take charge of her sewing; and glad was she to leave a place where constant toil but barely provided her with the means of living.

"Oh, what a fine roomy carriage," said Adelaide, as she took her seat, as they were about to start for home.

"This is the carriage, my dear, that was to have been sent for you and Caroline. I hope we shall all enjoy the ride the better for the thought, that you are to spend a longer time with us than the month's vacation."

CHAPTER XXIV.

CHARLES had determined to spend the winter in cutting and drawing timber, as he had made up his mind to commence the great work of preparing for himself and brother a home of their own. But, although his plans were pretty well digested in his own mind, he chose to submit them to his good friend Slocum, as he had so often found him a valuable adviser.

It was a fine clear morning, the ground covered with a light crust of snow, sufficient for a sleigh to run with ease; and Pomp being harnessed, in a short hour Slocum jumped from the sleigh in front of the old stone building.

"Ha! ha! I say, Charley, that colt 's a staver. But aint you afraid he will do mischief sometimes? he looks as if he wanted to tear things."

"Oh, he only feels in good spirits; he is as kind as a kitten. Just see now; Guss, call Pomp."

Augustus was at the barn, about ten rods' distance. He gave a peculiar whistle, and repeating it once or twice, the horse moved gently off, arching his neck, and trotting in a slow, graceful gait, stopped at his usual place for being unharnessed, and gave a gentle whinny, as much as to say, "Here I am."

"Ha! ha! ha! Well, if I ever! I 'll give it up now. How did you ever learn him that?"

"Easy enough. We always give him a taste of something good. Guss will, as like as not, give him an ear of corn now, or a handful of oats. I don't believe he would stir, if the wagon or sleigh should come upon his heels, if we were by him, and he heard our voices."

"I should n't like to try him, though."

"Nor I either; the safest way is to keep a good look-out for things, to see that there is no danger of breaking."

"I say so too; but what are you up to this morning, Charley? you would n't tell me till you got me here. I did n't know but you are so fond of fixing up old things that you had taken a notion of fixing up Aunt Casey's old house, and make it as good as new, ha! ha! ha!"

"It might be fixed very well, and make a very pretty place—the timbers are sound."

"Ha! ha! ha! upon my soul, patch the roof a little, straighten up the sills, put on a few clapboards, and then a coat of your patent paint, ha! ha! ha! how she'd look, Charley? would n't she? a neat, comfortable place;" and Slocum amused himself with a good hearty laugh that brought tears from his eyes.

"You 'll kill me laughing yet, Charley, you are so in earnest when you talk of making an old place look neat and comfortable. But say, what are you up to now?"

"Well, to tell you the truth, Slocum, I want to consult you a little about fixing things up here;" pointing, at the same time, up at the rough, uncouth looking building before which they were standing; "laugh away; don't be afraid, let it out."

Slocum, however, had done laughing for the present. He merely smiled as he cast his eye over the place, and then round upon the trees, which were sprinkled about in all directions, and then at the view which was presented from the spot.

"I tell you what it is, Charley, it is a plaguy pretty spot for a house, anyhow; a man can't ask for nothing finer than your view from here. And then, when these trees grow up a little, ding it, if it won't be taking, no matter. But the thing of it is, what you 'll do with the old jail here, as I call it; them stone and mortar is so welded together, it will be like digging into a rock; you 'll have to put powder in and blow her off; it will be the cheapest way."

"But I have no notion of taking it down, Slocum; my idea is to make an addition to it."

Slocum looked at him a moment, and then began to sing:

"Hie dum, diddle,
The cat and the fiddle,
The cow jumped over the moon;
The little dog laughed to see the sport,
The dish run after the spoon."

"You are a smart fellow, Charley, about most things, and folks say you are going to be 'forehanded; but if you can show me, in any manner of way, how this old stone barrack can be made into any such kind of a house as a decent; gentlemanly sort of fellow ought to live in, I am ready to hear it. But I guess you will trip up this time—it is no go, Charley, depend upon it."

So, Slocum took a seat on a log that lay there, and, shutting one eye, fixed the other intently on the building; and Charles, seeing that he was in earnest, took a seat beside him, and drawing a roll from his pocket, unfolded and presented a paper from it to Slocum.

"What is this? a drawing! who did it?"

"I drew it."

"You! now you don't! I should like to know what you can't do? It 's a pretty picture, though; what house is it?"

"It is a front view of this old one, as I mean to fix it; and it is all proportioned by rule."

Slocum looked at the picture, and then at the house.

"How many inches to the foot?"

"One-half inch to the foot."

Slocum jumped up in his spry way, and taking his rule from his pocket, opened it, and with great exactness measured the front, and then taking a pole ran it up to the eaves, carefully measuring the height; he then measured the picture.

"You are right to a fraction; but the plague of it is, my eye generally serves me truer than that."

"I tell you how it is, Slocum; you see, the house, as it looks now, appears top-heavy; the roof rising a gamble form, and the eaves projecting so far over it, give it an awkward, unnatural appearance. Well, this verandah in front remedies that; then this addition to the north side, which I design for a summer-kitchen, being thrown back a little to allow of a broad shed and stoop, helps to give a more correct proportion to the whole front; don't you think it does?"

"I don't know what does it, but something does it; it is as like to be that as anything. But the windows aint nowise comparing with those up there; they aint no bigger than the windows of a jail."

"Yes; but they must be enlarged. I have calculated them to be nearly five feet—they are not over three and a half now."

"But you don't pretend that your front is going to look like this picture. That old front is as rough as any stone fence need to be; this looks most like marble, or some grayish kind of smooth stone."

"Cement will do that. I read a receipt, not long since, by which, with a little coarse sand and lime, a composition can be made as hard, almost, as stone, and the cost will be trifling."

"Plague on it, Lovell, I want to go into the place, and look at it; are the rafters good, you suppose?"

"I guess you will find them so."

"These stairs aint very sound, though. My jimminy! who ever saw such rafters! why, there is timber enough to build a ship. Sound! they 're like iron, and there is space enough up here for three good-sized bed-rooms."

"When you have satisfied yourself here, I want to show you about the back building. In my plan here, I have designed for three good rooms, in addition to those in the body of the house. Here is the other picture. It is a side view of the house, showing the front of the back building, with its piazza."

"Well, this beats cock-fighting;" and Slocum looked at the picture, and then at the house, and burst into a hearty laugh. "Well, Charley, you have mistaken your calling; you ought to set up for a boss carpenter; you would take the wind out of my sails pretty quick. You will make a right down pretty place of this; and when it is done I would n't swap it for two such square, straight, staring looking places as Vanderbose has put up on Roder's point. And now, what do you want me to do? go right to work at it!"

"Not quite yet. This is the plan I design to accomplish, if ever I am able. But, to tell you the truth, I am afraid it will take me some years yet. I have no idea what it is going to cost, but my plan was to be getting logs along to mill this winter, and maybe some of the timber, so as to make a beginning."

"Well, I tell you what it is, Charley, I don't know how you calculate about the finishing; if you are intending to have much gingerbread work about it, why, you see, that counts up fast."

"Not a bit of it. I want it well done, but perfectly plain;

all its ornament must be in its proportions. I want the wood-work to be of the solid order; good, plain, heavy mouldings, doors and window-frames."

"That 's your sort."

"I want the timbers to be solid, and plenty of them, and the floors laid solid, and well grooved together, and the whole concern to match with the heavy walls of the main building. I want something that won't shake under me, or over me, and that will be a home for more than one generation."

"That 's the sort, that is just to my mind; and now I can tell you, Charley, that it is n't going to cost you a nation deal of money, after all. You see, you have got timber enough of your own, you need n't buy a stick; and then you have got white and yellow pine enough, that you can carry to mill and get sawed for joists and under-covering for the roof and sides. The most you will have to buy will be shingles, and clapboards, and lime, and some odd things. The shingles will be the heaviest bill you will have to pay for materials. I 'll bet the whole thing can be done for six hundred dollars outlay of money."

"You think so!"

"I know so. But I tell you what you must do; now is the time to be getting your timber along, and to get your logs to mill. The sooner you can get your floor plank sawed the better, and let it be seasoning; half the comfort of a house is to have it tight; I hate cracks staring at a fellow. What a pity it is that old Simon Duncan won't set his saw-mill a-going, it would be so handy for you."

"Perhaps I can persuade him?"

"Well, perhaps you may; you seem to have the luck with you about most things. But that puts me in mind of something I heard up town this morning. You know, some time ago there was some kind of a report that you was going into business with Frank Rice, in the great city. It 's well you did n't. They say Frank has all gone to smash."

"Oh, I am very sorry; I hope it is not true."

"I am afraid it is, though; the news has come pretty straight. You see there has been a terrible hubbub among business folks for some time; everything looks like our getting into a muss with England. Our Congress folks seem all hot for war; and if that should come, the mischief would be to pay with things. I tell you what, Charley, a little, and sure, slow and steady, is my motto; better keep where we can stand, strong and stiff. I always make my own scaffolding, and then I feel safe to go on it. A plague of this climbing up high, till a man knows what he has got to hold him, when he gets there."

Charles looked very sad. He felt a true interest for his former companion; and although he had not thought best to venture with him, most sincerely did he hope that Frank might succeed. Nor could he believe that so sad a catastrophe could occur in so short a time. But his doubts were put an end to, for a boy from the family of Deacon Rice rode up in much haste, and placed a letter in his hand.

"Well, good-bye, Charley; I must go now and see the colonel. When you want me I'll be on hand."

Charles opened the letter. It was from Miss Julia Rice, requesting that he would come and see them as soon as possible, as they were in great trouble. And, with all his feelings of friendship at once warmly roused, he lost no time in hastening thither.

The sight of a friend in the hour of adversity, of a friend whose heart we know to be true, and whose sympathy we are sure to have, is indeed a consolation. That friend may have no worldly substance to bestow, nor any very great skill in worldly matters; yet if he or she bring a true and loving heart, the grasp of the hand, the tender moistening of the eye, the soothing voice, have a charm to lull the troubled waters, and revive the sinking spirits. Why Julia Rice should send for Charles Lovell, she could scarcely have defined to herself; for the trouble which had involved her family was that which needed all the boldness of friendship together with the strength of substance, to afford such consolation as could really be of any avail. But she knew that Charles had a warm heart, that he felt a deep interest for her brother, and that Frank thought much of him. And, somehow, she had herself learned to look to him almost as a relative, so much had he endeared himself to all under his weekly instruction.

Julia met him at the door. Her voice trembled slightly as she addressed him.

"I sent for you, because I knew both my brother and my

father think a great deal of you, and will be advised by you sooner than by any one else."

"Is your brother here, Julia?"

"He is; but he keeps in his room, and I almost fear he will lose his reason. There is something terrible on his mind, and all we can say affords him no comfort."

"Do you think he would wish to see me?"

"I have no doubt he would; but I will see."

In a few moments she returned.

"My brother will be very glad to see you, but oh, the poor fellow!" And the lovely girl could say no more; but weeping bitterly, led Charles to the room where the sufferer had secluded himself.

Frank was walking to and fro as Charles entered. Cordially they grasped each other's hand, but no word was uttered. Charles took a seat, and for some time indulged in sad musings. He saw that it was no feigned grief. The pale and sunken cheek, the wild stare from his bright eye, the dishevelled hair, the unsteady step, and the loose and nerveless appearance of his whole frame, spoke too plainly of that sorrow which "maketh man's beauty to consume away as a moth."

At length young Rice took a seat, and placed it near to Charles.

"You have no doubt heard the news?"

"I have heard that you was in great trouble, and the report is that your business has been unfortunate."

"They are both true. I am a bankrupt—I am ruined, and many others, if not utterly ruined, will suffer greatly by me. Oh, Charles, death would be a welcome messenger. Life is too great a burden when the heart is dead."

"But, Frank, we must sometimes show our manliness by bravely meeting our trials, and doing our best under the circumstances."

"Yes, I know we ought. But to think how unwise I have been! to stake the comfort of my whole life upon such a venture! And now, in the beginning of my days, to find myself with a weight about my neck that I can never hope to throw off! Debt!—debt! Oh, how it sinks my heart, a debtor for life! to know that when my name is mentioned or thought of by many, it will only be as their debtor!"

"Will your father suffer, Frank?"

At the mention of his father the young man arose, and again walked the room, apparently in great agony, and then resumed his seat.

"I am heartily glad that you are here, Charles. My father thinks highly of you, and perhaps you can do what I cannot. You will remember I once told you that my father gave me five thousand dollars to commence with; that, of course, is lost. But, besides this, he is on my paper for ten thousand more. This being confidential, by our custom in the city, is secured. It is thought right by all our business men, that confidential arrangements must be attended to, in preference to others. Of course I have secured him for the ten thousand dollars. But what troubles me on his account is, that he must meet his endorsements before the securities can possibly be made available, and I know he has no funds. He is called a rich man, but you know how that is. His property is mostly in lands about here. He is probably worth twenty thousand dollars. And you know by our laws this can all be attached, and at once sacrificed; and if forced off at such a juncture, when money is not to be had, it would be his utter ruin. It would bring his gray hairs with sorrow to the grave. And how can I bear to think of the evil which I shall bring upon him?"

Charles knew not what to say; he was powerless himself, or how soon would he have interposed his aid.

"Might not your father, in justice to himself and family, make over his property to prevent its sacrifice?"

"He might do so; but you know he is very determined in his way. He thinks it is not right, and how can we attempt to persuade him against his moral sense?"

"Does he know that these payments must so soon be made?"

"He does not; and oh, Charles, how can I tell him?" And Frank covered his face, and groaned aloud in his agony.

"Would it be a relief to you if I should tell him; for it seems to me he ought to know the worst."

"It would be a great trial to you, I fear. You know my father is a man of strong passions; he cannot always command himself; but he has a great respect for you."

"I will do it, Frank, or anything else I *can* do. You know I have no pecuniary means, but my heart bleeds for you, and for your father, too. I am ready, if you say so."

"It will be a great relief to me."

Charles immediately left the room, and sought an interview with the old gentleman. He was kindly received, and lost no time in making known the errand with which he was entrusted. The old man heard him through, and, with great calmness in his manner, replied:

"You have told me sad news, my young friend. I did not, indeed, expect that the hour of trial was so near. I have worked hard for what little property I have, and I believe I have accumulated it by honest means. I am too old to get back what I have lost, and can only say, 'It is the Lord, let him do what seemeth unto him good.'"

Charles was much affected; there was something in his trembling tears and patient piety that was truly touching. It was an old man's trouble—an old man's piety. And Charles could no longer restrain his excited feelings.

"You have a warm heart, and a true heart, Mr. Lovell; and you are making many friends. And I trust you will never live to see the day when you will be obliged to say: 'no man careth for my soul.' I have not made many friends. I have, rather, I fear, been too careless in that matter. I have indulged my prejudices, and kept too much aloof from my fellows; but the Lord has met with me. It will, no doubt, be a matter of rejoicing with many, that Deacon Rice has been brought down. But I cannot mend the evil now; it is too late."

Charles would have proposed some steps to be taken, to save a waste of property by the selfish and unfeeling. But the calm and resolute manner of the old man clearly convinced him that his own mind was made up to bear the consequences of his own acts. The old gentleman grasped his hand very cordially as he departed.

"Whenever you can spare an hour, my young friend, to step in, you will be welcome. And if you can be any com fort to my poor Frank—"

He could say no more. Charles parted from him, and not knowing of what service he could be, left the house and proceeded on his way home. As he rode by the dwelling of

Colonel Johnson, he remembered that he had an errand for Lucy, and turned up to the gate. The old colonel heard his voice at the door, and called aloud for him to come in.

"I think you might, just once in awhile, ask if I aint in. It 's all Lucy, Lucy; but come, sit down. Lucy has gone down to that 'neat and comfortable' house, as Slocum calls it, which you and she have fixed up so for those folks from the island. The woman, it seems, is sick, and Lucy has gone to see about matters there; and that reminds me of something that happened to me a few days since, and I don't know hardly what to make of it. You see I have noticed that McDougall a little, since the stories you and Lucy have told me about him. He 's the oddest fish that has come on to my hook yet. But one thing is certain, he has never been used to hard work."

"Does he not seem willing to work sir?"

"Yes, yes, willing enough; he will work himself to death; he aint used to it. My heart really ached for the poor fellow the other day, as I was out in the woods, showing him a little where to cut. I could see every time he stopped a moment to rest, he panted like a dog after a chase; and although the weather was what I call pretty cool, the perspiration ran down his face in streams. But the queerest thing that ever I see was a little circumstance that took place as he was cutting down a small tree; as it fell he stepped a little one side, but the end of the lowest branch just grazed him and knocked off his hat. But, body-a-me! I was never so surprised in my life; the first thing I saw was a head of hair as black as my beaver. A black head, and red whiskers!" and the colonel put one hand on each knee, and looked most expressively at Charles. "A black head and red whiskers! the oddest sight it has ever been my luck to witness. I have seen brown hair and sandy whiskers, and I have seen whitish hair and red whiskers; but coal black hair and red whiskers! In all my born days, I have never seen such a sight before."

"Were you not mistaken, sir? I am very sure his hair is sandy, and very thick and bushy."

"Have you ever seen him with his hat off?"

"Yes sir, frequently."

"Well, it is very queer; my eyes aint in the habit of serving me such tricks. If his whiskers had changed color too, and all looked black together, I might have thought that my eyes had got some kind of a kink in them. And that aint all; he had quite a youngerly look. I should have taken him for a young fellow of twenty-seven. But it was only a glimpse I had, after all; for he sprang like a squirrel for his hat, and clapped it on as if his life depended upon it, and then all was right in an instant. I tell you, my friend, I never came so near misbelieving my own eyes. But I shan't puzzle my brains any more about it. So come, tell me what 's the news; anything stirring?"

"Only the news about young Rice—I suppose you have heard that, sir?

"Slocum mentioned to me that there was an unpleasant rumor of that sort, but I have hoped it might be some idle story."

"It is too true, sir; and I fear his father will be ruined too."

"The poor old gentleman! oh dear, oh dear! that is sad indeed."

Charles then related all he knew, as he saw the colonel was deeply interested. He told him that he had been there; of the state in which he found the young man, and of his interview with the father, and the sad prospect before them. The colonel listened very attentively, working his jaws very hard, until Charles had closed. He then got up and walked about the room, pulling up every now and then the waistbands of his small clothes, and making sad exclamations at the changes, and worryings, and vexations, that a man was liable to. At length he stopped suddenly, and asked:

"What do you really suppose will be the consequence to Deacon Rice, if he is not able to meet those endorsements at the time they fall due?"

"Why, sir, they are payable to people who will doubtless immediately attach all his property; and you know in such cases a man is rendered helpless, and his property recklessly squandered."

"Are you here with your horse?"

"I am, sir."

"Do you just drive down to old Shirley's—you know who I mean, Squire Shirley, you all call him—and tell him I want to see him just as soon as he can come here; tell him to lose no time."

The summons which Squire Shirley received was such a remarkable event that he had to ask Charles several times, "What under the moon the old colonel wanted of him." But as Charles could give him no satisfaction, he was obliged either to decline the honor or to go and risk the consequences. He concluded upon the latter course, saying to himself many times on the way:

"What under the moon is to pay?"

His reception, however, was very cordial. "I have n't sent for you, squire, to hold an argument to-day; you and I have squabbled long enough about Presbyterianism and Episcopacy, and we have called one another hard names enough. It is altogether for a different purpose; so come, sit down.

"I will sit down gladly, colonel, for it is something of a walk from my house. I am glad to find you in such good health. Mr. Lovell rather startled me with saying that you wanted me to come right off, and I did n't know what *was* to pay."

"You have done just the thing, squire, just the right thing. I am some years older than you, and they have gone off with my horse this morning, so I thought you could get here easier than I could get to you."

The colonel then arose, and took from the table a large Bible, and turning over its leaves until he found the first Epistle of John, read as follows:

"'Whoso hath this world's good, and seeth his brother hath need, and shutteth up his bowels of compassion from him—how dwelleth the love of God in *him?*'" and then shutting the book, he turned round and looked his visitor full in the face:

"Now, neighbor, what do you think of that?"

Mr. Shirley's countenance was what would be called an austere one. It was strongly marked with deep lines, as though the battle of life had been a hard one, and yet around his mouth the deep indentations might easily have been taken for those in which the smile could readily find its course, so that at times it would be difficult to say whether displeasure or mirth was the predominant feeling. It would have been impossible just then.

"What do I think of it? Why, I think it 's right—it 's good doctrine."

"Well, how do you understand it, neighbor?"

"Understand it? Why, it 's plain enough, aint it? it is as plain as the nose on your face."

"That it is our bounden duty to help a brother in distress?"

"I should say so—certainly."

"So should I; there is no getting round it that I can see; and, neighbor Shirley, if you or I should see a friend of ours about to fall, so as maybe to break his neck—he was hanging by his hands, and could n't hold on much longer, and we could, either by boosting from below or pulling from above, just get him out of the scrape, and set him tight and strong upon his legs again, don't you think we ought to do it?"

"I do so; and we ought to be in a hurry about it too."

"So I say. And now, neighbor, I suppose you have heard that our friend, Deacon Rice, is in trouble."

"No! he is n't though! But I have feared he would be. He has been endorsing for his son in New York, and I have been pretty sure that, sooner or later, the Deacon would rue it."

"Yes, perhaps it was not prudent. But what father is there, that deserves the name, that aint willing to risk something for a son or daughter?"

"That is true, very true."

"And now, if some one does not step in, and just hold up the old man for awhile, he will be utterly ruined." And the colonel, in a very business-like manner, detailed, so far as Lovell had revealed to him, the circumstances in which the good deacon was placed. "You understand it all now, friend Shirley. You know all about law, and what likelihood there would be that he would come off with a cent in his pocket."

"He will be ruined, broken to pieces, unless, as you say, some one steps in and gives him a boost or a pull."

"That is the thing of it, neighbor; and now who shall do it? I am not a rich man, but I can spare a few thousands for awhile. And, as you are one of his people, I have thought you might be willing to do the same, and perhaps we both together could give him all the aid he needs just now, and save his heart from a great deal of suffering."

"Well, colonel, I tell you what it is; friend Rice has never been a very particular friend to me, and I don't know as he has to any one. He has kept pretty much to himself. But he has certainly been no friend of yours, and if you are man enough to overlook all that, and come to his rescue, I 'll go you halves. I never liked partnerships much, and never had a partner; but, colonel, I 'll risk it with you. It shan't be said that an old townsman was left to go to the dogs, because Joe Shirley would n't risk a little for his help."

The colonel grasped his hand, and shook it heartily.

"That is a deal better than snarling at one another about apostolic succession, or ministers wearing gowns or round-abouts, or whether we should pray with a book or without one. And now, neighbor, what we do must be done quickly. I see Josey has come, and we will be right off."

"Who is Josey?"

"Josey! why there he stands at the gate. I 'll make you acquainted with him in short order."

It took the colonel a little while to get ready, for his beaver had to be smoothed, and his cloak brushed off, and his shoes dusted; at least the ceremony had to be gone through with.

"Whoa, Josey; just keep easy until I get in."

"I never knew the name of your horse before, but I have often admired him. You keep him nice and fat, colonel."

"And he carries me safe and strong; he treats me well, and serves me cheerfully, and I see to it that he has all he wants. Whoa, Josey; take your time, neighbor, and fix yourself; he won't start until I say the word."

"It don't take much fixing in this carriage of yours, for there is room enough for a man's pockets and his legs too."

"I don't like being cramped; there is no comfort in riding if you have to be squeezed. Come, Josey, ahead with you."

"Well, I declare, he seems to understand what you say; he goes off at a spanking rate, and through the snow too."

"I don't usually drive so fast, but somehow, just now I feel rather in a hurry."

When a man's heart is sad it is not the presence of every acquaintance that is agreeable. And if the feelings of Deacon Rice could have been spoken out, when it was announced to him that Squire Shirley and Colonel Johnson had called, and were waiting in the parlor to see him, they would have said "that he would a little rather they had stayed at home."

He, however, prepared to see them, as a necessary duty, which must be performed, however unpleasant.

It had been decided between the two gentleman, that the colonel should introduce their business; and after a few moments spent in the usual compliments, the colonel edged his chair up a little towards the deacon, and offered him a pinch from his box.

"Esquire Shirley and I have called upon you this morning, friend Rice, to have a little talk about business matters." The colonel just then was taken with a violent fit of sneezing, and the deacon had time to indulge his thoughts a moment.

"Business! ay, I warrant, in some way they think they are going to lose something; they 've heard the news."

"I suppose you will not think hard of us for alluding to what seems now pretty generally known; that your son has been unfortunate, and that you are somewhat implicated."

The deacon interposed abruptly:

"I have property enough to meet my responsibilities; people need n't feel so anxious; you 'll have your money if you are so unfortunate as to have any of my notes. I shan't shrink from my name, nor from any of my debts, that I can tell you."

"And it is for that very reason, friend Rice, that we have called upon you. We know you to be a thoroughly honest man, and that you will hold every dollar you own sacred to sustain the honor of your name. You don't owe me a cent, and I believe our friend here can say the same. But we have called upon you as neighbors; we heard that you was in trouble, and I will say more. I have heard through Mr. Lovell the nature of your trouble, and that you are in danger of having violent hands laid upon your property; and perhaps that which you have earned by your industry, and saved by your prudence, squandered to pay half its value. And we, as neighbors and friends, have come to let you know that we stand ready to prevent any such calamity. You shan't go down, Deacon Rice, if friend Shirley and I can hold you up."

There was something so perfectly unexpected in this announcement, that it was out of the power of the good deacon to make an immediate reply. He looked at both the gentlemen a moment, and his eye met their kindly gaze. Prejudice and distrust flew away. They were not the men to trifle in such an hour; and he knew they could accomplish what they promised. And Deacon Rice was not the man to hold out against kindness.

"Gentlemen, this is to me a most unexpected, and I must say most—" But the good man could go no further; the strong feelings of his heart—excited as they had been by poring over the state of his affairs, and now much more by this prospect of deliverance, and by the sense that he was not left to battle with his troubles alone—burst forth. He rose from his seat, and with the silent tears streaming down his furrowed cheeks, grasped both their hands.

"That 's it, neighbor Rice, that is a kind of shaking hands I like; don't you, squire?"

"It is a deal better than snarling at one another, and calling hard names; but, deacon, you must thank the colonel; it 's all his doings."

"Hut, tut, tut, squire, tut, tut, we are partners, you know; only think of that, friend Rice. Joe Shirley and old Colonel Johnson have entered into partnership. But, neighbor, let 's be about business; we will settle matters first, and then we will talk about other things. So sit down by us, friend Rice, and just let us know the upshot of the whole thing, and then we can see what is to be done first.

It required but a short time to place the statement of his affairs before them, to show the notes which had been put into his hands, and the assignment of them, and the goods to meet the responsibilities he had come under.

"And now, squire, you know much more about business than either Deacon Rice or myself; you see it all, now what is to be done?"

"It is all plain enough; the trouble with friend Rice will be to raise the money which must be paid in so short a time. It seems to be well secured. The goods, if not sold under the hammer, must amount to pretty much all his indebtedness. If he can be helped to means so that these payments can be met, and keep all hands off from his property here, and some safe persons found to receive for those who shall advance the funds, an assignment of the securities, so that they shall be made the most of, and sold to the best advantage, I don't see but all will come out straight yet."

Both the gentlemen agreed with Squire Shirley, but the difficulty of procuring the right man seemed for the time a serious one.

"Neither of us" said the colonel, "is of an age that will allow us to think of such an undertaking. But for my part I know of a man to whom I should be willing to trust my part of the risk; he is young, though."

Both quickly asked:

"Who is it?"

"It is one who feels most deeply interested for you too, deacon, a noble-hearted fellow; Charley Lovell."

"He is the man of all others I should choose," said Deacon Rice.

"He is a shrewd and stable young fellow. He is not acquainted with the city, but he would soon learn the ways."

"So I think, squire. He must be paid, though; we cannot ask a young fellow who knows how to make the most of his time, and his pennies too, to go off from his business for nothing."

"By no means," said Deacon Rice; "he should be well paid. But will he go, colonel?"

"Leave that to me, friend Rice; he and I are on pretty good terms. I will see to his going, and I will warrant if there is a penny to be saved or made, he will look out for it. And now, friend Rice, we must go. Only one thing I want to say; neither friend Shirley, nor myself, want you to say one word about this matter; your responsibilities will be met, and no body need know hów, or anything about it. And when this hubbub is a little over, and your mind gets settled, just come up and give me a call. We are both getting to be old men, and those who were young when we were, are getting scarce now. And I think we can have many a pleasant chat together."

"Colonel Johnson, I will say nothing now about the past. I have a great deal to regret, and to be sorry for. But if you and I have any more sparring in this world it shall not be my fault. You have taught me a lesson to-day, which I shall not be very apt to forget. And what I say to you, I apply equally to this good friend beside you. May God bless you both, and all that belong to you."

The colonel would insist upon driving Esquire Shirley home. And as the latter stepped down from the carriage, he looked up with much significance:

"They say, colonel, that when a certain personage begins to quote scripture, you must keep a sharp look out for mischief; now I don't want you to apply this to yourself."

"You need n't fear that, squire; I never make any application, but what I think suits me."

"But when you began upon a fellow so strong this morning, I must say I put myself a little on the guard; for though I have often heard you quote from the fathers, in favor of your notion about apostolical succession, I don't remember ever having heard you say much about the Bible."

"And for a good reason, squire; I don't like 'casting pearls before swine,' not that I mean to apply this to you."

"By no means, colonel."

"You see, friend Shirley, the fathers I have read pretty well, and I 've studied them mainly for the purpose of contending with such stiff-necked Presbyterians as yourself. But I take my Bible to find out what I ought to be, and the more I read it I find that there is better work to do than railing at those who don't see just as I do. And when I quote from it, you may always think I am in solemn earnest."

"I will after this, colonel; and whenever you have any little business on hand, like what we have been at this morning, just let me know. I would n't have missed that squeeze of the hand from neighbor Rice for double what it should cost, if we lose the whole. I shall sleep better to-night, colonel. And another thing, I aint a-going to wait any more for you to send for me, but I mean to drop in just as I feel like it."

"And I promise you, friend Shirley, to drop the fathers; and if you and I should be in doubt any time about what we are to believe, or to do, or to be, we will just open the good book, and see what that says. Whoa, Josey—good-bye, neighbor—go along, sir." This last was addressed to his noble beast, who bore off his master as if he was proud to have such a burden behind him.

Squire Shirley looked at the neat establishment as it rolled away, and then, turning to enter his house, could not help exclaiming:

"I never knew what was in that man before."

CHAPTER XXV.

The circumstances under which Frank Rice and Charles Lovell started together for the city of New York were so peculiar, that it might have been supposed much embarrassment would be experienced by them both. But the conduct of Charles had through the whole been so magnanimous, and the real reluctance with which he had yielded to the entreaties of Frank himself, and all his family, to take upon him the responsibility of his present position, had scattered every feeling but that of sincere regard. There was confidence, and a perfect good will, on one part, and a sincere desire to discharge his duty to those for whom he acted, on the other. As they had some business to transact with a gentleman who lived near the border of the North River, they concluded to take a private conveyance thither, and from thence the public stage to the city.

The day was a lowering one, and, as they progressed, the clouds assumed a more fixed and heavy cast; and by the middle of the forenoon, snow began to fall, and the wind shifting to the north-east, a regular storm set in. When snow falls in earnest, it gathers fast, and soon forms a serious obstruction to a carriage. The horses, after a few hours, began to lag, and were glad to walk when they could; and by the middle of the afternoon, it was only by constant urging that they could be kept upon a faster gait. At five o'clock they reached a village, where the driver advised they should remain for the night; but as their business was urgent, they induced him by extra pay to make the attempt to reach the place of their destination, about eight miles further on.

And on they went through the unbeaten track, the storm increasing in violence as the evening advanced, the wind whistling round the carriage, and roaring through the forests, and driving the fine snow so as to blind the horses, and make them unwilling to proceed. At length the carriage suddenly came to a stand.

"What is the matter, driver?"

"I fear the nigh horse is giving out; he staggers so that I am afraid he 'll be down next."

"Are we near a village?"

"I can't say, I was never on this road before; but I don't see any signs of one."

"Are there any houses near?"

"I see a light ahead, maybe it 's a tavern; as soon as my horses have rested a little, I 'll drive there."

With a slow pace they proceeded for some quarter of a mile, and bolted again. The gentlemen looked out and perceived by the lights from the windows, that they were before the gate of a large house, that stood a little back from the road, but it was evidently no public-house.

"It is a private mansion, Frank," said Charles; "shall I step out and inquire how near we are to a tavern?"

"Perhaps we had better; but let me go."

"By no means—I am more used to storms than you are;" and so saying, Charles sprang from the carriage, and proceeded to the house, and as he drew near perceived that it was probably the residence of a wealthy family. His summons was soon answered by a servant, to whom Charles put the question:

"How far am I from a public-house?"

Before the servant could answer, a gentleman arose from his seat in what appeared to be a large hall, into which the front door opened, and as he approached, Charles was struck with his fine manly form, and open, pleasant countenance.

"Come in, sir, come in out of the storm;" bowing at the same time, in a very courteous manner. Charles returned his salutation, and entered as requested.

"I only wish, sir, to inquire if we are near a tavern. The storm has proved more violent than we anticipated, and our horses are much fatigued."

The gentleman looked at him keenly a moment.

"There is no tavern, my young friend, within some miles, and that is hardly decent for a gentleman and lady to stop at."

Charles smiled as he replied, "I am very happy to say, sir, that my companion is a young gentleman."

"Well, sir, you might manage, then. But I fear you will find great difficulty in getting there; this road is narrow, and always blocks up in such severe storms. I can propose to you a much easier path; do you just bring your companion in here, and my men will take charge of your horses until the morning, and then we will see what can be done to help you along."

"Your offer, sir, is extremely kind; but I fear it will be taxing your hospitality too much."

"Not in the least, sir—not in the least; room enough, and provender enough, and ladies into the bargain, if you like their company; so ask your companion in at once."

It would have appeared like affectation to make any further resistance, and in a few moments the young men were seated before a good blazing fire in the hall, or ante-room of the house, enjoying its warmth, and looking round on the appearance of unostentatious gentility and comfort which surrounded them. The room was evidently designed as a passage-way to different parts of the house. It was a large, square apartment, with several doors opening into it, and a wide stair-case on one side, with a very heavy broad rail running to the upper story; a neat English ingrain carpet covered the whole floor; a large mahogany book-case stood between two of the doors; a round table, covered with newspapers, occupied a position near the fire, and old-fashioned leather-bottomed chairs stood at different locations round the room.

"What a delightful place this room must be in summer, or on rainy days, with that book-case so handy," said Charles to his companion, as he saw him looking round.

"I don't know as to that; but it is a most delightful place just now; this fire goes to one's heart after such a ride."

"Gentlemen," said their host, who then came in, having left them a few moments, "you have come in very opportunely; our cook has been late with the turkey to-day; our usual supper-time is half-past five; but I am happy, for your sakes, that it has so turned out. So soon as you are sufficiently warmed, I will introduce you to my family, and then we will attack the turkey."

Both young gentlemen immediately arose, signifying their readiness; and receiving their names he opened one of the doors leading from the hall, and ushered them into a large room, stepped up to his lady and introduced them individually, and then to the circle, at the head of which she was seated.

One is often so blinded by the lights, and that strange mist which spreads over everything at a first introduction to a company of ladies, that it is not often that a man, especially a young one, is able to distinguish either names or faces. It is not to be wondered at, then, that Charles did not recognize any one he had ever seen before, until a young lady stepped up, and putting out her hand, said:

"Oh, Mr. Lovell, how glad I am to see you!" Charles took the hand; we fear he did not realize that it belonged to a lady, for the dear little thing grasped his with such a true interest, that there is no telling how he returned the embrace. He had no thought for the moment of anything but the most exquisite delight. At length he replied:

"Is it possible?"

"It is possible; and now let me introduce you again."

"Mrs. Shawn, my friend, Mr. Lovell; Mr. Shawn, Mr. Lovell."

"Well, well," said Mr. Shawn, "this is a most unexpected pleasure. Little did I think, Miss Addie, that I was so fortunate as to be introducing, in a stranger, one in whom you claim such an interest."

"Oh, you know, sir, it is so long since I have seen any one with whom I was acquainted at my uncle's."

She could not hide the blush that spread all over her beautiful face.

"You are very excusable; I am only too glad that your *friend* has come along so opportunely. And now for the supper." And Mr. Shawn led the way at once into the eating apartment, where was spread a long table filled with a supply that would have been sufficient for very many hungry folks.

"Dear Miss Vincent," said a young lady, taking hold of her, and speaking in a low voice, "is this the Mr. Lovell I have heard you speak about?"

"Hush, Carrie dear."

"Introduce me; won't you?"

"Miss Caroline Shawn, Mr. Lovell."

Charles bowed low to her.

"Ah, but I must shake hands; if you are a friend to her, you must be a friend to me, too. I am going to love all whom she loves."

Poor Adelaide would have been in a sad condition if it had not been that there was some little confusion at the time.

Charles had leisure, during the long meal, to collect his bewildered thoughts, and to examine a little into persons and things. He found that the family proper consisted of Mr. and Mrs. Shawn, their daughter Caroline, and Miss Adelaide Vincent; the latter being treated by them with marked attention and respect. There was also a Miss Lawrence, who, with her brother, appeared to be visitors from the city. The young lady had a very agreeable countenance, and her manners were faultless; every grace of the lady shone from her; about the age, he thought, of Miss Vincent, to whom she seemed peculiarly attached, and on terms of great intimacy. The brother was, as near as he could judge, of his own age, of pleasant, easy address, free from affectation, and very attentive to those about him. It was, however, evident to Charles, that his attentions were more peculiarly directed to Adelaide, and he noticed some little passages between them which perhaps none others at the table thought of.

Eating did not appear to be the main idea; that part of the business was doubtless attended to by each, as far as necessary; for all hospitality was exercised by those who held the places of honor. And there was no reserve; perfect freedom from restraint seemed to be enjoyed by each of the circle, and a lively stream of conversation, and good feeling, flowed along through the whole entertainment, and continued until some time after the matter of eating and drinking had been finished. Never before had Charles seen such a perfect family party around a table; and when he arose, and gathered with them in the parlor, he could scarcely realize that, but two hours since, he was a stranger to nearly all of them. The same ease of manner he also noticed attended the social scene when they had collected for the evening. There was no attempt to get up amusements; those who pleased sat together and communed at their own ease, some resorted to the piano, and some, with light needlework in hand, sat by the round table near the lamp. Mr. Shawn arose, after chatting a little time with Charles and his companion, and left the room, merely saying, as he was about to go :

"Gentlemen, I am going to spend a little time in the hall with the newspapers; when you get tired of the ladies' company, I shall be glad to see you there. Make yourself perfectly at home."

Charles could have wished for a long and social chat with Adelaide, but he found no opportunity to be alone with her. He had no reason, indeed, to think that she avoided him ; her whole demeanor towards him was marked with the most perfect kindness and frankness. For she expressed much pleasure, when she learned that he was on his way to the city, and told him that she hoped to meet him often then, as she was expecting on the morrow, if the weather would permit, to accompany Miss Shawn on a visit there. Remarking, at the same time, that the family of Mr. Lawrence, where she expected to stay, was a delightful one to visit at. And Charles really thought, if the specimens he witnessed of that family then present were correct, it must be as she said. He had never met with those before, whom he thought exceeded them in true refinement. But—and dear reader, you would be tired, and perhaps disgusted with any attempt to define the workings of a mind in the state his then was—completely wrapped up in one lovely object, and that object, although within his sight, and listening to his words, yet acting independently of his will, and thrown by circumstances entirely beyond his control. He was, however, for the present, diverted from his uncomfortable thoughts by the intervention of young Lawrence, who in a pleasant manner whispered to him, so as not to be heard by the ladies :

"What do you say to a cigar?"

"I don't smoke, but I shall be happy to accompany you."

The young gentleman made the same application to Rice, and leaving the room, the three young men entered the hall where Mr. Shawn was enjoying the news in his large chair beside the blazing fire.

"I have been thinking, young gentlemen, that as you are all bound for the city to-morrow, you had better make a single party of it, and go together."

"Good," exclaimed young Lawrence; "I agree to that with all my heart, sir. But how shall we get a conveyance?"

"I can tell you. Let Peter put the bays to the large sleigh; it will hold six of you with ease. I think it more than probable you will find good sleighing all the way; but if not, he can take you as far as the snow has fallen, and then you can, no doubt, when on the stage road, find conveyance easily enough. But, perhaps you two gentlemen have business that may take you some other route."

"Thank you, sir," said Charles; "our business will require us to stop for a short time at the village of ——, probably not over half an hour. But it seems like taxing your kindness too much, sir, although it would be most agreeable to us to have the pleasure of such good company."

"Not at all, sir. I know that young folks like to flock together. The village you speak of is about half way to the city; and a half hour or an hour's rest there, will be just the thing for the horses."

"But would the ladies, sir, fancy such an addition to their party?"

"That is well considered, Mr. Lovell."

"I will soon put that matter to rest," said young Lawrence, leaving the hall. In a few moments he returned.

"The ladies, with one consent, each held up both hands; only Miss Caroline says that she shall put herself under the special care of Mr. Lovell. So you see, sir, you have made an impression already."

"She does me great honor."

"Well, gentleman, the thing is fixed then. But where are you going, Lawrence?"

"Oh, well sir, I have a little business to transact with these two young gentlemen in the library."

"Ay, ay, you rogue, I understand; but don't let your cigars keep you too long from the ladies."

Smoking is a very bad practice, and we would advise old folks and young folks to quit it at once. But we fear they won't, so we will waste no time in lecturing against the use of the abominable weed. But, good or bad, it has somehow a very comfortable look. A man seems so satisfied with himself, and all about him. There appears to be such a buoyancy to his thoughts, if one can judge from the complacency with which his eye follows the curling smoke, that really one cannot have the heart to scold very hard. It is also said to have a mighty charm in removing all that stiffness which is apt to attend a new introduction; like a third party, intimate with both, and bringing them through itself into close communion, and inspiring mutual confidence; opening, also, the flood-gates of the heart, and thus connecting itself with our happiest hours, the scenes of social intercourse. That it has such power, those who have had experience must decide.

There was probably, however, no need for any such medium to draw together the hearts of the young men assembled in the large and pleasant room dedicated as the haunt of literature, in this family mansion, more especially those of Lawrence and young Lovell. Frank Rice had too many burdens just then pressing upon his, to enter very heartily into any social scene; but he had too much good feeling to allow his own cares to interfere with the enjoyment of others. But with the other two life sat lightly, as the swan upon the glassy lake. They could sympathize, too, in their tastes, for both had cultivated a relish for literature. The fine ideas thrown out by nature's true poets, had been stored in their minds, and were ready "to come forth at their bidding." And as each, in turn, would bring out some passage of beauty that both could appreciate, they were imperceptibly linking their feelings in a pleasing chain. Charles thought he had not met with a more congenial mind; and young Lawrence more than once exclaimed:

"Lovell, you and I must see more of each other. How glad I am that this storm has kept us here, and driven you into the same harbor."

From poetry to love, is a very short and natural step for youth. Charles had accustomed himself to keep his thoughts in abeyance to his judgment. Not so, however, was it with young Lawrence. Both loved, but not in the same degree. With Charles, it had been a long, deep passion, kept in subjection only by strength of reason. With the other, it was a light summer cloud, tinged with golden rays. None could tell whether it might gather into the fierce thunder-storm, or melt away into the blue above. It was the thought, however, apparent in his mind now. At first it came out as a jest, but by degrees lapsed into expressions of deep earnestness, which could not be mistaken. Love must have an object, and, strange as it may seem, desires others to admire its choice, provided the admiration be indulged at a safe distance. It is not improbable, that on the present occasion, however, there was something more than the mere desire to give prominence to the name of a loved one. There were, no doubt, some little misgivings that one who had been called so emphatically a friend, might claim a more tender title; for after bantering awhile, young Lawrence assumed a more serious air:

"I don't know, gentlemen, but this subject is very uninteresting to you both."

"I think it cannot be to Mr. Rice," said Charles, "for I believe he is already engaged."

"And I don't believe," answered Frank, "that it is a very dull subject to Mr. Lovell; for, if reports speak true, he has chosen his mate, and a fine one too."

Charles knew well to whom he alluded. It was an old story about him and Lucy. He, however, did not think best at present to contradict it.

"Well, I must say," exclaimed Lawrence, "*that* is a great relief to my mind; for when I saw Miss Addie clasp your hand so cordially, and introduce you in such a particular manner, I feared that it was all up with me. But don't you think she is a lovely creature?"

"She certainly is." This remark was made by Frank, for Charles was so excited that he dared not trust himself to speak.

"My mother says she is too good for any young man she knows, and I know she is too good for *me*. But if I can gain her heart, I shall be a happy man. Whoever gets her, though, must gain her affections. If she don't truly love, all other considerations would have not the least weight with her. But come, I think, Lovell, you have had enough of our smoke; it don't agree with you, you look pale. Come, let us go back to the ladies."

Charles made no objections; he was glad of any change, just then, that would break the embarrassment under which he was suffering.

The morning proved as pleasant as the last evening had been stormy. The clouds had passed off, the winds had ceased, and the earth was covered with the virgin snow, reflecting brightly the rays of the rising sun. An early start had been proposed, and all were ready for it, and with gladsome hearts gathered into the roomy sleigh, and were borne off, after many a kind farewell—the noble beasts tearing their way through the deep drifts, and scattering the light snow before them like spray from the bosom of the driving boat.

Yet all were not happy. Charles did his best to assume a cheerful air; but when the heart is uneasy, it is a difficult task to bring the light and happy smile upon the lip. Adelaide, too, was much more serious than she had been the past evening, or than Charles remembered to have seen her; perhaps the realities of life, which were gathering about her, were too palpable to escape her notice.

CHAPTER XXVI.

Lucy Johnson had become a constant visitor at the McDougall's, in consequence of the indisposition of Mrs. McDougall. The change in their situation had not operated as might have been expected, especially on the mind of the latter. Her spirits lost their elasticity, and a deep and settled shade of melancholy settled upon her countenance; and, although at times she would smile, and try to be cheerful, yet Lucy could plainly perceive the change that was passing upon her.

One day when she called, Mrs. McDougall had not yet risen, and as Lucy entered her room, she was alarmed at the sight of her pale and emaciated features; she was evidently wasting away under the power of some hidden malady. Lucy earnestly addressed her:

"Do, Mrs. McDougall, let me call in our physician; you certainly need his aid; it shall be no expense to you."

She put out her hand and took that of the lovely maiden.

"Oh, thank you, dear; your kindness is very great; but I assure you that no skill of physicians can reach my case."

"Is there any *trouble* on your mind that you cannot tell *me?* I promise you the most sacred secresy."

As Lucy said this she put her hand on the forehead of the sick woman, and smoothed it gently, pushing back, as she did so, the long frill of her unsightly cap. She saw the tears starting from her long lashes, and stealing down her pale cheek; and, at the same time, her breathing became hurried, her breast heaved, the blue veins on her white temples swelled, and her whole frame seemed to be moved with some powerful excitement. Lucy was alarmed, but Mrs. McDougall feebly said:

"Take it off, dear, take off the cap."

And Lucy gently untied its strings, and drew it from beneath her head, and at once there lay before her, a young lady of her own age, with a rich head of hair of the purest auburn, whose long tresses fell down upon her pillow and around her shoulders, forming a beautiful contrast with her pale and delicate features. Lucy clasped her hands in amazement, while the other burst into a flood of tears.

"You shall know it all," she sobbed out; "you shall know it all. I cannot any longer deceive *you*, and I must have one heart like yours to pour my burden into. Fasten the door, and come, sit by me."

Lucy almost trembled as she obeyed her request.

"I had thought when, by the kindness of yourself, and that dear young man, Mr. Lovell, I came to this place, that I should be comparatively happy. I thought it would be such a pleasant change, to have occasionally a sight of you or him. But alas! I find I am like an encaged bird, only made more wretched by being placed where my mates are flying around in freedom."

"But you are with us, dear, and you shall be more with us; and if your present circumstances distress you, we will see what more can be done."

"Oh, hush, hush, don't speak of it; you have all done what can be done; no power on earth can roll back the dark cloud that shuts me from the world."

"Your mind is depressed by your sickness, dear."

"Oh, but you don't know. You see that I am yet young; life is yet in its freshness. No common circumstances could have impelled me to shut myself away from all who have ever known me; to endure the most bitter privations, and mingle with the lowest of my species. I have told you that you should know all; but how shall I begin! how shall I make you understand!"

"Perhaps you are not equal to the task now?"

"I feel that I shall never be more able to do it than at present. It is a strange recital, but you shall hear it. My mother died when I was but a child, and there lived with us a youth to whom my father was much attached. He was an assistant in his office, as well as a member of our family. He was most comely in his person, and of gentle manners, and pure in every thought. I know, I am sure he was.

Thrown much together, we became as brother and sister; he knew all my thoughts and feelings, and I knew his.

"As I advanced to maturity our intimacy became a strong attachment—stronger than death. My father saw it, and it met his approbation, and our union was to have been completed by marriage.

"A terrible change, without any warning, came over our fair prospect. My father, man of wealth, was defrauded of many thousands of dollars, and, horrible to say, the charge was so substantiated against him to whom I had given my heart, that there was no alternative for him but flight, or the walls of a prison.

"I saw him in the night, in a low place, and there he swore to me, by all that was sacred in our affection, that he was innocent of the crime, but felt that the circumstances were such as rendered it impossible for him to prove it; and he was about to bid farewell to me forever. I little knew until that moment how much I loved. I could not let him go; I knew my father's temper, his unbending will, his strong belief in his guilt. It was an awful moment; my reason seemed to have deserted me; and, even against the remonstrances of him I loved, I resolved never to leave him. We were both young, too young to act with judgment; we were married and fled in disguise together; we were utterly without means, and penniless; we threw ourselves upon the world. I need not detail all I have passed through. We have lived, we have suffered—suffered more than I can bear to think of now. At length we sought an asylum where you found us; and there, where nothing could remind me of what had been, with my husband's love, I had almost, I thought, forgotten the world; but it is now proved to me that I had not. My heart is yet alive to that which is refined and beautiful; it pants for fellowship with kindred spirits, and that can never—never more be mine."

She ceased, apparently much exhausted, and Lucy was so confounded by what she had heard, that she knew not what to say, nor how to administer comfort. She gazed, with silent pity, on the pale sufferer. She felt convinced that she had acted rashly; even wrong. She had probably brought her father in sorrow to the grave. She had violated a command of God, and the bitter fruit she was then partaking.

But it was not for her to upbraid; the past could not be recalled; the future, so far as earth was concerned, would now apparently soon be of little consequence. So she spake words of kindness to her; smoothed her throbbing temples with her soft hand, and prepared some nourishing draught to sustain her exhausted frame, and did all those little things which woman knows so well how to do either around the bed of sickness, or to ease the agony of the heart.

As Lucy had promised, she retained in her own breast the secret which had been revealed to her. She was constant in her attendance, whenever her duties at home would allow. But from day to day she could perceive that the object of her care was growing more feeble. The husband was not an unconcerned witness of the declining strength of her who had thus followed him down into degradation. Lucy could not tell whether he was innocent or guilty; but her heart bled for him, as she saw his sad gaze fixed upon his suffering wife, while bending over her pillow, in vain attempting to administer consolation, and revive her dying hope. She could not, nor did she try to hear what arguments he used, and only once was their meaning conveyed to her, by the answer of the sufferer:

"No, Robert, never; it will never be bright to me again in this world."

Soon after Charles Lovell had taken up his temporary residence in New York, the Reverend Mr. Foster was appointed by his superiors in the ministry to the charge of a congregation in a new part of the city; that is, a part which had been pushed from its outskirts, where a poorer class of inhabitants resided. It was on the north-east part of the city, where small frame buildings had been erected, to accommodate mechanics and laborers in ship-yards. Many of the inhabitants were of a decent class, but mingled among them were those of a loose and abandoned character. Mr. Foster not only preached to them in the small church which had been erected there; he also visited from house to house, talking to them as he found opportunity, and praying with the sick and dying; for death was very busy among those children of poverty and vice.

About the middle of this region stood a building, that had in its day been a favorite resort for young men from the city.

It had a kind of respectability attached to it, in its best days, because those who were the first people hesitated not to visit it; being one of the favorite drives from the lower part of the city. The old Belvidere may even now bring back, by the mere mention of its name, reminiscences to some, yet lingering in old age, of scenes that they could wish might not have been.

Its glory, however, had now departed. The green fields around it had been built upon, the knoll upon which it stood had been so far dug away as to leave merely an unsightly gravel hill, barely large enough to contain the building, and access could be had to it only by a long flight of rough steps rising from the level of the street below. It was still kept as a sort of tavern, and being within the bounds to which Mr. Foster was assigned, was not passed by unnoticed by that faithful watchman. Among its inmates lay a sick man, nearly advanced to middle age; he was evidently drawing near his end, and he was conscious of it. A "horror of great darkness had fallen upon him." The shadow from the unseen world was gathering around, and his spirit trembled beneath its cold and cheerless pall. All that the minister of Christ could say to him appeared to give no comfort. The cross of Christ, that hope for the perishing, was held up before him without effect. He did not despise it. He apparently tried to get the hope which it was told him it would impart; but some hidden power, some film about the mind, shut from his view what was in itself so omnipotent to save. Mr. Foster had spent much time with him by day and night, because he could not bear to leave him to the ministration of those who knew not how to deal with one, who, in the valley of the shadow of death, had no staff nor guiding star.

Charles Lovell had often accompanied his friend, Mr. Foster, at times when business did not demand his attention, in visits among the sick and suffering, and greatly strengthened the hands of the young minister in his arduous work. And as Mr. Foster had great confidence in his skill around a sick bed, or in dealing with the impenitent, he concluded to take him on a visit to the poor sufferer at the old Belvidere. Charles hesitated not to go, and finding that no suitable person was at hand, to spend the night with the sick and dying man, resolved to stay by his side. While he was awake,

Charles made every effort to get an understanding of his mental trouble. For his body there was little to be done; its energies were gone, and decay was marked upon it. But his mind was clear, and, like a criminal about to meet his doom, he looked about in restless agony, to find, perchance, some opening for escape. During some of the hours of the night, the sick man slept; but still his mind exhibited its restless state. At times he would utter incoherent sentences, the meaning only so far intelligible, that an idea could be caught now and then. And once or twice he spoke audibly a name that was in part familiar to the ear of Charles. He believed there was some burden resting on his conscience, and he resolved to do his duty by the dying one, and show him how alone he could have peace. As soon, therefore, as he awoke from sleep, at the breaking of the day, Charles approached him with all kindness in his manner and look, and told him what he thought, and asked him why he had called upon a certain name.

With a wild look, the eyes of the sick man were fastened on him.

"Did I? did I? Did you hear me speak that name? Oh! if that—but—" And then he closed his lids, and clasped his hands, and rolled from side to side as far as his weak frame could move. Again Charles urged, by all the motives which a present eternity held up before him, to do his duty; and if there was a wrong he could undo, to lose no time, but free his spirit from the burden before it was too late. Once more he settled into rest, and fixed a long, piercing look on Charles:

"I believe you are right. I will—I must do it. The injured man may be dead, but his name must be cleared. Oh! I must, I must." And Charles wiped away the big drops from his emaciated forehead, which had been forced out by the suffering spirit.

"Do you know Abijah Field?"

"I do not."

"He lives in —— street, No. —90; quick and bring him here. Tell him, if he hesitates to come, that —— is on his dying bed. Tell him I can give him information of great consequence to him, and his ——; go, be quick."

Charles lost no time. He easily found the place. Mr.

Field was an old man, and surrounded with every token of wealth. And when he heard that he was thus sent for, and to such a place, at first seemed reluctant to go; but when Charles told him all he had heard, and what he believed, he at length consented.

"Young gentleman, if you will accompany me, I will go;" and instantly ordered his carriage.

Charles was too much interested not to be willing to do as the old gentleman requested; and soon they were both ascending the long tottering steps of the old Belvidere.

It was a pitiable sight to behold the expression of mental agony, as the sick man cast his eyes on the tall, feeble frame of him who had once been his benefactor.

"Sin—sin—wickedness—a life of dissipation has brought me here, Mr. Field. Oh dear!"

Charles administered a little brandy and water, being the only medicine now prescribed.

"Oh, sir, I am dying, and I cannot go before my God till I tell you all. Robert Vincent was an innocent man. God forgive me! I plotted his ruin—I deceived you. But he is innocent. He is probably dead. But I ask you to bear witness to the world that Robert Vincent was innocent, and I call this young man to witness what I say. You believed *me*, Mr. Field, and you kept *me* in your employ; and all the circumstances were against *him*, who was to be your son. I got the money, but I lost what I wanted more; no matter now. Here I am, dying in poverty, in shame, in despair. Oh God, have mercy!"

Mr. Field sank down upon the chair which Charles had placed near the bed for his use, and covered his face, and groaned aloud, and seemed paralyzed with the tidings his own ears had listened to. At length Charles ventured to say to him:

"If what this sick man has just told you, sir, involves the character of an innocent man, whether he be living or dead, ought not his testimony to be at once taken down by competent authority?"

The old gentleman immediately aroused himself.

"By all means; and thanks to you, young man, for mentioning it."

"Shall I go for a notary, sir?"

"Or send for one; I should prefer to have you remain with me at present."

The proper officer was soon on hand, and a full and clear statement made. As soon as it was closed, Charles requested a private interview with Mr. Field. It was readily granted; and in one hour from the time he parted from the old gentleman, now most deeply interested in the object of his journey, Charles had taken leave of Frank, and was on his way to Melton.

At the close of one of those days that Lucy had spent almost entirely by the bedside of Mrs. McDougall, there was a slight tap at the door, and Lucy at once answered the summons. Putting up both hands, she exclaimed as she opened it, although in a low voice:

"Charles Lovell!"

He smiled as he took her hand, but his countenance at once assumed a more earnest cast than usual.

"Is Mrs. McDougall ill?"

"She is; I fear she is very ill."

"I can see her?"

"Oh yes; but she is very weak."

"I wish to communicate with her alone. Is her husband at home?"

"He has not yet come in. He has gone to procure some article which we think may nourish her a little; but I fear, Charles, she can last but a few days."

All this was spoken in a low tone of voice, so as not possibly to be overheard in the sick room. Lucy then entered, and informed Mrs. McDougall that Mr. Lovell had come, and wished a private interview with her. She looked very significantly at Lucy:

"You have been true?"

"I have, dear; not a word has ever escaped my lips."

"Let Mr. Lovell come in, by all means."

Charles was much affected by seeing the change which had taken place. He addressed her in the most soothing manner:

"You have confidence in me, Mrs. McDougall?"

"I have the utmost."

"The most urgent reasons require me to be plain, and to

ask you at once to tell me whether you have not assumed a feigned name. I beg of you to tell me if it is so. Circumstances which have transpired during our acquaintance lead me to think so; and it will be of the greatest consequence to you and yours if my surmises are correct. Give me your true name, and that of your husband."

She took his hand and drew him close to her, and whispered; and Charles immediately exclaimed:

"God be praised! your day of darkness has passed. Oh, Lucy!" And Charles, strongly excited, left the room, and gave vent to his feelings. Lucy followed him immediately.

"Tell me, Charles, is it true? Is her husband innocent?"

"He is innocent, and a deeply-injured man. But try to cheer up his poor wife, for wealth and happiness are yet before them. Try to rouse her spirits; tell her that her father lives, and is in an agony to know whether my surmises are correct, and his children living."

The interview with McDougall, or Robert Vincent, as he must now be called, was deeply interesting. Charles met him a short distance from his house, and there detailed the scene which had passed at the Belvidere, and the interview he had with old Mr. Field. Overcome with the sudden transition from disgrace and degradation to favor and a good name, he sat down on the ground, and gave vent to feelings that had long been suppressed by the energy required to support himself, and those entrusted to him; and then he arose and grasped the hand of Lovell:

"Dead be my heart to everything that can give consolation when I forget your generous kindness. God's blessing rest upon you to your last hour of life. And now I must see my poor Agnes."

It were but a vain attempt to paint the scene around that bed, when, with his disguise thrown off, he leaned his head upon the pillow, and received the tender embrace of her who had loved him but too fondly."

"Agnes, my dear one. Oh, cheer up, cheer up; the bright day has come!"

"And my dear father lives! and will come, if for nothing more, to let me see his dear face, and hear his words of forgiveness before I die. But must you leave me, Robert?"

"Only for a few days. Mr. Lovell can tell you I *must* go.

I must see your father, and assure him of all this. All he knows at present is, that Mr. Lovell, from circumstances, trifling in themselves, had strongly believed that you was his child, and I his."

"Well, go at once, my dear; hasten all you can, for my time is short."

Old Abijah Field had been a most kind and indulgent father; but he was a man of impetuous passions. Having wealth at his command, he had made himself believe that all dependent upon him must bow to his will. Agnes had been the idol of his heart. But when she fled, he thought his feelings were dead to her forever. But time wears out anger from a parent's heart, even if that hateful passion should ever get the dominion there. Long had he mourned over his lost child in secret. Again and again, in his hours of reflection, had he mourned over the hard words he had said to her, when he saw that she still clung to one whom he believed guilty; and the terrible threats he had made if she dared even to mention his name. But now the scene is changed; and, with him whom he once cursed, he is now hurrying on to see his own, his dying child.

"Hasten, hasten, driver; don't spare the horses. My life depends upon your speed;" and on, and on they go. Drive fast, thou fond, but rash old father; drive fast, for death is on his way too, and ye are both bound to the same abode.

"Do you think they will soon be here?" and the feeble sufferer looked up at the dear, kind Lucy. Lucy had not left her for a moment, as she promised her husband she would not.

"They will, they will."

"Do you not hear the sound of wheels?"

Lucy listened.

"I surely hear them," said the anxious wife and daughter. She doubtless did, and then Lucy heard it too; and in a moment more the rattling carriage halted at the door. With trembling steps, the old man, leaning on the arm of his son, descends, and Lucy is by them.

"You say she lives. Oh! let me see her quick."

"My dear, dear Agnes!" A faint smile has settled on her once ruby lips, and her eyes stare wildly.

"Oh, Agnes! my dear Agnes! It is your father, your own dear father. My love—my dear one!"

But the eye is fixed, and the lips are pale, and the breast heaves not. And the old man presses his lips, and drops his burning tears upon the cold, cold clay.

CHAPTER XXVII.

CHARLES LOVELL had not enjoyed much from the visit of Adelaide to the city. He saw her occasionally, but only went at the urgent solicitation of young Lawrence, for that youth had really formed an attachment to him that Charles could not resist, and, under other circumstances, would have been glad, and even proud to cherish. Surrounded with every luxury, and with wealth at his command, or which amounted to the same thing, at the command of an indulgent father, he seemed to be free from all thought of such external advantages; of an open, frank, and generous spirit, and above all that littleness which too often attends the inheritance of wealth.

But, although Charles took delight in the company of this new friend, it was really no pleasure to visit Adelaide, with the consciousness that every circumstance was conspiring against his heart's desire.

One evening, however, some weeks after he had been in the city, he received a polite note from Miss Lawrence, inviting him to a party at her home, and he felt, under such circumstances, compelled to go. It was quite a gay assemblage, and composed of a more polished class than Charles had ever found himself among before. Adelaide was very pleasant, but he fancied she entered too heartily into the engagements of the evenings, and was too ready too accept the offers of those who presented themselves for partners. Love is keen-eyed, a little too keen sometimes, and our Charley, much as we admire him, was to all intents and purposes human nature; he had a good deal of it about him. He could dance to be sure, a little, but he was very conscious that he would have made but a poor figure among those who had been trained to it, and who moved with poetic beauty through the splendid rooms. He, therefore, had declined to dance; but when the time for music had arrived, and the singers were hunted up, Adelaide whispered to young Lawrence, "that Mr. Lovell was a delightful singer." Charles saw the act and as his friend came up to him, and, with much politeness of manner, requested him to favor the company with a song, Charles replied; he did it, however, with a pleasant manner:

"That he really did not feel like it, and begged, as a particular favor, that he might be excused."

But in a moment Adelaide came up to him. She did, indeed, look beautiful. She was richly dressed. He thought he had never seen her look so lovely before, nor move with more grace, and a most winning smile was upon her lip.

"Did you realize that you were refusing a lady's request, when you declined favoring us with a song?"

Charles was just then so troubled with a palpitation of the heart that it was with great difficulty he replied:

"I presumed that Mr. Lawrence was prompted to do me the honor he did."

Adelaide noticed that he was very pale, and she thought his voice trembled; but attributing it all to his native modesty, she playfully rejoined:

"But you surely did not imagine that you were refusing the request of a friend? Do you know that I always expect my friends to comply with my demands?"

"I should have felt myself guilty of presumption had I classed myself among such favored ones."

Perhaps Charles tried to smile, as, bowing to her, he made this reply. But if he did, it was a failure; and the fair girl before him only saw his lip curl with an ironical expression upon it, that came like a bolt to her heart. She colored deeply, apologized for the liberty she had taken, and, retiring amid the circles in the other room, he saw her no more.

A few days after, he met his friend Lawrence, who rallied him a little on his dulness that evening, at the same time remarking:

"But I don't blame you; I never feel quite at home myself in those parties. I have no doubt you and I would enjoy ourselves much more in a little quiet confab by ourselves, and I must come and have a good talk with you. I am quite down in the mouth since Miss Vincent has gone."

"Has she returned to the country?"

"Yes—and taken my heart with her. Plague on it, Lovell, if you knew all, you 'd pity me. But it 's no use; I see clear enough there is no hope for me in that quarter; she has been 'spoke for,' or her heart, at least, is engaged, and that 's enough for me."

"Perhaps you misjudge; my opinion has been that you were quite a favorite."

"Ah, well, I know she treats one openly, frankly; there is no prudery, nor coquetry about her—she is a noble girl. But take my word for it, she has fixed her choice. It is an an old flame, from what I can learn; but who the happy fellow is, you nor I, probably, don't know. She has a cousin Montague, a lieutenant in the navy, that she talks much about. Did you ever see him?"

"I once was introduced to a gentleman of that name, and became quite intimate with him; but it was before my acquaintance with Miss Vincent. *He* was a fine fellow, indeed; a noble-minded, sensible man."

"Well, perhaps it 's the same. Heigh ho! Well, so we go; there is no getting all we want, at any rate. But I have n't told you that I am getting ready for Europe?"

"No, indeed!"

"Yes; my father has been anxious, for some time, to have me go off and see the world a little, and now I mean to clear as soon as I can. But I am coming to see you in a day or two, and have a good long talk."

This was the last, then, that Charles concluded he should ever see of her who had been so long the idol of his affections. He could not blame himself for the past; he had endeavored to curb his feelings by the effort of his own reason, but reason had always failed to suppress the passion, although it had prevented him from openly declaring it. He loved her still, hopelessly now indeed; but he could no more drive her image from his heart, than keep his mind from thinking.

His agency had come to its close, the money he had received was faithfully appropriated, and the good friends of Deacon Rice were fully refunded what they had advanced, and Frank was enabled to make a much better dividend to his creditors than he at first anticipated. He had, also, become strongly attached to Charles. His kind and unassuming manners, with his prompt and diligent habits, had won his respect and affection; and when Charles was preparing to leave, he could not refrain from again urging his former plea, to become his partner when he should commence business anew. But Charles could not be persuaded. And after listening to his arguments, he replied:

"I thank you, Frank, most heartily for your friendly feelings; and I assure you, that with no one would I so readily connect myself as with you, for I can testify to your noble conduct under all your trials. I can also assure you, that I see much in the business here that is very desirable. I find a generous, liberal spirit among the merchants—a disposition to assist the young and feeble. There is a manifestation of confidence in each other that is most grateful to the feelings, and less, much less of that littleness in bargaining which I had once supposed. And I do not at all wonder that you are charmed with it. But my tastes are still unchanged. The country has my heart. Its employments are more congenial to my feelings. Its labors are not irksome to me; I like them. You have my most hearty wishes for your success; but, as I feel, Frank, nothing but a sense of duty could keep me shut up, all my best and most joyous days, within your brick walls."

"And, Charley, you have my most sincere desire that your life may be as pleasant as your true heart and refined taste merit. I hope yet to spend many happy days with you at your country home, for I know it will be a spot hallowed by all that is noble and good."

The happy day at length came when Charles was to bid adieu to the city. It was but a day or two after the return of Mr. Field and young Vincent from the gloomy scenes at Melton, and Charles could not return without calling upon them. Great, indeed, was the change in the circumstances of him whom he had known as the fisherman of Oyster Island. But the blow he had received was just beginning to manifest its severity. He was now surrounded by every luxury; he walked amid all the elegance that money could procure; he was treated with the most tender care by his father-in-law; his independence for life was secured, Mr. Field having made an immediate settlement upon him. But, alas! of what avail was it all to a broken heart! His Agnes was ever before him. Her gentleness, through all her bitter suffering—her patient trust in his integrity—her sad departure just as their fortunes changed—all came over him with a power that was too much for a mind already overcharged with the burden of past years; and Charles saw too plainly, in his blank and sorrow-stricken look, that the present had no happiness for him. He was lying on a sofa when Charles entered, from which he quickly arose to greet him. But he seemed oppressed with weakness, and his hand was cold and clammy.

"Oh, how glad I am to see you! How kind in you to come! Sit down by me here, and let us talk together. When do you go home?"

"This very day."

He heaved a deep sigh.

"How I wish I could go with you! And yet, how could I bear to be there! There is no place in this world for me now; no more rest."

"You have been much excited; it is not strange that you should feel so now. It will take time to recover from such a blow."

"Time will never do it. The cup of misery has been too bitter. But 'His will be done.' I have, however, one more request to make of you. You will remember asking me one day about my connexions; and I was prevented at the time from replying by the intrusion of a third person. My only near relative is a sister; and for whom I feel deeply anxious. I can learn nothing about her from our aunt, to whom I have sent to inquire. It seems some misunderstanding took place between them, and my sister left her house—"

Charles interrupted him:

"Give me her name."

"Adelaide; she was—"

"A niece of Captain Halliday?"

"The same. Do you know anything of her?"

"I do; and you can set your mind at ease. She is in the family of a gentleman of fortune, a kind and noble-hearted man, and is treated with every consideration."

Young Vincent looked at Charles a moment, with the most perfect astonishment depicted on his countenance, and then hrew himself back upon his seat, while his eyes filled with tears.

"Ah! how merciful is God! Strange, strange, are the vicissitudes of human life!"

A few moments he was silent, and then he said: "I want to see her, and yet I am not able to go, and I am not even competent to pen a letter. Oh, my dear Lovell! what poor creatures we are, when the hand of God is laid upon us! I have not the strength of a child."

"Can I do anything for you?"

"Oh, you have done so much already, I cannot bear to burden you further. I was going to ask you, when you came in, just to pen an advertisment for me to put in the paper. But there is no necessity for that now. Strange enough, you have been enabled to relieve my anxiety. But where does this gentleman, this Mr. Shawn, live?"

"About twenty-five miles from here, on the banks of the North River."

"It is out of your way, then?"

"Would you wish me to see her?"

"It would be a great comfort to me."

"I am on my way now to Melton. I shall be occupied a day or two after my return home, and then, if you wish, will go there. Would you wish me to bring her here?"

"I will not ask you to do that; but if you could go to her, and tell her what has happened, and let her know that my character is redeemed from infamy, and that I have abundance to supply all her wants for the future, and—and tell her all you know, it would be indeed a great favor to me."

"I will certainly do it."

"You are very good. And now, before you go, Mr. Fields wants much to see you; he has been very anxious to do so."

Charles had made the promise to see Adelaide, but it was rather the consequence of his readiness to oblige, than from any choice of his will or judgment. He truly felt that the time had come when he must no longer indulge those fond and pleasing hopes which had so long been master of his heart. And to see again one whom he still loved so tenderly, when he felt assured there could be no return of affection, was only adding to his unhappiness. But he had promised to go, and he was resolved to perform the duty, cost him what it might.

In a few moments he was relieved from the tumult of contending thought by a request from Mr. Field, to whom notice had been given of Mr. Lovell being there, "that he would be very happy to see him in his own room."

The old gentleman was sitting with his grandchild on his knee. The little fellow quickly flew towards Charles, and caught him by the hand.

"Ah, Mr. Lovell, Mr. Lovell," said Mr. Field, rising to meet him. "The boy knows you, and I hope will never forget you; no, Abijah, you must never forget this kind friend," taking Charles by the hand, and grasping it cordially. "He has been the friend in need, the friend of your poor father and mother, when they were outcasts from the world." The old man's tears flowed freely, and he spoke with difficulty. "Love him, my boy, love him always, and, when you grow to be a man, pity the poor and the outcast. Come, my dear young friend, and sit down by me. I want to talk with you."

Charles took his seat, with the boy still clinging to his hand.

"There is no need, Mr. Lovell, to go over with the past; but deeds of friendship like yours must not be forgotten, and ought not to go unrewarded. I know money cannot repay you, yet it will be some relief to my mind to do something for you."

He arose before Charles could reply, and, opening a small drawer in his desk, took out a paper.

"Here, my dear sir, is a check for a sum that will give you a good start in life. And if at any time you may need a friend, remember that while Abijah Field lives, he will ever stand ready to meet your demand. Take it, and may God's best blessing attend you."

Charles was at a loss what to do. He took the little paper, but it was only for the moment. He felt the blood mantling his cheek, and a strange consciousness of doing that which his heart did not approve, at once came over him.

"Mr. Field, I thank you most heartily for your generous intentions, and I can sympathize with your feelings. But I hope you will not think me unnecessarily particular if I respectfully decline your gift. I am neither poor, nor am I above the desire for money honestly and honorably obtained. But this would be too much like taking advantage of your feelings wrought up by recent trials. All I have done, sir, was only what we are all bound to do for each other. I have not injured myself. And I have enjoyed untold comfort in the late development of divine providence. I have not acted from selfish motives. And I want still to retain the consciousness of having done a kind act for its own sake."

And, in the most respectful manner, he handed it back to the donor. The old gentleman saw that he was in earnest, and, when Charles held out his hand, he took the check back without objecting.

"I dare not, indeed, urge it upon you, if so you feel. May you ever retain such noble feelings; but here is something you must take as a memento of her who is now no more. I purchased it for her, a few days before the sad occurrence that parted us forever. This you cannot refuse me; take it and keep it, and let it go down to your children's children, as a token to them never to turn their backs upon the child of misfortune." And he held out to Charles an elegant gold watch, richly adorned with chain and seals. "Remember it was hers."

Charles took the glittering jewel; he looked at it a moment; he thought of the poor sufferer for whom it had been designed, and his overcharged feelings burst forth. He sat down awhile, and covered his face; but, as soon as he became sufficiently composed, replied:

"I will keep this, sir, most sacredly, as you request, and will ever look upon it as a precious relic of one for whom I have been so deeply interested."

The little boy still clung to Charles, as he arose to depart, and, as he stooped to kiss him for good-bye, he threw his little arms up to his neck, and hung upon him and sobbed bitterly. He seemed to feel, although he said nothing, that the friend he was parting with was associated with her he should never see more.

CHAPTER XXVIII.

When Adelaide Vincent left Charles Lovell, after the strange reply he made to her playful sally, on the evening of the party, she mingled with the company a short time, and then, asking Mrs. Lawrence to excuse her for the rest of the evening, as she did not feel very well, retired to her room, and there in a flood of tears sought relief for her wounded feelings. When her tears were spent, she busied herself in trying to unravel the strange mystery in which the conduct of one she had always so much respected, was involved. She could, however, think of nothing she had said or done that might or ought to give offence. Never before had he been deficient towards her in the most delicate attention, the most respectful and kind manner.

And thus, in perplexity, she sat and mused until the company had gone, and her friend, Julia Lawrence, found her sitting before the coal-fire, in their common bed-room, when she came to retire for the night.

"And are you not a pretty one to be sitting here all alone by yourself? Mamma said that you had gone to bed, as you were not very well; and you have been weeping! Now, dear Addie, just tell me what is the matter!" and the sweet girl threw herself upon her lap, and put her arm around her neck, and pressed her lips to hers.

"Now tell me, Addie, what is the matter! and there is a naughty tear stealing down that pretty cheek again. Do tell me, Addie, has our Willie been saying or doing anything to trouble you?"

"Oh, by no means—not in the least."

"I thought not, for to tell you the truth, Addie, he thinks too much of you—he feels too tenderly towards you. I don't know that I ought to tell you, but I love you so much myself, I want so much to have you for my dear sister, that I must tell you. Willie loves you to distraction, and nothing but delicacy prevents him from declaring himself, while you are here as a visitor."

"Dear Julia, you forget, you know, that you and I never jest about such things." Adelaide knew of no better way to turn aside the direct revelation, to her, of such unpleasant tidings. "Do not let us break what we have considered a rule of propriety. I know you do it to make me smile, but I had rather be amused by some less serious subject."

"You are right, Addie dear. I know we have made that rule; but, although I ought not to have said what I did, yet, truly I was not in jest. The expression escaped me thoughtlessly, and, since I have told you, I must assure you they are words of truth. No, dear, I will never trifle about such matters. But let it pass. Come, cheer up, and just tell me frankly what troubles you."

And Adelaide repeated to her, as well as she could, the occurrence of the evening that had so severely tried her, adding, as she closed:

"Oh, you cannot think, dear Julia, how very—very strange it was; so very different from what I had a right to expect; so totally unlike himself; and I have been trying to think what I may have said or done. He has, I know, very sensitive feelings, and I know I would not designedly have injured them."

Julia had taken a seat beside her on a bench that was at hand, and looked up at her with affectionate interest all the while she was speaking.

"You surprise me very much, Addie, and I cannot but think that you must be under some delusion yourself. He, certainly, is most gentlemanly in his bearing, and I should judge of a most amiable disposition. Willie says he is the best fellow he ever knew. If it was not, Addie, that he is engaged, I should say he was in love, and that this was merely a freak of that tormenting power, for it is said to worry folks almost out of their senses sometimes. But there! love again. Well, I expect we had better get upon some other topic, very different from that which leads us into the danger of breaking through our good rules."

And, in her lively way, with the sincere desire of diverting the mind of her friend, she recurred to other and pleasanter scenes of the evening; and very soon, as though all the world was at peace with them, and they with it, retired to enjoy that rest which is generally, by the young and guileless, so easily obtained.

To Adelaide, however, it was no night of rest. The revelation which her friend had made of the feelings of her brother were not by any means agreeable. She had no love to return for his. She liked his easy manners, his gentle attentions, his light and agreeable conversation, and she had great confidence in his pure morals, and the kind qualities of his heart. But none of these commanded the reverence of her heart. She could not look up to him, nor lean upon him with that confidence which she felt alone could satisfy the full expectation of her heart. She had never thought of him as a lover, and never could; and the idea that she had inspired him with emotions towards her which she could not reciprocate, was most painful to her sensitive mind. Again and again did she regret having made this unfortunate visit. And what course must she pursue? Julia had made known to her, although without thinking, the feelings of her brother; and it would not do for her now to receive his attentions, with the knowledge she possessed. It would be an unpleasant task, but her duty was clear, and she resolved at the earliest opportunity to let her sentiments be known.

But Julia had revealed another fact which she could not so easily dispose of. She dared not name it to herself. She could not reason about it. She could not throw it off. It pressed beneath its burden all her hopes. It took away from earth its beauty, and from her future all interest. Her tears flowed freely, but weeping gave no relief; and when she slept, and woke again, the same sad load was there.

Caroline Shawn was too young to be made a confidant, but she was strongly attached to Adelaide; and, when she noticed the change in her appearance, she clung around her, making constant inquiries as to the cause. At length she said:

"Has any one been unkind to you?"

"No one, my dear."

"Then I mean to write to my papa to send for us home, for I know you are not happy here. And I am tired of running round these dull streets, and we will ride the pony, and play with Rover, and go out in the woods and hear the birds. I heard them this morning, and I know they must have come in our woods, now the weather is so mild."

"But I am afraid, dear, you want to go on my account. I would not be so selfish as to take you away from so much pleasant company."

"Oh, well, I know it is pleasant, but one has to be so tied up here. It is just the same thing over too, day after day. It is all fine people, and fine dresses, and fine furniture; and it is company to dinner, and it is company in the evening, and I am just tired out with seeing people, and answering their questions about the country, and how we get along there through the dreary winters, just as if we had any dreary winters, or summers, or anything else. They don't know anything about the country, do they, when they ask such questions?"

"They are not accustomed to it as you and I are, dear; we are never lonesome there. And if you truly desire, Carrie dear, to return, I am sure it would be pleasant to me."

"Then I will write to papa this very day."

Adelaide bade adieu to the city with very different feelings from those which animated her when she came upon the visit. It had been a severe trial to her to make known to her friend Julia the true sentiments of her heart towards her brother. But it was done in such a proper manner, that it neither injured their affection for each other, nor lost for Adelaide the respect and kindness of any member of the family. They parted, as all had met, in the most pleasant manner.

Adelaide was not one who took delight in nourishing her grief. She would not cast away all the enjoyments of life because some things were contrary to her will. And she felt too sincerely desirous of cultivating a spirit of submission to the will of her Heavenly Father, to allow her disappointments, however bitter, to create a distaste for what of comfort was still meted out to her. She could not forget the past, although she would not permit its reminiscences to hinder the cheerful discharge of present duty.

A few weeks after her return, as she was one day engaged in the library with her friend Caroline, a servant entered, and said that her presence was requested in the parlor.

She waited not to inquire who was there? nor did she even

cast a glance at the mirror, to see how she looked; but, with a light step, passed down the broad stair-way, and through the hall, and at once into the room designated. A gentleman arose to meet her. She paused a moment; and then, with her pleasant smile, frankly held out her hand.

"Mr. Lovell! you are a very unexpected visitor."

"It is very unexpected to me, or it was so but a few days since."

Charles saw that a deep blush had suffused her beautiful face, and, wishing to relieve her from the embarrassment of supposing he had any business of his own, immediately added: "I have come at the request of one, with whom you are intimately acquainted, and should not have taken the liberty on my own account. I come at the request of your long-lost brother."

She looked at him a moment as though hardly comprehending what he said.

"What do you say? my brother! Oh! what do you know of him! Is he yet alive?"

"He is, and I must say at once, that the stain which has been upon his character is completely removed."

She sank upon the chair beside her, and gave full vent to her feelings; while Charles could only sit in silence, and bear, as he best could, the deepest excitement which the heart of man is susceptible of,—that of beholding the object of his adoration bathed in tears. So soon as she could command her feelings, with all the pathos of the most tender interest she addressed him:

"Tell me all you know about him; do tell me."

And Charles told her all that he knew; commencing with their first acquaintance, in his state of degradation, and detailing, as far as was necessary, the whole history.

She took not her eye from him nor lost a word that fell from his lips,—admiring, most of all, the slight notice he took of all that he himself had done in the eventful tale. And when he ceased, her eye still rested on his manly countenance, beaming with the interest which the recital had rekindled in his breast.

"And *you* have been the friend of my poor suffering brother! have stood by him when forsaken by all others!"

She could say no more, but, stretching forth her hand, Charles gently clasped it.

"What can I ever do to repay this deed of love?"

"I have already, my dear Miss Vincent, been richly repaid in the happy development that has raised one dear to you from degradation to honorable station. And believe me, for I speak in all the soberness of truth, to give one emotion of joy to you, I would make any sacrifice that was not sinful."

She still held his hand, and her eye gazed upon him. She was about to speak, but the words came not forth; and Charles thinking he had gone too far, was alarmed at his own rashness. He immediately added:

"Excuse me if my feelings have caused me to utter that which is painful to your ear."

Just then the step of Mr. Shawn was heard approaching, and at once he entered the room.

"Upon my word! right glad am I to see you, sir. Mr. Lovell, you are welcome here again. But," looking with an arch smile at Adelaide, "I fear I have intruded."

"Oh, by no means, sir; Mr. Lovell is quite through. He had an errand to me, bringing me good tidings from a lost friend, whom I have not told you about yet."

"Another friend, ha! Well, I think, Miss Addie, you will have a host of friends around you by-and-bye. If Mr. Lovell will excuse you a moment, I must ask you to accompany me, as there is another gentleman in the next room very anxious to see you. Please be seated, Mr. Lovell, I will be with you presently."

It was not long that Charles was left to himself, for Mr. Shawn soon returned, and requested him to go with him into the other room.

"It seems that the gentleman is an acquaintance of yours, too, and wishes to see you."

As they entered the apartment, Charles was surprised at seeing a young man in an undress naval uniform, and Adelaide leaning on his arm as they walked the room. The young officer, smiling as they approached each other, very cordially grasped the hand of Lovell.

"My dear sir, I am very happy to see you."

"Lieutenant Montague! Excuse me for not sooner recognizing you. I surely did not expect this pleasure."

It was, indeed, an old friend; and Charles, under other circumstances, would have been most happy. But the unaffected pleasure which beamed from the countenance of Adelaide, as she still clung to the arm of the officer, together with what he remembered had been suggested by young Lawrence, at once dashed all his hopes, and he could have wished—he did wish most heartily—that he had refused to come upon this untoward errand. But her words added to his dismay:

"Oh, how glad I am that you know each other. How is it that I have never heard either of you speak of the other? for I know of no two gentlemen so much alike."

"Not in looks, Addie dear," said the officer smiling, and turning towards the blushing Adelaide; "I think you hardly do justice to Mr. Lovell."

"Oh, I was not thinking of the looks; my friends all look well to me; but I think your sentiments and feelings are so much alike."

All three were now seated, and, after engaging awhile in conversation on the subject, principally, which had called Charles there, Lieutenant Montague recurred to their past acquaintance and old friends:

"How is the old colonel, and that charming daughter of his? and my friend Jamieson? and that old lady—let me remember—Aunt Casey, how is she? I often have thought of you, Lovell; how snugly you was living there, in that old house among the trees! What fine times you and I and Jamieson used to have there of an evening, on that little piazza, where everything was so beautiful and still, the moon shining on the distant water, and down through the trees about us. Believe me, there is no spot among all I have visited that is associated with such agreeable thoughts."

Charles replied to all his questions, and added as he closed:

"We did, indeed, spend many pleasant evenings together, and I hope I may have the same pleasure again. We change but slowly in the country; you would probably notice but few alterations."

"Is the old stone house there yet? I have often wondered whether you would keep to the views which Jamieson and I used to laugh about so. You remember how you talked about making that the nucleus to a good substantial dwelling."

"I am of the same mind still, and am now preparing to carry out my plan."

"Then you have not made a permanent change of your

business?" Adelaide asked this question, and Charles thought her countenance evinced deep interest, but whether for or against the change, he knew not.

"Oh, by no means. I have been in the city attending to some business for others; and I return to my old employment with greater zest than ever."

Charles could not tell how his answer had affected Adelaide; her countenance still retained a serious cast; she said nothing, and left the gentlemen to carry on the conversation. The lieutenant now arose, and bowing to Adelaide:

"I should like to see Mr. Lovell for a short time, and may we be excused, if we leave you for a walk in the garden?"

"Oh, by all means; only don't stay too long."

"What a sad and changeful world this is," began Lieutenant Montague, as soon as they were by themselves. "There is ever some thorn springing up in our path, or some ominous cloud rising upon our horizon, to annoy or fill us with apprehension."

"I should not have imagined, from the agreeable circumstances in which I met you but a few moments since, that there could possibly be either a thorn in your path, or a cloud on your sky."

"Well, I don't know why it is, but I am always cheerful when Addie is by me. There seems to be such sunshine about her, that one partakes of its bright influence, and almost necessarily falls in with her happy state of feeling. I was very sad, though, on my journey thither. I had been to see my sister, and found things in such a sad state there, that I was tempted to wish I had no relatives. I thought, of course, that I must come and see Addie; but all the way here, I have been planning and planning what course to pursue in reference to my sister. You know, I suppose, that she married Vanderbose?"

"I do; and would have prevented it if I could."

"Had I been here, Lovell, it never should have taken place. But it was all brought about through the means of our foolish aunt. I use the word purposely, and with a meaning. She is a woman without feeling or principle. But the deed is done, and regrets now of no avail. But when I saw my poor sister too feeble to rise from her bed, her cheek sunken and pale, alone in her large and splendidly-furnished room, with no friend to comfort her, and only selfish and unfeeling domestics to administer to her wants, while her wretch of a husband sat below with his companions, drinking and gambling, sometimes through the long night, it almost distracted me, and I was tempted to turn the whole profligate gang from the house, and bolt the doors against them."

"I feared it from the first. But can you not take your sister away; the law would certainly give you the control of her, under the circumstances."

"Perhaps it might; but there are difficulties in the way. If he had committed violence upon her person, the magistrate could at once interfere. But a man may kill a tender and delicate wife by cold neglect, and ruin himself and her too by debauchery; but if he keeps within his own dwelling, and does not disturb his neighbors, the law would be slow to move against him.

"But they have no neighbors; alone, as you know, the house stands on that point of land, and the miserable wretch has of late built a high wall across the isthmus or neck, that connects his property with the main land, and keeps the gates continually locked. He says he does n't want the rabble prowling around him. The laws, however, will do this. A conservation can be appointed over him, so that he cannot squander what property he has in Connecticut.

"And this must be done, for I learn that he has spent already a great part of his property. I intend at once to take steps for its accomplishment. But whom shall I get to accept the office? I am ordered on service in a few weeks, and cannot take it myself; and, to tell you the truth, Lovell, I have been thinking of you, as just the person I should choose. Could you undertake it?"

"I will do anything I can to aid you in the matter. But your sister, I fear, would only be the greater sufferer by any such step. It would greatly enrage her husband; and, if left in his power, I dread to think of the situation she would be in. Can you not get her away?"

"I can, and will. I must do it, if it cost my life."

"Will she willingly abandon him?"

"Oh yes; she has suffered so much more than I have the heart to tell of. Why, Lovell, her very home is made the resort of the most abandoned outcasts of the city. She asked me if I could not get her away. She cared not if it was only a hut I could put her in, so that it was a place of safety.

"There can be no difficulty then. Once away, he could have no control over her, and the property could be kept from being squandered, and, no doubt, a provision settled upon her.

"I care not for that, I can support her myself; but it would be a resource in case of my death."

Immediately their plans were digested; and then on other subjects they conversed awhile, as they walked arm in arm. What these were need not be told just now; but both came in, apparently with lighter hearts.

Late hours were kept at Mr. Shawn's that night. And yet, Charles was up by the breaking of the day, for he had asked Miss Adelaide if she would not like to take another ride behind the horse she had once admired so much. And she had said "She would like to very much; it would bring back old times." She seemed much confused, however, as she said it. But when the morning came, she had not forgotten the engagement, and was in readiness as soon as Charles.

Just at the hour of six, the servant of Mr. Shawn drove up the plain, but neat and comfortable establishment, which Charles had provided for himself. There was nothing showy about it but Pomp himself, and he seemed to be in high glee. And, as his master stepped towards the gate, with that lovely burden again leaning on his arm, Pomp began to toss his head, and manifested signs of great restlessness.

"Oh, how he has grown!" said Adelaide, as she was assisted to mount her seat; "but handsomer than ever."

It was a morning to make the heart, that had no oppressive burden, to leap for joy. Just cool enough to require a slight over-garment, but with all that brightness in the sky, and that mellow tint on the horizon, and that music in the woods and fields, which mark the days, the pleasant days of spring at the early dawn.

It was not far they rode, ere they reached a little copse of trees, standing at intervals from each other, and sufficiently distant to permit a carriage to drive between; and, attracted by the beauty of the spot, Charles reined Pomp from the road, and drove some little distance into it. It was vocal with those little songsters, who, silent so many months, and skulking in hiding-places from the storms of winter, now seemed to go mad with joy. Far off the blue tops of the highlands shot up their heavy masses against the amber sky, and the lovely Hudson sparkled through the branches which surrounded them. The sun, too, was just lifting his bright disc above the eastern hills, and gilding the summit ridge of the long line of the palisades. Whether it was to behold the pleasant view, that Charles drove in there and ordered Pomp to stop, is not worth while to inquire. But there Pomp stands, tossing his head, and pawing among the leaves. And Charles has dropped the reins, and holds instead a little plump, white hand, that makes no effort to be released. And oh, rash youth! he has raised it to his lips, and there he holds it, while its lovely owner has hidden her sweet face, and leans it upon his breast.

Sing away, you little warblers! Sing the happy union of two loving hearts. No eye but yours and His who made you looks upon them. In one sweet stream of bliss their souls now flow together. No more doubts, no more anxieties, no more jealousies, ever to mar their peace.

"And you thought I could not love you, because you had no wealth to give me. Oh, you naughty Charles. Did not I love you from the first hour we met together! And, ever since, you alone have filled my heart. Only be what you have been, the same Charles Lovell. I ask no more."

Charles spoke not. He had said all he had to say; and it was enough to hear her loving words, and feel her warm breath so near his heart.

"And now, you never more will have one jealous feeling? Never doubt I love you? Never think that wealth has any charm for me, unless you were its owner. I have spurned it from me, when offered by others. I have suffered the hatred of my friends, and ill-treatment of strangers, and have gone through more than I can bring myself to tell you, because I could not yield my hand when my heart was yours. And now I am happy. Oh how happy, dear Charles; my whole heart trusts in you."

And all that Charles could answer to these loving words was to press the little hand, and hold it to his lips.

But breakfast will be waiting, and they must leave this spot, sacred to them now through all their life to come. And again Pomp is in the road, and travels gaily on, and Charles has placed the reins in the hands of Adelaide.

"You are his mistress now, for you I have trained him; for, almost hopeless as my love has been, yet, strange to say, the thought of you has mingled with all my plans and purposes. See how proudly he arches his neck, and hardly seems at all to press upon the rein; as though he knew some gentle hand is guiding him."

"How delightfully he goes! it seems to be all play to carry us behind him. And this wagon! how very snug; and goes along so smoothly. There is no show about it, but I think I never sat so much at ease before,—but once."

And then she looks at him, with an arch smile upon her lip.

"You mean the sleigh ride?"

"To think how you tucked me in, and fixed my feet so warmly, and sat by me so demure, and drove so slow, and kept looking at the moon, and made me feel so strangely! But here we are, only think of it! back again so soon!"

As the young men wished to lose no time in attending to the business which they had resolved to accomplish, they concluded to depart for Melton immediately after the breakfast should be over.

Charles would have been happy to accompany Adelaide on a visit to her brother, but the kind-hearted Mr. Shawn, to whom they had communicated all their arrangements, entered into their interests, as though they had been near relations of his own.

He told them to "go on their way, and he would see to Addie." He was also delighted to hear that she had united her fortunes with Charles Lovell.

"Joy, joy to you, my dear girl," stooping to give her a fatherly kiss. "You have chosen a man after my own heart; and when Carrie gets old enough, I hope she may do as well. He is a man with an intelligent mind, and a warm and pure heart, if I am a judge. He will make his way in the world, and I am sure he loves you."

Caroline, as soon as she heard the news, knew not whether to laugh or to cry. She did both at times. "She was so glad," she said, " and so sorry too ; for now her dear Miss Adelaide would be going away."

When Charles was about to depart, she ran up to him and whispered:

" Have you got a brother ?"

" I have."

" Is he just like you ?"

" Not exactly. I hope he will be a much better man."

She then ran, and whispered to Adelaide:

" He 's got a brother, and I mean to have him, see if I don't; and then won't it be nice ?"

Adelaide laughed heartily at her childish notion, kissing her at the same time, saying:

" We will always be good friends, dear, wherever we are."

CHAPTER XXIX.

It was a warm and pleasant night in the month of April, and a boat containing six young men was moving rapidly along, impelled by the strong arm of two steady rowers. She was coming from the cove, that sets in around Roder's point, and nearly opposite the large house erected on the summit of that strip of land.

"Gently boys, gently now; make as little noise as possible. A little more to the west Charley; let her go to the shore easy, boys."

"What o'clock is it, Slocum?"

"I guess it is about the hour he appointed. Yet it wants five minutes to twelve."

"Then we are here just in time. Now, Slocum, strike your light."

The little lantern was scarcely elevated, before a light was seen in one of the upper windows of the house.

"He sees us; that will do; put out the light; and do you, Charley, lead the way. I almost wish we had a pistol or two, in case of need."

"Pshaw, Slocum," said a stout young fellow, as he jumped ashore; "a fiddle-stick for pistols; we should be as likely to shoot one another, as to shoot them. Let me but get a grip of them! that 's all I ask."

The little party having well secured the boat, moved in single file behind Lovell, who had arranged matters with young Montague, and knew where to lead them.

The lieutenant, having made an excuse for spending the night at the house of Vanderbose, had retired early in the evening, and before most of the companions of the master of the mansion had arrived.

He lay upon his bed without undressing, and watched anxiously for the hour of twelve. He had arranged with Charles to come in a boat, with a few trusty companions, as near to the house as possible. There might be difficulty in getting through the gates; and, in case of an alarm, or resistance and pursuit on the part of Vanderbose and his company, the object of his solicitude could much more readily, and with greater certainty, be conveyed beyond annoyance. Hour after hour rolled slowly by. Until ten o'clock, there was a great hurrying about the lower part of the house; servants running hither and thither; doors slamming, and the shrill voice of the house-keeper calling out to them, at times, in coarse language of abuse, and then again mingling with theirs in the loud laugh.

"Alas!" he thought, "and my poor sister, night after night, has been obliged to bear all this. But she shall bear it no longer."

As midnight approached, the noise of the servants died away, as one by one they retired to rest; and then, at times, there would come up from the room below a loud peal of laughter, and then a loud huzza, and then a confused mingling of angry voices, and oaths terrible to the ear, and heavy blows striking upon the tables, while the crash of glasses could be distinguished amid all the uproar; and then again the doors would be opened, and the wide hall would ring with obstreperous laughter, and confused moving of chairs and tables, and hurrying about, as of children in their frolics.

At the hour of twelve Montague arose and watched from the window, and soon a light near the shore gleamed upon the water. Immediately he struck his flint, and held the appointed signal for a few moments at the window, and then, taking the light in his hand, stepped softly to his sister's room. She was dressed, and, as he entered, arose and sat upon the side of the bed. She was deadly pale, and her whole frame shook with the deep excitement of the moment.

"Be calm as possible, my love; your brother will never leave you more in this horrible place, and there are strong hands to aid without. Be calm as you can; lean all your weight upon my arm."

And he put his arm around her, and with stealthy steps they walked along through the upper hall, and down the back stairway; his intention being to go out by the back door. To his utter dismay, it was locked, and the key withdrawn. He stooped and felt upon the floor, supposing it to have fallen out, but he searched in vain.

"Oh, Philip! hold me; I am so faint. Oh, I shall die!"

He took her up in his arms. But one way of refuge was before him, and that through the lower hall, and past the very room in which the rioters were assembled, and out of the more common passage of the front door. Every moment he expected to see the excited wretches bursting from their den, for they were in the midst of a tumultuous uproar. Bearing his precious burden, with his pistol drawn from his belt, and already cocked, held firmly in his hand, he hastened through, turned the latch of the door, and it opened; in an instant he was in the open air, and breathed freely. But a cry of "thieves! thieves!" from a female voice, told him that they were discovered. He called loudly for Lovell, who, true to his trust, rushed with his companions towards him; and at that moment his arms were seized hold of by several of the aroused inebriates, who, at the alarm, had rushed from the house.

"Here, Lovell, take my sister, and hasten to a place of safety with her."

Charles caught the once lovely girl in his arms, while two of his comrades walked beside him, to protect her from violence; and, freed from his burden, the young officer by a violent effort dashed his assailants from him, and laid them prostrate on the earth.

"You 're a robber, you 're a thief, you 're a villain. I 'll prosecute you for a midnight robber. I 'll have you in jail by the morning light; you thief, you robber, you villain, bring back that woman."

Montague knew by the voice that it was Vanderbose, who was thus letting out his feelings, irritated, no doubt, more by the fall he had received, than by the loss of her he called "that woman."

"Mr. Vanderbose, you have, by your infamous conduct, forfeited all claim to her who is unfortunately your wife. Don't stir one step nearer, sir, or I shall do you an injury. And keep in mind, sir, that nothing hinders me from chastising you as you deserve, but the fact of your being so nearly allied to my unfortunate sister. Stand back, each soul of you, for I will take the life of the first man who dares to follow me."

There was a ring to the tones of his voice that made each of the miserable gang step back, rather than forward. Montague turned at once, and went on his way; but he heard one of them ask Vanderbose:

"Where is your rifle?"

"That 's your sorts, Bob; run and get it—it 's in the hall; and bring the lights, and call the men; we 'll shoot the villain yet."

Only anxious to get his sister out of the way of all excitement, Montague hastened to the boat, although those around him urged him to let them run in upon them, and take the weapon from their hands; and even offered to stay and fight it out, while he went off with his sister to a place of safety. But he would not allow it.

"We have accomplished our object without violence, and I wish, for my sister's sake, to keep the law on my side. But let us hurry from the shore, for they may do great mischief yet."

"Jump in—jump, in all," cried Slocum; "they are coming—a whole gang of them, and may be the death of some one yet."

The boat flew from shore, for they felt that life depended upon every stroke.

"Straight out—right off shore; the further we get from their reach, the better. We can turn our course when at a safe distance;" and almost immediately Montague again called, but almost in a whisper, "Hold up—hold up your oars; they are trying to know in what direction to fire."

He was instantly obeyed, and in a moment more a ball struck the water near them, and the crack of a rifle was heard, and again another in the same direction.

"Now pull away as hard as you please; we shall be beyond their reach before they can load again." But no further attempt was made, and soon they saw the lights returning to the house, and heard their drunken shouts as they went back to their revels.

Julia happily knew nothing of what had happened, she had swooned just as they reached the boat; and when she was again conscious, her brother was bathing her temples with water, and telling her " she was safe now."

A carriage was waiting as they reached the shore, to convey her to the home of a respectable family, where she was to remain until some permanent provision should be made for her.

" And now, gentlemen," said Lieutenant Montague, stepping up and taking Slocum by the hand, as he seemed to be the leader of the company, " I give you my most hearty thanks for the service you have rendered to me and my unfortunate sister this night. I thank you from my heart; but you must allow me to do something more; anything you say—you have done me a great service—and so far as money—"

" Don't speak of it, sir; we have all got our pay, have n't we, boys?"

" Yes—yes," they all answered. " Only I should like to have had one good poke at the scamp; I only would have asked for one," said one of the young men.

" You would have done for him, Bill; that paw of yours is no joke, though I don't believe it has ever been laid on anything softer than a piece of timber."

" But, Mr. Lovell," said Montague, " surely I must, in some way, compensate these kind-hearted fellows. Tell me what to give them."

" My dear fellow," said Charles, " you do not yet quite understand a true country heart; it is like your own. This job has been undertaken in the true sailor spirit; you can understand what that is; and all they want as compensation is to know that they have accomplished a good deed. A cordial grasp of your hand is all the pay we want."

" And that you shall all have with a right good will. God bless you all, gentlemen."

A hearty shake of each offered hand, and Montague and Charles entered the carriage, and the band of social spirits that had risked their lives for a deed of kindness, walked along together, chatting in a lively manner about the events of the evening.

Old Colonel Johnson had some little business with his friend Squire Shirley; so, ordering Josey, he was soon seated in the easy chair, which the squire kept more especially for his own use. It was the morning after the scene just described, and the squire was busily engaged with some papers, in reference to an application to the court for appointing a conservator over the property of the wretched Vanderbose. He had already taken the deposition of his wife, and was anxious to get matters arranged as speedily as possible.

"Colonel, if you will excuse me a few moments, I will be back soon. The Judges of the Superior Court are attending to some business in the next house, and I want to hand these documents to them, and get their action without delay."

"By all means, neighbor; don't let me hinder any good work you are about."

The squire was not long absent, and when he came in, and threw his hat down on the table, and took his seat:

"Colonel," said he, "I tell you what it is; sometimes I get disgusted with my profession, because I come in contact with so much deviltry, for even roguish acts, you know, must be negotiated according to the strict letter of the law, to make them binding. Rogues would have nothing to do with law, I 'll warrant you, if they could help it. And then again, I like my profession, because I have a chance, once in awhile, to get the better, by means of it, of some villain who ought to be hung, or put where he can't do mischief."

"You mean Vanderbose, I suppose?"

"Yes, I mean him, and perhaps another that is not much better, though he has policy enough to conceal it. You see, 'this is the thing of it,' as you say, colonel,: I was called upon a day or two since, by Lucas, to make out a mortgage-deed for Vanderbose to sign in his favor, for ten thousand dollars, and Lucas in confidence, as he said, told me how it was. Vanderbose owes him five thousand dollars; he says it is for money he lent him, but most likely it is some gambling debt. Well, the only way he can get it, he says, is by loaning the fellow five thousand more, and taking a mortgage on his estate at the Point, for ten thousand, and Vanderbose has agreed to do it. Now, the probability is, if he gives him the money it will go right out of his hands as the rest has, for they say he has pretty much run through his estate in the city. Lucas will foreclose, and get that place for half its value; and I don't believe, between you and me, that he will have paid much money out of pocket either."

"And the poor wife have nothing left?"

"Just so; and that is the reason I was in such haste to get those papers through. If we can only once get a conservator placed over him, before he signs his property away, the jig is up. But I am in a terrible stew about it, for Vanderbose is to be here by twelve o'clock to-day to execute the deed, and it is ten now. But here comes Lovell and his friend."

Charles and Montague entered, and the latter received a most cordial greeting by the colonel. Charles immediately addressed himself to the business.

"Are those papers ready, Squire Shirley?"

"I have handed them to the judges, but they have a world of business on hand, and you know they must act with great caution, for it is a terrible power entrusted to them—that of taking away from a man the right to control his own property. And moreover, Mr. Lovell, bonds will have to be given by you for the faithful performance of the trust."

Charles colored deeply; he had not thought of that. He looked to Montague for an answer.

"Young gentlemen," said the colonel, "give yourselves no uneasiness about that. I understand the whole affair. You may offer old Colonel Johnson as security for Mr. Lovell, that he will fulfil his responsibility faithfully and truly."

"And I'll go you halves, colonel. I guess they will take Colonel Johnson and Joe Shirley for your bondsmen, if the property was twice what it is."

"Gentlemen," said the lieutenant, "your kindness is most unexpected, and I know not how to acknowledge it aright. If I was worth a hundred thousand, which I am not, I would not fear to venture it all in Mr. Lovell's hands. But, unfortunately, I have little besides my pay; my own responsibility would probably be of little account."

"No occasion for it at all, sir. The colonel and I know Mr. Lovell. Make yourself easy about that. But one thing do you do; go at once to the court—the judges are there—get a private interview with one of them—state the case—they have got the deposition of your sister, and let them know that there are urgent reasons for haste. Colonel, suppose you go with them; you are intimate with the judges, and a word from you will go further than a whole hour's pleading by a lawyer."

"That I will; come, gentlemen, let us see what can be done."

Time flies quickly when much is to be done in a given space, and it struck eleven before the old colonel was again back in the office of his friend.

"What luck, colonel?"

"Can't say, squire, can't say. I told my story, and they received it all very pleasantly, and said they would look over the deposition as fast as they possibly could."

"Did you tell them what was to take place at twelve o'clock?"

"I did, squire, but they said you must manage in some way to put them off."

"Manage! how can I manage? The papers are all drawn, and if they come here to execute them, how can I put them off? But who comes here? I hope it aint Vanderbose."

A carriage, driven rapidly, suddenly reined up at the office door, and a portly man, with a full bluff face, jumped in haste from it, and without knocking opened the door and entered. Bowing politely to both gentlemen, he inquired:

"Which of these gentlemen is Squire Shirley?"

"I answer to that name, sir."

"Your servant, sir," bowing again.

"Take a seat, sir."

"Thank you, sir, I have no time to sit. I have come to you, sir, as I understand that you are both a lawyer and a justice of the peace, to inquire how I am to get into a man's premises which has got a high wall that a man can't climb over, and high gates bolted, and three or four bull-dogs loose in the day time, and ready to fly at you the moment you enter?"

"Better keep away; a man that shuts himself up in that way shows that he don't want company."

"Yes, but I must get through, and into the house too, if there is any law in the land. Does the law allow a brute of a husband to abuse a dear little inoffensive wife, and crush her to the grave? And cannot an old uncle, who loves her as his own child, be permitted to go to her and take her away, and give the fellow his deserts?"

Squire Shirley felt almost at first disposed to smile, but when he heard the voice of the stout man trembling with emotion, he entered seriously into his feelings.

" The law, sir, doubtless would give redress under certain circumstances. If it could be proved that the wife was cruelly beaten, and she should swear that her life was in danger, it would no doubt interfere."

" But a man may destroy a woman without beating her, or cutting her throat, or poisoning her; he may break her heart by neglect; he may leave her alone upon a bed of weakness, while his house is filled with gamblers and outcast wretches; he may frighten her out of her reason, by allowing base debauchees to prowl about his dwelling. Heavens! it is too bad. I only want to get at the villain. I only want just to get within reach of him."

" Your hand looks as though it might do some execution upon him; and yet, my dear sir, the penalty of the law might have to be borne by you instead of the culprit. Come, sit down, my good sir, and let us understand your case."

" Why, sir, I am the uncle of that poor unfortunate girl married to Vanderbose. I have just returned from a long voyage, and have come up here to see her, but such stories as I have heard about her have set me almost distracted."

" Sit down, sir, sit down; I can tell you all about it. Your niece is not there, sir; she was taken away by her brother in the dead of night, and is now in a place of safety. I saw her this morning. She is more comfortable than could have been expected, and I and others are doing what we can to get justice done for her."

" God bless you, sir, and them too," rising, and grasping the hand of the squire.

" May I be permitted to ask," said Colonel Johnson, rising, and offering his hand, " is this Captain Halliday?"

" The same, at your service, gentlemen, and I hope you will excuse my rude manners. I have been terribly excited. That dear child, sir, was one of two darling creatures that I nourished from infancy. They were lovely as cherubs, and dear to me, for all I know, as own children could possibly be. I was obliged to leave them to the care of a wrong-headed relative, a sister of mine, who encouraged one to marry a fool, and, because the other would not do so too, has turned her off upon the world; and Heaven only knows where *she* is, for I can hear nothing about her. And now, here I am home again, with abundant means to make them and me comfortable for life, and they are gone. But Julia, you say, is safe. The Lord be praised for that. But where is she? for I must see her, and tell her that her old uncle will stand by her to his dying day."

And the tears started freely, and both he and the old colonel had to use their handkerchiefs in spite of their will; the colonel, however, making as if affected by a bad cold. At length the old colonel stepped up, and taking the captain by the hand:

"The Lord has been better to you, my dear sir, than your fears. I know all about your nieces, for whom you are so much interested. One of them is out of the hands of the scoundrel whom she married, and the other is as happy as a lark, in the family of a Mr. Shawn, who loves her as a daughter; and she is engaged to be married to one whom I believe you know, as fine a fellow as ever breathed the breath of life, Charles Lovell."

"Gentlemen," said Squire Shirley, "I must ask you to be seated, and keep mum about all these matters while a certain person I see coming is in here."

They immediately complied, and retired to a corner of the room where they could converse in private.

"Good morning, squire."

"Good morning, good morning, sir; take a seat."

The gentleman helped himself to a seat.

"Vanderbose not come yet?"

"Hardly time, is it?"

"It wants five minutes to twelve. He was to be here, you know, by twelve. Ah, good morning, colonel, how are you to-day?"

The gentleman smiled very complacently, but the old colonel merely replied:

"Well, I thank you, sir."

"Are the papers all ready, squire?"

"Pretty much."

"I wish he 'd come along; I am confoundedly anxious, between you and me, to get this thing along as quick as possible, you understand?"

"I understand."

"Things looks squally;" and then, raising his voice, "pretty stirring news abroad this morning, Colonel Johnson."

"Indeed, sir!"

"They say Vanderbose had his wife stolen from him last night. Things have come to a pretty pass here. By George, I should like to catch any one playing such a game with me."

As quick as thought, Captain Halliday was by his side, and holding out his clenched fist:

"And, sir, if you deserved it as much as that scoundrel does, I should like to be the man to tear the helpless being from you, be you who you might."

"Hout, tout, gentlemen, there is no need of this. Captain Halliday, will you and Colonel Johnson just step out and see those gentlemen about our business, and tell them the sooner they can get along with it the better."

And, obedient to the request of Squire Shirley, the two gentlemen addressed immediately departed.

"A testy old fellow, that! Who is he? I did n't know but he was going to fall foul of a fellow. But here, it is getting past twelve; why don't Vanderbose come? Yes, by George, there he is; he drives fine horses, don't he?"

Esquire Shirley was too deeply excited to reply. All the ingenuity of his mind was tasked to prevent, if possible, the completion of the arrangement between these two villains, as he thought them both. But the carriage of Vanderbose now drove up, and in a few moments he entered the office.

"How are you, my good fellow?" said Lucas, rising and giving his hand. "Squire Shirley has got the papers all ready."

"Well, I suppose I must read them. How is it, squire? you think they are all right? best to read them?"

"Every man should take great care how he puts his name to paper. I should advise you, and any one else, to read every word of any article—I don't care who writes it—before signing it. When a man's name is once down, there is an end to it. No, no—read every word."

"Well, let us have it."

"In a few moments, sir; I perceive an error or two that I have made, which must be corrected before signing. I can do that, however, after you have read them."

"Shall I read it to you, Van?" said Lucas, who was pale with the excitement of the moment, and, being too uneasy to sit, was walking about the office.

"No—I guess I can read the thing; but whether I shall understand it is another question. Lawyer's writings, I believe, were never made to be understood."

He laughed as he said this, and turned towards the squire; but that gentleman took no notice of the remark; he had too much to think of just then, and was very busy looking out of the window, and contriving how he should manage to delay matters. Lucas was also looking out, but from another window, and just then remarked:

"Yonder comes your testy friend again, squire."

"Where!"

"Down street—don't you see him, and a whole posse with him; they aint coming here, I hope." He made this remark, because he saw Lieutenant Montague among the number, and he judged there must be such a state of feeling between him and Vanderbose, as might lead to difficulty, and prevent the accomplishment of the business in hand.

"Come, Van, aint you most through?"

"Yes, I 've done; where 's your pen?"

"Stop—stop, Mr. Vanderbose," said the squire, with earnestness; "it will not answer to sign that instrument until the errors are corrected;" taking the paper from his hand for the purpose of making the corrections. At that moment Charles Lovell, followed by Montague, entered the office; the former, as he handed a paper to the squire, asked with much concern in his manner:

"Is it too late?"

"No—just in time; all correct."

The attention of Vanderbose was now arrested, by looking up and beholding close beside him the person of "his mortal enemy." He sprang from his seat, and began to pour forth a volley of the most abusive language at his command, but was at once stopped by the owner of the premises.

"Mr. Vanderbose, this is no place for such language; nor will I allow my office to be thus polluted. And, sir, I can tell you further, that there is no business that need detain you here any longer. I hold in my hand an injunction from the court, forbidding you in any way to dispose of your effects in this State, either real or personal, until you shall show cause why a conservator shall not be placed over you; that is all, sir."

At that moment Colonel Johnson, followed by Captain Halliday, walked in. They had sent the young men ahead, and then took their own time. The captain cast his eye around, and the moment it fell on Vanderbose, he made a rush towards him. His nephew, however, and Charles Lovell, each seized an arm:

"Captain Halliday! my dear uncle!" and both exerted their utmost strength to hold him back; but it would have been in vain had not Vanderbose, in great terror, sprung from the office and into his carriage. All in the room now, with the exception of Lucas, who, pale with rage and disappointment, kept aloof, surrounded the captain, begging him to be calm.

"My dear sir," said Squire Shirley, "he has got part of his deserts, and the rest will follow. Do no violence, and we will get the whole thing fixed to our mind."

"And I am to understand, then, Squire Shirley, that I am to be cheated out of my debt, and partly by your connivance, after employing you as my counsel?" said Mr. Lucas, looking quite fiercely as he spoke.

"I do not consider myself, sir, as ever having had that honor. If you had consulted me, Mr. Lucas, I should have advised you not to loan money to gamblers; and, further than that, not to associate with them. We are apt to get somewhat soiled by engaging in dirty work."

"What is your bill, sir?"

"Nothing, sir. I am but too glad that the whole matter has been quashed."

The gentlemen clapped on his hat, and walked off at a very spry gait.

"And now, gentleman," said the colonel, "this has been a pretty busy kind of a day; and, as things are so well fixed to our mind, I want you, Captain Halliday, as soon as you have seen your niece, and you, Lieutenant Montague, and you, Mr. Charley, and—"

"And me too, colonel?"

"Yes, and you, too, Squire Shirley, to dine with me to-day; and I shall send for our good minister, Mr. Jamieson, your particular friend, Mr. Montague, and we will have a nice time of it. At three o'clock, gentleman remember the hour."

CHAPTER XXX.

Time, like a mighty stream, bears its voyagers along in various connections. Sometimes at scattered distances, and apparently unequal speed, and then a favoring gale to some, and the dead calm to others, gathers them together, and they come to anchor side by side.

Dear reader, we have come to the last chapter in our story. Those in whom we have been interested through its course, are clustering near, that they and we may say farewell. And if there be some tokens of confusion, or some last words unsaid, is it not thus in all our partings here? And if, when under the excitement of such occasions, the common order of the social scene is broken, we take it all in good part, thinking more of the sad adieu, than of the little proprieties of life. So must your author crave the same indulgence in a parting hour. It is no easy matter to let go one's grasp on those with whom we have been in strict converse for many months, when by the lone fire-side, or in the still watches of the night, or by the silent river, or through the green fields, or amid the lonely solitude of the deep woods, they have been with you, and made your loneliest hour cheerful by their presence, and associated themselves with your dearest haunts. It must not be a marvel if the last word and look cause deep regret, and the reluctance to say farewell create some stiffness in the manner.

It was a scene of mingled joy and sorrow, when good old Captain Halliday first, after his long absence, embraced his pale and feeble, yet still lovely Julia. She threw her arms about his neck, and kissed his weather-beaten cheek, and could not let him go; and when her sobs would let her speak, her only words were:

"Dear, dear uncle!"

"There, there, now, Julia dear, there, hush now, that 's a darling; let the tears go now; we will have nice times again, for I am going to get a home for us; and mamma and I are going to have you and Addie with us once again.

"Oh, Addie, too, dear uncle?"

"Yes, Addie, too, until that noble fellow, to whom she has given her heart, shall get his things in readiness to take her to his own home."

"Oh, how lovely that will be!"

"Yes, and I am about to get my old place back again. It will seem more like home than any other spot, and I shall live just in a plain, snug way, and keep my mind free to enjoy its beauties. And there, you know, are the trees which I planted for you and Addie, and there is the pretty garden that you both used to tend, and there are the fine walks down among the rocks and cedars, where we used to look upon the broad water, and see the boats sailing so sweetly on a summer day."

"Oh, dear, dear uncle, how sweet it used to be."

"To you it was, no doubt, for you had no care to trouble you; but to me it will, I hope, be pleasanter than ever, for I have learned some lessons from the past. We will make no more show, my dear."

"Oh, how glad I am, dear uncle, for I never wish again to do anything for display. My heart sickens at the very thought. I want to live for something better, for *Him* who has had pity on me, and I hope has pardoned my sins; who has been with me in the hour of my trouble, and granted me a great deliverance."

The wretched Vanderbose did not wait to make any opposition to the appointment of the court, but fled at once to the city, where he dragged along a miserable life among the abandoned there, for a few months, and then his wasted life was brought to a close. Rich relations followed him to the grave, in their coaches, and, as they went, said to each other: "What a pity that such a handsome property should be so soon squandered!"

The place at Roder's point was sold, for Julia said she never wished to put her foot in it again, nor see an article she had ever looked on there. And Charles, by judicious management, with the advice of Esquire Shirley, gathered from the wreck of her husband's estate a few thousand dollars, which were loaned out for her benefit. And even that she could not, for a long time, be persuaded to touch; and would much have preferred, if her uncle had permitted, to earn her living by her own efforts.

The only shadow that came over the little family, and especially Julia, was the departure of her brother for the seat of war, upon one of our northern lakes.

It was his lot, however, to be among the favored ones who, by their station as well as prowess, made themselves conspicuous before the whole nation. Unharmed through terrible dangers, and victorious over a gallant enemy, he returned at the close of our struggle, to be crowned with honors.

The brother of Adelaide never recovered from the oppression of his early misfortunes. He mingled with no society, and spent his time in seclusion with his father-in-law, endeavoring by every means in his power to solace his declining years. The false step made in his early career, and its consequences, destroyed the buoyancy of youth, and he ever carried upon his brow the marks of settled grief.

Charles Lovell found, on his return from the city, that his faithful brother had been, as every one said "as busy a bee;" drawing logs to the mill, and joists and boards from the mill, and gathering timber and stone around the old place, and getting everything in readiness for operations in the Spring. Charles had received a handsome compensation for his services in the city, as also a commission for the settlement of Vanderbose's estate, which, added to what he had previously made, enabled him to commence his building with confidence. He would have a surplus still left as a capital to work with.

Slocum was ready to begin at the time appointed. And he said to his hands, as they were about to commence hewing the timber:

"By jingo, I never was in such a hurry to get at a job in my life. I tell you, boys, I know it looks dark how anything is going to be made at all ship-shape out of this old concern, and I don't wonder you laugh. I 've laughed at Charley many a time about it; but he is not a fellow to be laughed out of his notions."

"You know we laughed too, Slocum, about these trees. You remember how they looked! like poles sticking up here and there. And now just look at them, and only think how they will be a few years hence."

"That 's the thing of it, Bill. Charley looks ahead; he has had a plan about this place all the while, and what he has done has n't cost much; but it tells more and more every year. He will have a beauty-spot here, see if he don't."

"Take care, boys, that you don't cut too deep; keep outside the line, for I am going to have this timber as smooth as a house-floor; but there comes Charley himself."

"So he does, and Guss with him, and they have both got their axes. Now you 'll have to put it, Slocum. You had better let me take an adze, too, for those fellows will make the chips fly."

As the house had ever been a favorite idea with Charles, it was very natural that now it was begun in earnest, he should make it a subject of frequent conversation when at home. At such times, Aunt Casey did not join in. Her countenance would assume a serious cast, and often a heavy sigh would escape her, and she would in many ways manifest great uneasiness.

One evening, when Charles was more than commonly elated, in consequence of having that day completed the exterior of his building, and received the assurance of Slocum, and all hands engaged in the work, that it was even much prettier in reality than the sketch he had made of it, Aunt Casey became so restless that Charles could not forbear speaking.

"Why is it, aunty, that you appear lately so different from what you have been? You hardly ever laugh now, and everything seems to trouble you."

The old lady had, before he spoke, as much as she could do to keep the tears back, but this finished the matter, and at it she went in right good earnest. Charles waited until the shower was about over. At length, in a playful tone, he asked:

"Perhaps, aunty, you think I am not going to be happy in my new condition? Did you see anything in Miss Addie the day she spent with you, that gives you uneasiness on that account?"

This only added to the trouble, and Aunt Casey started off to her little room, and there had a time of it all to herself.

Charles was indeed perplexed, for he knew not how to account for her singular conduct. It was so unlike anything he had ever noticed in her before.

At length she again entered the room, wiping her eyes with her apron, and trying to put on a cheerful face.

"It is very wrong in me to do so; it 's very childish and foolish, and it is very selfish, too. But one thing I must say; don't you never think that I have anything against that sweet young creature; for a sweeter, lovelier young darling, I never see in all my born days. And to think how she took an interest in everything, and see how I did everything, and asked me in her pretty way how I did this, and how I did that; and to see how delighted she was to see me feed the fowls and the chickens, and would take the bowl out of my hand, and throw the stuff out all around her feet, to get them up to her, as close as she could; and then she wanted to see the heifer, and so I took her out to the barn, and you never see how delighted she was. And I tell you what, she notices things; for she looked all around the barn, and granary, and all over, and then she turns to me: 'He keeps things in their places, don't he? I hope,' says she, 'I shall be able to keep things as orderly in the house; but,' says she, 'I hope, aunty, you will come up, won't you, and just show me how to manage, for you know the help I may have, perhaps will not know much, and he has been used to your ways.' But, oh dear."

"Well, I hope you will, aunty, and I wish it was so that you could be with us all the time."

"Oh dear! do you wish so?"

"Yes, I do most truly; and Miss Addie thinks it would be almost too good just to have you live with us."

"The dear, blessed creature; then it 's done. And now, Charley, just hear what I 've got to say. You see I have been thinking the thing all over; it 's been upon my mind all the time since you 've been getting ready to go away, and the more I think the worse I get, 'till I 'm a most done over. You see it has been such another kind of a life to me, since you boys have been here; we have lived so happy, and

I have got along so smooth and easy, and I have been a-laying up all the time, too, that come to think of you going away, and me living all alone, only once in awhile when Hetty comes home, that I can't stand it; and so I have been thinking how much better it would be for you to have me there, doing all that has got to be done, making your butter, and seeing to things just as I have done here, only I shall have your dear little wife take all the management, and I will see that it is done as she says."

"Well, aunty, I feel, now, as if I should be perfectly happy."

"Oh dear, how glad I am to hear you say so. And you won't go to hiring no help; I don't want them round."

"Just as you say, aunty."

And the old lady went off into one of her short chuckling laughs, her sides shaking, and her apron wiping away the tears at the same time.

The Spring and Summer have passed away. Their bloom, their showers, their flowers, and their fruit, have been enjoyed, and silently, but with steady progress, the tints of autumn have been stealing on, until upon the hills, and over the fields, and by the roadside, and wherever a forest tree reared its branches, were bright and varied colors.

The dwelling of Charles Lovell had received its finishing touches. The plain, but neat enclosure, which encircled the large yard, had also been put up, and the eye could now take in, at a single glance, the design of its owner. To one not acquainted with the process by which it had all been accomplished, it would have appeared a costly place for a farmer. And, doubtless, had any one attempted, in a single season, and by the purchase of every article, and hiring all the labor, it would have been so in reality. But, as Charles went forward by a fixed plan, and with his own hands, as opportunity offered, did something towards it, the real outlay of money did not much exceed the estimate of Slocum.

As the brother of Adelaide had placed in her hands a sum sufficient for a handsome outfit, she furnished it to her own mind; and Charles had as much reason to be satisfied with the neatness of its house-keeping arrangements, as he had with the completeness of the finish which his friend Slocum had imparted to every item of his work.

It had been a very lovely day in the latter part of October, and as Mr. Slocum had some business at the old mill, just before evening he walked leisurely around that way, casting his eye occasionally back as he passed the house and grounds, where he had been at work so long.

"Jingo! it looks well, and I hope Charley will have many happy days there. It is finished, upon honor, anyhow, and paid for too." This he said to himself, as he turned into the lane which led from the highway to the mill.

He found Mr. Duncan at work with some logs he was sawing into slit work, and he stood and looked on a moment until the log had passed through, and then, when the noise ceased, saluted the miller:

"A pleasant evening, Mr. Duncan. You keep hard at it, I see."

"Yes, I have to; what between the grists inside, and the logs outside, a man has to step pretty lively."

"Well, that 's the way; but I never thought you could have been induced to set the saw a-going."

"Nor I either."

"I used to be sometimes almost afraid to come here with a grist, you used to grumble so about the dam being out of order, and that you had n't but one run of stone, and all that. But now, they tell me, you have had to hire a young fellow to help you."

"Well, it 's true, Slocum; but, you see, I 've been over-persuaded. That fellow, Lovell, got at me first about fixing up my old oven for kiln-drying corn; and then nothing would do but I must rig up the old saw again, because he wanted some sawing done. And you know what a fellow he is! What can you do with him? You see he 's right into you, and he 's got such a way with him."

"Charley 's a fine fellow."

"Well, now, Slocum, how is a body going to say 'no' to him. Gosh! I can't. Only just see how it is. He 'll come right up to you, and the first thing you 'll know, he 'll up with a bag of corn and over with it into the hopper; or he 'll maybe catch off a bag of meal from my back, saying, 'Uncle Jo, I am younger than you, let go,' and off he 'll clip with it into somebody's wagon; or he 'll catch hold of the lever, and whip up a log, and on to the cradle with it—'You go in, Uncle Jo, and tend to the hopper.' "

"That 's his way."

"It beats all creation what a fellow he is. And then when there 's sickness, he 's right in among it, doing something or other. I 'll tell you, Slocum, just what he did: Last spring we had a hard time of it, I tell you. There was Jemime, she came home, and was took down with the measles, and was as sick as death; and then Sue, she got the cankers, and was all swelled up in her throat, so that she wheezed like a broken-winded horse; and right in the midst of it, Bill falls down through the trap-door of the mill, and snaps his leg. There we were, three on 'em all on their backs to onst. Well, what does Lovell do but down he comes, and at it he goes—off coat, and the first thing he did was to take the baby—and what do you think?"

"Rocked it to sleep?"

"No, gosh; he could n't do that; it aint in the power of mortal man to do that. It 's never slept yet to my knowledge. But he stopped it's hollering; only think of it!"

"Does it cry much?"

"I guess you 'd think so? Why Slocum, it 's screeched ever since it 's been in the world. It come screeching, and it 's been screeching ever since, and it 's my opinion it will screech itself out of the world again, if it keeps on. But only think, Lovell stopped it; the old woman was clean beat. She ran out of 'tother room to see what was the matter. 'She did n't know,' she said 'but it had stopped for good. Oh dear!' says she, 'what is it! it aint dead?' And there was the little sarpent, looking up at Lovell and laughing; only think of that, Slocum!"

"Now, you don't!"

"True as the Bible; how he ever got the critter to stop bellowing is the greatest wonder I 've seen this many a day. And there he was; sometimes he would stay all night, and then again he 'd bring all kinds of nice things for the sick ones, and they 've all got so fond of him, that it is nothing but Charley Lovell, all day long. Now, what can you do with such a fellow! I can't, he 's got clean round me. But I 'll tell you one thing, Slocum."

"What is it?"

"The old thing begins to pay. I never was so 'forehanded in my life; and I've fixed the old dam, and mended the wheel, and put in a new run of stone, and fixed up the saw, and things begin to look bright. But what upon earth, Slocum, are you doing with your Sunday clothes on?"

"Going to the wedding."

"What wedding?"

"Why the great wedding or weddings. Did n't you know that Charley is to be married this evening and Priest Jamieson too. And it is to be in the church. But what now, Duncan?"

"I'll tell you what in a minute." And the miller fairly ran into the mill, and was out again instantly. "I'll tell you what it is. Charley has been at me this good while to go to church. You see I have n't been this ten years, and Lovell says I'll be a heathen yet, and my family too, if I don't turn over a new leaf, and go to meeting Sundays, and I believe he is about right. But the thing of it is, when to begin. Gosh, if I should go there in the day time they'd all turn round and stare at a fellow so that I should wish myself back to home."

"Well, then, suppose you begin to-night; it will kind of ease the way."

"That's what I'm thinking; break the ice like. But come along over to the house, and we'll talk about our business on the way, and you just wait 'till I put on my best. But don't lisp a word to the old woman, or she'll want to go too, and take that screeching brat with her."

"I'm afraid you will get it, Duncan, when she comes to find out."

"I shall get it, anyhow, for the matter of that."

Duncan was not long in putting on his best. But so seldom did such an event take place that it necessarily excited the curiosity of his good woman.

"What upon earth, Duncan, is to pay now! Your best clothes on, and your new hat that you have n't never yet had on your head? Where are you going?"

"Oh, I am just going to take a little turn with Slocum."

"Take a little turn with Slocum! It aint no such a thing; there's something to pay; you know there is, and you're ashamed to let me know."

" Maybe I 'm going to church."

"To church! catch you to church! you 're ashamed to be seen there, you know you are. Aint Lovell talked enough about that; but never mind, you 'll catch it."

" Oh, Mrs. Duncan," said Slocum, " he is only just going a little ways. You see Charley Lovell is to be married in the church this evening, and Mr. Duncan and I feel like going to have a peep at it."

Mrs. Duncan threw the baby down on the bed, and clasping her hands together, exclaimed:

" Did I ever? And now, Duncan, you 've done this a purpose. But—"

Mr. Slocum and her amiable husband either did not hear what else she said, as the baby, being left to scratch and kick by itself, was sending forth noise enough to drown even the clatter of the old mill—or, being in haste to see the ceremony, took French leave and were off.

As the Reverend Mr. Jamieson, and his much-loved Lucy, had determined to celebrate their nuptials in the house of God, Charles and Adelaide had prevailed upon Captain Halliday to forego the pleasure of having the ceremony of their marriage at his house, and to allow it to take place in company with that of their two friends. A company of invited guests, from both Melton and Wellgrove, were to escort Charles and his lady from the residence of her uncle to the church under the pastoral charge of Mr. Jamieson, and, after the ceremony, to repair for a short time to the house of Colonel Johnson, and partake of refreshments, and then to the house of Captain Halliday, where a feast, consonant with the notions of the old captain, was to be in readiness for all who chose to come.

" There 'll be a nation sight of folks there, I 'm a-thinking, Slocum."

" I should be ashamed if there was n't. It aint often such fellows as Parson Jamieson and Charley Lovell are married, nor such girls as Lucy Johnson. And if there aint a raft of folks at the old colonel's to-morrow, to take the old fellow's hand, and heartily wish him joy, then I'm mistaken, and I 'll bet there won't be a horse and gig in all Melton, to-morrow, that won't be on the way to give Charley a call, and bring him and his lovely girl to their new home. It will be a sight, Duncan, that aint often seen, I tell you."

"Punch plenty, too?"

"I don't know about that. Charley, you know, never was a roysterer; but there 'll be enough to eat and to drink, I 'll warrant; and them that are enemies or jealous of Charley, if there be any such, had better keep out of the way, for we mean to give him such a 'welcome home' as aint been seen here before."

They were now near the church, and the bright, long, painted windows shining through the trees which surrounded it, formed, indeed, a fairy picture. Clusters of people could be seen ascending the steps, and wagons and carriages driving towards it.

"I 'm most afeard there won't be room, Slocum."

"As much room for us, as for any of them; and if there is any squeezing, Duncan, them that get against your old bones will have the worst of it."

As Slocum was the pilot, he led the way up the stairs, and through the gallery to its further end.

"Now, Duncan, we have got a grand seat; we can see the whole thing."

Duncan probably did not hear him, for he was staring at the lights in the chandeliers, and at the gilded pipes of the organ, and at the people gathering in the pews, and at the bald foretop of old Mr. Somers, who, with his head powdered, and in an extra neat black dress, sat within the altar, looking pleasantly on the smiling faces of the multitude. At length Duncan turned to his companion:

"Where 's the folks, Slocum? Where 's Charley?"

"He has n't come yet."

"Gosh, how them lights dazzle a fellow's eyes!"

"Turn your eyes t'other way then, and whisper what you have got to say, Duncan. You aint in the old mill now."

The pews below had all been filled, and an almost breathless silence reigned within the church; when suddenly the pipes of the organ sent forth a lively air, and all looked round.

"They are coming now, Duncan."

And immediately a procession was seen advancing up the centre aisle.

"Who is that fellow in black, with them satin small-clothes on. He looks sleek, don't he?"

"That is Mr. Jamieson; and the lady leaning on his arm, with that white veil on her head, and hanging down her shoulders, is Lucy—Miss Lucy Johnson; and that is the old colonel on t'other side of her; bless his old heart, how trim he looks!"

"Look, Slocum, look! who upon earth is that?"

"That 's Charley; don't you know him? his head is powdered, aint it! I tell you, Duncan, that blue coat, with the light small-clothes, looks well on Charley. I did n't think he was so much of a man."

"Gosh; I should never know him. He looks taller."

"Yes, he does. And that beauty by his side, aint she a picture?"

"Charley goes the whole figure, don't he? But see there, Slocum, if there aint Guss! sure as I'm alive, and he 's got a gal too. What a nice plump little rosy thing she is?"

"I guess that 's the daughter of a rich man off where Charley's girl has been staying. I heard say that they had come to the wedding."

A long train followed the happy couples up the aisle and arranged themselves before the altar. As soon as the organ ceased, Mr. Somers arose, and in his expressive manner, with simple fervor, but very appropriate words, united in the bonds of marriage his loved brother in the ministry with the fair Lucy. The organ, accompanied by a choir of singers, immediately chanted the Gloria Patri, during which Mr. Jamieson left the circle, and entered the vestry-room which opened from the altar. In a few moments he returned, dressed in his silken robes, and Charles Lovell and his long-loved Adelaide with their attendants, circled about him. His voice trembled slightly, but its rich tones could be heard distinctly through the house, and the beautiful service lost none of its interest from the evident feeling which he manifested.

Proudly did old Captain Halliday resign the hand of his lovely niece to the manly youth who stood ready to receive it. And they, who had so long and steadily loved, were united in those bands which death alone can sever.

"Did you hear that, Slocum?"

"Hear what?" Slocum had been too concerned a spectator to be disturbed by any common occurrence.

"Gosh! she 's come;" and old Duncan bolted out of the pew, and although the organ was again pouring forth its loudest notes, Slocum could distinguish, above its highest peal, the shrill scream of a baby.

"Duncan will take it now!"

THE END.

www.ingramcontent.com/pod-product-compliance
Lightning Source LLC
LaVergne TN
LVHW021136110826
845150LV00005B/1045
9781425548599